HOUSE TALES

SCARLET DARKWOOD

CONTENTS

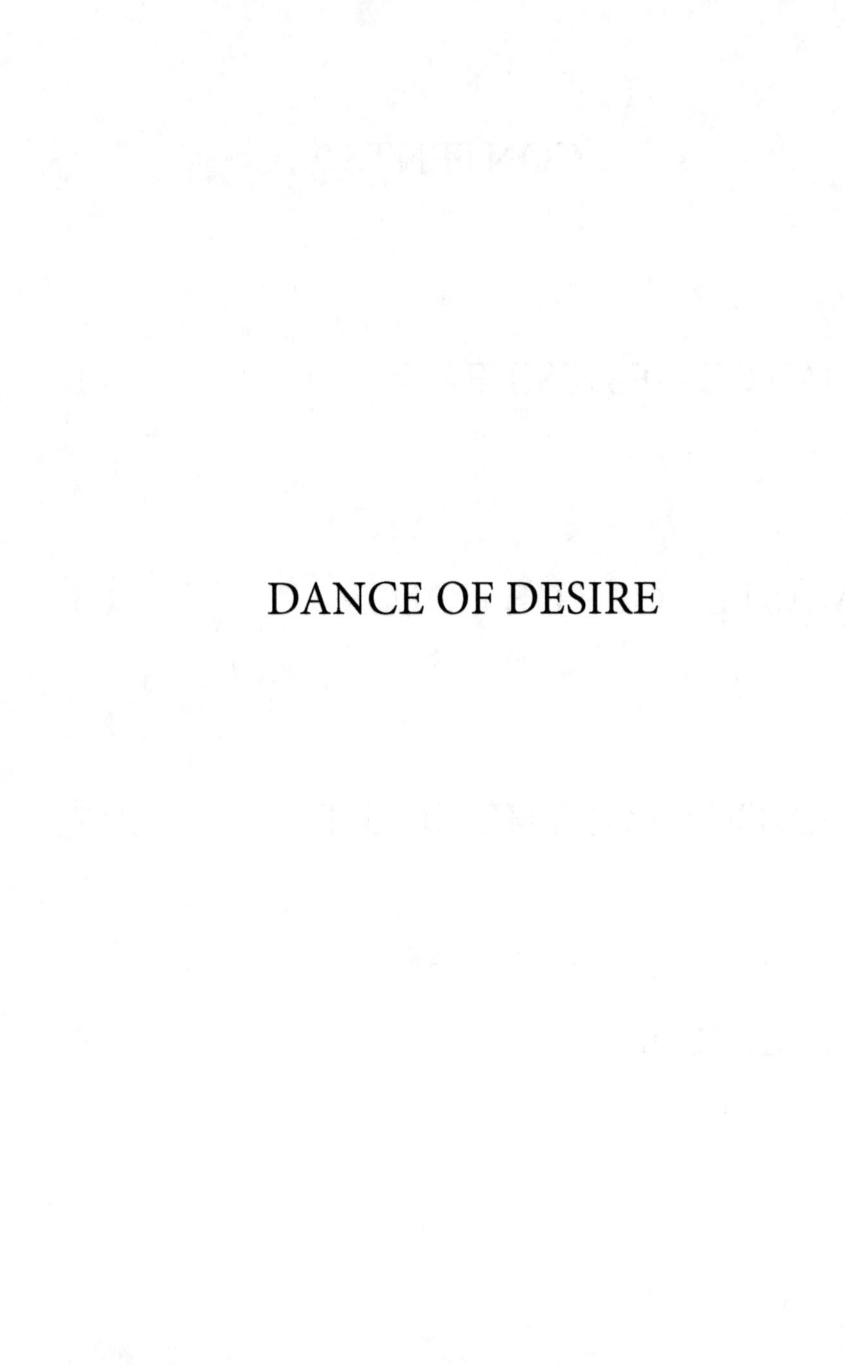

DANCE OF DESIRE

CHAPTER 1

Daren sat hidden in the shadows, transfixed by the vision before him. Several nights ago, he'd stumbled upon this clearing while wandering the grounds of The House. Unable to sleep and craving a new sense of adventure, he headed outside, taking in the nightlife around him. No amount of wild imaginings had prepared him for the treat he'd discovered. From that moment on, he had vowed to return with high hopes of seeing the object of his fascination.

On that night, up high in the inky sky, a voluptuous moon had cast beams of light on the ground below, giving the twirling figure before him an almost eerie, ghostly appearance. A young lady with a flowing scarf had danced and swirled. After observing her smooth, swaying movements those previous nights, his fascination with her had turned into an obsession. He vowed he'd have her, this lithe, nimble body swaying in all directions, oblivious to anyone or anything.

She passed the scarf behind her, stepped to the right, gave a light jump forward, and spun to the left, swinging the airy fabric in front of her. A few more executions of fancy footwork, and the dance ended. Daren held his breath, eyes widening. The lady stopped a moment, turning her head up to the moon. The scarf slipped from her hands, floating down to the ground, catching on sharp spindles of grass. Without hesitation, she lifted the hem of her dress and whisked off the shapeless garment, tossing it to the ground next to the scarf.

Daren clapped his hand over his mouth, eyes darting around to see if anyone else might be watching. She'd never done this before. He turned his gaze back to the naked lady in the moonlight. Curvy, with full, pert mounds, she reminded him of a moving sculpture, one that flitted and floated through the air. She picked up the scarf, and began her dancing ritual all over again.

What a beauty! Her long hair wafted behind her, competing with the fluid movement of the fabric she bore. Her breasts bounced a little with each small jump, her powerful legs lifting her into the air. Between his thighs, Daren felt his cock stiffen. He fingered the silky flesh of his tip, deciding if he wanted to save himself for someone else or spend right then and there. From the looks of her clothing, she didn't reside where he did. Those incarcerated on her wards wore poorly made clothing created from stale-colored fabrics, accented with stains from wear and little washing. Residents on his side of The House dressed in simple, sensual attire, functional and serving one purpose. Unlike her world, filled with malodorous bodies, scattered minds, and broken spirits, his offered ample opportunity for indulging in lusty pleasures in a luxurious setting with any beauty of his choosing. Should he approach this lady now and introduce himself, or should he find out more about her first? After all, she wasn't fair game, like his own kind.

His eyes widened. She stopped her strange gyrations and settled down on the grass, using her shapeless, dull dress as a blanket. As she rested her hands behind her head, basking in the moonbeams, she stretched out, bending one of her knees up. Her legs parted a little. She moved one of her hands from behind her head and trailed her fingers between her breasts, over her abdomen, and down between her thighs. At that moment, a soft, warm breeze filled the air, carrying soft scents of wildflowers that made him nearly swoon. While watching her, Daren had mimicked her same hand movements on his own body. The struggle to contain himself ended in failure, and with hard, rhythmic contractions, he released thick, white jets of lust on the grass. He closed his eyes and caught his breath. He resolved to find out more about her, and he knew the very person who would be able to shed some light on this intriguing nymph.

CHAPTER 2

W hat, you don't have enough beauties around you that you have to go find new sensations elsewhere?" Dr. James, The House physician, leaned back in his leather chair with his feet propped up on his desk, a wide smile across his face. The afternoon sun peeked through the windows of his office; its rays bringing out the earthy, red grains of the wooden panels along the wall. Rich, heavy furnishings dotted the room, showing off the doctor's impeccable taste in decor. He chuckled. "You're right, this young lady is an 'admit' on the other side. Due to her personal circumstances, we didn't place her on the side of The House where we address the sexual appetites. Her family dropped her off here because they believed her eccentricities made her unfit for normal living within the community."

"So what makes her eccentric?" Perplexed, Daren stared back at the doctor in disbelief, running a hand through his wavy locks of fiery red hair.

"Let's see," the doctor said, getting up from his massive desk and heading toward one of his wooden filing cabinets. After searching through the drawers, he pulled out a folder and leafed through the papers. "Ah, yes, here it is. She's abandoned religion, engages in ritualistic behaviors, and prefers other odd and unusual forms of worship. That's probably why you've see her outside carrying on the way she does."

"Dr. James, I have to tell you, this girl is beautiful. You should see her move, the way she glides over the grass, the way the moon shows off her, um, assets."

"I'm sure you'd be more than capable of showing her some new moves yourself. But Daren, remember she's housed on the other side, not on yours. So if you're thinking—"

"No," Daren said, holding up his hand, "you don't understand. I saw her naked."

The doctor raised an eyebrow. "Really? What else did you see?"

"She stopped dancing and all of sudden stripped off her dress. Of course I don't blame her. Those dresses you make the women wear over there are absolutely hideous. They're nothing like what our women wear over here."

"Okay, she removed her dress. Is that all?"

Daren leaned forward in his chair like he was sharing the most precious secret to a friend. "There's more. She began feeling herself, including her—" He pointed down between his legs.

"I see." Dr. James's cheerful expression left his face, and he sat upright in his chair. Rubbing his chin, he eyed the young man sitting across from him. "What do you want from her? You're a handsome man, Daren. You have a way about you. I've heard other women talk about being with you. But I'm not quite sure if this particular young lady might feel so inclined, regardless of what you've seen her do."

Daren turned his eyes towards the floor, thinking a moment. He finally looked back up at the doctor. "I think you know all too well what I want from her. I want to learn all about her, feel her, taste her, experience her completely."

Dr. James opened a drawer of his desk and pulled out a sheet of paper. "I'll tell you what, given the story you've just told me, I'll give you permission to engage with her, but first you must get her signature to ensure confidentiality and consent. Because she'll be transferring to this side of The House, her signature means everything. It's not like the other side where residents are deemed incompetent. She's not allowed to reveal what she's experienced with you to anyone outside The House. This is important, because we don't need outsiders interfering with what we offer here. People don't understand the magnitude of how our treatment methods help others, no matter how unconventional it may seem."

"Don't worry. I'll make sure she's in agreement and get her signature before I try anything. I don't want our work here destroyed, either. I like my job and what I do. We help lots of people."

"Excellent." The doctor handed the paper to Daren. "I'm sure this young lady, if she consents, will be in for a real treat. You just let me know how it all goes or if you run into problems."

Daren smiled at the doctor. "Again, you have my word. Everything will go off without a hitch. I'll see to that."

CHAPTER 3

Anew moon hung in the night sky, lighting up the clearing in bright, white light. Daren hid among the shadows and waited. He fidgeted, growing restless and impatient. She was late tonight, and he cursed the situation causing her delay. The more he thought about her, the more he desired her, to hold her, kiss her lips, suckle those sweet breasts. A soft rustling sound came from several yards away. His heart pounded hard in his chest. In the distance, he made out the dark outline of a figure trudging toward the clearing.

He lifted his lip in a prayer of gratitude before sitting back to watch. Just how to catch her, he hardly knew, with each option appearing more ludicrous than the previous. Should he just go up and introduce himself? Perhaps an ambush by surprise might work. Confused, he shook his head and continued staring into the clearing. The trees formed a bewitching backdrop while the soft grass served as a stage on which this mysterious lady would soon dance.

The performance began with the girl lifting her head toward the sky. When she finished her invocation, out came the scarf, trailing like the tail of a kite on a windy day. She twirled round and round, slowly at first, then faster and faster until Daren thought she might tumble to the ground, dizzy and ill. Though the spinning came to an abrupt halt, her head continued moving in broad circles. Waving her arms above her head, she swung the airy fabric, first in one direction, then the other, before taking the same steps to and fro as she had those previous nights.

Daren studied her pattern of movement in more detail, determining which step might serve best as his point of entrance. She still wore her ugly House attire. Perhaps he ought to act now, before she decided to shed her clothing. He smiled to himself. Whether a woman kept her clothes on or tore them off, he knew how to control and care for his admits, instilling in them a wish to follow his orders no matter what. The present moment served as good a time as any. She pranced out the last of her steps before swirling around once again, the scarf flowing out from one of her hands.

He struck out from his hiding place in one bold move, feet pounding hard against the ground. She never suspected anyone around her. As he grabbed the end of the scarf, he pulled her, gliding and twirling, into his arms. She let out a loud shriek. He clapped his hand over her mouth, holding her fast in an iron grip. With her back pressed against his chest, he caught the stale smell of her hair. The fabric covering her right shoulder had a large tear along the seam. She jerked against him, thrashing from side to side. "Sh-h-h, silence," he said, breathing the words in her ear.

"Let me go," she said, with muffled screams.

"I said stop. Be still." Daren jerked her harder against him, holding her close, glancing around to make sure they were still alone. "I'm not going to hurt you. Calm down." The girl stopped, her chest heaving hard between soft sobs and fear. "It's okay. You're safe. You really are." He rested his cheek against hers for a moment before turning her around to face him.

Her mouth fell open in surprise. "You're ... where ...? Do you always run around naked?"

Daren released his vise-hold and stepped back. He glanced down, perusing his own physique. "Well, I wouldn't say I'm totally naked. I always wear my loincloth." He flashed her a bright smile. "We can't run around nude where I stay."

"You live here too?"

"Actually, I work here. I'm an attendant on the other side of The House. That's why I probably look rather odd to you."

"The other side of The House?" She narrowed her eyes. "I've heard people on my ward talk about the other side, and how there are wild orgies and nothing but unbridled sex. Where I stay, all you hear is the constant chattering of staff and rants from those who are truly insane." Leaning in closer, she said, "So it's true, then, that this House has two sides?"

"It's true. I live a life of pleasure every day."

"You do? Really?" Her eyes sparkled in the moonlight and the breeze played through her hair, tousling stray locks across her forehead.

Stepping in closer to her, Daren said in a soft voice, "I think you're beautiful."

With eyes steadfast on his, she answered back, "You're quite handsome too."

"Let's sit down a minute." He guided her onto the grass. "I'm sorry I haven't introduced myself. My name's Daren."

"I'm Serena."

"Serena. What a beautiful name." He brushed a finger against her cheek. "I've been watching you for the past several nights. Why do you come out here by yourself? And for that matter, what staff person in their right mind even lets you out after dark? I know they watch you like hawks over there."

Her eyes widened. "You've been watching me, even when I ...?" With a huff, she moved to get up and leave. Daren jerked her back in place, holding her close.

"Don't run away from me."

"That's just like staff. Never letting us have a moment's peace. You're no better than the rest." In the moonlight Daren caught a quick glimpse of the hostility in her eyes before she turned away.

Daren caught his finger under her chin, gently propelling her face toward his. "Trust me, Serena, I'm the least of your worries. Of all the people who could have seen you, I'm the best one."

Serena stared into his eyes. "You won't rat me out? If anyone knows what I do out here, I'll lose all my privileges. And I worked hard to get them." Her lower lip trembled.

Daren's voice softened. "I'd never do such a thing. Helping people enjoy their sexuality is my job. It's what I enjoy doing more than anything. It seems like you take this so-called private time to do just that."

Her eyes narrowed. "Why did you keep coming back? Just so you could watch me undress? You have other women, why keep an eye on me?

"I'll explain in a minute. Right now, let me remind you that you have a freedom unlike others on your side. They'll never have it."

"Maybe you're right, but at this point, I still don't have as much of it as I would like. You don't live your life here like you would if you were somewhere else."

"True enough. You haven't told me why staff let you out at night, and I'm really wanting to know."

"If you have good behavior, follow the rules, and don't give any trouble, they let you do more things unsupervised. You have to earn the staff's trust, I guess."

"Earning trust is important in any relationship," he said, nodding in agreement.

"I've earned enough to have some time alone."

"Mind telling me what you did to earn such trust? That's a pretty big privilege, to be allowed out after dark, especially by yourself."

She ran her fingers through the grass. " I've had to pay a price."

"A price?" He raised an eyebrow. "And what exactly do you mean by that?"

Serena closed her eyes, gathering her thoughts. She opened her eyes and stared at Daren. "This is a little awkward, telling you all this. We've just met."

"It's okay. There's probably very little you could tell me that would shock me." He rubbed her arm with reassurance, studying her face. Though she seemed hesitant, he sensed a deep need in her for a listening ear, someone who might actually give a damn about her.

"Good point." She gave her shoulders a small shrug. "Okay, I'll give you a quick explanation. Over time, I befriended one of the maintenance staff. He came to our ward several times to make repairs. He began making small talk, trying to be friendly. One day he made an offer I had to think long and hard about before refusing him flat out."

"What kind of offer?" Daren squared up his shoulders, intrigued.

"He said if I granted him some special favors, he'd find an excuse to get me off the floor for a little while, but I had to pick a set time. I thought about his proposal. He wouldn't tell me what he wanted, so I took a gamble: free time off the ward or stay where I was, pining away in grief. I took the gamble."

"Oh, dear, I think I can see where this is going." Daren pursed his lips and shook his head.

"I selected nights, the time you've observed me coming here. I have no idea what he told the attendants, but they didn't interfere or try to stop us in any way. He took me straight to his room, where he questioned me about men, asking if I knew how to please them. With the things he asked, I just knew he was up to something."

"I'll bet you did." Daren grimaced, rocking back and forth. "And by the way, how old are you?"

She grinned. "I'm twenty-three."

"Good to know."

"At any rate, we spent the time fondling each other. He wasn't the most handsome, but doing whatever he asked let me off the ward. I just dealt with it. Besides, when I closed my eyes and let him have his way, I liked his finger filling me up inside. I especially liked him fingering my clit. Sometimes he used his tongue. I came so hard when he did that."

Daren stretched out, leaning back on his elbows. "Is that why you pleasure yourself when you come out here? You're simply imitating what he did?"

"Pretty much." She gazed hard at Daren. "I love a good hard

orgasm. Once I got into the mood, I tolerated stroking his dick, feeling his tip. It was so silky. When I come out at night, I make sure my body doesn't starve for attention."

"Do you find that if you aren't satisfied physically, sex becomes an obsession?"

"Yes." Serena nodded, her eyes filled with a dreamy expression. "I hate that ache when it's not satisfied. It hurts, but it feels so good at the same time. When I come, everything in me settles down again, and I can sleep better at night and concentrate more."

She lay back on the grass, positioning herself close to Daren. "As long as he got what he wanted, I got what I wanted."

Daren played with a few locks of her hair. "Did you ever allow him to enter you?"

Serena laughed. "He was much older. I know this isn't funny, but he couldn't get an erection. He didn't even attempt to enter me at all. I believe he thought it was pointless to try."

"Or he didn't want to embarrass himself. This is a big concern for guys, you know."

"I'm sure you're right. I think he just got off on touching a woman and having someone touch him back."

To Daren's surprise, she stroked his arm with her finger. A sense of relief flooded him. At least she was warming up. He remained silent, gazing up into the sky. The touch of her hand sent chills down his spine and a jolt of heat to his cock. "I'll ask you this question too. Have you ever had a man's full length inside you?"

"Only once, before I came here. A friend and I were curious to see what it was like. He told me he'd passed by his parents' bedroom late one night, where the door was open enough to peek inside. He knew better than to do that, but the temptation was too strong. He did it anyway." She let out a small laugh. "He told me everything he had seen, and suggested we try it. It sounded exciting to me. I didn't see any harm, so I agreed."

"How did you two get together?"

"We slipped away one afternoon to a meadow on his property. His family owned a lot of land, and there was this one place where we knew we wouldn't be caught, a secluded area a good distance from his house. The minute we settled under an old oak tree, he unfastened his trousers. I'd never seen a naked man before. He was beautiful, fascinating, really. He told me to finger his cock and give his balls a good squeeze. Looking back on it now, I know he needed that to get in the mood and prime himself up."

"Did he do anything for you so you'd be in the mood?"

"Sure. When I nearly had him to the breaking point, he told me to rest on my back. When I lifted my hips, he pulled off my panties. I felt a little strange with my cooch exposed like that. It was a little embarrassing the first time. I knew one thing. I wanted to do the dirty deed with him first. I liked him, but I don't think he suspected.

"Anyway, the more he stroked me, the more his touch drove me wild. I felt a strange, pleasurable ache. When he spread me open and flicked his tongue over my clit, I nearly screamed. The spasms inside took me to another world. I'd never felt anything so good. He smiled and worked a finger inside my pussy, feeling all my hidden bits.

He whispered to me about being nice and wet, and told me to get ready. When he settled himself between my legs, he pushed, working himself all the way in."

"Did you enjoy yourself?" Daren said with a knowing smile.

"He was gentle, but I thought he'd rip my hooch right open. God, what pain! Nothing romantic in that. I'd never suspected it would be like that for a first time. Nobody every told me, but I swallowed him whole."

Daren laughed. "That's too bad for you lovely women, but a most great experience for us men. Nothing better than having your cock squeezed hard by a tight muff."

"He liked it, all right. I loved the look on his face when he came, so happy, satisfied."

Daren returned her strokes, his cock stiffening as he ran his fingers over her satiny thigh. Swallowing hard, he took a deep breath, hoping to contain his lust. "Are there other reasons you come out here at dark? And what's the scarf for?"

"Oh, that," she said. "Have you ever heard of the whirling dervishes who spin as part of their spiritual practice?"

"I think I have heard of them. My family and I have done quite a bit of traveling."

"I don't do exactly what they do, but I create my own dance in order to find connection. The scarf is used for added effect and motion, something extra I can do with my arms too. I like coming out at night when the moon is full. I love the way it makes me feel. I feel spiritually recharged."

"You're quite lovely when you dance."

"Thank you." She fidgeted, shifting her body in different positions, wiggling her feet up and down and side to side.

"If I didn't know better, Serena, I'd say you seem distracted. Am I keeping you from something?" He smiled. Their conversation had disrupted her routine.

"No, I'm fine. Just trying to get comfortable."

Not one to discourage a woman's routine, especially when it involved potential nudity, he continued. "You're lying." He took the liberty of running a finger lightly over her breast, feeling the stiff nipple beneath her dress. "After the first time with your friend, have you continued doing what I've seen, even once you got here, finding ways to satisfy yourself when staff weren't looking and everyone was asleep? I'm sure in some ways, the old man was an added bonus." He sat up, giving her a pointed look. "Tell me, Serena. It's okay if that's true."

"Maybe," she said, her voice cold.

"Good for you, that you know what you need. That's the beauty of my job. I, too, understand what your body wants." He rubbed tenderly over her other nipple.

Serena sprang up, gathered her scarf, and started to leave, but Daren, possessed with quick reflexes, pulled her down, pinning her tight between his muscular thighs.

"Get off me," she cried out, reaching to strike a blow at him.

He caught her arms, pressing them back down against the ground. Keeping calm and collected, he said in a soothing tone, "Please don't run away from me. I'm not trying to take advantage of you. I can help you exercise your spiritual and sexual appetite. You're a beautiful creature."

"Please stop. You're hurting me." She panted, small sobs catching in her throat.

"Serena, listen to me." Daren's tone became more insistent. "Let's share in carnal pleasures together. You don't need to fondle ugly old fools to get what you want. If you sign an agreement with me, I can take your body to the heights of ecstasy. I'm well-trained in what I do."

Without waiting for any protest, he placed a hot, passionate kiss on her lips, slipping in his tongue for good measure. She relaxed against his grip, all her pent-up energy slowly releasing as she sucked his tongue, accepting him as he explored her mouth. He sensed her straining against his thighs. His balls ached. It wouldn't have taken much coaxing from her to slip between her legs and plunge his swollen cock inside a hot, wet channel. But he was bound by protocol. Until he had her signature, he couldn't do much more.

Daren ended this kiss. "So what do you say?" With her arms free, she reached up and ran her fingers through his hair.

"Such magnificence, your hair. I love it."

Her hands found their way to the flesh between his thighs, but he caught her just in time, repositioning her arms behind her head. "No cheating. We don't have an agreement yet."

She smiled, a renewed sparkle dancing in her eyes. "We have an agreement, then."

"Not so fast. You seem to jump into situations much too quickly. I have to know you'll have no regrets."

Her smile turned to a frown. "Well, what do you want from me?" She struggled against him again.

"What I want from you is not only your consent, but a promise you'll do what I tell you to do, and enjoy yourself to the fullest while we're together." He quickly kissed her, gently squeezing one of her breasts. "That's all I want from you."

"You've got a deal, I promise." She gazed up at him, trying to catch her breath.

"Before I take you into my world and obtain your signature as our covenant, I need for you to do one more thing to show me that you mean everything you say."

"I'll do anything."

"I want you to finish your nightly ritual. I want to watch everything you do."

She nodded.

"You'll begin when I release you." He loosened his hold on her wrists.

Without another word, she stood up and slipped off her dress and panties. Daren caught his breath as she stood naked before him. He gritted his teeth, stifling the urge to ravage her body right then and there. Knowing the value of patience, he allowed only his eyes full reign.

Serena clutched the scarf and began the last phase of her dance. The swoosh of the material whispered through the air, and the soft thudding of her feet against the ground drummed out its own unique, rhythmic cadence. Now for the grand finale.

In silence, she reclined on the grass beside him. She inhaled a few deep breaths and, parting her legs, she trailed her hand over her body until she reached her slit.

"Go on, please continue." Daren whispered the soft command in her ears, his lips brushing against her skin.

With delicate fingers, she parted herself, searching for the sensitive knot hidden inside her cleft. With circular motions, her finger teased the bundle of nerves. She closed her eyes, lifting her hips at intervals as her arousal grew. As he watched, his cock grew rigid and his balls ached. While she strummed away at her own flesh, he did likewise. Her breathing, though soft, became faster, and with a little moan, she pumped her hips in time to a strong orgasm. Daren squeezed his sac with one hand, taking several deep breaths, stalling his own release.

"I'm done." Serena turned her head in his direction, paying attention to him for the first time since she'd begun. Her eyes locked on the sight of his hands, focusing with intent on the way he gripped himself.

"I'm not, so watch closely." Daren released the chokehold on his sac, continuing with the soft tugging and manipulation of his head. Serena propped up on one elbow, watching him with amazement.

"Here's a good load for you." He gave a soft grunt, shooting his emissions high in the air. With a sigh, he loosened his hold and sank back into the grass, regaining his breath. "So do we have a deal or not?" He smiled at her.

She moved to straddle his thighs. Pressing her lips next to one of his ears, she said in a whisper, "Take me into your world, Daren. We have a deal."

CHAPTER 4

Daren arrived at the clearing first, fidgeting again while he waited. Was she toying with him, making him squirm? Maybe he should have brought the sacred paper with him last time, and that would have solved everything. But he had to know for sure if she wanted a transition as much as he wanted it for her. Until he had her signature, he didn't have charge of her, which made the waiting even more frustrating. He took a deep breath and tried to relax. She'd been holding up her end of the bargain with the old handyman up until now, so why would tonight be any different than before? Surely she wouldn't suddenly change her mind.

He relaxed at last, catching sight of her outline coming toward him in the darkness. His heart leapt at the thought of becoming her attendant, caring for her and nurturing her in learning more about the pleasures of the flesh. When she arrived, he enfolded her in his arms. "Are you ready?"

"I'm more than ready. I've been dreaming about this moment." She snickered a little. "The old man must have sensed something because he seemed to take his own sweet time tonight. I gritted my teeth through the whole ordeal, reminding myself of the reward at the end."

Daren kissed her. "Sign this, and you won't have to bother yourself with him again." He reached into the leather bag he'd brought with him and removed a small light. He turned it on and held the glow over the page as Serena scribbled her signature on the dotted line.

"There, it's done." She looked up at him, a broad smile lighting her face.

"Welcome to my world, my sweet pet. You belong to me now." Wrapping his arm around her, they made their way back to The House.

§ § §

In the entrance hall of The House, Serena stood entranced by the beauty of the room.

"Quite lovely, isn't it?" Daren paused to let her acclimate to the new surroundings.

"This place looks very familiar."

"Yes, everyone enters The House through this room, but the difference lies in which side you end up on."

"I barely remember this room. It's been a while." Her eyes wide, she gave herself time to bask in the beauty. "This place is so big. I almost feel like I'm in a castle of some sort. I can't imagine how quickly I'd forgotten about it." She stared up at the ceiling over the staircase landing. "That crystal chandelier is the most beautiful thing I've ever seen, like a million sparkling diamonds." Glancing around at the portraits on the wall, she stifled a giggle. "And those paintings! You can just tell those subjects are up to something naughty."

"Yes," Daren said in agreement, "their special parts seem rather inflated. Unless you're paying close attention, you almost don't notice."

"And the staircase. Is it marble?"

"Fine Italian marble, I believe. You can come back here anytime you want, and we'll be passing through as we do things together, but let's go on up to our room, now."

When they reached the first landing, they made a left turn and climbed up another set of steps. They backtracked to the right, heading down the hallway to a door located at the end. Twisting the handle, he opened the door and motioned for her to step through.

"What a gorgeous hallway. Look at those tiles on the floor. And the decorative artwork." She cast her eyes up toward the ceiling, marveling at the attractive lighting. "This is just beautiful, nothing like—"

"You'll find your experience here like no other you will ever have, especially once you're outside these walls." Daren gave her a warm smile and continued to lead her down the hall.

As they walked, Serena's face reflected an expression of worry, but she remained silent.

"What's wrong? You look like you have something on your mind." Daren stopped.

"Where are the doors?"

"Excuse me?"

"Doors. These rooms don't have doors. You can see everything." She peeked quickly into one room before jumping back in place next to Daren, shaking her head. A light flush covered her cheeks.

He rubbed his chin in hesitation. "Well, no. There are no doors."

Her face clouded. "This is all going to be interesting." She sped on down the hall, turning her head right and left as she passed each doorway.

Daren caught up to her and grasped her arm. "Feel free to watch any of this. You're allowed to, you know."

Following his suggestion, she lingered in one doorway to watch a young couple devour each other. A young lady, her hips straddled over her male partner's face, busied herself taking in the full length of his cock. As she bobbed her head up and down, passing his shaft in and out of her mouth, he focused his attention on flicking his wet tongue inside her open gap, giving her clit a good tickle. An occasional moan or giggle from one or the other provided the only testimony to their pleasure.

Tapping her arm, Daren said with a wink, "I bet you and the old man never tried this, did you?"

"You're disgusting." Serena turned out of the doorway, a look of annoyance covering her face.

He let out a soft chuckle, before quickening his pace to catch up with her again. They passed a few more rooms before he pointed out theirs. "And here is home sweet home." He picked her up in his arms and carried her over the threshold.

"Do you really think that was necessary?" She laughed as he placed her feet back on the floor.

"I'm sorry, I couldn't resist. So what do you think?"

The light on the nightstand by the bed filled the room with a soft glow. She looked all around, touched the thick covering on the bed, and moved across the wine-colored carpet to the other side where she ran her hand across the wood grain of the chest of drawers. The tiny sink with its ornate knobs attracted her attention. She turned one of them, smiling as she held her fingers under the cool water pouring from the faucet.

"This is quite cozy, and looks so comfortable."

Daren stood by the bed, turning down the covers. "Come here and help me turn the other side down." Serena smiled and grabbed the other corner, admiring the crisp, white linen sheets. "I guess your man always returned you back to the ward once you finished your time outside?"

"Oh, yes. He never asked me to spend the night with him, thank heaven." She paused, staring at the bed. "I guess you and I will be sleeping together?"

He stepped around and placed his arms around her tiny waist. "Of course we will. As a matter of fact, we'll do everything together, unless there's an activity where we have to separate."

"You have activities here?"

"We always have fun. You won't be bored like you are on the other side."

She rested her head against his chest. "Interesting, and I like the idea of not being bored all the time."

"It's late, precious girl, let's get some sleep. But first, you have to take this thing off." He reached for the hem of her dress and jerked the unsightly covering off her body. His eyes widened. In the glow of the light, she seemed even more beautiful, her skin flawless and smooth, her breasts topped by pert, pink nipples. He gently rubbed over one of her breasts, watching as she accepted his touch. She surely wouldn't be too hard to manage as an admit. With any luck, she'd go along with the teachings of The House. So far, so good. Catching his fingers over the top of her dingy undergarments, he pulled them down to her feet. She stepped out of them. "Again, you won't be wearing these clothes, either." He placed the clothing in a neat bundle next to the doorway and turned back to face her.

"You don't have much to remove," she said, teasing.

"True." He grinned at her, pulling her closer.

"Now can I see you? I've been dying to, you know." She moved her finger over the loincloth, tracing over the outline of his cockhead. "I didn't get a good look in the darkness the last time we met."

Daren gave her a warm smile. "I'm all yours."

Reaching for one of the ties on the side, she gave it a gentle tug, and the cloth came unfastened; revealing a beautiful full sac cupping an ample shaft, topped by a shapely pink head. She opened her hand and enveloped the mound of flesh, kneading and tugging with gentle determination. "So nice to see a handsome man, to feel a stiff cock." Serena beamed up at him. "I bet you know how to use this to your advantage, don't you?

Daren closed his eyes. "Yes, I do. You'll be missed by someone to-morrow tonight, and luckily, it won't be me."

Serena chuckled. "You're so silly."

"Your hands are divine." He sported a full erection. "Come on. Let's get into bed. We still have a little work to do before we go to sleep."

She loosened her grip and crawled in between the sheets, Daren climbing in behind her. Requiring no further instruction, she rested on her back, spreading her thighs wide open.

"Well, you're definitely not wanting to go nice and slow are you?" He gave her a playful, light smack on the outside of her thigh before settling into position over her.

"I don't think it will hurt so much this time, will it?"

"I'll be as tender as I can. You just try to relax and let me in." He placed his hands on either side of her shoulders and wedged his full pink tip inside her folds, aiming for her entrance. "Ready?"

She nodded, gazing up into his face with gleaming eyes.

Taking a deep breath, he pushed in gently but firmly, moving his hips back and forth with a firm rhythm until his total length lodged firmly inside.

With a gasp, she pulled his face down close to hers. He delivered slow, even thrusts; she arched her chest and sank back down into the sheets.

"Yes. Keep going. Easy. That's it." She gripped him tighter. Their rapid gyrations fell into unison. Daren closed his eyes, paying close attention to the sensations of her tight walls enclosing around his shaft, hugging his flesh with each advance and retraction. He liked the way she yielded to him, accepting all of him with barely a whimper. As he moved faster, the regions between his legs filled with a heavy, thick sensation, the tension mounting until he found himself at the breaking point.

He slowed the pace, wanting to make the pleasure-pain last. Nothing better than losing oneself to another dimension. His pace quickened, the urge to come overpowering him. A few quick thrusts, and he pressed hard against her, emptying his lust with full force. She embraced him, pulling him close. "Stay with me."

"I'm not going anywhere." He gave her earlobe a soft lick; she giggled.

He pulled out and reached over to turn off the light. Cuddling her into his arms, he gave her a soft kiss. "Now, we sleep."

CHAPTER 5

A new day dawned at The House. Inside one of the vacant tub rooms, Daren and Serena luxuriated in a sumptuous claw-foot tub. He rested his back against her, settling easily between her thighs. He knew a hot bath would be a nice introduction to his side of The House. They'd already enjoyed a tasty breakfast. He adored watching Serena eat as she savored every bite like it might be her last.

Most of the night had passed smoothly with her curled up in his arms. When she awoke one time, he'd taken her in his arms and reminded her that she didn't need to be scared anymore. Serena had taken on a different appeal for him, someone he'd hand-picked and saved from the brink of destruction. His only wish was restoring hope and igniting in her a desire for true sexual adventures. Great skills in the bedroom positioned her for power and keeping a relationship exciting once she left The House. Unlike the other side, where residents were kept indefinitely, she would leave; free to exert her skills on someone deserving.

Serena hugged him closer, popping a small kiss on his cheek.

"You've done that how many times now?" He laughed as he splashed some water back toward her head.

"I'll stop if you want me to, but I can't resist. I still can't believe I'm here." She rubbed his abdomen with some soap he had placed in her hand. "You'll have to pinch me so I can see if it's all just a dream."

"I can turn you over my knee and give that sweet ass of yours a good spanking. Then you'll know you're not dreaming."

She delivered a sharp bite to his earlobe, laughing when he jumped.

"You wouldn't do that. Or are you just that evil?"

"I'm that evil." He let out a loud laugh.

"I love this tub room, as you call it. And what's in those cabinets along the wall over there? Do all the tub rooms on this side of The House look like this one?"

"Yes. And there's all kinds of things in those cabinets. Towels, various sundry supplies you wouldn't understand right now, and all kinds of concoctions we can use in the bath water."

"What on earth would you put in bath water?"

"Relaxing agents, herbs and salts infused with aromatic oils, that sort of thing."

"I didn't see you use any of it for us. Why not? I would have loved some wonderful smelling oil."

"Because I chose not to right now. I promise we'll have plenty of time for experimenting with the supplies in the cabinets."

"Daren, what's that iron grid in the corner?"

"The iron grid?" He craned his neck to the left corner of the room where she indicated, staring at the metal bars in their neat crisscross pattern. His pulse quickened as he thought about times he'd used the screen for sessions on discipline and pleasure. Every 'admit' experienced lessons involving those bars. The drain in the floor definitely came in handy for "messier" jobs. "Oh, that. Um, I'll show you soon. Don't concern yourself with it right now." He caressed the outsides of her legs. "What are bath times like on the other side?"

"You wouldn't believe the horror of our tub rooms. I haven't had a warm, clean bath in ... oh, I can't even tell you how long it's been."

"Really, what do you mean?"

Shuddering, she said, "The staff fill the tub up once with cold water. After that, we all take a turn."

Daren glanced around at her, a look of dismay on his face. "You take a turn? You mean to say that all of you share the same water?"

"That's right, all thirty-something of us."

"Oh, dear god, that's just disgusting."

"It doesn't matter what's going on with someone, whether they're sick, or—"

"Okay, stop, I get it." He relaxed back in her arms. "You'll never have to experience that here. You'll only be sharing a bath with me, and I aim to see that we're both clean and cared for."

"Hey Daren?"

He closed his eyes, smiling as Serena massaged his shoulders. "What, darling?"

"Why doesn't anybody help the people on the other side, like you did me? You rescued me, you now."

Daren's eyes flew open in alarm. "I know that, Serena." How would he answer this question without sounding so callous?

"Tell me again why you brought me over here. Would you have saved another girl if you'd seen her instead of me?"

He felt a flash of irritation. Couldn't she just be happy that she was here and leave it at that? Her question challenged him. More than that, it reminded him of his own selfishness.

"First of all, remember, neither I nor anyone else can save the world, but I believe taking small steps can help a lot. Dr. James saw an opportunity to serve people who want to understand their sexuality and grow as a result. So he came up with this program here. If he thinks anyone can benefit from treatment on this side, he'll definitely see to it that they do. Not everyone is suitable.

"Why was I suitable?"

"I think you know that perfectly well." He splashed a little water over himself, warming the parts of himself that had grown cool.

"No, I don't. Tell me again."

"Let me put it this way. I'll admit that lust played a part at first. But through that lust, I also saw you as one who embraced her sexuality, one who had an internal hunger so strong you'd stop at nothing to satisfy it. Even the handyman played his role. Don't lie. You know it's true."

"Fair enough, I guess." She kissed the back of his head, running her fingers through his hair.

"I saw potential in you, that you'd be a stronger person with treatment on this side. Does that answer your question?"

"It does." She sighed and hugged him tighter. "I love sharing a bath with you, Daren. I especially like squeezing that full sac of yours, and giving those precious plums inside an extra tweak."

He grinned and let out a soft gasp, happy that she'd finally changed the subject.

"I like playing with your cock too, and fingering that silky head." She wrapped her hands around his shaft, pulling at the flesh, trying to coax out its full length.

"God, that's great. Rub harder and faster around the ridge. Yeah. Good." He hung his legs over the side of the tub, sinking down deeper into the water. She kept at him, stroking with more determination as he voiced his pleasure. His cock had reached its full length. His balls ached; he tensed his hips.

"Let's see how long you can hold out, Daren." Her hot breath brushed against his ear. With a quick move, she grasped his shaft with one hand, encircling and tugging his sac with the other. "I remember how you did this the other night in the clearing."

"You're wicked." Daren gasped. He reached for her hands.

"Don't even think about touching me, or I'll squeeze the life out of you." She teased him, nuzzling his hair and licking the nape of his neck. "Where did you get such shocking red hair? It's incredibly beautiful, like hot flames."

"You've got my cock and balls in your hand, nearly killing me here, threatening me, and you want to talk about my hair?" Daren panted in between chuckles. "Are you going to let go? Because I'm boiling over here."

She gripped tighter.

"Serena, I'm not kidding. I'm begging you to let go." He let out a groan as she tugged at him.

"I like hearing you beg." She delivered a firm nip to his shoulder. "You're so hot and sexy when you beg. You think you're so powerful and all that. I can handle you, sweet boy, I really can."

"Please, you're hurting me."

She released some tension, but continued stroking until he pumped out his ejaculate, sighing with relief.

The moment he finished, he scrambled up, climbing out of the tub. "Let's go, now," he said, clapping his hands.

"What? No, I want to stay here some more. Get back in here." Lifting her hand, she splashed some water at him.

"Get up. We're done with the bath." He gripped her wrists, jerking her to her feet. She let out a shriek. "I'll show you what powerful is, pretty lady!" Encircling her waist, he lifted her out of the tub and onto the floor. He snatched up a couple of towels.

"Why are you in such a hurry?"

He stopped long enough to give her buttocks a soft swat with his hand, smiling all the while. "There, is that good enough for you?"

"Ow!"

"Here we go. " He scooped her up in his arms and, tossing her over his shoulder, headed over to the iron screen. "Ah, what have we here? Must be my lucky day!" Daren reached for some handcuffs dangling from one of the bars. "Apparently someone forgot to put these back, but so much the better for me." He lifted one of Serena's hands and fastened her to the screen.

"What are you doing?" she said, her voice filled with concern.

"Just making sure you don't bolt and run. I don't quite trust you yet." He tapped her under the chin. "You wanted to know about this screen, so I thought I might as well just show you while we're here." He strode across the tile floor and headed toward the cabinets. "Since you seemed concerned that I hadn't done enough for our bath, I thought I'd make it up to you."

"Oh, Daren, I was just kidding. Our bath was wonderful."

"Don't try to backtrack with me, dear girl. I know disappointment when I hear it, and you reeked with disappointment. I want to please my ladies." He pulled some towels out of the lower cabinets and opened up several drawers, retrieving various items.

"What have you got?"

"You'll see. Just do everything I tell you, and you'll be fine." He returned to the screen and placed some towels on the floor before unfastening her wrist. "Now, lie down."

She did as he instructed.

"Do you have to use cuffs?" She sounded annoyed. "I like my hands free, please."

"Really? That's nice to hear." The loud sound of cuffs snapping shut filled the room. He stood up and gazed down at her. "So beautiful you are, but there are a few little things I want to do to make sure you're extra perfect." He reached for a bag of fluid he brought from the cabinet and attached a long rubber hose with a slender, bulbed end. He donned some rubber gloves, tore open a pack of lubricant, and applied a generous amount to the bulbed end of the tube. "Spread your legs apart for me."

"Will this hurt?"

"Of course not. Just do it." Aiming the end of the tube at her anal entrance, he pushed gently.

She gasped.

"Don't panic." He rubbed the outside of her thigh. "Take a deep breath for me." He continued pushing, advancing the tube until the bulbed end rested deep inside her rectum. "You'll feel something cool inside. It's okay, though." He lifted the bag and hung it on one of the bars of the screen.

"Oh, that's cool, all right." She squirmed. "And why am I itching?"

"I want you clean inside and out. There's a reason for this. I'll soon show you."

"I'm so full. Can't you stop?"

"Not yet. The bag's not empty."

When the bag was empty, he removed the tube and quickly insert-ed a gloved finger. "Now if you can hold on for a bit."

"Daren, I don't think ..." She twisted from one side to the other.

"Hey, calm down." He gave one of her nipples a gentle squeeze.

"I'm about to ..."

"You won't be doing anything. I've got you."

"Will you be waiting long? I'm beginning to rumble inside."

"Let's wait just a few more minutes." He tried distracting her with small-talk, but that idea didn't work as well as he wanted. Glancing at the clock on the wall, he determined it was time to end this pro-cedure. "Good. I think we're ready now. Luckily for you, The House has a special quicker acting formula we use for times like this." Before un-snapping the cuffs, he took up a couple of the towels and secured them around her hips and crotch. "Get ready because here we go." He grabbed her wrists and pulled her to her feet. Filled with horror, she squeezed her eyes shut as she released herself.

"Oh, god, I can't believe this. How could you?"

"Don't worry, Serena, it's just me. There's nothing to be ashamed of." He reached for a spare towel and, dampening one end, cleaned her off. "Now, can I trust you to just stand here a moment?"

"I promise I won't do anything."

"Good, because you'll be in huge trouble if you do." He popped her again on her buttocks, and busied himself removing the soiled towels, only to replace them with some clean ones from the cabinets. "I'll need you to lie down again. There's one more thing I want to do before we head back to our room." He pushed her thighs apart and applied a thick layer of cool gel. "I think it's time we remove this little bush of yours. I think you'll have a better experience with a silky, clear mound." Lifting up the hair, he applied a sharp blade to the roots, taking great care to avoid cutting her skin.

"That feels so strange." She rested, relaxed and quiet, with her hands behind her head. "I think I'll like having a smooth muff."

"You will, and I'll like seeing it." He grinned at her, making a few more strokes. "There, I think we're done with this. Go ahead. Touch."

Her lips turned into a wide smile; her eyes sparkled. She stroked the soft skin, grazing her finger back and forth, first one side, then the other. "You're right, that does feel nice."

Taking up a small, green glass jar, he said, "Here, let me put on some ointment to keep the skin soft." She opened up her legs wider as he caressed her flesh, stroking each large lip with firm but gentle fingers. Unable to resist, he took a moment to pay some attention to her clit, teasing the sensitive knot with soft caresses. He watched as she closed her eyes, no doubt preparing herself for a good, hard orgasm. He stopped short. "Now, back to our room." He patted the outside of her thigh.

"But aren't you going to finish?"

"I'll finish you off when I choose to do so." He leaned in close over her face. "Just remember, I call the moves here." Before she could protest, he pulled her off the floor, scooped her up in his arms, and headed back down the hallway.

When he entered their room, Daren tossed Serena on the bed. "Don't move!" He trotted over to the chest of drawers and removed a pair of cuffs, some lubricant, and a double-end phallus.

"Oh, for godsakes, do we have to use those cuffs?"

He snapped the cuffs around her wrists and attached them around the iron bars of the bed. "Just for your complaining, I'm going to use these." He ran over to the chest of drawers and retrieved a ball gag and blindfold, applying them promptly to his charge upon returning to the bed. "It's more fun if you don't see, and besides, I really don't feel like hearing you scream."

She writhed, trying to pull away at the cuffs, her cries muffled by the gag.

"You have the prettiest pink bits down there, if I say so myself." He rubbed a finger inside her, enjoying the sounds of her muffled cries as he grazed her clit.

"Now, for a new sensation, Serena. I think you'll like this. Something tells me you're more ready than you'd give yourself credit for." After applying lubrication to the phallus, he gently inserted the ends, one into her anus and the other deep within her folds. "Nice and easy, here I go. And stop wiggling around so much."

Her muffled cries excited him further. "Easy, dear one, I'm not going to hurt you." He pushed the phallus in deeper, entering inside her by degrees. She twisted her hips, trying to snap her legs together. Daren stopped his advances long enough to push her thighs apart. "Open up!"

The cuffs rattled against the bars, filling the room with loud clanking sounds. She pumped her hips, trying in vain, to pull herself away. Tired of the struggle, Daren gave her buttocks a swift, hard blow. "Stop!" He positioned her on her back once again and straddled her hips. Cradling her face in his hands, he said in a soft voice. "You're resisting far too much. This does not hurt. I need you to relax and take this in." He stroked her hair away from her face.

She sobbed a little, trying to say something against the gag. Daren, filled with a sudden bout of compassion, removed the gag.

"I'm scared." Her chest heaved.

"Am I really hurting you, or is it fear talking?"

"I don't know." Her words came out in a loud wail.

"I'll remove the blindfold, then, but not the cuffs. Do you think you can be still long enough and let me finish?"

She nodded.

"Good, now calm down." Giving her a light smile, he resumed inserting the phallus. "Besides, I'm using some smaller sizes here."

She let out a small whimper. "There's larger sizes?"

"There are larger sizes, and I'd never consider using them on someone as new to this as you are." He gave her a small kiss. "We're in this to have fun, not endure pain." He gave the phallus one last gentle push. "There, it's in now." With a small tug, he moved the toy in and out, watching her face for any signs of discomfort. She gave a quick jump, her eyes staring straight at the ceiling, her hips tensing under his touch. With each push and pull of his hands, she relaxed a little more. At last, her strained expression gave way to one of lust. In the silence, the only sound consisted of the phallus stirring her internal fluids. He moved the phallus quicker, coupling his motions with manipulating her clit.

"Oh. " Her eyes glazed over, a faint smile lighting her face.

"You like this, after all?"

She swallowed and closed her eyes. "Not bad. Not bad at all."

"Is that little hot trap of yours aching?"

A small moan slipped from her lips as the swirling sounds from her nether regions grew louder. "Keep on, Daren."

"As I said before, I'm not going anywhere, and right now I aim to make you come hard."

"I think it's working." Panting, she rocked her hips in time with the orgasm overtaking her body.

"Let it out. I'm not stopping until you let it all out. I want to see that pretty muff of yours chew this dick up good."

She cried out, tossing her head back and forth on the pillow; her hips writhed harder and faster. Daren moved his finger in rapid circles over her clit. She stilled, trying to catch her breath.

He gently slid the phallus out. "We're done."

"Being double-banged wasn't so bad." She smiled and took in another deep breath.

"Interesting term coming from you, but yes, I'm glad you finally enjoyed yourself. I was beginning to worry." He lay beside her, caressing her abdomen, taking a moment to play in her navel. Her breasts called out to him, the pink flesh on top teasing his carnal appetite. He straddled her thighs, dipping his head down toward one of her nipples. His tongue covered her flesh, and the occasional hard sucking from his mouth extracted cries of pain mixed with pleasure.

Running her fingers through his hair, she said, nearly breathless, "I love the way you suck my tits. Your mouth feels so good." Serena arched her chest as Daren suckled harder. Roving over his abdomen and down between his thighs, her fingers reached around to his anal entrance, where she paused a bit before slipping one of them inside. He jerked his hips and pulled away.

"Oh, you tart! How dare you?" He gave one of her nipples a firm bite. She cried out between laughs.

"Can I fuck your ass, Daren?"

"Excuse me? What did you just say?" He gave her soft swat on the outside of her thigh. "You know what, getting double-banged makes you a dirty girl, you know that?"

"So when do I get to make you howl?" She gave him a sheepish smile. "I want to, you know."

He smiled and kissed her. "You already make me howl. You don't know how much I thought about you when I came to the clearing and saw you dancing. Just watching you made me hard, and one night I even jerked myself off."

"Really?"

"Really." He dropped down next to her. "But you know what pushed me over the edge?"

She shook her head.

"When I saw you finger yourself. I thought to myself, anyone who does that is definitely someone I want to meet."

"So seeing me twaddle my pussy made your dick spew?"

"God, your way of saying things is unbelievable." Daren threw back his head and laughed. "And I thought you were a nice girl."

"I am, really." Her expression turned a little more solemn. "But there's something about you. You bring out the naughty in me."

"From the way you carried on a few minutes ago when I tried to impale that sweet twat of yours, I'm not really sure I bring out the naughty in you." Leaning in close to her ear, he whispered, "I'll never hurt you. I may ask you to do some unusual things, but I'll never hurt you. Just know that much."

CHAPTER 6

"Where are we going?" Serena held Daren's hand as he led her down the grand marble staircase. This afternoon, Daren intended to take his admit on a new adventure. The rainbow flashes from the magnificent crystal chandelier above played against the walls, giving the room an almost magical glow.

"I know how much you like being outside, and I thought letting you spend some time in the light of day might be beneficial." He shifted his trusty leather bag over his shoulder. "You know the sun has its own health benefits, don't you?"

"Yes, I've learned that. Unfortunately, I didn't get to spend much time in the sun when I lived on the other side."

"Then I'm sure you also know how the rays enhance your energy and your disposition."

"What's wrong with my disposition? Are you telling me I've been too cranky lately?"

He laughed. "No, silly, but the sun is known for lifting melancholy moods, and I wanted us to enjoy the rays for good measure."

They turned right at the foot of the stairs and headed down the hallway until they reached the end, where they passed through a side door leading to the outside. The sound of birds twittering filled the air, and a gentle breeze blew all about.

"What a pretty day." Serena sniffed the air. "The flowers smell so good, and they're so pretty too." She stooped down, burying her nose inside an open pink rose.

"The sun may have its benefits, but you have to admit that hiding in the dark under a full moon allows one to ... how did you describe it? Oh, yes, "twaddle your pussy." That's it, I remember now."

"You're atrocious." She wrinkled her nose in disgust, taking an opportunity to pop his backside with her hand.

"Now you're taking after me. No copycatting."

She laughed. "I'm only learning from the best."

"Flattery gets you everywhere, and trust me, your learning has only begun."

They strode over the lawn, past the ornate gardens, and headed toward the woods, leaving behind the songs of falling water from one of the many fountains dotting the grounds. Daren, with the exception of a few other attendants, knew the House grounds well, having explored and taken advantage of every hiding place and attribute, using many of these areas as a backdrop for his sexual escapades. In his mind, nature got him in the mood the quickest, while putting his admits at ease. Nothing better than transgression out in the wild.

"You haven't told me where we're going." Serena tugged at his hand.

He turned to her and smiled. "I'm taking you to a hot spring. Not many people know about this place, and I'm sure we'll be alone, with only trees and flowers as Peeping Toms."

"Hot spring?" She stopped in midstride. "Is that like a pond or creek with hot water?"

"You could say that. There are hot spots in the earth where the water runs through, and it comes up into a pool, all nice and warm. I love that place."

She kicked at a small twig in their path, then picked up a stone and tossed it into some bushes, eyes widening as a small lizard scurried away. Daren watched her face light up in animation as she turned her head in all directions, taking in every tree, animal, and sound. He saw deeply into the young woman who enjoyed nature as a gift, like a big box at Christmastime, filled with smaller gifts that delighted the eyes and soothed the soul. He liked this about her, a willing spirit ready to experience life to the fullest. He'd sensed it somehow as he watched her dance those few nights, veiled in moonlight, sailing over the grass as she moved.

His heart stirred, and before he could shut off the vision and the emotion following it, he saw in his mind's eye the two of them in another world outside The House. He stopped to catch his breath and calm the surge of alarm racing through him. This attraction to Serena was highly unusual, one that came uninvited. Though he enjoyed all of his admits on many levels, he'd never experienced this before. The House had strict rules: no falling in love with admits. Unless he wished to end his career, he needed to put any thoughts of her as more than an admit out of his mind. He could enjoy her to the fullest, but for only a little while. She really belonged with someone else, not him.

"What's in that bag?" Serena sidled up, tugging on the strap. "And what are you thinking about? You drifted off a second."

Daren shook his head. "Not thinking of anything but what fun we'll have. I brought a little food. A picnic is nice on a day like this, don't you think?"

Giving him a nod, she sniffed the breeze again. "I like the smell of the woods, so nice and earthy." She threw her arms around Daren's neck, giving him a wet kiss on the lips. "Thank you for bringing me out today."

His heart nearly caught in his throat. "My pleasure, pretty lady." He pulled her along, quickening their pace. "Come on, we're nearly there."

Rounding a bend, he picked up the beginning of a small trail and followed it until they came upon the spring nestled in the heart of a grove of trees.

Serena cocked her ear in the direction of the water. "I can hear it, the soft bubbling."

"Let's get in." Daren moved to the edge, stripped himself of his loin cloth, and helped Serena out of her dress. "Though I like these short, red, form-fitting dresses we have you wear on our side of The House,

I love seeing you without clothes even more." He tugged at the neck strap, loosening the knot. "Sometimes I wish we were allowed to go nude."

"You practically do." She giggled, trailing her hands over the sides of his thighs.

"Hey, I cover up enough."

Shaking her head, she said, "I don't understand why nudity isn't allowed. They allow everything else, it seems."

"The directors who run The House have standards, and they, too, believe leaving something to the imagination is a good thing."

"Oh, everyone seems to make good use of their imaginations from what I've seen." She held on to Daren for support while she dipped a dainty toe into the water. "It's really warm." Smiling, she stepped down onto a large flat rock peeping out of the water. "This should be safe, I think."

After helping her onto the rocky ledge, Daren climbed in behind her, settling himself first before guiding her down beside him.

"M-m-m, I love it. So warm." She closed her eyes and stretched out, wrapping her arms around his for security. "Has anyone ever drowned in here?"

He thought for a moment, stroking his chin. "Now that you mention it, I think there has been at least one drowning. They say the bones rest ... let's see ... right near where your feet are, I think."

Serena let out a scream, jumping into his arms. "What are you laughing at?" I nearly had a heart attack.

Laughing, Daren clapped his hands, his eyes filling with tears. "You should have seen the look on your face. I really had you going."

Grimacing, she pulled herself free. "Hateful thing."

They sat together in silence while a squirrel rummaged under the leaves of an old oak tree. Up high in the sky a couple of birds chased each other, the scolding cries of one filling the air.

After soaking for a long time, Daren said, "Are you hungry, because I know I am."

Serena smiled. "Now that you mention it, I could use a bite." She leaned over and kissed him. "Have anything good in that fun bag of yours?"

"I always have good things in this bag of mine." When he stood up, water dripped from his limbs, running down every muscle and curvature of his body. He stretched out his arms toward the sun, while she stared at him, her lips slightly parted. "What are you looking at? Is there something wrong?"

"You're so handsome, Daren, absolutely beautiful, really. And I love the way your cock and sac sway every time you move. I could watch you for a long time."

"I think you're beautiful." With a grin he held out his hands and pulled her out of the spring. "I see a wonderful patch of moss under that tree over there where we can dry off and rest."

The sun's rays flashed through the trees, casting a golden light on the mossy patch beneath a gnarled old tree. Daren rifled through his bag and pulled out a small container of fruit. "This will be yummy on a warm day like today."

"Did you bring anything else to eat with it, or do we just pick out of the bowl?" Serena sat stretched out, resting on her elbows. Neither had taken the time to put clothes back on, basking in the solitude of the woods where the only sounds were breezy whispers through the tree limbs and animals frittering about. "I didn't realize how much I've missed the outdoors. It's a far cry from the lusty panting and love noises I've heard lately."

"Couldn't agree more, but enough about lusty panting and love noises on the ward. It's time for us to make some of that out here." He patted the space next to where he sat. "Come closer. I want to show you something."

She crawled over to him, waiting for the next set of instructions.

"Lie down on your back, bend your knees, and spread your legs apart."

"So you can do what?"

"Just do what I tell you to do," he said, giving her a light push with his hand. "Good, now don't panic." He positioned himself next to her hips, admiring how her nether lips cupped the wet, pink flesh showing through her open slit, just enough to entice him. "Now for the fun part." He spread her apart and began inserting the fruit.

Serena gave a small jump and stifled a yelp as Daren slid in a tiny piece of melon, guiding the piece as far inside as he dared.

"God, that's cold."

"Sorry, I tried to keep everything on a small container of ice." Smiling, he gave her lip a gentle squeeze. "Here I go again." With nimble fingers, he inserted a strawberry, a grape, and continued with a few more pieces of fruit until he knew she couldn't hold any more."

"I'm about to burst. I'm glad you stopped." She twitched her hips a little, the juice from the fruit running out and trickling between her buttocks.

"Now stay flat on the ground. I want you to feed me your fruit."

"Huh? You want me to what?"

"You'll see." He turned himself around so that his head hung over her slit, and his shaft bobbed at her mouth. He lapped at the fruit hidden inside. She let out a cry, soon cut short by his entrance into her open mouth. He closed his eyes and sucked in his breath through clenched teeth. The stroking of her tongue against his sensitive tip sent jolts of warmth throughout every region of his body. With a soft lick, he consumed the juice between her folds. She pushed out the fruit, piece by piece, as he sucked each one into his mouth, quickly chewing before swallowing each luscious mouthful.

"You taste good, Serena," Daren said between breaths, licking her flesh clean. In answer, she tried to bury the tip of her tongue into the little slit on top of his cockhead. He closed his eyes and steadied his breathing. Her sucking became more in earnest. She lifted her hands and squeezed each ball hidden inside his plump sac.

"You're killing me here." Daren groaned. Her resolve firm, she kept at him, tormenting him until he quickly pulled out of her mouth.

"Hey, what the ...?" She gave the outside of one of his buttocks a light smack with the palm of her hand. "What are you doing? I was just ..."

Without answering, he reclined on his back, working himself with his fingers, coaxing his loins to pump out his lust into a tiny puddle on his abdomen. The heavy rise and fall of his chest calmed to a light rhythmic breathing. Serena stared at him for a moment. Struck with an idea, she snatched up the bowl of remaining fruit and selected a piece. Her eyes sparkled, and on her lips twitched a mischievous grin. She dipped the sweet fruit into his thick ejaculate and brought the passion-laden morsel to her mouth, taking her time to chew and savor the tiny bite before swallowing every bit.

"Did you just do what I think you did?"

"Uh-huh." She licked her lips first, then her fingers. "Sweet and salty, an interesting combination!" Cocking her head, she thought a moment. "I think I'll have the rest of this fruit the same way." Not stopping until every piece was gone, she finished off the remainder of the meal, then licked his abdomen clean.

"There, I wanted to make sure I got every bit off you."

Daren laughed. "I can't believe you. That was pretty creative." He sat up, grasped her arms, and pulled her on top of him. "Is that hot cooch of yours hungry? Somehow I can't help but believe that a good cock-stuffing would top off a great day out."

She spread her thighs apart and glided on top of him, tossing her head back, smiling as he pierced her with sharp, deep thrusts. "You feel so good, Daren. Your cock's so thick and hard. You can stuff my hooch anytime." Holding his hands like the reins of a horse, she undulated her hips, riding him hard and steady, pushing down as he pushed up. Relaxing her muscles, her body allowed him to forge deeper until he hit her back wall. The breeze tossed her hair, sending tiny wisps flying behind her head, giving her an almost ethereal look. Her serene smile, at times, turned into light grimaces of pain—or was it pleasure? Either way, he didn't care, falling prey to the perfect moment of two bodies in unison, in total connection.

Matching her rhythm, he moved his hips slowly at first, then faster, maintaining the pace until her walls contracted around him, wringing out thick streams of passion. She dropped her head on his chest. "Fantastic," she said between breaths.

"You're fantastic." He held her in his arms, feeling the vibrations from her beating heart pounding against his chest. Pulling her face over his, he smothered her lips with a soft, deep kiss. Within each other's embraces, they rested until the sun set low in the sky.

CHAPTER 7

Darkness enveloped the House, and the new full moon lit the grounds with a soft, eerie glow. He had failed to take her out for several nights, and the toll of this deprivation on her spirit began to wreak havoc with her temperament. Not only her body, but her soul craved this special union with the night and the brilliant moon that ruled from above. Daren and Serena wound their way through the trees, crunching small twigs and pebbles beneath their feet as they made their way to the old, familiar clearing.

With only the moonlight to guide them, she broke loose from his grip and ran to the center of the clearing, trailing the scarf behind her. Daren smiled, watching her move like a gazelle, skipping her way to the grassy stage where she enjoyed performing her personal ritual. He caught up with her and grabbed her hand, interrupting her initial twirls.

"I have a bargain for you, if you're interested."

"Oh, and what would that be?" She stopped and turned to face him.

"Come down here by me and I'll tell you." She dropped to the ground and crouched next to him. "You've mentioned wanting to plunge into my ass. Tonight, I'll let you—if you win."

"And if I don't?"

"I take you, if you understand my meaning."

"So what do I have to do to earn the privilege of piercing that sexy rump of yours, Daren?"

He chuckled as he reached into his leather bag, which he usually brought with them on their outings, and pulled out three metal balls made of steel. Soft chimes rang in the air as he shook them in his hand. "You have to hold these inside you and not drop one."

She furrowed her brow, confused at his proposition.

"Let me try to explain this better. You see, these balls are heavy, and when they're in a wet environment, they tend to slip around—a lot. You'll wear these while you dance, and when you're finished, you'll still need to have these little darlings tucked away in that tight little snatch of yours. If you're still holding them, you get a shot at my behind."

"Okay, you've got a deal," she said, starting to sit down on the ground.

"Not so fast. There's one other thing I want you to do."

Impatient, she let out a small huff. "What else do you want from me?"

"You'll need to wear these." Daren reached into the bag and brought out a pair of small clamps with bells on them. As he jiggled them, they emitted a tiny tinkling sound.

"What are those?" She moved in for a closer look.

"You'll remove your dress, and I'll place these on you."

"Where?"

"Don't ask so many questions. Do we have a deal or not?" He jingled the clamps and balls again.

Without another word, she snatched her dress off and stretched out on the ground, where she opened her legs, parting her own nether regions for good measure. "Go on, let's get started."

Daren smiled, admiring her naked, nimble form. Wasting no time, he applied some lubricant and, one by one, slipped in each ball. "Feel okay?"

"So far, so good. You're right, they are smooth."

"Now for these." He applied the bell clamps to her pert nipples.

She let out a small shout, wriggling when he placed the second clamp. "Ow! Oh, lord, those are tight."

"You'll dance for me with all this, and remember, you drop anything, you're mine. So get up now."

She started to rise, but stopped short. "You're right," she said between clenched teeth. "These little monsters will be hard to hold, and these clamps are demons on my tits." Taking a deep breath, she attempted to stand. "Finally, I made it up." She breathed a sigh of relief. "I had to tighten every muscle *down there* to do it."

"Now, you dance for me." Daren stretched out on the grass, watching with great interest.

Serena moved over the grass to the center of the clearing with more deliberation, almost too cautious for her free spirit. The light of the moon cast a silvery glow, making her appear like a ghostly goddess. The bells on her breasts sang with every twitch of her body. She gazed up at the moon for several moments like one in prayer. The night breeze caught up the ends of the scarf, whipping the airy fabric around her. When she determined the right time to start her dance, she shook the fabric free and began her steps in the same pattern she created in the beginning. Giving a small jump, she propelled herself a few inches into the air.

Daren held his breath. He'd only heard the soft thud of her feet hitting the ground instead of a steel ball. She twirled, raising the scarf over her head, letting the fabric flow in the breeze. Breaking from her normal routine, she lifted one of her legs, kicking it out and following suit with the other. She jumped once more, landing on her feet before spinning around again. Still no sounds of steel balls hitting the ground, only the chimes from the bells anchored to her breasts. After a few more minutes, she ended her dance with a final spin and flourish of the scarf. She made her way back to Daren, stepping easily as she moved.

Marveling at her success, he clapped his hands in approval. "Unbelievable. You win."

Serena stretched out on the grass, laughing. "You didn't think I could do it, did you?"

"I wondered. I even had my doubts, but you won, hands down." He kissed her. "You were incredible, as usual."

"I have a question for you."

"What's that?"

"Will you tickle my clit? I want to know how it feels when my pussy tries to crush these steel bits." She let out a giggle.

"I have a better idea. First of all, let's remove these steel bits, as you call them. Here, stand up and give a little push." He pulled her to her feet. With a soft grunt, she popped out the steel orbs, one by one, into his hands. "Now I need you to lie back down again." From inside his bag, he pulled out several smaller balls attached to each other, resembling a string of large beads with a ring anchored at one end.

"What are those? I've never seen such a thing before." She spread her legs apart, allowing him to insert the balls.

"These treats are used to heighten orgasm. You'll see in just a moment how they work. Are you ready?"

"I'm ready." She wriggled her hips while his fingers worked over her clit with vigorous, circular motions.

"That feels so good," she said, whispering. "Keep going." Serena closed her eyes and whimpered, lifting her hips off the ground. Daren kept an eye on her face, showing the signs of an orgasm about to erupt. He stroked faster, teasing her until she cried out. As he sensed a tug on the ring around his finger, he slowly slipped out the balls. She let out one loud, final cry and fell silent.

"Feel good?" He rubbed the outside of her thigh.

"Y-y-es. God, that was incredible. Those balls felt so good when you pulled them out."

"Didn't I tell you they'd make you come harder? And your tight snatch bit down on them hard, too."

"Thank you for being so generous, but now do I get my chance to ride you from behind?" She smiled, tugging at his arm.

"I'm as good as my word, so yes, you get your reward." He reached into the bag and retrieved a large phallus and some more lubricant. "Now you get to learn how to use a strap-on." She gazed at the phallus with interest. "Here, I'll help put this on you." In a couple of minutes, Serena found herself with the likeness of a man's cock resting against her pubic area.

"This looks so odd." Grinning, she pinched the tip, feeling the springy texture beneath her fingers. Daren applied some lubricant before dropping to his hands and knees on the soft grass.

"Okay, Serena, let me tell you what to do first."

She knelt on the ground close beside him to catch every word.

"Go in nice and slow. Even though I've done this a lot, you still want to be as gentle as you can."

"I'll be easy. Don't worry."

He nodded, positioning his body for her invasion. The thoughts of her penetrating him already stiffened his cock. Silence filled the air, with only the sound of crickets for music. "What's wrong? And why are you taking so long back there?" He glanced back, impatient.

"I don't know. I'm scared for some reason."

Turning around, he let out a small chuckle. "You've nagged me all this time, you win a bargain, and now you're scared?"

"Don't laugh at me." Her voice took on a shrill, urgent tone, accented by a trembling lower lip. "I'm just afraid I'll hurt you or something."

He took her wrists in his hands and moved his face close to hers. "You'll do fine. Just spread me apart, find my entrance, and slowly start pushing inside. It's not too hard. I'll tell you if you go too far."

She nodded again. "Okay, let me try again."

He turned around and waited, jumping slightly when she touched his skin. She paused once more before starting again and spreading his buttocks apart, fingering around for his anal opening. He sucked in his breath and squeezed his eyes shut, the tickling sensations nearly driving him mad. With a deep breath, he concentrated and relaxed his whole pelvic area. Success! With tender but firm determination, she worked the head of the phallus inside his entrance.

"That's great, Serena, just keep going. Nice and smooth. Move your hips like you see me do. As a matter of fact, pretend you're me."

She stopped, stifling a laugh. "Now that's a thought if I ever heard one. Pretend to be you. Okay, here I go." Taking his suggestion, she pushed against him with a little more force. He let out a soft moan, which encouraged her, yet scared her, too, as she moved with confidence, only to slow down again. With a few more thrusts, she glided inside him, burying the phallus to the hilt.

"Oh, yes, That's it, sweet girl." He let out a gasp. "Now start moving. Easy and smooth."

She rocked her hips, mimicking a male in coitus, slow at first, then a little faster, her confidence building. As she advanced and retreated, the tinkle of the bells on her chest matched each thrust. She reached around and grabbed his cock, running her hands over his swollen flesh. The gliding of the phallus in his backside speeded up his heart, and the simultaneous teasing of his cockhead created a feeling of light-headedness. These two sensations always managed to get the better of him, but he'd decided long ago he'd rather run the risk of showing a little weakness in nearly passing out from pure delight than not experiencing the sensations at all.

"Easy, precious, you're killing me here." He let out a groan and shook his head, hoping to clear his mind. In and out the phallus moved, stimulating his prostate, teasing him, mocking him. He started to pant, the heat rising in his face. As his heart pounded harder, he lowered himself until he could rest on his forearms and dropped his head down, resting it lightly on the ground. Deep inside, a soft, aching pressure rose. Her hands moved over him with more precise determination, with fingers grazing over all the right areas. He groaned louder, struggling for self-control. The desire to ejaculate nearly got the better of him. His breaths fell from his lips, rapid and heavy. From behind, the tinkling of the bells came faster, louder.

Serena slowed down, stroking his back a little. When he raised his head, she leaned down and kissed his earlobe. Leaning over him, she toyed with his nipples, caressing and squeezing. With one hand, she encircled his sac, cutting off the potential flow of passion. He caught his breath as she resumed passing in and out of him, stirring up his internal fury. He closed his eyes and gritted his teeth.

"I think I'm about to come," he said between breaths.

"I've got you, Daren, just hold on." She squeezed and tugged a little harder. "I'm helping you. Don't come yet. Not yet." Her hips moved faster, grinding away inside him. The dizziness set in, and he felt faint. He dropped his head, breathing harder. "Are you ready?" she said, not letting up her speed.

He had barely sounded out a *yes* when she loosened her grip, allowing him to spill his lust onto the ground.

"Good?" She spooned herself over him, encircling one arm around his chest while stroking his hair with her other free hand. She whispered in his ear, "I loved fucking you, Daren. Squeezing those plump balls of yours makes my pussy dripping wet."

"You're such a lady, Serena." He laughed.

She popped his buttocks. "Saucy boy!"

He freed himself and faced her. "Saucy boy, eh?" Without warning, he grabbed her in his arms, managed to free her from the phallus she wore, and forced her to the ground, smothering her with kisses while she tried fighting him off, shrieking and laughing. Enveloped in his embrace, she stilled at once as he slipped in his tongue, hot and wet. For a brief moment, they lost themselves in the kiss while the moon smiled down in approval. Daren inhaled the fresh fragrance of her long, sandy hair. The sound of her sighs with each bump of his flesh against hers heated his blood. He wrapped his hands around one of her breasts, kneading the satiny flesh with his fingers.

The sound of tiny bells broke the spell. With a smile Daren plucked the clamps from her chest, squeezing each nipple with enthusiasm.

Serena jumped, wincing with pain. "What's the matter, those sweet cherries of yours sensitive?" He licked one of her peaks, ending with a soft bite. She arched her chest, begging for more. Taking her in his arms, he nuzzled close. Her skin felt damp, and the taste of salty perspiration stung the tip of his tongue when he licked the top of her shoulder. Best of all, he liked toying with each nipple, sucking and biting each fleshy bit.

She threw her head back, eyes closed, lost in the heat of the moment as she gave herself over to him, opening her thighs to entice him further. As the pressure built inside his shaft, he slid into place, pressing in his engorged tip. Hot, slick walls hugged him with each advance, yielding without resistance.

"Fuck me hard. Make it hurt." She panted in his ear, lifting her hips to meet his thrusts.

"You want a pounding from me, sweet girl?" He pulled out a little and slid into her with lightning speed.

"Yes. Hurt me good." Her thighs opened wider, and she reached up to tug and play with her nipples. "That's it. Hit me hard." Daren repositioned her hips before plunging in and out of her depths again, hitting her back wall at intervals. Her body shuddered, filled with a mixture of pleasure and pain. The sight of her toying with her own flesh brought him to the edge. He slammed hard against her, passing in and out in a more rapid rhythm. His loins, filled with an aching heaviness, succumbed to a series of spasms.

"I love feeling you come inside me, Daren." She reached up and stroked his hair, pulling his face over hers, smothering him with soft kisses on his lips and cheeks.

"That fine pussy of yours knows how to lick and groom my cock, for sure." He kissed her hard and loud in return. "But you know what, it's getting really late. It's time we get to bed."

"Can't we sleep out here, under the stars?" She held him close, wrapping her legs around him.

"I find a soft, warm bed more preferable. If it's fresh air you want, we can open the windows in our room. And you know what else I can do?" He stood up, dusting himself off. "I can put up a temporary curtain in our doorway to block out additional lights and sounds from the hallway. The staff allow some privacy like that on rare occasions."

"I guess that'll work, then." Serena smiled as she reached up for Daren's outstretched hands. A soft breeze blew from the North. Shivering, she slipped her dress back on and wrapped the scarf around her bare shoulders.

CHAPTER 8

Daren pushed the curtains back, gazing out the window. The day was getting on, sending his impatience soaring. He turned back around, viewing the bed holding a curvy body beneath soft covers. Her face rivaled an angel's, so peaceful, so innocent in appearance. Just looking at her tempted him to consume her right then and there, but he stalled. He had made plans for the day, which included ways to curb his lusty appetite.

"Get up, Sleepyhead." He crossed the room and climbed onto the bed, straddling over Serena, tousling her hair and patting her buttocks hidden beneath the covers. She stirred, forced open her eyes, and yawned. "It's time to play again today," he said, whispering in her ear.

"We play every day. I'm sleepy. Go away." Trying to ignore him, she closed her eyes and threw the blanket over her face.

Not one to be put off, he jerked back the covers and dived in for one of her breasts.

She opened her eyes again with a start. The expression softened on her face while she wrapped her arms around him. One hard suckle from his lips extracted a wince and a groan. Her legs jerked underneath the covers. He moved to give some attention to the other breast, flicking his tongue in rapid succession. From under the covers, she pushed her hands toward his hips until they met the fullness between his thighs. Curving her nails upward, she grazed over his flesh. He closed his eyes tight. The more her hands worked, the harder he breathed, cheeks flushing with excitement.

He lifted his hips, pulling himself away, laughing. "No you don't.

No touching." Cradling her head in his hands, he pressed a soft kiss on her lips. "Get up and get ready, I want to take you to a special place today. Most people around here don't even know about it."

She smiled up into his face. "You said that about the hot spring. Are you the only one who knows anything around here?"

"Of course!" He smiled, delivering a quick bite to her neck.

"You're always full of surprises."

"Trust me, you'll be in for a surprise, all right. Now get up and let's go!"

Serena yawned one last time, cast the covers aside, and stumbled her way to the sink, where she concentrated on cleaning herself up. The sound of Daren ruffling his way through the chest of drawers distracted her.

"You're awfully noisy. What are you looking for in there?"

He straightened up, running his fingers through his blazing locks. "I'm pulling out some special treats for us. Just go back to doing what you were doing, and don't mind me."

"You're also full of naughty secrets, in case anyone has never told you."

"I've been called naughty. Secretive ... Well, I can't readily remember, but perhaps so."

She turned around and stuck her tongue out at him. "So what plans do you have for us, other than this special place and the treats you're trying so hard to find?"

"I'll share that secret with you when the right time comes. Hey, hand me my leather bag by the bed, won't you?"

She tossed him the bag and returned to grooming herself. "I just love the brass sink here, and the pretty handles to turn the water on. This side of The House has some simple, attractive furnishings."

"We believe in beauty, but also functionality." Inside his leather bag, he plunked in the last of the supplies selected from the drawers before he sauntered up behind her, pulling her close. Her head fit snugly under his chin. The warmth of her back heated his chest. He loved holding her. Again, the same earlier vision haunted him. Would he be happy waking up to the same woman every day? He focused his eyes on the reflection in the mirror and placed his hand underneath one of her breasts. Desperately needing a distraction, he entertained himself by kneading the nipple between his thumb and forefinger.

"You like a nice set of tits, don't you?" She turned her head back, trying to see him.

"I think most males like those sweet treats you ladies carry around. What can I say?" He smiled, trailing his hand over her pubic area. "Hurry and get your dress on. The day's getting on."

"You're so impatient." She turned around, facing him head on. "We have plenty of time. Could you hand me my dress that's over there, please?" Daren helped her slip on the form-fitting outfit, threw the bag over his shoulder, and pulled her toward the door.

"Get ready for some unique fun." He winked and led her out of the room, toward the marble staircase.

Taking their usual route downstairs, they reached the foot of the stairs, turned down the hallway to the right, and headed toward the door leading outside. The sun blazed high in the sky and the scent of trees and plants filled the air. Serena closed her eyes and took in a deep breath, a broad smile sprawling across her face. "What a pretty afternoon. And not a cloud in the sky, either."

Daren took Serena's hand and led the way over the lawn, heading toward the woods. The route to his chosen destination was longer than the one to the hot spring they had visited several days earlier. Re-adjusting his leather bag over his shoulder, he strode across the grass, eager to make use of the time left in the day.

Once they reached the edge of the woods, Daren selected the trail. They marched off, losing themselves into the dimness ahead. The wild arrangement of nature proved a stark contrast to the neat, prim gardens surrounding The House. Birds and small rabbits twittered and scampered at every turn. A stream popped into view, flowing onward, sounding off a soft gurgle as the water traveled deeper into the heart of the forest.

"This walk will be wonderful, but what I'm going to show you is even better." He squeezed her hand tighter in his.

She skipped a little. "Can you at least give me some kind of hint? Just a little bitty one?"

"Of course not. Not even a little bitty one."

"Daren," she said, her tone turning more serious, "do you enjoy being here at The House?"

"Of course I do. I wanted to work here, so that should say a lot." He turned and smiled at her. "I love the lusty, physical nature of my work."

"I can see that. But I have a question for you, if you don't mind."

"Ask away, dear girl."

"Do you plan on staying here forever?"

Licking his lips, he thought while he walked, never breaking his stride. That's a good question. I really don't believe anything is forever, but if you're asking me if I plan on staying here longer, then yes would be the answer."

"Do you ever intend to settle down with one person?"

"You know, I haven't given the issue much thought, really."

"Oh." She stared straight ahead, her face expressionless.

"Is there a reason you want to know?" He stopped a moment, turning to face her.

She shrugged her shoulders. "No, I was just making conversation. We've never really talked about things like this before. I just wanted to know more about you, that's all." A grin twitched at the corners of her mouth.

They started walking again. Daren stared straight ahead, avoiding her face. These questions bothered him, pushing the boundaries of his comfort level. Confused emotions never set well with him, and he usually avoided them. He knew, whether or not he liked it, he'd have to come to terms with how he felt about Serena, one way or the other.

"Honestly," Daren said, "I enjoy all types of women, and if the right one comes along some day, perhaps I'll change my mind." He drew up enough courage to glance at her. "What about you, do you have plans for the future?"

She gave him a look of disgust. "Are you serious? Really? I have no plans for the future. I'm stuck here, remember? I was abandoned here by my family, which proves nobody gives a damn."

Filled with deep regret at asking her such a thoughtless question, he stopped short and pulled her into his arms. "Serena, I really didn't intend to have a conversation like this. I'm not liking where this is going. This is supposed to be a fun day, without a worry in the world."

"That's all easy for you to say. You're happy where you are, and let's face it, I'm sure you'll grow tired of me and send me back to the other side of The House soon. This all can't last too long, I'm sure."

Her comment startled him. He'd never considered this before. Most of the admits were situated on his side of The House because of their heightened sexual awareness, dropped off by their families with hopes of vanquishing this side of their nature forever. Little did they suspect that The House embraced this basic nature of one's being, seeing sexual pleasure as healthy and good. With luck on their side, most admits ended up back in the community, reclaimed by their loved ones or someone who cared about them. Her situation was, indeed, different. What would happen if he grew tired of her? Worse, what would happen to her once she completed treatment?

Nobody wanted her back home, so she wouldn't be discharged like the others. How could he send her back to the other side? That notion didn't make sense at all. Such a thought revolted him. Actually, such a thought had never entered his mind, until now. Not even Dr. James had broached this subject. For once, the consequences of his decision to bring her into his world frightened him. He'd never considered the responsibility. He held her tight as the sound of light sniffles reached his ears.

"Have you been worried about this the whole time?"

She nodded.

"Why didn't you say something before?"

Tears streamed down her cheeks. She pulled away from him, covering her face with her hands. "I don't know. I don't think I really wanted to hear the answer, because I'd die with grief if I knew."

Lifting her chin with his finger, he said, "Serena, I'll promise you this one thing: no matter what, you will not be sent back to the other side. I won't let that happen."

Her eyes, wet with tears, searched his with an imploring gaze. "You really mean that? You promise?"

"Precious one, I give you my word with all my heart. I'll never cast you aside that way." He leaned down and kissed her, his seal of promise. "Let's go on and not worry about this right now. You're with me, and I'm taking you on an adventure you'll never forget."

Daren grabbed her hand and pulled her along, picking up the pace. The conversation had left his spirit a little ruffled. Just how would he live up to his pledge? He'd never been in this situation before, and now he felt trapped, stifled almost. The reactions roiling inside amazed him. Thoughts of commitment brought up the opposite question. If staying indefinitely with Serena didn't totally suit him, how would he react to her leaving forever? Did he sense sadness, or a twinge of relief? He shook his head, hoping to shake off the uneasiness lurking inside him. One thing he knew for sure, he needed to do some planning for the future, and what those plans entailed, he didn't quite know.

The trail turned rocky, with the woods and vegetation spreading farther apart, eventually leading them to a large, yawning hole in the face of the mountain. To the right, a few more yards away, the forest line began again. In the distance, the soft sound of the swirling of a stream floated through the air.

"We're here at last." He gave Serena a gentle push forward. "So what do you think?"

Standing in silence, she turned her head sideways and up and down, taking in the landscape. "Well, it looks like we're in front of a large cliff of some kind, and that big hole in the rock wall could be the doorway to a hidden cave, perhaps."

"You're exactly right. We're going to spend our day in that cave. There's a lake in there too."

"Really?" Her eyes widened. "But isn't it dangerous to go into places like this? If something should happen, nobody would ever find us."

"In most circumstances, you'd be right. But I've been in this cave several times, so I know what I'm doing. Besides, I let the staff at the front desk know where we were going, just for safety. The nice thing about this cave is that the directors of The House went to great pains to install lighting and place other things inside to make it more useful and enjoyable for all of us. For those who know it's here and want to use it, that is."

"This is unbelievable. Everyone should know about a place like this."

Daren pulled on her arm. "Let's go in so you won't find it a mystery anymore."

The light of day disappeared with each step forward into the cave. At one point, he flipped a switch, illuminating the room. Serena stopped and stared all around, her mouth open in surprise. Large stone formations dotted the area, some hanging from the ceiling, others standing proudly at attention, rooted to the earth. Off in the distance, her eyes picked out what appeared to be a walkway leading to other rooms. Tiny pebbles littered the ground, and off to the right, she caught a glimpse of the lake, shimmering in the light.

"There it is, the lake you mentioned before."

"Come on, we're going for a ride."

"On the lake? Now?" Her mouth turned up into a wide smile, eyes sparkling with excitement.

"Follow me."

The pair made their way along a path beside the lake, crunching over small stones as they walked. On the back side of the cave, a small rowboat, anchored to a post, floated in the water. Daren tossed his leather bag inside, and ushered Serena to the back seat. He climbed in behind her, settling himself on the seat closest to the stern. Taking up the oars, he rowed toward the entrance to an adjoining room, making sure he arrived at the left side of its rocky wall. Reaching over, he flipped another switch. From strategic places behind boulders and select stones, the glow from the lights gave the room a friendly ambience.

"What a magical place." Serena took a deep breath, running her fingers through the cold water. "How deep is this lake?"

"That part is the secret Mother Nature won't tell us. Nobody knows how deep this lake is." With a few more swift strokes, he pulled up to the edge of a small dock. "Here, let me tie this boat down, and then I'll help you out." He tied off the boat to the posts, tossed out his bag, and stepped out. "Give me your hand. Be careful so you don't fall." She offered him her hand and stood up. Lifting one leg first, then the other, she made her way out onto the dock.

He led her to a large, flat area, making sure he placed everything near the brightest of the lights. "Help me spread out this blanket." Daren stretched out, propping himself up on his elbows. His eyes darted around, surveying every nook, cranny, and stone slab. "I absolutely love this cave. It's one of my favorite places," he said, taking a moment to close his eyes and turn his face up so the cool air brushed across it.

"I can see why." Serena's eyes wandered over the cave walls, her face filled with awe. "Are there any other rooms here, or is this the only one? I could have sworn I saw more when we came in."

"There are others, mostly found in the main room where we came in. Did you see the bridge at the back?"

"I thought I saw what looked like a bridge, but I couldn't be sure. Anyway, my mind was taking in everything so fast, you know." She scooted closer beside him until her shoulder touched his.

His eyes fell on her face. With a pounding heart, he studied her features, her sandy hair, the soft outline of her pink lips, her satiny flesh, her delicate form. The more he stared at her, undressing her with his eyes, the more he wanted to just rip the red dress right off her. "How about some fun, now?" Cradling her in his arms, he smothered her with a round of kisses. "Take off your dress." He reached for the neck straps.

"Only if you remove your cloth." She giggled and tried to roll away.

"Fair enough." Grasping at the ties, he stripped himself free from the loincloth.

"Good. Now, my turn." With fluid motions, she stood up and removed her dress, breasts bouncing lightly as the fabric brushed over her skin. Daren watched with anticipation. Her naked form, with slender thighs, pert nipples, and curvy waist, always took his breath away. He could almost taste her. She dropped back down on the ground, where he caught her up in his arms again and kissed a trail from her lips, over her breasts, and on down to her abdomen. Her body relaxed in his arms. As he gently pushed her back down on the blanket, she spread her thighs apart. He moved his head to the space between her legs and worked the tip of his tongue inside her slit until it rested on top of her firm clit. She closed her eyes, encircling her hands around his head to hold him in place.

"That's it. Right there. Yeah. Oh, lick it hard." She shifted her position at his touch, opening herself wider. With eyes closed, she smiled, lifting her hips. "Keep on. Suck it hard. Yes, hard. Oh!"

Daren worked his tongue and jaws until a sharp cry filled the air. She loosened her hands from his head and began kneading her breasts, tugging at her nipples. A few more draws on her clit with his tongue, he succeeded in bringing on a hard orgasm. She pumped her hips, keeping time to her internal spasms. He sucked hard on her clit one last time before she stilled, her face filled with a smile.

"God, you're good."

"You think so?"

She nodded, her eyes glinting with lust.

"How good do you really think I am?"

"Very good," she said with a whisper.

He pressed his lips close to her ears. "You taste good."

"Do I?" Her fingers wound their way through his hair. Even in the dimness of the cave, the lights caught the surface of his locks, lighting them up in a brilliant flame.

"You do." He licked the side of her neck. "You've never tasted me, though."

She frowned a little. "I most certainly have. What about our little outing by the spring?"

"True enough, but you had fruit to blend in with the taste."

Her eyebrows rose with surprise; she blinked a moment before saying anything. "Does that matter?"

He nodded. "Yes, I want you to taste me as I am, with no mixture of anything else but me."

"And just how do I do that?"

"It's easy enough." He reclined back on the blanket. She sat up, perplexed; then she spied the rosy pink tip between his thighs. "Your turn, my darling." With that comment, he closed his eyes, spread his legs a little, and waited.

The touch of her lips on the tip of his cock built up a thrill of anticipation. Her mouth, slick, warm, and wet, consumed his entire length. As she flicked her tongue over the very topmost part of his tip, his fluids roiled inside him. "God, Serena, that feels good!" He reached out and stroked her hair. "Keep going. Don't stop, pretty one!"

Her sucking became more fervent, her tongue-flicking equal in vigor. He fought against the urge of surrendering to a quick release, wanting to savor the anticipation longer, no matter how hard the ache surged between his thighs. He let out a groan. Her work on him proved relentless, and he drowned in the happiness of losing the battle against his own urges. His fingers wound around the locks of her hair, curling them up and unwinding them again to their full length. Her tongue traced over his swollen veins, bringing him to a point where he couldn't contain himself any longer. With a light cry, he released himself into her mouth. Without flinching, without blinking an eye, she swallowed every drop.

"Just salty. Not sweet this time, but a rather odd texture." She sat up, a little dazed. "I've never tasted a man's cum before."

"A little thick by itself, no?" He smiled, rubbing his hand over his pubic area, a new gleam playing in his eyes. He sat up, the smile replaced with a sober expression. "I think you need something to wash it all down, don't you think?"

She shrugged. "I guess a little water would be nice. Did you bring some with you?" With a light toss of her head, she indicated in the direction where the leather bag lay.

Daren also glanced over in the direction of the bag and slowly turned his head back to face her head-on. "A little water would be nice, indeed." He stood up and stretched a moment. "You want water? Then I want you to get on your knees and do what I ask you to do."

Her eyes clouded a moment, unsure of the reason for his request. "And why do you want me to do that? Can't you just pull some out of the bag?"

"Don't ask so many questions. Just do what I tell you to do."

Serena complied, kneeling in front of him. He moved in closer, grasping her head between his hands. Turning her face up to meet his, he stared down at her. "I'll offer you the water."

"You'll what?" Her face turned pale, and she shrank back.

"Don't pull away from me." His grasp tightened around her head, pulling her closer to the tip of his shaft. "Take me in your mouth again."

Without further argument, she slipped her mouth over him, eyes never leaving his, and wrapped her hands around his hips for support. He sucked in his breath, as her tongue flicked over him, indicating her readiness, her submission. "Now, I'm going to offer myself to you. You'll drink every drop. Do you understand?"

She let out a sound of affirmation.

"Good, now here I go." He closed his eyes, relaxing his muscles, encouraging his water to flow. With control, he let out a small stream, giving her a few seconds to acclimate to the taste of human fluids. She seemed undaunted, swallowing without any show of revulsion. He released more. She began swallowing. Comfortable in their rhythm of intake and release, he poured himself out, totally and completely, until his body sensed the comfort of emptiness. He let out a sigh and opened his eyes. "How was it?"

She just stared up at him, saying nothing.

"Well?"

"That's the strangest thing I've ever done." She sat back down, gazing up at him.

"What did you think about the taste?"

Running her fingers through her hair, trying to collect her thoughts, she said, "I'm not exactly sure how to describe it. Tart, lemony, salty. Not exactly bad, either."

Daren knelt down beside her. "Do you know there are healing properties in our own fluids?"

She raised an eyebrow in doubt. "Oh, really, I just looked at it as waste."

He shook his head. "No, it's not just waste. It's stated in certain practices and teachings that consuming these fluids can be beneficial." Another smile lit his face. "Now I want you to lie back on this blanket, with your legs turned toward the light."

"What are you going to do now?" Her brow furrowed a little.

He whispered, "Just do it!"

With a light huff of impatience, she did as he instructed.

"Now bend your knees and spread your legs wide open." He reached for the leather bag and brought out a few packets of supplies, each sealed for protection and cleanliness. While he arranged every-thing in proper order, he saw the expression of anxiety on her face. "Don't worry, you'll enjoy this. Just open yourself up to me, and don't fight me in any way." Her face tensed up at the sound of wrappers tear-ing, and the snapping on of rubber gloves increased her fear. When he brought a pad of cleanser down against her skin, her hips twitched. "Ah, careful, sweet one, no jumping, because I don't want to hurt you."

She took a deep breath, letting it out slowly with pursed lips. He cleansed her with great care before extracting from one of the packets a thin silver rod with a rounded end. He'd taken the opportunity to cover that end with lubricant. The other end he held in his fingers curved up slightly.

He said, "This rod is, in fact, an antique sterling silver catheter. During one of my travels abroad, I purchased it in an antique shop specializing in medical collectibles. I liked the quality of the metal and the design. House staff are so kind in making sure this special piece is sanitized and in good working order at all times. It's special and pre-cious to me, and because you are too, I intend to use it today."

Her eyes widened, and her face flushed; her breathing becoming more rapid.

"Don't be scared. I think you'll enjoy this. Relax, because here I go."

She let out a whimper and closed her eyes.

Daren, with the steady hand of a physician, aimed the end at her tiny orifice and guided the tip inside, advancing tenderly, watching her face for any signs of discomfort. Her hips twitched ever so slightly upon its entry; a gasp slipped from her open mouth. "Feel good?"

Her face said it all. As he gently pushed in the silver catheter, tak-ing a few seconds to move it back and forth, her face showed signs of pleasure, her mouth turning into a smile. Working the metal instru-ment by degrees, he pushed it into her bladder. She winced. From his experience, this always happened, as the entrance of the tip created a strong urge to urinate. He held his finger over the top while he lowered his face, slipping his lips over the end as if he were using a straw. Controlling the flow of her fluids by placing his tongue over the top, he began sucking, drinking in her golden liquid like an offering from the gods.

She remained still, processing the sensations inside her brain, her face and body giving him the signs of pleasure and submission he wanted to see. When he finished, he stopped and pulled out the catheter, taking his time so she could savor each sensation of the metal rubbing against her most delicate walls.

"Again, you taste good." Daren placed his prized toy in a special bag for cleansing.

"Those were the strangest sensations I've ever felt, almost like little flurries in my tummy." She started laughing. "I can't believe I let you inside my pee hole."

"Pee holes are fun, aren't they?" He gave the outside of her thighs a small, friendly pat. "That area of your body is very delicate, and highly sensitive. I like my silver catheter because it not only allows me to drink from someone, I can also use it as a sounding device."

"Sounding? What on earth do you mean?"

Daren assumed a philosophical air. "Urethral sounding is a wonderful way to enjoy sexual gratification. A sound is nothing more than a smooth metal rod with rounded ends. Usually these are used for medical procedures, but The House approves of their use in sex play."

She sat up. "Do you ever let anyone inside your pee hole?"

"You bet I do," he said, laughing. "I love the sensation of a metal rod inside me. I sometimes use sounding rods on myself."

"Can I use one on you?" Her lips turned up into a sly smile as she rubbed her finger over his shaft and tip.

"You won't leave me without learning how, so don't worry about that right now. We'll play with rods later." He took her in his arms again, pulling her back in a reclining position on the blanket. His fingers stroked over her body, making their way inside her slit once again. As he fingered through her folds, he said, "Tell me more about the gentleman you were with before you came to The House."

"Gentleman? Oh, you mean Martin?" She placed her hands behind her head, arching her chest ever so slightly in the process, leading Daren's gaze from her bottom to her top. "Let's see, what to say about Martin." Lost in thought, she grimaced at times, until she came up with her story. "He and I didn't live too far away from each other. As I mentioned before, his family owns a great deal of property. Though we grew up together, we hadn't paid much attention to each other until recently." She turned to Daren and smiled. "I guess that's just the way it is, isn't it? You don't really start paying attention to someone until a certain time in your life."

"That's true," he said in agreement. "Maturity seems to heighten your awareness, including sensations in your body." He slipped her a quick kiss. "But go on. Don't let me interrupt."

"As of late, I had started paying more attention to him, especially the way he was built, so solid and strong. I loved his face when he smiled, so pleasant, and his eyes came alive with a life of their own. I think he'd begun having the same interest in me, but like I said, I didn't let on. The more I think about it, I went along with him because I wanted him to be my first love. Maybe my only love."

She stopped a moment. Her eyes filled with tears.

Daren wiped a thumb across one of her cheeks. "Are you okay?"

"I guess," she said, trying to keep herself from crying harder.

He sat up. "What's wrong?"

"I miss him. When I touch myself, I pretend it's him. When I spent time with the handyman, I'd close my eyes, pretending he was Martin." She wiped her eyes and sniffled. "From what you told me the first time, Martin sounds like a man who's a quick learner." Daren smiled, welcoming any levity at this moment. "Did you two ever make it back together before you came here?" He stroked her hair, giving her a light kiss on the top of her head.

"No, that was our only time." She wiped away a stray tear trickling down her cheek. "My parents sent me away before we could have any chance together again."

"And just why did they send you here? I don't think you've ever told me that."

"Being devout in their religion, they didn't like my lack of interest in church, and they didn't like the fact that I enjoyed my dancing. They'd catch me at it in my room or out in the yard sometimes. I'd get a scolding, that's for sure. They said nice girls didn't act like that, and that I'd be better off spending my time studying things we learned in church."

Daren wrapped his arms around her again and held her close. "Just exactly what are your beliefs, Serena?"

Her face flushed as she started to answer him. "Daren, I don't embrace a philosophy based on strict Christianity. I'm more of a spiritual person who believes in the laws of the universe and nature. I don't accept the dogma you get in church. It just doesn't sit right with me, you know?"

He nodded. "I think I know what you're saying, but how did you come to a different understanding?"

She smiled at him. "I befriended a lonely elderly lady who lived at the end of the lane about three streets over from my home. Her house, because of its location, was separated more by woods and country fields. Everyone else thought her eccentric and odd. If we had lived in a much earlier time, I think she would have been burned as a witch." Serena shook her head, turning her eyes to Daren's "I'm sure of it."

"Burned as a witch?" Daren frowned. "That doesn't sound too nice." He scratched his head a moment, thinking. "So what kind of things did you learn from her?"

She stretched out on her back, wiggling her hips into a more comfortable position. "Well, she taught me about how we all fit into the universe together, about soul personalities, love and what it really is.

She gave me a better understanding of natural laws and how they influence us, and how we're bound to abide by them."

"I see," he said. "Does Martin feel the same way?"

The soft smile faded from her face as she sat up in a hurry. "Oh, dear, I don't know that for sure." She glanced over at Daren. "Does it matter?"

"Well, I'll only suggest this. Two people sharing a common belief makes for a better union."

"A better union? What do you mean? And why are you using such a word talking about me and Martin?"

Daren concentrated on tracing his finger over an imaginary shape on the blanket, hesitant about how to continue this conversation. He looked up at her and said, "Serena, do you have a desire to be with him someday, permanently?"

She blinked in confusion. "You mean, like, be his wife or something?"

"Yes, like his wife, bear his children ... you know ... that sort of thing."

Her head hung low, her lips trembling. "I don't think I'll ever get out of here. Nobody has even come to call on me while I've been here. For all I know, he's most likely found someone else by now."

He rubbed her shoulder, trying to offer some form of comfort. "Serena, maybe there's still a chance. How do you know he's not missing you?"

"I don't know that he's not, but why hasn't he tried to come and see me, then?"

"Most people don't find The House the most comforting place to visit. Besides, he may not think he's allowed to. Does he even know you're here?"

She shot him a withering look. "I don't know. If he did find out, wouldn't it have been nice if he had made an effort to come and visit?"

Daren took her face in his hands, landing a tiny kiss on her cute, button nose. "If you two were beginning to enjoy each other physically, he's bound to have missed you when he didn't see you around anymore. I can't believe he'd be that oblivious. On the other hand, I hate to admit it, but sometimes it seems like we men just don't get it, do we?"

Turning her eyes up to meet his, she said, "Do you think your work here at The House is based on love, or just lust?"

He threw his head back, chuckling. "Now that's a trick question if I ever heard one."

"You mentioned while we were walking that you love the lusty, physical nature of your work, but do you know what love is?" Serena grabbed his hand, pressing it between hers. "Who would be the right one for you?"

Filled with alarm, he tried to pull his hand away, but her grip tightened. Overcome with a strange notion, he blurted out, "Who would be the right one for *you*?" He faced her head on. "Do you love *me*?"

"What?" Her mouth fell open in surprise, and she dropped his hand like it had burned her.

Daren stood his ground. "You heard me. Don't look at me like that. Do you love me?" His eyes narrowed as he viewed the discomfort on her face, her fingers fidgeting, cheeks flushing bright pink. He moved in close and took her in his arms. Whispering in her ear he said, "I need to know where we stand with this. I sense you want something, Serena, and you want it bad."

She gave him a light push. After regaining her composure, she stared him in the eyes. A slow smile formed at the corners of her mouth. "What an interesting question. I think you'd be a wonderful person to love, and I like the qualities that you have. You remind me somewhat of Martin, only you're much more skilled in the naughty ways than he is. But then again, you practice lust like a religion."

"So you don't love me, then?" Daren feigned a look of disappointment.

She fell back laughing. "I don't think you really mean that as a serious question. Maybe my questions led you to believe something different."

"Well, all this talk of finding the right one and settling down. I know how you women are, how you go about finding out certain things."

"I'm sorry, Daren." She clasped his hand in hers again. "Honestly, I think I use you as a yardstick, a means of comparison. I enjoy being with you, and I think when I imagine I'm with Martin I feel the same way, only a bit more."

Daren breathed a sigh of relief. "Good, because that's the way it should be. You need to be with someone you love." He lifted her chin with his finger. "And as for me, I teach people how to enjoy the most basic parts of their nature without feeling shame or disgrace. Experiencing sexual pleasure is the foundation of our being, and if you can't embrace it and love it, you'll have a difficult time developing the higher aspects of yourself."

"You make this sound so serious and philosophical. Do you really believe what you're saying?" She gave him an incredulous look.

His face solemn, his words intense, he stated, "Yes, I believe what I say; and most of the other attendants on our side of The House believe the same." He reached out and placed his hands on either side of her shoulders. "You may think we revel in perversity, engaging in activities with no meaning, but it's just not true. Everything we do serves a purpose. And I'll let you in on something else. We're not allowed to fall in love with our admits."

"I see." She nodded. "But you have to admit, your methods of teaching are not in keeping with the community's stance on the subject of sex."

"Yes, they see physical union much differently than we do here at The House. The community would be horrified if they knew all our secrets and the philosophy behind it. That's why I had you sign the agreement before I brought you over with me. We have to keep our teachings here private. Only people who are allowed on my side of The House learn what you are now. Returning home and sharing your experiences here could create a problem if outsiders rallied against us. That's why we would have the authorities pick you up, and you'd be placed back on the other side of The House once again."

"Oh, really? You would go that far?"

"This is serious, Serena. Yes, we would go that far. It's one thing to receive visitors on your side, but on our side, we're careful how any visits are planned."

She let out a deep breath and settled back down again. "Well, no one will hear a peep from me, so don't worry about it."

Daren wrapped his arm around her. "Good, I'm glad we understand each other." He glanced around the room before reaching for his leather bag and gathering up his used supplies. "Here, let's get this placed cleaned up and head on back. I think we're done for the day."

CHAPTER 9

S erena, get up. Wake up. Now." Daren gave her shoulder an extra firm push, trying to rouse the form sleeping beneath the covers. "Um-m-m, what's going on? And why do you keep poking at me like that?" She sat up, rubbing her eyes with the back of her hand.

"I have something to tell you, but I want us to eat breakfast first." The food trays rested on the floor at the foot of the bed, where Daren always preferred to eat in the mornings. When he removed the covering from the plates, he inhaled the aroma of freshly cooked food. Mornings at The House allowed everyone to wake up at their own pace, with no rush or stress. Because the directors believed a good mood at the start of a day ensured a happy one for the rest of it, they created the rule for breakfast being served in rooms.

"So now I have to spend our meal-time in suspense, dying of curiosity?"

"That's right, you've got it. Now get out of bed and come on down here by me." He patted the empty space beside him with his hand.

"You know what, you're making me wait. Maybe I can just close my eyes and rest in bed a little longer." She rolled over and threw the covers back over herself.

"So help me, don't make me get up from this floor." Daren's stern tone didn't seem to bother her. She didn't make one move. He sighed and pushed the plates out of the way. No sooner than his hand touched the covers, she sprang from the bed, seating herself down by one of the plates."

"You did that just to irritate me, didn't you?" Daren's eyes flashed with annoyance.

She shrugged and chewed on a small slice of bacon, pretending to ignore him.

He sat down beside her and snatched up a bowl of oatmeal, swallowing the bites from his spoon in silence.

"So what's the big secret?" She kicked at his foot with hers.

He turned away, his back facing her.

"Daren, I'm sorry. I didn't mean to make you mad."

"You like pushing me to the limit at times, don't you?" He kept his back toward her. "It seems to be a sport of yours."

"Sometimes, but honestly, I don't really mean to upset you." She put her plate down, crawled over, and wrenched his bowl away. Taking his face in her hands, she kissed him, licking off the faint film of butter coating the bottom of his mouth. "You're one of the few people I know who sweetens their oatmeal with butter and honey." She dipped the spoon in the bowl and passed a hot bite into his open mouth. After feeding him several spoonfuls, her curiosity kicked in again. "Can't you at least give me some idea why you wanted me out of bed so fast? What do you have planned for us today, anyway?"

He turned around, smiling. "I think I should ask *you* what you have planned for the day."

"That's all? You woke me up just to tell me that?" She plunked the spoon back in the bowl and handed over his meal with an expression of disappointment.

"Trust me, you're in for the surprise of your life. Here's the twist: you'll be planning the events of today on the fly." Daren reached for a croissant, placing some of his egg inside.

She said nothing but stared at him, chewing her food. When she swallowed, she said, "You make absolutely no sense whatsoever, you know that?"

"It'll all make sense soon, I guarantee you." He pushed away the plates and stood up. "Come here." He moved toward the chest of drawers. "You'll need to put this on." Reaching down to the bottom drawer, he pulled out her old House attire, dangling the dingy, unsightly garment between his fingers.

Shrinking back in horror, Serena gasped, clapping a hand over her mouth. Big, hot tears welled up in her eyes, and her lower lip trembled. "You ... you're ..." She gulped before speaking again. "You're tired of me already? I have to go back to the other side now?" Her chest heaved.

Daren stared at her.

Her fists clenched at her sides. "I knew this would happen. You have no intention of keeping your promise." She lunged forward, her voice nearly reaching a shouting point in between sniffles.

"Whoa! Hold on a minute." He held out an arm, warding her off. "When will you learn to trust me?"

"Never!" Her eyes seemed to flash hot, red bullets in his direction.

"Just get over here and put this on, will you? And would you please stop crying. You look like an absolute wreck."

"Oh, I have to get dolled up to face those bastards on the other side, do I?"

Daren strode over, ignoring her comments, and began helping her slip on her dress. "Here, hold up your arms."

She flinched and backed away, teeth clenched. "I'm not going back over there. I'll do whatever it takes to get out of here. So help me, I'll never land back over there again, even if it kills me."

Daren paused, taking her in his arms. "Do what I tell you to do, and you'll get your wish. You'll understand in just a minute." When he'd slipped on the dress and tugged out the last wrinkle, he stood back and cocked his head, studying her appearance.

"Stop gawking. I know I'm nothing to look at." She hung her head, pouting.

"Well, I must admit, I like you better naked, but I can't let you out of this room like that." He grabbed a brush from the counter next to the sink and ran the bristles through her hair. "There, I think that helps a little." He opened a drawer to remove a wash cloth. "Wash your face off.

I don't want you having tear stains on those beautiful cheeks of yours. When you're done, I want to explain something to you."

Snatching the cloth from his hands, she yanked at the faucet, turning on the water. While she washed her face, he moved to his side of the bed, dropping to his knees to retrieve his leather bag from underneath. Tossing it on the bed, he waited until the sound of running water stopped. "Come here" In silence, she crept toward him, eying the bag with mild interest. He placed his hands on either side of her shoulders. "I need you to pay very close attention to what I'm about to tell you. Do you understand?"

She nodded.

"Serena, we've invited Martin here today."

Her face went pale; her knees weakened. Daren caught her in his arms and guided her to a sitting position on the bed. "This will most likely be the most important day of your life. It's a make or break deal, really. He can't know you've been on this side of The House. This is why you're wearing your old dress." He picked up the bag and handed it to her. "In this bag, I've placed some handy supplies, food, and your scarf. I want you to feel him out, see if he's happy seeing you again. When or if you think the time is right, you might try a few moves on him."

"A few moves?" Her brow wrinkled.

"Yes. If he's missed you at all, he'll be itching to have a shot at you. No man in their right mind would ever turn you down, especially if they've been with you before."

"Looking like this?" She scowled. "I never looked like this at home. I had pretty clothes, kept my hair neat."

"You're in an asylum. He'll understand, and I'm sure he won't be expecting you in fancy garb and make-up."

"Why did you invite him here?" Serena's eyes narrowed. "And what if I screw things up? What if he doesn't want me anymore?" Her voice rose.

"Serena, stop it." Daren admonished her, eyes intent on her face.

"Dr. James and I thought long and hard about this. Your situation is unique. When we got in touch with Martin, he was more than willing to come. And you'll know how to handle him. Don't doubt yourself so much. Go nice and easy." He hugged her close. "Just keep in mind, though, failure is not an option. If this works, this could be your ticket out of here."

She took a deep breath, nodding, turning her face toward the door. Daren pulled her off the bed, propelling her forward. "Go down to the entrance hall, and he'll be waiting for you. When you two are finished, you'll bring him back to the hall, and a staff member will be there to take care of the rest. As for you, you'll return here to me." As she headed out of the room, he grabbed her arm one last time. "Remember, go with your gut and believe in yourself—and him."

§ § §

Serena turned out of the room and headed down the hallway, making her way to the marble staircase, her thoughts racing. Would spending a whole day with Martin prove a successful venture? Had he come out of pity, or did he really want to see her? The fact that her freedom from The House hinged on winning him over frightened her. Options were limited at best, if not basically non-existent. There was no choice but to succeed. The handyman had offered some solace in her grim world, even if it meant prostituting herself. But Daren had been her true savior, and she knew staying with him indefinitely was out of the question. She'd grown to admire him, had almost fallen in love with him, but her heart kept leading her back to Martin. Since she had joined Daren on his side of The House, she hadn't been with any-one else. Many of the activities at this time were optional, and for some reason he had chosen not to participate, keeping her to himself. She shook her head and hoisted the leather bag over her shoulder. What did he have in that bag, anyway? Eager to see the supplies Daren had selected, she placed the bag on the floor and unbuckled the flap. Inside lay her scarf, packets of lubrication, and a small bottle of oil. She also found a light lunch of fruit and tiny finger sandwiches, covered and tucked away on a container of ice.

Smiling, she re-buckled the flap and repositioned the bag over her shoulder. When had Daren placed these items in here? His quick wit and skillful planning always fascinated her, and this time proved no exception. As she walked, the bottom of her dress flapped at her knees, and the sleeves and collar held her body in an unrelenting grip. She'd grown accustomed to wearing the short, sparse clothing in Daren's world. The light from the magnificent crystal chandelier loomed ahead, and from the prisms, her eyes already caught the first rainbow flashes playing along the walls. She turned a corner and started her descent down the stairs, her eyes staring straight ahead. Inside her chest, the hard pounding of her heart filled her ears with a soft drumming sound, echoing the rhythmic thump-thump.

Near the main door stood the figure of a man who busied himself examining some of the paintings on the wall. His back faced the staircase. Because of her light steps, he didn't hear her until she reached him. To attract his attention without startling him too much, she lightly touched his shoulder. The young man whirled around in surprise. Summoning up every ounce of will to calm herself, Serena smiled. "Hi, Martin."

CHAPTER 10

The young man smiled and nodded. "Serena, good to see you." His eyes roved up and down her figure, making her all the more self-conscious about her appearance.

"I'm sorry, they make me wear this hideous thing. I know I look nothing like the way I used to." She wrinkled her nose in disgust.

Martin placed a hand on her shoulder, giving her an intent look. "You're still beautiful to me." He reached for the leather bag. "Here, let me carry that for you."

"What made you decide to come? This is such a surprise. I would have never believed it."

"We can talk about that later. Is there a place here for us to sit and visit, or will we go somewhere else?"

"Um ..." She stalled a moment, confused. Daren had always planned their outings. Struck by an idea, she said, "You know, Martin, it's such a beautiful day outside, so warm and breezy, let's have a picnic lunch. As a matter of fact, I know of a perfect place close by where we can visit without any interruptions from others."

His eyes twinkled with their old, familiar warmth. "Point which direction, and I'll follow you anywhere."

They stepped out into the sun, greeted by the sound of the outdoors, birds calling to one another from the treetops and insects buzzing. In the distance, water gushed from a fountain. From every direction, rows of colorful flowers flaunted their petals, perfuming the air with the sweetest scents. "These grounds are simply amazing, like something you'd see in a palace. I never would have guessed how pretty this place really is." Filled with awe, Martin turned his head back and forth, checking out everything in sight.

"This place is a world unto itself. We have gardeners, dairymen, doctors, nurses, attendants, cooks, handymen. You name it, we have it."

"Really?"

"Really. We're pretty much self-sustaining."

He nodded. "I can see that." Without word or warning, he took Serena's hand in his. She fought the urge to faint. The additional years had matured him, fine-tuning every aspect where looks were concerned. She'd forgotten what being around him was like. Her eyes took in his features as they walked, and she admired the deep mahogany color of his neatly cropped hair, the pink flush in his handsome cheeks, the strong, sinewy build of his body.

"Any idea where we're going?" He smiled, squeezing her hand tighter..

"I do have a special place, but I want to keep it a secret. I've spent some time there, and you'll enjoy yourself as much as I have." Her heart leapt as he paused and kissed her on the cheek.

"Sounds like fun. Let's go."

Serena located the trail she and Daren had traveled. Together they followed the path through the woods, winding themselves deeper into the heart of the forest. She liked the fact that they would be quite alone. Just the sight of him stirred the lust inside her. His eyes and facial expression hinted at the old desire he'd had for her the last time they enjoyed each other, carefree and easy in the meadow. Today they could relive that time, continue where they left off, pave the way for a future. In the distance, she heard the soft gurgling of water. "We're nearly there." Excited, she pulled him along until they found themselves at the edge of the hot spring.

Martin gave her a puzzled stare. "Okay, it's a pond. It's pretty, but is there anything more to it?"

Her eyes lit up. Taking both of his hands in hers, she said, "Yes, it's a hot spring. I want us to get in, but before we do, I'd like to spend some time and catch up on things. How does that sound?"

"That works for me." Martin helped her down to the ground and settled down beside her. "I didn't realize how big this place was. There's not a lot of talk about it at home."

"Oh, really? That's interesting. I wonder why not." Serena tried to sound surprised.

"Who knows? Maybe they swear you to secrecy or something!" Martin's eyes stared hard at her; his grin brought out a dimple in his left cheek.

With a forced smile on her face, she gave a light shrug of her shoulders. "I've never been sworn to anything that I can remember." Then her face clouded. "But on the other hand, I don't know if anyone ever leaves here to tell about it, either." She gazed off into the distance. Much to her dismay, a lump in her throat nearly strangled her as she struggled against the hot tears welling up in her eyes. His presence, though comforting on one level, only reminded her of her solitude and abandonment. He would soon return to a normal world filled with the warmth of family and a secure home, while she remained alone, spending her time wishing for a life that may never come to fruition.

Martin reached over and brushed aside a lock of her hair. "I'm sure people don't stay here forever. They're probably so glad when they get out, they don't even want to think about this place once they leave."

"Maybe you're right." Serena turned her eyes up at him, her heart pounding. Did she dare ask? Her stomach lurched at the thought, but she had to know. "Tell me, Martin, what made you come here today, after all this time?"

He smiled and leaned over, kissing her softly. "I've been thinking about you. I wanted to see you, see how you were getting along."

"I know the staff here called you. They told me."

He nodded. "And when they did, I jumped at the chance to come see you."

"Do my parents know you're here? And why didn't they come with you?"

Martin sat back, staring off into the hot spring, running his finger over a small patch of moss. The light smile on his face waned, as did the sparkle in his eyes. "Honestly, they don't know I'm here." He grinned. "I think some things just need to be our little secret, don't you?"

She studied his face, noting the subtle change in expression. "Do they ever talk about me or wonder how I am? Or have they forgotten they even have a daughter?"

He fidgeted, digging deep into the moss with his fingers. "You know, I've been so busy with my own life lately, I haven't seen much of anyone except my own family, so I wouldn't know."

Silence fell between them, with nothing but the sounds of nature reminding them they were still part of the world. Serena's heart sank. She had read the powerful message in his eyes as he'd tried to make light of the situation. With a heavy heart, she hung her head in despair.

Martin, sensing her sadness, reached over and wrapped an arm around her. Lifting her chin with his finger, he said, "I want you to know something. You're not forgotten. Things will work out for you, I'm sure." He hugged her close. "We're together now, and I want this afternoon to be special, one we won't forget."

She looked up at him with a light smile. Though things seemed calm on the outside, Serena's nerves wreaked havoc on the inside. He made a good observation. Their time together was indeed limited. The mood needed to change fast. Teetering on an emotional precipice, she knew every word, every action from this moment forward held great weight in determining her future. Dwelling in bitterness would only seal her fate with a bleak outcome.

How would she handle the remainder of the afternoon? How should she behave? What would they talk about? What plan did she have to win his heart, and leave The House and its world behind forever? Daren's words haunted her: *'It's a make or break deal.'* She fully understood her mission, and he was right, she had to be wise in her words and actions. With steady determination, she closed her eyes, took a deep breath, and braced herself.

Resting her head against his arm, she said, "So you've been thinking about me lately, eh?"

Martin squeezed her tighter. "I think you're a nice girl, Serena. I was shocked when I learned you'd been sent here. I've missed you." He kissed her again, longer this time. She cast her fears aside, focusing on his kiss, the way his tongue teased hers, caressing the roof of her mouth. His lips felt soft and warm over hers, determined, almost greedy.

When they finished, she breathed a small sigh of relief. He'd missed her. So far, everything he had said and done suggested they stood a chance of picking up where they left off. The soft, bubbling of the spring called out a reminder, and she glanced at the water. "Hey, how about a dip in the spring?"

His broad smile warmed her heart. "You bet, but you know what that means, don't you?"

"What?"

"We'll have to get totally naked this time." He winked and placed the bag under the same tree she'd shared with Daren.

Serena felt her face flush. "Yes, that's true, but we've seen each other. What else is there to see?"

"You got me there." He paused a moment, surveying the area one last time before pulling off his clothing. "We're so far out, I'm sure no one will see us. What do you think?"

Her breathing nearly stopped as she viewed him in his entire nakedness. His physical features showed more beauty than she had imagined, the flesh between his thighs being the most prominent. His flaccid shaft, instead of hiding inside, draped over his sac, showing great promise in length and girth. Somehow time had dimmed her memory of how his body had looked, the excitement of their first union blinding her to anything else. Transfixed, she just stood there with her mouth slightly open.

"Um, Serena, are you okay?" He snapped his fingers in front of her eyes.

She shook her head. "Oh, I'm sorry."

"You were staring hard down there. Is there something wrong with me?"

The question made her laugh. "You know what, Martin? I'm going to be perfectly honest with you. You are the most beautiful man I've ..." She stopped short and just smiled, not about to share with him just how many she'd seen.

While she pretended to be distracted by kicking off her shoes, he moved in close and unfastened her dress. "Thank you, and I'm sure you're even more beautiful." He whisked off the garment and tossed it to the ground next to his clothes. It was his turn to stop and stare. She blushed, raising her hands to cover herself. "No you don't. No hiding from me, young lady." Martin grabbed her hands and held her arms apart on either side of her body. "Now I must say, you are quite a beauty. I'm ashamed to admit that I'd almost forgotten." Pulling her into his arms, he whispered in her ear, "You won't hold that against me, will you?"

"Of course not. I think the same happened to me." The touch of his shaft teasing the inside of her cleft surged her lust, and she pressed in closer, trying to tame the giddiness and lightheaded sensation overtaking her.

"Well, then, I think that makes us even." He pulled her to the edge of the spring. "Any safe way of getting in here? I'm dying to try this out. We don't have any of these hot springs on our property. Just old oak trees." He squeezed her hand again, fixing his gaze on hers.

She swallowed, forcing herself to smile. Her head nearly spinning, she used him for support, climbing onto the rocky ledge just under the water. "Here, follow me and go where I go. The drop-off is a few more feet out." She settled into the water and closed her eyes while he seated himself next to her.

"Oh, this feels good. I'm glad you suggested this place." He reached his arm around her, pulling her close beside him. Closing his eyes, he dropped his head back, soaking up the sun's rays as the warmth of the water covered him. Neither one said anything, both listening to the bubbling of the spring as it conversed with Nature.

"So tell me, Martin, what have you been doing lately?" She cringed on the inside, trying to make casual conversation as if she'd been in the community all this time, living as if she'd never been abandoned by anyone in her life.

He opened his eyes and smiled at her. "Not as much as you'd think. Life has been pretty mundane, but I'm thankful I've at least been able to make it on my own."

"On your own? What do you mean?" As she shaded her eyes from the sun, her heart started to sink. The last time they'd been together, he wasn't on his own. He resided with his family, helping them out with their business. Was he preparing for someone else in his life, some other lady, perhaps?

"Well, I've got my own place now, but I still work in our dry goods store. I also help Dad out with the livestock on our property. What little we have, anyway." He chuckled. "You know how Dad is. He likes to dabble at being a farmer, but can never commit to going all the way with it."

"Yes, it's difficult to commit sometimes, isn't it?" She nearly choked on her words.

"It certainly is." His arm tightened around her.

"So how do you like living in your own place?"

"Not bad, but it gets lonely a lot of the time."

Her heart sped up. Did she risk asking why? She cleared her throat. "You, lonely? I can't believe that for one minute."

"Well, when you live alone in an empty house, it can get rather lonely." He rubbed a finger over her back. His touch sent her swooning. Did he also think about her at night, fondling himself as he remembered their last time together? If she had her way, his nights would never be lonely again. With the skills she'd acquired, his body would know true ecstasy.

She wrapped her arm around him for support. "Are you having any fun besides working with your father, like pursuing interests of your own?" Did she just hear her voice squeak during that last sentence?

He didn't seem to notice if it did or not. "Um, let's see. No, not so much. I live a pretty simple life, really. But enough about me, what about you? What have you been doing lately?"

Serena wanted to sink into the water and drown. "As you can pretty well guess, we don't do a lot here, either. We live simple lives too."

"I see." He stared off into the distance.

She swallowed hard. "It's pretty much the same, day in and day out. Boring to the point of insanity." God, this conversation had to end. She moved her fingers over his chest, lingering over the tip of each nipple. A new flush spread over his cheeks. Was it from the heat, or her touch? Her hand slid from his chest to his thigh, stopping short of his cock. Should she tease the pink cockhead? Overcome with a severe attack of nervousness, she stopped. "You know what, I'm a little hungry. I bet you are too."

"I could use a bite."

"Let's go settle under that old tree over there where we left the bag."

Serena led the way. When they reached the tree, she sat down on the ground and reached into the bag for the tiny finger sandwiches. Martin plopped down beside her. "Here, for you." She guided a tiny sandwich into his mouth.

"M-m-m, these are good!" He licked his lips, opening his mouth to receive another bite. After he swallowed, he said, "Now it's your turn." Reaching down, he plucked up one of the treats and popped it into her mouth, which she chewed and swallowed down fast.

Martin stretched out on the moss, making good use of the sun to dry himself off. "Serena, you've never told me why your family sent you here. Why did they do that?"

A twinge of nausea hit her stomach. She fidgeted for a moment, occupying herself with putting the empty sandwich container back in the bag. He waited for an answer, giving her an expectant look. "It's complicated, really."

"Why can't you tell me?"

"Surely you're not interested in all that, are you?"

He propped himself up on one elbow. "Yeah, I am interested. Since we have the afternoon all to ourselves, I think I have more than enough time to hear your story."

Licking her lips, she sucked in her breath. Part of her was already tired of fighting this situation. Unbeknownst to Daren, she'd spent many a night, many an hour, pondering over Martin, dreaming of what could be, what might not be, and how she might have to live out the rest of her life. Exhaustion flooded her like a tsunami, instilling a desire to just lie down and sleep for a very long time. Should she allow her mental side to take over, weighing and calculating everything, or should she practice what her lady friend had taught her, to be true to yourself and just let go, putting out your heart's desires so the laws of the universe could rule in your favor, or not?

She pushed the bag aside and snuggled up to Martin, nuzzling his cheek. "You know how families can be if you don't follow their way of thinking. In this day and age we live in, they can put you away for that, declaring you're crazy when you really aren't. The truth is, my parents were extreme in their beliefs, and I didn't share the same ideas with them. I didn't conduct myself the way they wanted me to. I wasn't religious enough to suit them. They didn't like some of the things I did or the people I befriended, so they dumped me here for the rest of my life." Her words poured out in a bitter tone, souring on the end of her tongue.

"What did you do, exactly, that they didn't like?" He stroked her hair. The warmth of his breath in her ear heightened the desire to curl up in his arms forever. She'd give anything for time to stand still this very moment.

"You know old Hortense who lived at the end of the road a few streets over from me?"

He nodded.

"My parents detested her, said she practiced witchcraft and other such nonsense. And you know that wasn't true."

"Oh, yes, I know who you're talking about. You were friends with her?"

"Martin, she wasn't a witch or anything like that. She was a good, kind lady who understood things differently from most people. "

"You know, I kind of liked her myself. Personally I found her rather interesting." A wide smile spread across his face. "Believe it or not, I kind of like eccentric people. I find they're usually smarter, and much of the time I agree with their way of thinking." Martin stared at her, silent. Leaning over, he kissed her, slipping in his tongue. When he finished, he propped up on his elbow. "Okay, you've told me about a friend your folks didn't like, but what kind of things did you do to make them so unhappy?"

"They didn't like me dancing."

"You dance? Really? How come you never told me that?"

"You like to dance?" She turned up a raised eyebrow in his direction.

"Well, no, I don't dance, but I sure would like to watch you do it." His fingers trickled over her breasts, teasing the soft flesh of her nipples. Serena closed her eyes, nearly melting at his touch. She stifled the urge to cry out. He whispered in her ear once again, "Why don't you dance for me? Won't you, please? I want to see you." His fingers squeezed her flesh harder now, kneading with more determination.

Her eyes widened, blood rushing to her face, and from deep inside, her arousal rose. Should she do it, or give an excuse and decline?

Now was the moment. *'It's a make or break deal.'* Serena made her decision. She reached over and pulled open the bag, dragging out the scarf. "Fine, I'll dance for you." Moving several feet away from him, she prepared herself to perform in the light of day what she usually reserved for the darkness of night and a full moon. She lifted her face to the sky, closed her eyes, and after a few seconds, began the dance. Her feet and arms moved according to the pattern and rhythm she'd created long ago, and the scarf sailed merrily along, flowing in the direction guided by her hands.

She lost herself in the rhythm of the dance, her dance, the one created from the depths of her heart and soul, the one that expressed all the desires and frustrations she held inside. Her feet tapped against the ground as she moved; her arms sailed the scarf easily over her head, and lightly around her.

Caught up in the whirl and heat of her own excitement, time stood still, with no worries about the past or the future. She commended her spirit to the universe and nature, even for just a short time, wishing never to return. But, like all things, time and the universe stay still for no one, and she would soon be compelled to return to her communion with the inhabitants of her present world.

When she finished, she returned to Martin's side. "I'm not quite done yet."

"Fine, then show me all of it. Everything." His eyes glowed with passion, and a soft smile lit his face.

She reclined on the moss and spread her thighs open. Trailing her hand between her breasts, she wandered over her abdomen and landed between her legs.

"Go on. Don't stop," Martin commanded with a whisper, his eyes glazing over with lust. Her fingers worked the hard knot of flesh nestled within her folds, each stroke encouraging a dull ache and a heavy thickness inside her. He took her nipples between his fingers and squeezed in time with the soft rise and fall of her hips as her orgasm gained momentum. Within minutes, her hips writhed in time to each internal spasm while his fingers squeezed her flesh harder. She let out a small whimper of pain. Martin smiled at her with approval. "Just let it all out, it's okay." As he moved closer, his flesh bumped against her, breaking the spell of her trance. She relaxed on the moss and took some time to catch her breath.

Lust held her in its unrelenting grip. She turned to Martin, pushing him back against the ground. "I need you to lie back." Without protesting, he did as she instructed. She guided his arms over his head and bound his wrists together with the scarf. Reality hit her senses as she reached for the bag. What should she do next? Did she run the risk of going too far with him? With no time to think, she pulled out the tiny amber bottle of oil. A smile lit her face. Martin eyed her with curiosity, but said nothing. She moved closer to him and straddled his hips. With a twist of the cap, she opened the bottle and poured out a generous amount of oil into her hands. A nutty, woodsy smell mixed with mint wafted through the air, and she rubbed the oil into his skin.

Working her way from the top to the bottom of his torso, she paid extra close attention to his nipples, caressing and squeezing, much like he'd done to her. He closed his eyes and sighed. "Wonderful."

"You like this?" She rubbed the insides of his thighs. In a surprise move, she added a little more oil to her finger and slipped it inside his anus. He gasped. His walls felt hot and moist, clenching her finger as she moved in and out. Turning her finger upward, she stroked the area near his prostate. He tensed at the sensation, but as she kept up her persistent movements, his body relaxed.

"Oh, god that feels good." Martin closed his eyes in submission, his cock growing rigid between his thighs. Just when she'd brought him to the brink of release, she stopped. His eyes flew open, and he looked at her surprised. "You're stopping now? Come on, Serena, no teasing." His face held a look of pain mixed with pleasure.

"I know those balls of yours are full." She squeezed them. "I love the way your fat plums spring between my fingers." Her fingers worked over his shaft, teasing the top of his cockhead.

"That's it, baby, just keep going." Martin closed his eyes again, shifting into a more comfortable position. She worked him harder and faster. Grasping his cock, she rested her forefinger against the ridge of his tip and settled her thumb on the opposite side, applying a light pressure and moving in circular motions. A few more maneuvers with her fingers, and she watched with excitement as his ejaculate landed in a small puddle on his abdomen.

"I know what goes good with cum."

"Oh, and what might that be?" He watched with interest as Serena reached inside the bag and pulled out the container of fruit. She slipped out a piece and placed it against his lips, pushing it inside his mouth. He licked his lips after swallowing and looked at her, indicating he'd like another bite.

"Nice to have something so cool and wet on a warm day." Like she did with Daren, she selected a piece of fruit for herself, dipping it into his lust before swallowing the whole bite.

"For the love of ..." He didn't finish his sentence because she'd already placed another lust-covered bite into his open mouth.

"Have you ever tasted yourself before?"

He managed to chew and swallow the morsel she popped into his mouth. "You're crazy, that's what."

"But I thought you liked 'em rather crazy."

He laughed. "Can I please just have another piece of plain fruit?"

"Of course you can." She offered him the last piece and ended by kissing his lips, licking off the juice trickling out from the corner of his mouth. "I'll untie you now."

He stretched and worked his hands, relieving the stiffness of being in one position. Just as she put the last of the containers and supplies back in the bag, he grabbed her arms and gently flipped her on her back.

"You're quite a little devil, aren't you?" His smile showed beautiful, straight white teeth. Serena marveled at his strength, his muscular thighs anchoring her in place. He gazed at her for a moment. "I think you've learned more here than you're willing to tell me." The smile on his face faded. Catching the sight of her breasts, he lowered his head and took each one of her nipples in his mouth, sucking and licking, ending with a soft nip.

The warmth of his mouth excited her. She loved the way he touched her, as if he did it every day, as if they'd never been separated. "Suck me hard, Martin. I like that." He drew hard enough to make her cry out in pain.

"I bet you like a lot of things I don't know about." His expression, stone cold, startled her.

Meanwhile, the inside of her slit throbbed hard, begging for his fullness. She reached for the thickness between his thighs, spreading her legs wide open, preparing for the final consummation of the afternoon.

But it didn't come.

He lifted his hips, pulling himself off. "Here, let me help you up. We need to get dressed and head on back."

Time stopped. Did she hear him right? Did she believe what just happened or, rather, didn't happen? She gulped, blinking her eyes to fight back the tears. "But Martin, what about ... like last time?"

"Serena," he said with a calm voice and sober expression, "Maybe what happened last time shouldn't have happened then." He grabbed her wrists and pulled her to her feet. They dressed in silence. Martin took up the bag over his shoulder and reached for her hand. Together they walked back to The House, neither one saying a word to the other.

CHAPTER 11

Serena climbed the stairs of the marble staircase, her heart heavy, her eyes blurred with tears. She'd managed to hold them back in Martin's presence, but now they streamed down with no restraint. The beauty of the crystal chandelier did nothing to make her feel better, and the thoughts of facing Daren filled her with shame. What would he think of her now? Her body felt heavy, and each lift of her foot to reach the next step felt like a major undertaking. The leather bag hung like a stone weight around her shoulder, almost mocking her, reminding her of failure.

At last, she reached the top, and began the walk back to her room. She tried to ignore the glances and smiles from other residents who passed her on the ward, wishing they'd all go away. The room seemed miles away, and every passing second seemed like hours. Within moments, she arrived, finding Daren resting comfortably on the bed, reading a book.

§§§

He jumped up to meet her. "So, how did it go?" From her facial expression and red eyes, the answer was clear. "Uh-oh, not so good?" His heart sank.

Trembling, Serena lost the last ounce of control she possessed and collapsed to the floor, falling on her knees. Hard, heavy sobs racked her body, her chest heaving with each breath. Daren steadied himself against the wall. His blood ran cold; the room spun before his eyes. He managed to sit back down on the bed, helpless, witnessing the scene before him.

The view of Serena in total shambles broke his heart. He cursed the first time he ever saw her. What had he done? Even Dr. James had seemed hesitant to let him bring her over here to his side of The House. He had his choice of beauties over here. Why had he been so intent on having her? What would he do if Martin never returned? The idea filled him with horror and dread. He'd lifted this girl's hope for love and a normal life. From the looks of her current behavior, it seemed that all of it had somehow slipped away as quickly as it had presented itself.

Taking several deep breaths to clear the chaos in his head, he knelt down beside her. "Serena, can you tell me what happened?" He put his arms around her and helped her up to the bed. "Please stop crying for a moment and talk to me." His voice, soft and gentle, seemed to work its charm. She calmed herself down and joined him on the bed.

She sniffed, wiping away a stray tear. Daren got up and brought her a warm, wet cloth for her face. "I'm not sure what happened. It all seemed to start off fine. We made small talk, he started asking me about why my family sent me here, and one thing led to another. But in the end, he didn't do what he did the last time we were together." Tears streamed down her face again.

"Tell me more about how the evening ended, before you left to come back here."

"Well, we ate the food, and I used the oil in a little round of anal play. I even did my dance for him like I do with you. Remember the way I ate the fruit when we were at the spring?"

"Yes." Daren's eyes never wavered from hers.

"I did that with him too."

"You did all that?" Daren pursed his lips.

"He seemed responsive to everything I did, even encouraging me in some cases. Then when we got to the end, he was on top of me, but the expression on his face had changed. He talked about me liking a lot of things he didn't know about."

"Did you share anything else about this place with him, other than what I gave you to share?"

"No, of course not. I did just as you told me to."

"So finish telling me the story. What exactly happened at the very end?"

"I thought he would follow through, that we would fully come together like we did the last time at home, but he stopped at the last minute. I asked him if we were going to finish up like we did last time, but all he said was, 'Maybe what happened last time shouldn't have happened then.' And that was it. He helped me up, we got dressed, and then we came back here. We said goodbye and, like you said earlier, a staff member took him away down the hall while I came on up here."

Daren sat in silence, running his hands through his hair. "*Maybe what happened last time shouldn't have happened then.*" He repeated the sentence under his breath a few more times, trying to decipher the meaning. "You know, Serena, sometimes things aren't always what they seem, and men don't always express themselves in the clearest manner." He turned his face back to her. "By the way, who called the shots this afternoon? You or him?"

"What do you mean?"

"I mean, did you take the lead or did he?"

"I did. He followed, and he didn't seem to have any problems doing it. He enjoyed everything I did."

"Maybe he meant something different with his comment." Daren snapped his fingers, his face looking like one who'd just had an epiphany. "I'm willing to bet if you were the one taking the lead, Martin may have been simply trying to take control back by stopping when he did. That makes sense to me. It's always that way with roles of dominance and submission. You have to decide who's playing what."

"Roles or not, it was all pretty clear to me. You should have seen his face. He was aloof and reserved, when he'd been pretty pleasant before. He even said he liked my lady friend I told you about."

He nodded. "Yeah, the witch lady."

"Her name's Hortense."

"Hortense, is it? How interesting."

She turned to Daren, laying her head on his shoulder. "I don't know what will become of me. I think I'm doomed to die here. I can't seem to find my way home, and nobody cares."

Hot tears hit his arm, and he held her close. "Please don't say that. It can't possibly be true." He got up, pulling her with him. "Let's get you undressed and ready for bed. Do you want anything substantial to eat? I can get something for you."

"No, I'm not hungry. As a matter of fact, I'm sick to my stomach."

"I think you're sick with a broken heart. And I'm sick of seeing this dress on you. Let me help you out of it." Within seconds, he helped her slip out of the ugly dress and pulled back the covers, leading her into bed. She settled into his arms, ones that held her tight, making her feel safe for the moment, comforting her in her darkest hour.

"Serena, did you two ever talk about why he came here today?"

"Yes. He said he'd missed me, and that he was lonely now that he had his own home."

Daren stroked her hair. "I still think there's more to all this, and he held back for a reason. Men get squirrely when their emotions get the better of them. It sounds like you kept him occupied, made him do some thinking."

"Well, I guess my occupying him is the reason he left. He'll probably never come back." Her voice grew louder, her energy more charged.

"Sorry, I didn't mean to upset you again. I had hoped that inviting him here would have been a good thing."

"You did all you could. So we're done with it. Besides, how on earth did you manage to find him?"

"We have ways of getting things done."

Her face turned red, and her eyes narrowed in anger. "How could you be so meddlesome, asking him to come here, like I'm some charity case? If he hadn't come here by now, it was because he never intended to."

"Now hold on." Daren sat up beside her. "Did he tell you that he'd been wanting to come here for quite some time, but just didn't know how to go about it? He didn't feel comfortable asking your parents, for fear they'd be angry at him."

"So what? Let him be a man and come on his own."

"Serena, you're being unfair. Men aren't princes in fairytales. We feel pain, we love, we hate, and we have fear. It's that simple. You can't sit here and wait for a knight in shining armor to whisk you away."

"Why not? There are plenty of men who'll stop at nothing to get to the one they love."

"They're usually considered crazy. And besides, just because someone keeps coming after you doesn't necessarily mean you'll want him for a mate." He put his arms around her. "Listen to me. He's been thinking about you all this time. He wanted to come, or he would have refused our invitation. You couldn't have found a more willing person."

"Well, he came, and now he's made up his mind that I'm not the one for him. I probably scared him off."

"I highly doubt that for one minute. If anything you probably got him thinking."

"Thinking about not wanting me."

"Okay, I see we need to give this conversation a rest." He pulled her down, cuddling her into his arms once again. "I have another question for you."

"Fine, what is it?"

"Is there any chance you'll let me finish where he left off?"

She jerked her head up, glaring at him. "I can't believe you said that. Have you no mercy?"

"Oh, I have lots of mercy. Unfortunately, I have an uncontrollable urge to take you here and now, and somehow I have a sneaking suspicion you won't be dancing for me tonight."

"And I have a sneaking suspicion you're exactly right." She dropped her head down again, but popped it up a few seconds later to say, "And just for your impertinence, no, you cannot finish where Martin left off."

"Didn't think so." He sighed.

"And again for your lack of sensitivity, I'm not giving you anything again until I'm ready. How about that?"

"Suit yourself, but you know that won't work well here, if you know what I mean." He heard nothing but the sounds of soft breathing next to him. "Serena?"

She didn't answer. He smiled to himself, relieved she most likely hadn't heard his last comment, for she was fast asleep, lost in fitful dreams.

CHAPTER 12

The sun blazed through the windows, filling the room with bright light. Outside in the hallway, people went about their business. Daren straddled himself over Serena's thighs, trying to rouse her from sleep. "Get up, Serena. Wake up."

"Hm-m-m." She yawned and stretched beneath the covers. The last several days had been torture for her, causing her to sink into a bout of depression. She'd even refused to let Daren take her to the clearing when the moon was full. Now he loomed over her, his hair blazing as brightly as the sun's rays. "What do you want?"

"Let me in with you." He pulled the covers back and settled in over her. She gave him a sleepy smile and opened her thighs for him.

He looked at her in surprise, and with relief. "So you're opening up to me, are you?" He leaned over and whispered in her ear, "You've been true to your word. You really haven't let me in."

"Well, it didn't seem to stop you. I notice when you're gone. I wake up in the middle of the night, and you're not here. You give me excuses much of the time, telling me you need to take care of something, and I'm waiting, giving you more than enough time to finish any business you need to take care of."

"I get it," he said, "but I want you to let me in."

She laughed and pulled him close. Her loins throbbed. She had missed being with him, and now she was ready. With eager anticipation, she spread her legs wider, ready to receive his full length. Closing her eyes, she thrilled at his advances, penetrating her with eager, full thrusts. After going for a while without anything inside, her core longed for a hard, fat shaft, and Daren's did the trick.

"Fuck me hard and good, Daren. Make it hurt."

"I see you're getting back to your old self again." He laughed, and slid into her with lightning speed. She closed her eyes and groaned.

"God, I love it when you do that. You take me to another world."

He glided in and out, the soft thumping sounds of flesh against flesh echoing throughout the room.

"You feel so good." She squeezed her eyes shut and tightened her jaw. "Keep going. That's it."

Lowering his head for a moment, he stopped thrusting so he could suck the tips of her breasts. His tongue flicked over the flesh, and he drew long and hard on each one, hanging on as though he never wanted to let go. "I love sucking your tits as much as you like me to," he said, coming up for air.

She ran her fingers through his hair, while she stared at him, but not quite seeing him. "I think it would be so much easier to just be with you, Daren. You know, just us."

Daren stopped a moment and smiled down at her. "Don't say anything else for a moment. Let me finish in peace. I want to enjoy this moment, just you and me. Just let me fuck you hard and good, okay?"

She nodded, and stroked his hair.

He closed his eyes and started again, slow, nice, easy. He moved a little faster, a little harder, moving until he lost himself into a quick, flowing, steady rhythm. Serena relaxed, taking in all of him, enjoying his flesh inside her, refusing to give any more thought to what had happened several days ago. She stared at Daren's face, his closed eyes, and the way his expression suggested he'd lost himself briefly to another dimension. His hips moved as if they had a mind of their own. He tensed; his eyes shut tighter; he smiled. Inside her center, she sensed the pulsations of his fluids against her walls as he ejaculated into warm, moist darkness.

"I'm done. And you know what?"

"What?" she said, whispering.

"We're finishing the way we started."

"Okay." She didn't quite hear, let alone understand, the magnitude of his words.

Daren stopped smiling a moment and stared down at her. "Did you hear me? We're finishing the way we started."

"What are you talking about? You confuse me sometimes, you know that?"

He pulled himself off and hopped out of bed, making his way to the chest of drawers. He opened a drawer and pulled out some clothing.

"Oh, for godsakes, not that hideous dress again! This is it isn't it?"

"Put your clothes on."

"Daren," she said, starting to sob, "please don't send me back to the other side. I won't ever refuse you again, I promise."

"Get up and put *your* clothes on."

She sat up, blinking for a moment at what he held before her eyes.

"Do these look familiar to you, or have you forgotten?"

"I think those are the clothes I wore when I came here."

"Right. Now put them on, please." He smiled at her, while she still stared up at him in confusion.

"I don't get it. Why am I putting these on?"

"Serena, what can I tell you? Ugly clothes are for the other side of The House, sexy clothes are for this side of The House, and street clothes can only mean one thing: you're leaving."

"I'm leaving? To go where?"

Daren laughed. "You'll see."

She got out of bed, washed off her face, and brushed her hair. Daren helped her into her street clothes, which felt so restrictive compared to the skimpy attire she'd been wearing for so long. Numbness had enveloped her body, and her mind didn't work so well on its own right now. The joy she felt couldn't be described. Her whole body tingled inside. She was leaving, but with whom? Did her parents have a change of heart? Her life was about to begin again, and The House would soon be nothing more than a bad dream. All except the moment she met Daren. He'd always have a special place in her heart. She smoothed out the wrinkles in her clothes and glanced up.

"There," he said, "now you look like someone from the community." He pulled her close and cupped her head between his hands. His voice, kind and gentle, soothed her soul. She stared into his amber eyes, marveling at their warm beauty. She'd always liked Daren, appreciating his humor, his level head, his strong sense of compassion. Was all that going to disappear? What would the future hold for her now?

"Serena, my sweet girl, I'm going to miss you and everything about you, your beauty, your grace. You're one who deserves to be treasured and adored. When you leave this room, you'll need to go downstairs to the entrance hall. Take a right at the foot of the stairs and proceed to the steward's office." He paused a moment to give her one last kiss. I have a wonderful announcement to make. Your new master is waiting for you."

"My new master?" She gave him a blank stare. "You sure like to talk in riddles, don't you!"

"No riddles this time, precious one. Just go, you'll see."

"Are you not coming with me?"

"We aren't allowed to accompany admits when they leave, but you know the way to the office. We've passed it many times on our way outside." Daren smiled and led her to the doorway.

"This is all so sudden." She shook her head and stood there a moment, staring at the floor. After a few seconds, she lifted her head to gaze around the room once again, trying to sear the image of this sacred place she'd shared with Daren in her memory forever. Finally she made her way to the door, and as she turned out of the room, she paused one more time to glance back at him. "Thank you for all you've done for me. I'll miss you too."

He smiled at her. "The pleasure was all mine. And the next time you find yourself alone in the moonlight, do a special dance for me."

With a small grin and a wave of her hand, she left the room. Her mind whirled in a state of confusion and disbelief, her future still uncertain. Who was waiting for her? Would this journey of hers really have a happy ending? Maybe this was all a dream, and she'd find herself back on the other side of The House, waking up in a cold, hard bed. The walk down the hall to the marble staircase now seemed surreal. The flashes of rainbow light from the crystal chandelier rained down around her for the last time. Her heart pounded; her mouth felt dry. Upon reaching the bottom of the stairs, she turned right and headed toward the steward's office and stepped across the threshold.

Her eyes fell upon Martin as he stood up, quickly making his way toward her. Her vision grew fuzzy, and dizziness overtook her senses. She struggled to maintain her balance, but he caught her up in his arms and held her tight, the warmth of his body nearly intoxicating her. His face beamed down with a bright, new smile, the light in his eyes dancing with excitement and anticipation. "Let's go, Serena, it's time to go home."

MASTER OF THE HOUSE

CHAPTER 1

The door slammed, jarring the silence within the isolation room. William Strumpkin, known as "Willie" to his friends and acquaintances, tensed with apprehension as he eyed his House attire resting in a heap on the floor. Stripped of all clothing, with his wrists cuffed to an iron bar above his head, he awaited his fate with a sense of uneasiness and a twinge of excitement. He pulled against the bar one last time, hoping the cuffs might release as if by magic. Not a chance. They held him fast like a trapped animal. The cool air whipped around his naked body. Part of him wanted to hide in shame. The other part of him liked being bare, while the lady in the corner watched with gleaming eyes.

Places like The House normally wouldn't have suited him, or so he'd thought. But over the past several days, he'd learned more about human sexuality than he could practice in a lifetime. He glanced down to the space between his legs. On second consideration, maybe he cared more than he'd like to admit.

Located in the countryside, hidden from the community, The House remained an enigma to most people. Its ornate, massive, chevron-shaped construction and glorious grounds rivaling those of a European palace hid its secrets well from prying eyes. The public viewed this place as mainly a dumping ground for housing those with lesser mental faculties, and ones who failed to conform to societal norms of the day. But Willie made a startling discovery after his arrival, one that filled him with intrigue while allowing his lusty nature to function full throttle. Today, the lady in his presence had ordered him here, with no hint of why she'd chosen a cold, empty room with nothing but a bar between the stone block walls. The chill from the tiles under his feet stung with the vengeance of a hundred hornets, but the core of his body radiated heat like a freshly stoked furnace.

Only a few moments earlier, accompanied by an escort, he'd made the descent from the upper wards down to the bowels of The House where the isolation chambers lay hidden. His imagination had run amok as he viewed the closed doors lining each side of the deserted hallway. The environment here had struck his senses as menacing and dark, nothing like the opulent beauty of the upper levels of The House, with its grand entrance hall featuring a magnificent crystal chandelier and marble staircase. Even the wards upstairs displayed artful, tiled floors and a pleasing decor.

Delores, his attendant, stepped toward him, her black stilettos clicking against the tiled floor. Tight black shorts hugged her hips, and her matching corset pushed up her ample breasts, showing off a tempting cleavage. Fishnet stockings hugged her legs, and her alabaster skin glowed.

Her cerise lips turned up into a sultry smile. "Well, well, what have we here? My, aren't you a fine specimen of male humanity." She pranced back and forth, eyeing him up and down, taking a brief moment to give one of his nipples a hard pinch.

Willie winced; his heart pounded. The sight of Delores had pleased him the moment he'd entered The House and made her acquaintance. The fact that she'd be his attendant, caring for him during his stay, made the bargain even sweeter.

"So it's time we get down to business," she said, tapping the handle of a whip against the palm of her hand. "You've been here, oh, about four days, and I've been quite gentle with you, giving you time to adjust." She lifted her face to his, her straight, white teeth flashing between smiling lips. "I know how hard it must be for you to acclimate to our surroundings, especially when you've been uprooted from your family and home—and I hear you have quite a nice one. Home, that is."

Willie said nothing, but kept his eyes on her.

"But what disturbs me is what I heard from your family when they left you here. They say you live alone in that big beautiful house." She pulled back a little, taking in his full frame. "They're worried about you. Is it true, Willie? Do you live all by yourself, a handsome man such as you are?"

Willie remained silent, but closed his eyes as the handle of the whip caressed the outside of one of his thighs, its bulbed end smooth against his flesh.

"Answer me!" Delores gave his thigh a sharp swat with the other end of the whip. Willie jumped.

"Yes, I do live alone." Willie clenched his teeth, smarting from the sting.

"That's better. When I ask you a question, that's your cue to speak." She grazed the handle of the whip against him once again. "Know what else I've heard about you?"

"No, ma'am, I don't."

"I've been told that living alone in a big house makes you a dull boy."

Willie raised his eyebrows, but said nothing.

"Are you a dull boy, Willie, all work and no play?"

"I-I'm not sure what you mean." A rush of confusion overpowered him. What business did his family have sharing his private life with a stranger—and a woman at that? And why he had even let them talk him into coming to The House confused him more. Tired of their badgering and nonstop complaints about his solitude and dour mood, he'd relented and allowed them to sign him into treatment.

"Tell me again why you're here." Delores pressed against him, peering up into his face. "I want to understand you better."

Willie swallowed, taking a moment to formulate an answer. "Well, I do work long hours as an accountant in my father's business. I'm actually purchasing the house from my family. And yes, it's quite nice." He paused a moment.

"Do go on, dear, I'm intrigued already." She ran a finger down the middle of his chest, ending with stroking movement inside his navel.

His stomach lurched at her touch, and he began to sweat. The air in the room, which had earlier cooled his bare flesh, felt hot and dry. "Apparently, I don't get out enough to suit them. I'd rather stay home and have a drink by myself or read a good book. Sometimes I bring extra work home with me because I'm tired of being in the office all day."

She licked her lips, tilting her head to one side. "I see. So it's true. All work and no play *has* made you dull."

He nodded in silence. She rubbed one of his buttocks with her hand, the warmth and tenderness nearly causing him to melt.

"So you prefer to stay home, you don't get out much, and I guess I'm correct in my assumption that you have no special female in your life." She cupped his face in her hands and stared straight into his eyes. "Is that true, too, no female for you?"

"Yes, it's true." He averted his eyes, casting his gaze to the floor.

She stepped back and, with a solemn tone said, "You know in this day and age, fits of melancholy and isolation usually get you placed on the other side of this House, where the insane ones reside."

He jerked himself up straighter, eyeing her with alarm.

"Yes, my dear. There are two sides to The House, and the lucky ones end up here."

Without thinking, he blurted out, "Permission to speak, ma'am?"

After giving him a hard look for a moment, her face warmed into a smile, and she bowed her head, indicating her permission for him to talk.

"The House has two sides? I've heard some tales about this place, but no one ever seems to tell the whole story. Why?"

"The side you're on assists people in learning more about their sexual aspect. We believe carnal desire in man is good, and should be nurtured so his spirit can continue to grow."

"A most peculiar philosophy. I've never heard of such a thing, and apparently no one else has, either." He shook his head a little, thinking.

Pacing back and forth, she continued her historical lecture. "And why the secrecy? Because the community could interfere and shut down our practice. We offer wonderful treatment, and our staff is highly trained, no matter how unorthodox it all may seem. Our admits, which is our term for patients, all benefit. While they are in this environment, they learn to take risks and explore their deepest desires without censure or judgment. When they leave, they continue on as successful members of society. Since you're on this side of The House, you signed a confidentiality agreement in those papers we gave you, remember?"

"It's all such a blur, but yes, I think I do remember that now." He straightened himself up and asked, "So what exactly will I learn here?"

She grinned as she walked up to him again. "You will be highly trained in pleasures of the flesh. We guarantee that when you leave us you'll have a fire in your spirit and a new confidence, capable of winning you anything you want. You'll get your power back."

He smiled. "I'll get my power back?"

"Yes," she said, bowing her head once again.

Willie sensed the flush rising in his cheeks. Had his family suspected this would happen when they signed him in? Doubtful. Delores spoke the truth. He'd, of late, been stripped of his power—exhausted, and dominated by his family. Though they meant well, wanting only the best things for him, he had begun to feel smothered, longing for a sense of freedom. He stifled a chuckle. Perhaps this serendipitous turn of events might be his good fortune after all, with him gaining the upper hand in the end.

Delores studied his expression in depth and spoke again, a new gleam in her eye. "So, are you ready to begin?"

With an air of humility, Willie answered, "Yes, I'm more than ready to begin."

"Excellent, we begin now." Her eyes lit up and she held out the whip in front of her, grasping both ends in her hands as she walked back and forth in front of him once again. "Now, my dear Willie, there's one subject I want to pursue and that is the one concerning women." She returned, delivering a soft thrust of the whip against one of his thighs. "You have quite a muscular body, with strong thighs, rippling chest, and a chiseled, handsome face."

Willie lowered his face in submission, but he was beaming inside. No one had ever commented on his appearance until now. But what she did next turned his cheeks scarlet. With one end of the whip, she caught up his flaccid shaft, lifting it up to admire its appearance.

"My, what a beautiful cock you have! I like the way it flows over that sweet, plump sac of yours." She reached out and gave his flesh a firm squeeze, rolling the spongy contents between her fingers.

With gritted teeth, Willie silenced a groan. He'd never been touched this way before by anyone, and this woman was bold, with no reservations.

"Tell me, darling, do you ever fantasize about women? Do you have a special someone who makes your heart flutter and your cock swell?"

Her question took him by surprise, and he stood there, dumbfounded, almost losing himself in another dimension. Another swat from the whip jarred him back to reality. "Um … well …" He licked his lips, swallowing hard.

"Answer me!" Her tone of voice turned into a snarl. "Do you have a special love?"

Willie cleared his throat. "As a matter of fact, I do have someone special I think about from time to time."

"I thought so." She gave him a satisfied smile. "And what kinds of things do you think about?"

Startled by this question even more than the previous one, he had to think a moment. Just what did he think about when he thought of her, this young lady who'd attracted his attention for quite a while now? "I'm not sure. I've never given the matter much thought before."

Delores threw back her head and laughed. "I find that hard to believe. Any man smitten with a woman always has plenty to *think about* when he's alone without her." She moved in closer and whispered in his ear, "Even more, any man smitten with a woman always finds plenty *to do* when he's alone without her."

He narrowed his eyes. "Plenty to do?" He knew blurting out his comment might irritate her, but he took the chance anyway.

"Yes, plenty to do." She lifted up his shaft with the whip one more time. "Now, I want you to be honest with me. No more games and being coy. I want you to show me what you do when you're alone thinking of this special lady you admire so much."

Stunned by such a request, he glared back at her. His jaw tightened, and his whole frame tensed at such a suggestion. Undaunted, she unfastened one of his wrists, freeing it from the cuffs.

With a stern voice she reiterated again, saying, "Do what I tell you to do. Now. Move!" She brought the whip down against his buttocks.

He winced, the sting searing throughout his backside. "What would you have me do?"

She leaned in close to him, her nose nearly touching his. "Take that free hand of yours and show me what you do when you're alone in bed at night, filled with lust, thinking of her." Taking the end of the whip, she gave his sensitive tip a few light taps.

Willie, distraught by a sudden bout of shyness, paused. What had happened to the eagerness he'd possessed a few moments ago, wanting his power back, thinking his admission to The House a fortunate one? Did modesty pose a problem, or did part of him rebel against taking orders from someone else? Either way, his current situation had put him in a submissive position.

"Are you going to follow my instructions, or shall I whip you harder?"

He gave a small jump, shaking himself from his brief reverie. "Uh, no, ma'am, of course not. I'll … I'll do as you wish."

"Then get stroking, pretty one. We haven't got all day, and you won't be here forever." She gave him a knowing wink.

Fueled with embarrassment tinged with indignation, he gazed straight ahead, numb, wishing for the floor to swallow him whole. It was one thing to stand naked in front of her, but to show her what he did in the privacy of his own bedroom? He held himself for a moment with his free hand, almost paralyzed. Before Delores could bring the whip down on him again, he began working his fingers up and down over his flesh, paying special attention to his head, each series of tugs and manipulations sending bolts of pleasure throughout his loins. Within moments, his cock bloomed into a beautiful erection.

"What a beautiful pink flower you're sporting on top." Delores fingered the silky flesh. "Keep working, darling, you're far from finished."

Closing his eyes, hoping to shut himself out of his current situation, he continued showering his shaft and tip with firm tugs and earnest squeezes, creating a heaviness inside. He knew this feeling, this pretense at lovemaking, pleasuring himself alone in bed at night while wanting Louise the whole time. Images of her face flashed inside his mind, accompanied by more images of how she might appear naked before him. He worked himself harder, his breathing more rapid, his face flushing hotter. Without warning, something unseen entered his backside, invading and tickling his walls as it traveled upwards, kissing his sensitive flesh. Startled, he stopped, his heart pounding hard.

"Keep going!" She continued inserting the bulbed end of the whip handle deep into his rectum, grazing over the area near his prostate.

Stifling a groan, he squirmed, trying to pull himself away from his new invader. A blow to the side of his thigh with her hand encouraged him to stand up straight.

"Don't even think of stopping. You had a great rhythm going; don't lose it." Delores's hot breath filled his ear, and the wet lick of her tongue against his earlobe suggested he surrender to the moment and leave modesty behind him forever. He no longer cared if her eyes witnessed him in the throes of his own passion. She already knew what he practiced in private. The whip handle moved faster inside him, tickling his walls, keeping time with the rapid movements of his hands against his own flesh.

"Here I go," he whispered, hips jerking. In a shameless display of relief, he released his ejaculate in thick streams onto the floor.

"Quite nice," Delores said, grazing a crimson fingernail over his back. He shuddered at her touch. "Feel better now?" In one smooth move, she slipped out the handle of the whip.

"Do you always stick things inside people like that?" He turned his head in her direction.

She swatted his buttocks with the palm of her hand. "Are you always an impudent little prick, asking someone like me such questions?" Another blow, a little harder than the last.

He hung his head, regretting his retort. In another second, his body jerked at the familiar touch of the whip handle sliding inside him once again.

"In case you must know, yes, I stick things inside people ... like that." In a round of slow up-and-down movements, she guided the whip in and out of his passage as he sucked in his breath. "Your training starts at some point, and I decided bringing you down here to the chambers might be a nice way to break you in." She nuzzled in close to his neck, licking along the side, ending with a sharp nip to his earlobe. "But we really must work on your manners."

"Yes, ma'am." Willie closed in eyes, discovering he rather liked the rectal stroking from the small pole lodged deep inside. To his surprise, he found his cock stiffening again.

Delores removed the whip and unfastened the other wrist. Giving his nipples a soft pinch, she gazed up into his eyes, smiling. "I think you've had enough down here. We'll head on back upstairs."

He stretched his arms and legs, relieving his stiff muscles before slipping his clothes back on.

She linked her arm through his and led the way to their private room on the upper wards. As they walked together, she noted, "You performed beautifully, but let me warn you now, your treatment has only begun."

CHAPTER 2

Willie turned, stretching out on his back. In the same bed, Delores rested next to him, curled up beneath the crisp, white linen sheets. From the windows, the first rays of sunlight shone through the curtains, illuminating the room in soft light. Dark, wavy hair framed her flawless face. A set of thick lashes accented her closed eyes. As she lay in a deep sleep, he admired the contours of her breasts, and the gentle curves in her hips. Her face suggested one of an angel, though she'd proven herself a relentless taskmistress ever since his footsteps had graced The House. She had earned his respect, creating in him a fondness and deep appreciation for her tender but firm tutelage.

Willie felt a tug at his emotions, the vision of her stirring a deep longing he'd kept to himself for quite some time. He caressed a nipple, gently squeezing the nub between his thumb and forefinger. She stirred, eyes fluttering open.

"You're awake early." She ran a soft finger over his cheek.

"I guess I got enough sleep after all. I'm surprised how comfortable these beds are."

"Or do you just like having someone next to you?"

He thought about her question before answering. "You may have a point there, Delores." Leaning over, he gave her a soft kiss. "Maybe I do like having someone next to me, sharing a bed." He frowned, adding, "I still can't get used to rooms with no doors. People can see and hear everything if they want."

"True, but I think most people are too engrossed in themselves to worry about what we're doing." She returned his kiss and settled in closer to him. "I like boldness in you. You're well suited to taking control."

"What do you mean?"

"Like kissing me, or making tiny, endearing gestures every now and then."

"Can I be honest with you?"

"Of course, I wouldn't want anything else from you." She ran her fingers through his sand-colored hair.

"You confuse me sometimes, and scare me at others. I'm not sure what you want."

Delores sat up, smiling, taking his hands between hers. "Willie, isn't that what most women do to men? You find us both alluring and frightening. But a strong man isn't easily put off by a woman and her take-charge spirit. He learns to appreciate all of her, including the feisty aspects of her nature. This only intrigues him, leaves him filled with fascination and adoration. You'd find a totally submissive woman a complete bore."

"I think you have a point there." He sat up, staring into her face. "I've never thought about it before, but it does make sense."

"And remember, there is a give and take to it all, one playing off the other, each one understanding the other. It's a sensual game of hunter and hunted. No one dies, but each emerges more loving and trusting." Her eyes sparkled in the glow of the morning sun, and her smile rivaled its brightness.

He cleared his throat, shifting his hips to a more comfortable position. His eyes remained fixed on hers. "I think I'm slowly understanding."

"You've been here several days now, enough time to start absorbing what I'm teaching you."

Licking his lips, his gaze trailed off into space for a moment, his mind preoccupied.

"Something's on your mind, Willie. I need you to tell me. I've seen you drift off like this. Quite frankly, it bothers me." She gave his hand a firm squeeze.

"Why haven't you tried to make love to me? Lord knows you've teased me every other way."

With gleaming eyes, Delores sat in silence, rocking back and forth.

Willie turned his eyes from the ceiling and gave her a questioning look.

"I have the same question for you. Why haven't you tried to make love to me?" She resumed her stretched-out position, waiting for his reply.

He frowned. "Are you saying you've been waiting for me to make the move? You're my attendant, the one in charge of me. Isn't that your job to call the shots?"

She laughed. "Excuses, excuses."

His eyes flashed in annoyance.

"Oh, come on. Willie, it's not like this is your first time. You're just in the middle of a dry spell, that's all."

He grimaced, shaking his head. "It's not like I'm an expert at this, either. I've only done this once, and that was a while ago."

"Tell me what happened? Why only one time?"

"A female friend of mine and I had a little too much to drink one evening. We were at a party. One thing led to another. We sneaked away to a private place. Most of the parties I attend are hush-hush, more so because of the alcohol served rather than the indiscretions that occur. I wasn't so intoxicated I couldn't function, but I regretted the incident after it happened. This lady had been around, but I think she wanted more than just a one-time fling, and I really didn't. After that, I thought it best to keep what was in my trousers to myself." He placed his hand over hers. "I don't ever want to do something like that again, so thoughtless, hurting someone's feelings."

"I see." She looked at him directly before continuing. "So you're afraid, not very confident of yourself."

"You think so?" He gave her a weak smile. "I like to think it's because of my sensitivity."

"Mastery of your flesh and your self-control is what you need to learn, and that's what I can teach you. I can also teach you to master someone else, the object of your desire." She stretched a little, arching her chest, showing off her ample breasts. "You mentioned earlier a fondness for someone, and I'm guessing the lady from your first tryst wasn't her."

"Correct. Thank goodness."

"Tell me more about the lady of your affections. Who is she and what's she like?"

He took in a deep breath. "Her name is Louise Carnwell. We all call her 'Lulu' for short, except for me. I call her 'Lou.' And if you want to see someone who's confident and opinionated, she's the leading lady. She annoys a lot of people, but I find her fascinating." Willie smiled at Delores. "Personally, I think Lou has a good heart, means well. I think she pushes her ideas on people because she cares. And she believes she's right."

"Does she share your feelings?"

Eyes narrowed in thought, he said, "I'm not sure, really. Sometimes when we're at a party or other social events, I catch her staring at me when she thinks I don't see her." He turned on his side and faced Delores, smoothing back her hair with his finger. "You remind me of her: your face, your smile." His eyes gazed straight ahead, his mind drifting off into another time and place.

"What would you like to do if she were here with you right now?"

Her voice lulled him back. A lusty smile crept over his face, watching as she threw off the top sheet. Her form teased him from the top of her plump nipples down to the wet slit between her legs. Memorizing every inch of her, he saw Louise in each line and curve. How could Louise not look as enticing and delicious as the one who lay open before him?

Delores gazed up at him in silence, lips showing off a light smile. Her chest rose and fell with each gentle breath, reminding him of her vitality, an energy he found appealing. Blood rushed to his cheeks; his heart pounded. This was his moment, one he could have had several times with her, but had been too nervous to follow through. Between his thighs, his morning erection raged.

When he touched her, she gasped. A drumming pounded in his ears, and a hard ache urged him on. She opened her legs wider, inviting him. Spreading her apart, he lit his tongue down on her pink flesh, moving up and down, focusing on teasing the hard clit hiding within her folds.

§§§

His hot, wet tongue coursing over her sent searing bolts of heat radiating throughout her pelvic region. Delores stifled the desire to scream. Unlike the male attendants who usually initiated their female admits into intercourse on their first night at The House, she preferred to make her male charges wait, believing patience and self-control served a man much better than satisfying sexual urges on a whim. In her opinion, Willie, like the others before him, had been well worth the wait. Through his own foolhardy actions, he'd already learned the lesson of using caution before rushing into the heat of a moment.

She closed her eyes as his tongue probed with urgent determination, swirling at her entrance. At the top of her sex, the tiny, hard bundle of nerves ached, tormenting her into an agitated state. With a gasp, she pressed her head into the pillow, opening herself up more as he slipped a couple of fingers into hot darkness.

"You're dripping wet, and you taste as sweet as you look." Willie stopped teasing long enough for a quick smile. "Are you ready for me?"

"Yes," she said, eyes squinting as the pleasure-pain flared between her legs.

"Good, because here I go." Steadying himself with his arms on either side of her shoulders, he pressed his way inside with one firm push. She cried out, gasping for breath. "You like that, me plunging my hot bullet into you?" With a light chuckle, he leaned over her face, popping a quick kiss on her lips.

Delores giggled, lifting her hips upwards, meeting his undulating motions with perfect timing. Grazing her nails along his buttocks, she grinned as he shivered between thrusts. He moved his hips in a slight, circular twist. She gazed up into his face, smiling, held captive by the lusty glow in his eyes as he gave himself over to his own rhythm, his own pleasure, his flesh slapping against hers. She ached hard as an avalanche of internal spasms rolled between her thighs. At that moment, his hips shuddered, his shaft releasing its passion deep inside her.

Willie collapsed down beside her, catching his breath. "That's the way it should be," he gasped, "not rushed with a head clouded by drink."

"Were you able to feel more, sense more?" She smoothed his hair back, feeling the dampness of sweat.

"It's much better to keep your wits about you, this much I know for certain, now."

Delores waited a moment, savoring the feeling. Time to get back to his training. She turned over, propping up on her side. "Has this Louise of yours ever been with anyone?"

He rubbed the side of his mouth, eyes narrowed. "I'm really not sure. And I've certainly never asked her. We haven't had many moments alone, come to think of it, but I've never heard any talk of her being with anyone. And you know how rumors get around."

"I've been with many men, but with fresh ladies, be gentle," Delores said with a warning.

"Oh?"

"Yes, and when you enter her the first time, you'll understand."

He grinned. "I'll keep that in mind." Nuzzling close, he sniffed the soft floral fragrance in her hair. "You take such pains with your appearance, making sure everything comes together with perfection. I like that about you. Louise is the same way."

"I take pride in my appearance. I want to be my best at all times. You have high standards, Willie. Louise seems like your type."

"Delores, why did your parents give you that name? I've been wondering about that."

She let out a light laugh. "My name means 'sorrow.'"

"Is there anything you're sorry about?"

"No, but my mother was saddened by my being a girl instead of a boy, thus my name."

Willie wrinkled his nose. "That's awful! But I think most fathers want sons." The heat crept into his face. "As much as I hate to admit this, there's a part of me that believes women are to be owned and mastered."

"And that's exactly why I came to The House. I learned that women can be dominant, and men can be subservient. I like the freedom I have here. I can express my sensual nature in a setting created for tolerance, regardless of gender—or gender preference."

He smiled and pinched her cheek. "Hm-m-m, gender preference. I'll admit I've seen some pretty odd things here. What about you? Ever tasted another female the way I've tasted you?"

Delores sighed, repositioning herself on her back, and focused on the ceiling again. "Let me put it this way, many of us here have experimented with all kinds of ways to enjoy pleasures of the flesh, including same-sex coupling. As for me, I like men."

"How come you haven't made me do something with another man as part of my training here?"

She glanced over at him, fluttering her eyelashes. "If you remember, we take a thorough history of an admit's personal preferences and past encounters. House directors believe same-sex experiences should be an individual choice, with the admit initiating this contact with a consenting partner. If you voiced a desire to try an alternate union, it could be arranged. We attendants never force this on someone, not even for training purposes."

"I think that's a wise decision," he said, nodding in agreement. "For me, it's women all the way."

CHAPTER 3

Two months had passed. Willie had seen all aspects of The House, from same-sex activities to cross-dressers in flowing gowns and styled hair. The more he witnessed the differences, the more he accepted them while staying true to his own preferences. That was the beauty of The House. No individual or group experienced persecution like they would outside The House walls.

He'd followed Delores's stern advice to keep his emotions at arms' length. According to her, falling in love at The House was forbidden. The attendant's job was for training purposes only, nothing more. While playtimes with Delores were welcome—expected—he saved his heart for Louise.

From the bed there emanated loud clanking sounds, followed by Delores's giggles as she strained against the cuffs anchoring her legs to the iron headboard. Looming above her, Willie smiled, giving her plump nipples a resounding pinch, followed by a kneading of the springy flesh between his fingertips.

"Oh, god, Willie … that …" She burst into laughter.

"You like that, you dirty girl? You like having those tasty tits of yours squeezed, don't you?" He rolled her over a little and swatted her buttocks.

"I like you tasting my tits." She pulled his face over hers, aiming her lips toward his.

He jerked back, teasing. "No you don't!" He bent over one of her breasts and suckled the pert tip, tugging, licking, ending with a sharp bite. "There's one for you."

"Ow, that …"

Willie dove in, performing the same series of actions on the other breast. "There, now they're equal. We don't want one getting jealous of the other, do we?" Another swat to her buttocks.

Delores laughed. "Really, you think these mounds have minds of their own?"

"Sh-h-h, don't talk about my precious darlings like that. You'll hurt their feelings." He trailed his tongue over her abdomen and into her navel, teasing the sensitive area with vigorous strokes. Her body tensed beneath him, writhing, as she tried to stifle another round of giggles. *Clank!* went the cuffs against the iron bars of the headboard.

Willie, seized with an idea, lifted himself off the bed and headed over to the chest of drawers on the other side of the room. Though filled with modest furnishings—a bed, chest of drawers, nightstand, and a small brass sink—the room proved a cozy place to relax. But as days passed, he'd found himself missing his home, with its spacious rooms, rich furnishings, and high ceilings. Most of all, he was missing his privacy and his lifestyle, attending parties when he wanted to or enjoying his time alone. None of that existed for him here at The House.

Digging through one of the drawers, he pulled out a small bottle of oil and a wand of beads. He returned to the bed, straddling her head between his knees while leaning his face over her moist slit. "Now for some final finishes." With a light tip of the bottle, he covered the beaded wand with the oil before gently inserting the piece inside her anus. The grazing of the beads against her flesh caused her to jump. "Here, let me warm things up a bit for you." He moved the wand back and forth.

"You're wicked … oh, that's the hot oil you're using, isn't it?" Delores twitched her hips as the oil covered her flesh with each caress of the wand.

"I'm not done with you yet." Willie assumed the sixty-nine position, spreading her nether lips apart and applying some of the oil to her clit, rubbing his finger over the sensitive bud. "Feel good, now?" He chuckled as he watched her hips tense under his touch. Just as she began to moan, he dipped his shaft into her mouth. In silence, she suckled him, running her tongue over his swollen veins. He closed his eyes, sucking in his breath. With a small tug and push, he manipulated the wand in and out, grazing her clit with his finger at the same time.

He smiled. Delores had stopped her sucking, hips bucking as a hard orgasmic wave set in, consumed her, and receded. She resumed her tongue movements, turning up his internal heat. The muscular pull from her mouth stimulated his tip to the boiling point; within minutes, he emptied himself. "I love it when you swallow me whole," he said, lifting his hips away from her.

"I love the taste of you." She tickled his buttocks with her nails. Her chest arched as he slipped out the wand. "I love those beads. They give the inside of your ass a good tickle."

"It's payback for what you do to me," he said with a chuckle. "And yes, I've grown to like a good plunge in my ass." He disposed of the supplies according to House protocol for sanitization, and settled down beside her.

"Aren't you going to release my legs?" She jerked her ankles a little, clanking the cuffs against the bars.

"No. I think I'll just tease you some more." He winked at her.

"Fine." She laughed and shifted herself to a more comfortable position, keeping her thighs spread apart. Several moments of silence passed. She rubbed his arm. "I want to ask you something. You've seemed preoccupied lately. What's on your mind?"

Willie rested by her side, fingering the inside of her crotch. "You think so? In what way?"

"I just sense a restless spirit about you lately. I can't quite put my finger on it, but I see the lackluster gaze in your eyes. I feel it in your energy." Her face lost all expression of its former mirth as she gave him a quiet, thoughtful look. "When we're together, you seem like you're somewhere else far, far away from here." She rested her hands behind her head. "Are you getting tired of being here, or perhaps you're tired of me? We can arrange for you to have another attendant if you wish."

He grinned and shook his head. "You're definitely not one I'd like to leave. Actually, I tend to grow restless at times. I'm not sure what the problem is, but don't take it personally."

"Do you often think of her?"

"I think about a lot of things, like what my future is going to be like, what do I want out of life, those kinds of things."

"That's a good thing. I hope you're coming up with some answers." She licked her lips and fixed her gaze on the ceiling. Neither one said anything. Delores broke the silence. "During your time here, you've seemed happy," she began carefully, "but maybe it's time to practice your skills outside these walls." She looked at him in the eyes now. "What do you think about that?"

Willie scratched his head, not sure if he wanted to share his true feelings with her or not. For the most part, he wasn't even sure what his true feelings might be, except that his spirit had grown weary, longing for home, the familiar. "You may be right. My time here has been well worth the experience, but I'm truly happiest when I'm the ruler of my own domain, in my own house."

Delores reached up and stroked his cheek. "Tell me, Willie, what have you learned while you've been here?"

He squinted his eyes in thought, rubbing his lower lip as he turned her question over and over in his mind. "I'm not sure I know how to answer that," he finally replied. "I'm not even sure where I'd begin."

"You're not sure?" She shot him an incredulous look. "You've been here for a while now, perhaps it's time you began to consider these things. If you returned home tomorrow, what would you do with the skills you've learned? You must admit, we've put you though some rigorous training during your stay."

He nodded. "I agree with that, and you've been quite a teacher. The best, I'd say." At this point, he kissed her, and released the cuffs from her ankles.

"Ah, freedom at last," she said, laughing and stretching out her legs. Pulling him close, she snuggled in his arms, running her fingers over his chest. "Thank you for the compliment, but I know you'd have something to show for your time with me, whether or not you realize this yourself."

"True enough, no doubt."

"I suspect you'd most likely win the love of your heart, if fate put you to the test."

He chuckled. "I hope so." He tightened his hold on her. In his mind, he wasn't so sure. How would he behave without Delores around? She always made things appear so simple when she took charge. But when she did, part of him deep inside always rebelled, creating this emotional paradox. In the end, though, she knew the thoughts of his heart: it was time for a change—soon.

CHAPTER 4

Willie reclined on the floor of the common room at the end of the hallway, resting after the round of lovemaking in which he and Delores had engaged moments before. A light film of sweat clung to his skin. Both of their scents lingered in his nostrils. A post-breakfast tryst in this room had become a ritual between the two, the prime time before others used the space as a setting for their own lusty tumbles. He thought about his stay at The House, replaying in his mind the previous conversation with Delores. Just exactly how would he apply his learning to the outside world? How would he stake his claim and take ownership of everything that mattered in his life?

"Oh, Willie, can you come here, please?" Delores's voice rang out across the room. From the windows, the bright streams of light from the early morning sun cast her curvy form into a magnificent silhouette as she stood in the doorway.

He got up from the floor and made his way in her direction. "What is it? You've been gone for a while."

"I need you to follow me back to the room. We have to talk." She grabbed his arm and pulled him along at a rapid pace.

"What's the hurry? And you seem so serious … so …"

She stopped a second, turned around, and said, "I'll explain it all to you in a minute, but we don't have much time to spare. Your family is on its way here to pick you up."

Willie pulled her back into his arms. "What are you talking about? I'm sure you're mistaken. They wouldn't be coming back for me so soon, would they?"

"You've been here longer than you realize. Let's just get back to the room. We'll talk more there." Delores, her face filled with urgency, turned back again, heading down the hall.

When they entered, Willie spied his street clothes on the bed. He turned to her in alarm. "You weren't kidding, were you?"

"We never joke when someone is leaving us." She handed him his shirt. "Here put this on." Her tone was almost matter-of-fact now.

Willie, still not believing this turn of events, slipped on the shirt he'd worn when he had first arrived. The fabric hugged his skin as he slipped each button through a hole. Immediately he detested the sense of constriction, barely able to breathe. Unfastening the front panel of his House trousers, he harbored a grudging moment for having to give them up. The idea of unfastening the front panel and pulling it all the way back to expose the entire pelvic region still impressed him. He'd been able to take care of sexual business quickly and efficiently. Perhaps he'd hire a designer to create a pair once he returned home.

"I'm dressed. Is there anything else for me to do?"

"Don't forget these," Delores said, handing him his socks and shoes.

"Oh, those." Willie frowned. The thought of wearing shoes again didn't appeal much to him, either.

Delores leaned in close to his face, smiling. "Willie, you've received the best training here. When you return home and you're settled in your own environment, please don't forget what you've learned." She delivered a kiss on his lips.

He returned the embrace, before pulling back for a last look into her eyes. "I'll miss you, Delores. Is there any way I can talk you into leaving this place and coming with me?" He smiled and kissed her forehead.

"But my darling," she reminded him, "contrary to what you may think now, it's not me you want. You know your heart's desire, and you have the means of obtaining it. Be wise in your actions and thoughtful in everything you do. Remember, though you may use what you've learned here, you're not to share *where*." With a wink, she led him to the doorway and gave him a light push. "You know the way to the steward's office. Your family will be there waiting for you." Willie paused, waiting for her to come with him.

Noting the hesitation, she said, "Unfortunately, I'm not allowed to go with you. But you'll be fine, and I wish you all the best."

"I'll need all the luck I can get. And, Delores, please know that our time together has been the best thing that has ever happened to me." Viewing her radiant smile for the last time, he turned out of the room and headed toward the entrance hall.

His head whirled with an onslaught of thoughts. How would he continue his life outside The House? For the first time, he embraced his accounting work with a grateful heart. At least that pursuit held some possibility of occupying his mind while he settled in at home once again. He reached the top of the marble staircase, descending one step at a time, savoring each moment left to him, basking in the rainbow glow cast from the prisms of the crystal chandelier. Stifling a chuckle, he viewed the portraits hanging on the wall. He'd thought the artist quite clever, creating subjects who appeared so normal to the casual eye. It was on closer inspection that one saw the naughtiness: the females showing off more than ample bosoms and each male sporting a pronounced fullness between his thighs. Perhaps he might find out the name of this artist and commission him to paint such a portrait for his bedroom at home.

At the foot of the staircase, he turned right and headed to the steward's office near the end of the hall. From inside the room, sounds of voices reached his ear as he neared the doorway. In silence he entered, greeted by smiles from his parents. His travel bag rested at his mother's feet.

"Willie, my boy. " His father stepped forward, offering his hand. His mother intercepted first, showering him with a big hug and some light kisses peppered on both sides of his cheeks.

"We've missed you, son." His mother's eyes, soft and warm, welled up with tears. "As we promised when we brought you here, we've come to take you home."

"Mother. Father." Willie nodded, accepting his father's hand. Surprised, he discovered he'd actually missed his parents, even their nagging.

The steward came out from behind the desk. "All the paperwork is signed. You are now free to leave." Offering his hand, he said to Willie, "It's been a pleasure having you, and we hope your treatment here will serve you well."

"I'm sure it will, sir." Willie returned the handshake. He picked up his bag, and he and his family turned out of the office and headed out of the building.

As the car sped away from The House, he turned around, gazing one last time at the place he'd called home. His old home, his true home, awaited him, and thoughts of returning filled him with a mix of anticipation and anxiety.

"So tell us, Willie, did they treat you well?" His father turned to give him a quick glance as he drove down the road winding through the countryside.

"Yes, the staff treated me well." His eyes followed a small brook on his left, spying a doe and her fawn drinking at its edge.

"What kinds of things did you do there, son?" his mother said, her voice trilling out the words.

Willie said nothing for a moment, unclear as to how to answer her question. Clearing his throat, he finally answered her. "Oh, nothing much. We just talked a lot about why I'd been feeling so dissatisfied, what I wanted out of life. You know, those kinds of things."

His father shrugged. "That sounds somewhat helpful. I hope you'll have some new life in you, because we were really worried there for a while. It's not right for a man to be so down and out the way you were."

Mrs. Strumpkin turned around and gave Willie a broad smile. "Just so you know, dear, we're holding a welcome-home party in your honor."

"You're what?" He sat up straight in his seat. "Why the need for that sort of thing?"

"It's okay, we're having the party at our home tomorrow evening. You'll at least have one night's rest."

"Thanks for giving me that, at least." He scowled and sank back, trying to distract himself with the scenery, which had now changed to show some semblance of city life. The small office building where he and his father worked every day came into view. Somehow he'd also forgotten how much he'd liked coming to the office, dealing with the clients, running the numbers. Stroking the keys of an adding machine always lit up his face with a smile as he tapped away at the numbers, trying in earnest to ethically come up with the most desirable figures. If he'd been so content, why had he become so despondent? Perhaps what Delores suggested might be true: living alone didn't sit well with him. But just how to put his newly acquired skills into action still remained somewhat of a mystery.

They rounded a bend and began riding over the streets toward Willie's home. The residents in this area enjoyed their pedigrees and connections to old money, flaunting their abundance with large dwellings and the newest model of vehicles made in the present day. The Strumpkin's fortune came by way of a substantial inheritance from a deceased family member, which only made it easier for his parents to purchase one of these fine homes for their son. His success in the family accounting business had substantiated his sense of responsibility, and their making him pay a modest monthly payment to them for his home had only served, in their minds, to round out his initiation into living as an adult in a precarious world.

Mr. Strumpkin pulled into the driveway and continued around to the back of the house. He turned off the engine and stepped out of the vehicle. "How does it feel to be home again, Son?"

Willie climbed out, scanning everything around him, feeling like a foreigner in his own backyard. "Good, very good," he said, trying to hide his uneasiness.

"Let's go on in. Do you mind if we sit and visit with you a little while, catch up?"

"No, of course not." He smiled at his parents. "I guess Judith has minded the place well while I've been gone?"

"She's the best housekeeper you'll ever find, and yes, she's guarded your things like they were gold!" Mrs. Strumpkin laced her arm around her son's and followed him into the house. They entered a spacious living room filled with the finest quality furnishings, both of the Victorian and Art Deco style.

Catching a quick nod of her husband's head toward the kitchen, Mrs. Strumpkin released her arm from Willie's. "I think I'll go see what Judith is up to, and let you two men talk."

Mr. Strumpkin proceeded to the small bar along the back wall and filled two small glasses with whiskey. Before seating himself in a leather chair, he handed one of the glasses to Willie. "Ah, some of the finest batch around!" He lifted the glass, peering at the amber liquid, and took a sip.

"You always manage to have the best connections to the finest things in life." Willie chuckled, tipping his glass to his lips. How he'd missed the taste of good liquor on his tongue. And this particular brand of sipping whiskey gave him a heady orgasmic sensation almost as good as the ones he'd experienced at The House—almost.

"You know we've kept your whereabouts this long while a secret from all our friends and family," his father began.

"Oh." Willie cleared his throat, enjoying the relaxing effects of the alcohol. "And just what have you told our good friends and family?" The words slipped from his lips, bearing the stinging hint of sarcasm.

Mr. Strumpkin shot his son an irritated glance. "No need to get snippy with me, young man! I just wanted to make sure you, me, and your mother are all singing from the same page here."

"Fine, so what have you told everyone?" Willie polished off the remaining drink in his glass and rose from his seat to pour himself another.

"Your mother and I have just said that we sent you away to the country to spend some time with distant relatives, that you needed to rest and get your vitality back."

"Sounds like a good enough line to me." Willie sighed and plopped back down in his seat. "Count me in."

His father half rose from the seat, thought the better of it, and sat down. "Damn it, Willie, must you be such a wise guy? We've been trying to help you. Are you that wretchedly ungrateful for all we've done for you?"

"I'm sorry, Father." Willie shot his father a look of apology, hoping he'd calm down. "My remark was uncalled for." He shook his glass, tinkling the ice inside.

Mr. Strumpkin leaned toward his son. "I'm hoping that where you've actually been has helped you rest and get some spunk back in you."

Willie flashed him a toothy smile. "Oh, I've got plenty of spunk in me, and yes, where I've spent my time helped, more than you'll ever know."

Mr. Strumpkin settled back in his chair and took a draw from his glass. The afternoon sun from the window lit up his face, illuminating fine, distinguished features, an elegant straight nose and refined pink lips. The rich, silvery gray in his hair matched the neatly trimmed mustache above his mouth. With piercing, steely blue eyes, he gave his son a steady look. "So tell me, now that it's just the two of us in here, what exactly did they do with you while you were there, at The House, you know?"

"I've already told you. Nothing much. We just talked about why I'd been out of sorts. Really, there's nothing more to tell."

"I can't quite put my finger on it, but I can't help but suspect there's more to all this than you're telling me." There was almost a twinkle in his father's eye.

Willie found himself wondering for a moment how much he might know, then set the idea aside. He shifted in his seat, feeling the burning heat of his father's stare, gazing at his glass and wishing for a way to get off this topic of conversation. "Tell me more about this party you're planning for me tomorrow evening. How do I need to dress? Is this formal or a casual thing?"

"It's more on the formal side. We like to do things with style," Mr. Strumpkin said, beaming as he spoke.

"More like showing off, if you ask me." Willie shot him a wide grin. "You like flaunting your new money, don't you, old man?"

Mr. Strumpkin laughed. "That, I do. I'll tell you something else, Son, money is money, whether you've made it yourself or it's handed over to you. Either way, it gives you power." He took a last swig from his glass and set it down on the table beside him. "And you do want power, trust me on that."

Willie pursed his lips. "Yeah, I've heard that's true." Deep inside, he laughed. One thing he knew for certain, money wasn't the only thing that gave you power.

His father got up and placed his empty glass back on the bar, knowing Judith would come by later to tidy everything up. Willie followed his father to the front door, where his mother and Judith had already been conversing in hushed tones. Willie's gut clenched, his anxiety rising. Were they talking about him?

"You heading back to the office, Pops? Maybe I can come with you, get caught up on all my accounts."

Mr. Strumpkin nodded. "Those numbers don't roll by themselves. But stay home and get some rest. The work won't get up and walk away." He grinned at his son. "See you at our place tomorrow evening at five o'clock sharp. Again, welcome home!"

CHAPTER 5

With his parents gone for the day, solitude came crashing down— consuming, suffocating. As soon as his parents had left, Willie coaxed Judith into taking the afternoon off. He took his time, wandering around all the levels of his house, checking out each room to see if anything had changed during his absence.

The high ceilings instilled a sense of smallness in him, and though The House had its merits in fine architecture and interior design, he gloried in the beauty of his own home, with plush carpet and ornate rugs, fine artwork, unique lamps and curiosity pieces, and furnishings that reflected his own taste, elegant, unpretentious.

On an accent table, he picked up a small porcelain Rosenthal nude, admiring the detail in the female's hair, the curve of her buttocks, and the allure of her breasts, right down to the rosy tinted peaks. In a curio cabinet, he beheld an ivory netsuke of a couple engaged in one of the *Kama Sutra* positions he'd seen not only in carvings adorning doorways of The House, but displayed by admits and attendants as they learned each of these positions like a student learning a history lesson.

He smiled. His mother had been correct. Judith had changed nothing; his home had been waiting for his return. In the silence, he caught the sound of his own breathing.

As much as he disliked the thought of spending his first day home alone, left to his own devices, he needed this time to get his head together. But something had, in fact, changed. What? He used to enjoy his time alone, with no one else around, entertaining himself as he wished. Or had he? Delores's words came to mind once again. All work and no play had, in fact, made life dull. The realization hit him. He needed a new change going forward, one that would endure.

He gave a jump at the unexpected sound. A long time had passed since he'd heard a doorbell, and the ringing left him confused for a moment. Laughing to himself, he trotted to the door, and opened it to find … Louise Carnwell!

"Hi, Willie," she began, "I'm not catching you at a bad time, am I?"

He stood in the doorway, stunned.

Uneasy, she glanced past him, craning her neck for a peek inside the house. "Is it all right if I come in for a bit?" She shifted from one foot to the other, holding a large basket in her arms.

"Oh, of course," he said, returning to reality. "How rude of me. Um, here, let me take that for you. Yes, please come in." He took the basket and stepped back, allowing her to pass. "I'm sorry. I wasn't expecting anyone."

"Well, I'm sure you weren't, but I had to come over and see if you needed anything. I didn't know if Judith had prepared something for you to eat yet, but I thought I'd bring food over to you anyway. I've told your mother countless times before that you can't always rely on hired help to do everything the way you'd like things done. And Judith … God love her, but well … it's just not the same as getting the personal touch."

She stopped a moment, and eyed him up and down. "Well, Willie, I must say, you are looking quite rested. I think your time away did you some good, after all. I'm glad your parents finally listened to me. I told your mother before you left how weary you were starting to look. 'Lorna,' I said to her, 'I really think Willie should take some time away from here, get out of town. He's working far too much, and I don't see the old spark about him anymore.'

"It's true, you know, Willie. You'd stopped coming to all the parties; you seemed to mope around a lot. At least I thought so every time I saw you. And I see things, you know."

Drawn in by Louise's monologue, Willie smiled. He knew most people found her meddlesome, even irritating in some cases. Yet he couldn't help but wonder what it would be like to possess an ability to calm her frenetic energy, curb her penchant for presenting small speeches to listening ears. Something about the urgency in her eyes and the intent expression on her face always attracted his attention, especially the way she cocked her head at intervals as she spoke, her special way of making a point. Watching her lips move tempted him to kiss her into silence. He waited as she continued on, smiling wider with each word.

When he managed to find her at a good stopping point, he interjected, "So what do we have here in the basket?"

She gave him a bright smile, eyes sparkling with pride. "I brought you some homemade soup, fresh bread, and some cookies I baked. I made them all myself, using a recipe I created. If you didn't know already, I'm known for my good cooking. 'Lorna,' I told your mother, 'I know Judith is probably a good cook, but I could teach her a thing or two when it comes to preparing a good meal …'"

And I could teach you a thing or two … Willie, startled by his own reaction, clamped his teeth together. Thank goodness he'd managed to keep his mouth shut. He cleared his throat and nodded toward some swinging doors. "Lou, why don't we head on to the kitchen table and eat. I'm starving."

Louise's eyes sparkled with satisfaction. "See, I knew it. Judith is good, but you need the personal touch. Like I told one of my friends the other day …"

Willie stifled the urge to laugh, but ignored the rest of her ramblings, leading the way to the kitchen. Her chatter didn't matter to him. It never had, actually. Right now, the only element about her standing out in his mind were those plump breasts, cherry-red lips, chocolate eyes, and that charcoal bobbed hair. The only thing he really wanted to taste was *her*: all of her, from the nape of her neck all the way down to that sweet spot right between her curvy thighs.

" … Willie, are you listening to me? And why are you looking at me like that?" The expression on her face challenged him.

"Huh?" He averted his eyes, setting the basket on the table by a large picture window overlooking an enormous English garden.

Not waiting for an answer, Louise continued her search. When he thought it was safe, Willie turned around toward the cabinets where she stood on tiptoe, opening one door at a time.

"Where do you keep your dishes and silverware?"

"Um …" He ran his fingers through his hair, trying to remember. Had he really been gone that long? "Oh, yes, over there on the far left … Yeah, that door. That's the one. And the silverware is in the drawer right under it."

As Louise reached up to grab a couple of dishes, he continued gawking at her tiny waist … and those long, slender legs, as her dress crept up even more the higher she stretched.

"There, I think I have everything." She headed toward the table where she placed two porcelain bowls, two bread plates, matching spoons, and a butter knife. "Willie, do you have any butter in the fridge?"

"Yeah, I think so. I can't imagine Judith ever letting things like that run out. Oh, and can you bring out some milk? I'll get a couple of glasses." He made his way to the cabinet and pulled down two large glass tumblers.

They both made their way to the table where Louise promptly took charge, preparing everything in just the right portions into the bowls and on the plates.

"Food at last!" Willie said, sitting down.

"I love your kitchen," she said as she sat opposite him at the table. "The white tiled floors, and the stove and refrigerator. You always have the latest models of everything, don't you?" She swallowed a spoonful of soup and wiped her lips on a napkin she retrieved from the holder on the table.

"Yeah," he admitted, "even my car. I love it better than anything." He picked up some bread, slathering a generous helping of butter on top. "This is all so good. Thanks for bringing it over."

"I don't like seeing someone spend the first day at home alone after they've been gone."

"Oh?" Willie glanced up at her, his lips slick with butter. Louise reached over with a delicate finger and wiped away a small amount clinging to the corner of his mouth. He nearly choked. She'd never touched him like this, and her caress sent a hot bolt of heat ricocheting down between his thighs.

"As I told my mother, 'Someone ought to go and give Willie some company. It's hard coming home to an empty house.'"

"I do have Judith," he said, teasing.

"You know what I mean."

An uncanny, wicked desire consumed him. He wanted to continue teasing her, get a sense of where she stood emotionally. They'd been acquaintances for a long time, but had never ventured into spending any time alone together. What would it be like to possess her, subject her to his command? But the one big question burned in his mind the most: Why had she come to him now?

"So you thought you'd be the perfect one to keep me company, huh?" He looked directly at her. "Why you?"

She stopped chewing her slice of bread and studied him a moment, gathering her thoughts. "Well, it's just that … I mean, I supposed you might …" Confused, Louise became silent.

Willie laughed. But deep inside, her soulful gaze urged him to sweep everything off the table and ravish her, right then and there. "I'm glad you came," he assured her. "And you're right, I was already trying to figure out what to do with myself." He kept his eyes on her, spooning another bite of soup into his mouth.

Louise gave a little smile, and continued. "Anyway, did you enjoy your visit with your relatives?"

"Huh?" he said, his memory lapsing a moment.

"Didn't you spend time with family? At least that's what I've heard." She tipped her glass for a drink, waiting for his answer.

"Um, yeah, I did." He turned his eyes back to his bowl, trying to calm his mind. He'd nearly forgotten his parents had chosen that story as an alibi. *Did she have to ask such questions? Wouldn't it be easier just to lay her on the floor, rip off her blouse and taste those sweet breasts?*

"What did you do while you were there?" She continued, filling the silence again. "Anything fun and exciting?"

His heart caught in his throat. "Oh, a few fun things while I was there. You wouldn't believe how exciting things can get in the country."

"Like what?" She persisted. "And why are you hedging so much? You almost act like you've been caught with your hand in the cookie jar or something." She leaned over close to him. "What really happened, Willie? You seemed to go away so fast, no word, no warning. Just one day, then Poof! you were gone."

Her insistence triggered an urge to strike back. With a sly gleam in his eye, he gave her an inquisitive stare; yes, now was the moment. His voice took on a new, calculated tone. "Do you always watch people, questioning everything they do, everything that goes on? I'd have never guessed for one minute that you paid that much attention to my business or to what I might or might not be doing."

Stunned, Louise stared at him, wide-eyed with surprise. The only sound in the kitchen came from the clock ticking on the wall. She turned her attention back to her bowl, stirring through the remainder of her soup.

He'd struck a nerve, and moved to soften the blow. "It's okay, Lou." His voice released its accusatory overtones. "I'm not mad at you or anything." He laid his hand on hers, hoping his smile would heal her wounded spirit and make her feel better again, all the while imagining his lips kissing hers. Her breasts rose and fell with each rapid, shallow breath she took, while her porcelain skin glowed from the soft flush on her cheeks. He continued soothing her. "I just didn't know you cared so much. Just wondering, that's all." He watched as she struggled to keep her emotions in check.

She swallowed hard, pulled her shoulders up, and smiled back. "Thank you, William. I didn't mean to make you mad. And yes, to answer your question, I tend to watch people a lot. I don't know why I do that, but I do." She shrugged a little, plunging the last spoonful of soup into her mouth.

He kept the tone light, sensing a breakthrough at hand if he played it right. "Hey, how about one of those cookies you made? I'm dying to taste one of your sweet treats." He tipped his head toward the basket as he fidgeted in his chair, trying desperately to stifle the erection forming in his pants. The way he'd shocked her with his questions had shot his lust to soaring heights. As far back as he could remember, he'd never seen or heard of anyone challenging Louise Carnwell as he just had. Filled with a new sense of power, he discovered he liked making her squirm—just a little, anyway.

Louise pulled back the wrappings from the plate, revealing several cookies, each one topped with a pert chocolate drop in the middle. "Here you go." She handed the plate to Willie.

"Beautiful. I love the cute drop on top. It looks just like a lady's …" He put the cookie to his mouth and caressed the chocolate peak with soft strokes of his tongue.

Louise fixed her sparkling eyes on him long and hard, watching him with intense interest.

"They look like a lady's what, Willie? You never finished that part." She smiled at him as their eyes met.

Realizing what he'd just said, he stopped for a moment, shaking his head to help him focus better. "Did I say something?" He mustered up his most innocent look.

"Never mind." She laughed, grabbed a cookie off the plate, and took a bite.

CHAPTER 6

Willie climbed the stairs, unbuttoning his shirt as he took each step. When he reached the top, he strode down the hallway to his bedroom. It was dark when Louise had finally taken her leave, and much to his relief, no other awkward moments had surfaced for the remainder of the evening. No more direct, personal questions from her. He had also been careful with every word he spoke, not wishing to toy with her emotions as he'd done earlier. Afterward, he'd busied himself for another couple of hours, sipping some fine wine while leafing through his accounting ledgers. The thought of getting back to work invigorated him, giving him a renewed sense of purpose. But thoughts of her gave the flesh between his thighs quite a different sense of purpose. The vision of her face, her smile, the feminine curves in her body had all burned their impressions hard in his memory.

He stood near the bench at the foot of his ornate bed and slipped out of his clothes. When he eyed the emptiness waiting for him, another round of loneliness hit his senses. With a heavy heart, he grasped the brocade covering on the bed, revealing crisp, clean sheets. How he wished for someone now: a warm body to hold, lips to kiss, and a good moist crotch to swallow his swollen cock. He crawled into bed.

The fire between his legs raged as thoughts of Louise taunted him. He tossed and turned, but his erection strained hard against his undergarments.

Disgusted, he threw aside the sheets and stripped himself free from his underwear. Instead of returning to his place beneath the sheets, he rested on top, hoping the air hitting his skin might cool him off. Moonlight stole through the windows, lighting the room in a soft, silvery glow. In the dim light, he saw his thick shaft standing stiff at attention.

His thoughts turned back to Delores, who had always remarked how much she liked holding his fat length inside her. On a whim, he swatted at himself, watching how he swayed, bobbing from side to side until he stilled again. At the very top of his tip, he fingered his pre-cum, rubbing the slick moisture between his thumb and forefinger. He gasped, fingering his slit, enjoying the sensation. Between his thighs a dull pleasure ache mounted, growing stronger by degrees.

His resolve gone and lust running amok, he grabbed the head, tugging and rubbing around his ridge. At intervals, he let out a light groan. He closed his eyes and encircled his length with his hand, coursing over his swollen veins, switching out to finger his tip and play in his slit some more. After several minutes of tormenting himself, he climaxed, releasing thick streams of lust. He pulled himself out of bed, heading toward the bathroom for a towel to clean himself up. Relief at last. To-morrow he'd spend more time thinking about how to involve Louise in achieving relief. Better yet, he'd think more about how to pleasure her, imagining how she'd behave in the throes of passion as his fingers and tongue roved over her flesh.

§§§

The next morning, Willie awakened. Between squinting lids, he turned over to pull Delores close, but reached out to nothingness beside him. He lifted his head in confusion, before sinking back down into his pillow. Now he remembered: he was home, in his own house, his own bed, his own domain. Downstairs, he heard Judith rustling in the kitchen, pots and pans clanging gently as she worked on today's meals. Willie pulled the covers over his naked body, grateful for at least one living soul in the house besides his own.

He remembered the big welcome-home party at his parents' house. His face clouded over. Cursing under his breath, he tried to reason with himself why he should even show up. Maybe he might beg off, with some minor ache or illness. His eyes widened, and his body roused fully awake. He couldn't forego this party. Louise had promised him she'd be there too. That settled it. Spending the evening at his parents' home wouldn't be so bad after all.

"Sir, will you be dining downstairs, or shall I go ahead and bring your breakfast in now?"

"Huh?" Willie jumped at the sound of Judith's voice. "I'm sorry, I didn't hear you knock." He turned in her direction and gave her a warm smile, grateful he'd sought shelter beneath his covers. "Sure, I'll eat in here. You can put the tray over there."

"I saw your door open, and I thought it might be okay to check in with you." She entered the room and placed a tray on a table by the window. "I'm sorry if I disturbed you or caught you unawares."

"Oh, Judith, you never inconvenience me in any way."

"How was your stay in the country?" She walked over to the bed and stood next to him, arms folded behind her back.

"Um, fine. Yes, I had a wonderful time away." He studied her for a moment, taking in her features, the pristine housekeeper's uniform over a thick, stocky frame, the gentle expression on her face. For the first time he acknowledged the sense of comfort her presence provided him. Just knowing she came every day to his home to see to his well-being and care for him filled him with peace.

"You look much more refreshed and rested. How did you fare after I left yesterday? Did you eat any dinner?"

He smiled, seeing the look of concern on her face. "Actually I had a wonderful dinner with a nice visitor."

"You had a visitor here? And who was that, if I may be so bold as to ask?" Judith's arms slipped to her side, and she stepped closer to Willie, a concerned expression on her face.

"Louise Carnwell. She brought over a basket of food. She fixed the most delicious soup I've ever eaten, and we ate it with fresh bread and butter. For dessert, we ate some homemade cookies, with fat chocolate drops in the middle." His mouth watered at the memory, and not just because of the cookies.

Judith sniffed and turned up her nose. "Miss Carnwell, is it? If you don't mind my speaking a bit out of turn, sir, I think she came over here just to see what you were up to. She's a nosy thing, and she thinks her cooking is better than anyone else's. Well, let me tell you, sir, mine beats hers, hands down, any day."

Willie nodded, stifling a laugh.

She lowered her voice, shaking a finger at him. "I think she has designs on you, Mr. Strumpkin. I'd be leery if I were you."

"You think she has designs on me? Why on earth would you ever think that, Judith?" Willie rested on one elbow, intrigued.

"I get out more than you think I do, and I hear things, sir. And besides, when I've helped your parents out with their parties recently, I've seen her give you the eye when you were there, all hungry and lusty, like a starving animal." She sniffed again in disapproval. "Mark my words, sir, she's bossy and demanding. Why, you won't be able to get rid of her."

"Now, now, Judith, she's surely not that bad, is she?" He dropped back down and rolled onto his back, laughing.

"You won't be laughing when she's wormed her way in and smothered the very life out of you. She's a force to be reckoned with!"

Trying to appear more serious, he stopped laughing for a moment and tried to keep a straight face. "So you don't think I can handle her? Is that it?"

"Mr. Strumpkin," Judith said with a wide smile, "you're such a gentle man. Your nature is soft and quiet. She's a persistent thing; you'll have no chance against her." Judith stepped away and headed toward the door. Before leaving the room, she turned around one last time. "Just mind what I tell you. By the way, I'll have one of your good Sunday suits pressed and ready for you to wear tonight." She walked away, as if her task had been accomplished: he had been warned.

Willie settled back down on the bed, lost in thought. He chuckled to himself, especially at the remark about Louise trying to "worm her way in." As far as he was concerned, the only one trying to worm in anywhere was him—straight into that hot slit hidden underneath "Miss Carnwell's" skirts. But his lighthearted view took a more sober turn. Why had he, during these past few years, chosen to keep his distance, watching her from afar, engaging in trivial conversation whenever chance seemed to put them alone together in a corner of a room? Judith was right. Louise had glanced his way many times at parties, giving him a light smile before turning back to converse with her friends. Did they both share the same interest in each other? Was she just as scared to make a move?

She had always come across as a walking whirlwind, hard to grasp, hard to handle. Willie now saw her in a new light, as a new challenge. The gleam in her eyes the day before told him everything he needed to know. After his training at The House, he trusted his ability to master her wayward spirit. The more he studied the matter, the more he suspected she secretly longed for someone else to wield the upper hand for a change.

CHAPTER 7

Dressed in his best clothing, Willie slipped onto the seat of his 1926 Studebaker President, excited about the prospect of driving again. He loved this car, the look of it, the high performance as it graced the roads. Running his hands over the hard steering wheel, he smiled, breathing in the scent of leather seats. The late afternoon sun shot blinding rays of light and heat through the windshield, and with a tingle of anticipation, he started the engine and pulled out of the driveway.

As he traveled the road to his parents' home a few miles away, he realized how much he'd missed driving and the sense of freedom it brought him. Through the open window, the air hinted at smells from the outdoors. Visions of old familiar homes and neighborhoods calmed him, but not enough to totally squash the twinge of anxiety he held about the evening ahead. How would he handle himself with guests casting sideways glances in his direction, engaged in hushed conversations about where he'd been? They'd be questioning him with utmost discretion. He knew all his clients and friends wondered about his sudden disappearance. Louise, more than anyone, wanted this answer too, though she presented as the least of his concerns; squelching the burning curiosity among the others might prove a tougher dilemma. Better to be polite and evasive, while offending no one. His business and good standing within the circles of society depended on his fine-tuned execution of the social graces.

In the distance, he spied the entrance to the driveway of Strumpkin manor. He passed through the gate and made his way down the long drive toward the house. A fine example of gothic architecture, this home was much bigger than his, more stately and more elegantly furnished, a most suitable place for lavish parties. Several cars sat parked, one of them being Louise's. True to her word, she had shown up for the festivities. At least if he chose not to mingle with the other guests too much, giving most of his attention to her would serve as a wonderful diversion. When he parked his car, he headed toward the door. Closing his eyes and muttering a quick prayer to get him through the evening, he walked on in. "Well, here he is, the guest of honor. Come on over here, Willie, my boy!" Mr. Strumpkin held up a glass of gin in one hand while motioning him over with the other.

Willie smiled and walked toward his father, nodding and smiling at some of the guests as he passed. Across the room Louise, seated in an elegant pose, spoke to a small group of young ladies. As usual, she held the floor while the others listened with the occasional discreet grin or eye-roll passing from one girl to the other. The green color of her dress brought out the luster of her dark hair and milky skin, making her even prettier. He admired the way she wore cosmetics, adding just enough to accentuate her luminous eyes and pouty lips. What would it hurt if he ignored his father and spoke to her first? On second thought, he decided to wait, play it cool. No need for him to appear overeager. He joined his parents and another couple who turned to give him a warm greeting.

"Good to see you back again, Willie." Mr. Lars Anderson, one of his father's oldest clients, gave him a hardy pat on the back. "It looks like time off has put some new energy back in you, old boy."

Standing next to her husband with her arm through his, Mrs. Ingrid Anderson gave him a warm smile. "You do look rested. Did you have a nice time away?"

"I had the most wonderful time away, Mrs. Anderson. Thanks for asking." Willie gave her a polite nod and smiled back at her. He'd always thought she was such an attractive lady, with soft, light brown hair, full lips, and deep, searching eyes. She and Mr. Anderson still seemed to hold a genuine affection for each other, even after twenty years of marriage. What would she be like in bed? Did she know how to pleasure her husband in ways that would make other women blush with shame? He imagined himself enfolded in her arms, nestled between soft, plump breasts, with slender fingers caressing his most sensitive areas. Time at The House had affected his thought processes; he'd never quite see situations or people the same way again. He blinked a few times to clear his mind, trying to pull his attention back to Mr. Anderson.

"I hear you'll be back in the office next week. It'll be good to see you back behind your desk again, plugging away at those numbers like you used to do. We've all missed you, you know." The gentleman took a sip from his glass, but kept his eyes on Willie.

"I'll be happy to be back, sir. Even though the country's nice, I enjoy city life myself." Willie gave them all a wide smile, catching the smug, secretive look of approval from his parents. The touch of a hand on his back steered his attention to the guest who'd stepped up beside him.

"Well, well, you're back among us once again." The hearty baritone voice of an old family friend filled his ear. "We thought you'd left and gone forever."

"Mr. Carnwell, good to see you again." Willie took the outstretched hand before him and gave it a firm shake. "I'm glad you made it tonight."

"I wouldn't have missed this for anything. To show you what a good sport I am, I even let Louise drive us here. Can you imagine that?" Mr. Carnwell burst out laughing.

Willie laughed along with the rest of the group, but deep in Mr. Carnwell's eyes, he detected a flash of cold hostility. George Carnwell held a reputation for being overbearing and protective when it came to his daughter's interests. What few suitors she had managed to gain, he'd scared off after a few visits. But like any caring father, he still indulged her willful nature at times. No doubt he'd come to the party not only to maintain his social connections, but to learn more about her friends.

Time to chat with someone else. Willie excused himself. "I think I'll get a drink."

Louise stood at the punch bowl, her audience having dispersed to other parts of the room. Willie slipped up from behind, placing an arm around her shoulder. She gave a little jump, smiling when she saw him.

He'd been waiting to go another round of wicked teasing, and now was as good a time as any. "Well, did you give your friends some insightful knowledge, great words to live by, things they can hold near and dear to their hearts?"

"Huh?" A light frown covered her face as she ladled some punch in a cup. "Why do you ask that?" She flicked her moist, pink tongue over one of her fingers, licking off some drops that had splashed on her hand.

Willie felt a rise in his pants. He moved in closer. "You just seemed to have everyone so hypnotized by your speech, I thought it had to be something good. That's what I like about you, Lou, you're never at a loss for words when it comes to a listening crowd. I wanted to hear you too, but I got waylaid by my parents—and your father." Hemming her in between himself and the table, he brushed his cheek against hers, reaching for a cup and the ladle.

He kept his eyes pinned on the crowd in front of him. To his satisfaction, everyone seemed caught up in their own moment, tuned in to their own gossip. Louise's father and his parents had their backs turned away, Mr. Carnwell nodding with enthusiasm, apparently engrossed in some juicy tidbit Willie's father shared.

The smell of Louise's soft perfume filled his nostrils, and, for a brief second, he turned his face to touch her hair and take in a deep breath. As he pressed in closer, the hardness between his thighs ground against her buttocks. He filled up his cup in silence and stepped back. Bold? Yes. Fate couldn't have presented a more opportune time than this one for him to make a move; his heart raced at the challenge.

She turned around to face him, eyes flashing with lust. A pink flush rested on her cheeks. From beneath her blouse, Willie almost swore he detected the strong beating of her heart—a heart that pounded behind a set of succulent breasts.

"What's the matter, Lou, did I say something wrong?" Satisfied with her reaction, Willie smiled to himself, enjoying the opportunity to throw her off guard.

"Um, no … but …" Confused at his comments, she fixed her eyes on his.

"You seem a little lost for words. Like I said before, you're not usually like that when I see you with other people." He pushed a stray lock of her hair back in place and trailed his finger down the side of her cheek. The color on her face turned a deeper red.

She cleared her throat, took a quick sip of punch, and tried to regain her composure. "I guess I never thought of myself as one who draws a crowd." She swallowed, quickly regaining her pose. With a lecturer's detachment, she continued, "But you know me, Willie, when I have something on my mind, I just say it. I study up on all kinds of things, and when I can share what I know, I like to take the opportunity to do just that." Louise warmed up to her new topic, dismissing her previous shaken composure as a mere brief inconvenience. "Take Clara's hair, for example. That's probably what we were talking about when you came in. She dreadfully needs a new style to make herself not look so frumpy and all that. You'd agree, too, wouldn't you, Willie? The latest style magazine only proves I'm right in what I was telling her and the girls tonight …"

With her nervousness subsiding, Louise had regressed to her old self, the lusty gleam in her eye somewhat dimming.

He went with the casual flow of her speech. "You see, there you go again—good information. I'm sure Clara was grateful, and the next time I see her, she'll most likely be a changed woman, all because of you." He smiled and chucked her under the chin.

With her eyes now narrowed into slits, she opened her mouth to say something else. He waited a second and continued with his own banter.

"Like I said earlier, you've always got words of wisdom for anyone who'll listen."

Her face clouded with indignation. "What's gotten into you to-night? You've never talked to me this way before." Her tones snapped at him like one of Delores's old whips. The charged words cracked against his ears.

Easy does it. Willie knew his unchecked cockiness might put him at great risk of losing her. *Time to put this train in reverse.* He chuckled. "Oh, Lou, I'm just yanking your chain a little. I don't mean anything by it." He gave her an affectionate pat on the arm, hoping to brighten the mood. "Hey, let's go outside for a bit. I don't know about you, but I'm feeling hot and stifled in here all of a sudden."

She glanced down at her cup, licking her lower lip in hesitation.

He repeated his request in a softer tone. "Please come outside with me so we can be alone for a bit. I promise I'll be nice." He smiled at her, motioning with a toss of his head. "Come on, let's go."

He grabbed her hand and led the way through a set of doors, step-ping outside into a large garden similar to the one he had at his house. Night had fallen, and a full moon hung in the sky. A light chill filled the air. Louise shivered. He put his arm around her and pulled her close. "Maybe I can help keep you warm." The warmth of her body next to his sped up his pulse, sending his spirit soaring. Maybe she was a forgiving soul. He turned his eyes up to the moon and smiled. "I don't know about you, but I think I love autumn the best of all the seasons. The air just seems so pure and fresh this time of year."

Louise didn't answer, but out of the corner of his eye, he caught her looking up at him with curiosity. A new softness filled her face, and the irritation seemed to have dissipated. In silence, they wandered down some stepping stones, following the path until they reached the far end of the garden. He turned and lifted up her chin with his finger. "I didn't mean to hurt your feelings back there, really I didn't. I'm not sure what got into me." Lying seemed to be a new sport of his, it seemed, and he hoped his expression and tender tone convinced her more than it did himself.

She lowered her head. "Are you sure? For some reason, I'm starting to get a sneaking suspicion you actually like doing that to me." Lifting her eyes she said, "Why do you do that? You did it when I came over yesterday too. Why say things like that?"

He said nothing, but kept his eyes on her as he took a quick sip of punch from his cup.

After a quick breath, she continued. "The truth is, I've liked you for a long time, Willie. You've always seemed so genuine, so kind, so nice. Not a mean bone in your body. But now, I'm not so sure. I'm usually a good judge of character, you know. Like you said yesterday, I watch everybody and everything, but maybe I've made a mistake this time. You've changed. Maybe I shouldn't have come to visit you yesterday."

He winced before blinking a few times and swallowing hard. "Louise, I'm really sorry. But I have to say that you always seem so sure of yourself, so confident, always with an answer for everything. Don't you ever feel scared or unsure of yourself? Ever?"

She let out a light chuckle. "Oh, Willie, I guess I've always been opinionated and strong. Girls get called out for that, don't they? People just don't seem to like it." The moon showed off a wide smile and cast a new glint in her eyes. As the breeze stirred, she pressed in closer, encouraging him to tighten his arm around her slender waist.

"Lou, I've been wondering, do you ever feel like you're the one always in control, the one taking charge of things?"

"That's an odd question, but now that you ask it, yes, it seems like I'm usually the one taking the lead. I'm not sure why that is, exactly. But then again, you say it's because I seem to hold the answers to anything and everything." She grinned at him, rubbing her hand up and down his back.

Willie nearly dropped his cup of punch. He took a short breath and asked, "Do you ever just wish, for once, you didn't have to worry about that, and let someone else take charge for a bit?"

She pursed her lips a little then shook her head. Pulling away from his embrace, she peered off into the empty field in front of them. The seconds passed before she arrived at a response. "I don't know. I never thought about it much, but now that you mention it, it sounds a little appealing. Might be a nice change for once, at least someone other than my parents, you know?" Turning back around to face him, she giggled. "As for you, William Strumpkin, it seems like, since you've gotten back home, you've taken on a more challenging tone. As I said, I've never known you to act that way before."

Willie smiled. "There's a lot of things you don't know about me yet, but I'll promise you this, my intent is never to hurt you." He kissed the top of her forehead. "I do have to ask you something, though, Lou. Why did you come over yesterday?"

Sipping some punch, she faced the open field. "Like I said, I've always thought highly of you. While you were gone, I guess I missed seeing you. I even wondered if you'd ever come back. When I heard you were home, I wanted to see you right away. I thought bringing you food would serve as the perfect excuse, I guess."

He turned her face to his. "Lou, we've known each other for a while. Let's make a promise, you and me, to play it straight with each other from this point forward. I'll start by saying that you don't ever have to think of an excuse to come see me."

He placed their cups on the ground. Taking her in his arms, he leaned down and pressed his lips against hers. She pulled back a moment, never taking her shining eyes off him. After a quick breath, she moved into his arms and placed her lips on his. He slipped in his tongue, caressing the inside of her mouth. When she reciprocated, he intercepted the soft, wet flesh, sucking gently. His loins ached, and he pressed against her, trying to wedge himself inside the hot cleft hidden beneath her skirt. Much to his surprise, she accepted his advances, holding him tighter, and pressing just as hard against him as she ran her fingers through his hair.

No amount of fantasizing had prepared him for the reality of holding her close against his chest, soaking in her radiating heat until the bulk of it settled in the space between his thighs. The flurry of her slender fingers through his hair made him weak in the knees, and even the rush of a cool breeze failed to calm his excitement. He continued to smother her with kisses, and for just a moment, he wanted to drown himself in her vitality, become united in body and spirit. The low hooting of an owl in the distance broke the magic spell that seemed to hold them captive to only each other.

"I have to confess something to you, Lou." He gazed down at her with a smile.

"What's that?" Her eyes sparkled with anticipation.

"I've liked you for a long time too. When you left last night, I couldn't stop thinking about you."

"Really?" The moonlight showed off her delicate figure, and a light, cool breeze ruffled through her hair.

He smoothed a tousled lock back into place. "Really."

The sound of his mother's voice rang out through the night air. They both glanced in the direction of the house. Had they been outside long enough for the other guests to miss their presence?

"I think we better head back inside, Lou." He landed a quick kiss on the tip of her nose and led the way back to the party. He paused. "Just know one thing, though, you haven't seen the last of me."

CHAPTER 8

Louise and Willie came through the back door, laughing and stumbling over each other as they made their way into the kitchen. Another fine evening crossed off, leaving Willie satisfied at how well his time with Louise had passed. They'd been seeing each other for a few months now, going to museums and the opera, and taking long picnic lunches in the park. His world was coming together, filling his spirit with a sense of completion.

"I simply loved that play, Willie. Thank you for taking me."

"I thought you'd enjoy experiencing theater in the round, where the audience sit around the stage, and the actors are so close you can see every detail in their clothing, their faces. You feel like you're part of the story, you know?"

She caught her breath from laughing so much. "I know, and I can't stop thinking about that last funny line before the play ended. How clever the writers were."

Willie pulled her into his arms, swaying from side to side as he held her close. "You know what I liked best, Lou?"

She nuzzled against his neck. "What? What did you like best?"

"I liked being close to you." He placed another soft kiss on her lips. "Me too."

"What say we have a glass of wine and settle down by a nice, warm fire? If you pour the glasses, I'll go get some wood."

"That would be fantastic. Are you sure it's not too late?"

"It's not late at all." He turned his wrist, viewing his Rolex watch. "It's only eight o'clock, and we have the whole weekend ahead of us."

"I just don't want to worry my father, that's all."

Willie sighed and shook his head. "Yeah, we don't want mad daddies, do we?"

Louise laughed. "Oh, he's not that bad."

"You don't think so? I hear he's run off every man who wanted to see you. And he doesn't seem all that keen on me, either."

"He's harmless, really. He thinks if a man can't take a little heat, then he's not a real man. And then he's not worthy of me, that's all." She shrugged a little, and made her way through the kitchen to the bar in the adjoining room.

Willie shook his head again, choosing to let the subject stop right there. He had to admit he'd managed to stay with Louise longer than most, bearing the cold stares, barbed comments, and a host of other hateful prejudices he couldn't quite understand.

"Hey, are you going to make that fire yet, or am I going to have to do that too?" Louise stepped inside the kitchen, hands on her hips. Her smile disarmed him, warming his heart. The site of her stiffened his cock.

"I'm on it, never fear." He swung out an arm, sashaying his way into the living room.

"You're so silly. I love your sense of humor." Louise popped him on the rear as he passed by.

§§§

"I love this wine. You can't beat Chateau Mouton Rothschild, a 1924 vintage. I paid a pretty penny for this baby." Willie held the Steuben crystal glass up to the firelight before taking a sip.

"You have a great collection, some of the most expensive and rare vintages around. You need to show me that cellar of yours some time." Louise stretched out, resting on one elbow, and took a drink from her glass. The light of the fire cast a warm glow throughout the room, encasing the pair in a soft, golden embrace.

"You know what's the most fun? Drinking on the sly. I don't advertise this to everyone, only people I choose to tell. And you're one of the lucky few."

"I'm glad I'm one of the privileged. And you know I'd never tell a soul. Don't want any authorities spoiling the fun, do we?"

"Yeah, you can't be too careful these days. I hated it when they made this stuff illegal. Good thing our circle of friends is tight." He took another sip. "We value the fine things in life, and good drink is up there along with big homes, fancy cars, and luxurious vacations."

"How does it feel to suddenly find yourself with money, Willie?" Louise cocked her head up in his direction. "Most everyone else around here seemed to be born into the right family. But you and your father started out with such humble beginnings—there's nothing wrong with that, either, don't get me wrong." She rubbed her finger around the rim of her glass. "I just wondered what it's like to have something that all of a sudden changes your life."

He stretched out beside her. "Good question. I guess I haven't given it that much thought. But I guess you're right, it's nice to have the means to do things you want to do, or to have the things you want, but just couldn't buy at one time because you didn't have the money.

"And then there are some things you want that you simply can't buy." He gave Louise a pointed stare. She said nothing, but turned her attention on the glass in her hand. The continuous motion of her delicate fingers coursing over the rim inflamed him, sending a heat searing throughout his body. More than ever, he wanted to cast aside his wine glass and dip his tongue elsewhere.

Surely enough time had passed so he wouldn't be violating the boundaries of decency. As he continued to watch her, he sensed anticipation rising inside her, too, with the way she shifted her position on the floor, the way she peered up into his eyes, the way she'd been coming on to him throughout the night with tender gestures.

With a sigh, she tilted her head back, concentrating on the ceiling. For a moment, nothing resounded in the room but the crackling sound of the logs in the fireplace. Inside his pants, Willie felt his cock stiffen, the furious carnal ache plaguing him again. The rise and fall of her chest flaunted a pair of firm, plump breasts, and, beneath her blouse, he detected the hardness of her nipples. He had reached a point where he needed to make a move, wanted to make a move. All their flirtations with each other up to this point had hinted at a mutual interest for more than just a platonic relationship. Was she ready? There was only one way to find out. He set his glass aside and leaned over to kiss her. As the kiss became more passionate, his hand brushed over a breast. She stiffened at his touch. He slipped in his tongue, and she reclined all the way down on the floor, resting easily on her back. This was her cue, unmistakable, for him to have free reign. While he kissed her, he worked the buttons on her blouse, undoing each one until he'd exposed her bra.

He stopped the kiss and gazed down at her. She smiled up at him, lifting her arms and placing them behind her head.

"It's okay, Willie. Go ahead." Without any further persuasion, he pushed up the undergarment and feasted his eyes on a pair of beautiful, smooth breasts, each topped with a plump nipple. He encircled one of them, massaging with his fingers, ending with a firm squeeze on top.

"Remember when you brought the cookies over the first day I came home?" He continued his exploration of her breasts as he spoke.

"Uh-huh. What about them?" She squinted her eyes at him, puzzled.

"What I did to them is what I wanted to do to you that day. They way I licked over that chocolate drop on top is the way I wanted to taste you, like this!" Dipping his head down, he opened his mouth and latched onto the other nipple. His vigorous licking and sucking extracted a cry from her throat. Willie stopped and smiled at her. "Of course, that would have been so forward of me, don't you think?"

She chuckled. "I wouldn't have minded if you had done it."

"Oh, really?" His eyes widened in surprise. "Why is that?"

"Like I said, I've liked you a long time."

With a smug grin, he turned his head toward her thighs. She'd bent up her knee and turned it out a little, opening up her skirt just enough to tease him. "You know what else I wanted to do to you that day?"

"What, Willie?" Her eyes blazed as hot as the flames in front of them, flashing hot sparks of lust.

"Then you wouldn't think me too forward if I remove these?" He reached beneath her skirt, catching the top of her panties.

"No, not at all." Her words barely a whisper, she lifted her hips.

"What's this? A smooth mons?" With his forefinger, he lightly grazed her skin. "You've just shaved yourself, haven't you?" He rubbed over her again. "This is smooth as glass." Without a trace of expression on his face, he moved so his lips nearly touched her ear. "Why, Lou? I've heard most girls only do this for one reason. What's yours?"

She avoided his eyes.

"Louise, I want to know why you did this to yourself?" He pressed his lips closer to her, his tone more insistent. "I want an answer, and I want it now."

She swallowed hard, glossing her tongue over her lips. "I-I wanted to look nice, that's all. I take pride in my appearance, so I want to look good."

"Down there? Who would see you there?" Willie smiled inside. On the other hand, he waited with bated breath for her answer.

She fluffed her hair, eyes steadfast on the ceiling.

He gently turned her face toward his. "Talk to me, Louise. I want you to tell me why you did this?"

"I just wanted to be prepared, in case …"

"In case what?" He reached down and rubbed her again, delighted in seeing her legs part.

"In case … you … we might …"

"So you thought at some point we might find ourselves like we are now, is that it?" His voice trailed out softer, less demanding.

She nodded.

Willie leaned down and kissed her. "That's okay, Lou. You don't ever have to be shy, or worry about what I might think about you."

"You don't think I'm trashy or unladylike for doing this, for thinking we might …?"

"Of course not. I'd never think about you like that." He gave her another quick kiss on the lips. Willie wedged his finger inside her cleft, sliding over wet flesh. She let out a small gasp and closed her eyes, spreading her thighs as wide as her body allowed. "So what else did you want to do to me that day?" Her smile dared him to continue.

He moved his head down between her thighs. Parting her with his fingers, he slipped in his tongue and caressed her gently. Under his body, she tensed her hips, crying out when the tip of his tongue probed and washed over her clit. Between soft licks and gentle sucking, she settled into a light, undulating rhythm, hips moving in time with each stroke of his tongue.

"That's good, Lou, let that ache ride itself out. You're a good girl. That's it." He stopped to let her catch her breath. "Now open up for me again. I'm not finished yet."

"Oh, Willie, I'm not ready for that." A look of panic filled her face; she slowly moved her legs together.

"Don't worry, doll, I know you're not. But you're more than ready for this." With a light push, he pressed her knees apart. Ever so gently, and with great tenderness, he slid his finger inside her until he'd reached the end. Louise made no sound, but her rapid breathing said it all. He slid his finger around. "You're so tight. And wet. So nice and wet! You taste sweet too." Turning his finger upward, he stroked her walls until she let out a cry and succumbed to another series of pelvic twitches. "Gotcha again, didn't I, Lou?"

"Oh, god, Willie, this is so …" She stifled a groan, lifting her hips as an orgasm consumed her. He removed his finger and stretched out beside her, the erection in his pants grinding against her thigh. She stifled a giggle.

"Feeling more comfortable, I see."

"I feel more than that, actually. I've felt it before too."

"What's that?" He smiled and stroked her cheek, knowing exactly what she meant.

"That hard bump you've got. I may not have let on, but I've noticed it hard and strong, like at the party we had the day after you came home. And you've gotten awfully close to me several other times since then too."

Willie grinned at her. "Sorry, sometimes I can't help myself."

"Is that what I do to you?" In the glow of the firelight her eyes sparkled like the finest gems. Without another word, she sat up, grabbing for his belt. "My turn." With a quick tug, her fingers pried the belt loose. "I want to see what I do to you. You've seen me, so now it's only fair."

"I can't argue with you there." He chuckled and reclined back, allowing her free reign. She lost no time in wrenching down the zipper, catching the first vision of the bulge between his thighs.

"So this is what …" Louise gazed at him, glassy-eyed with wonder.

"Here, let me make this easier." He lifted up and slid the pants and briefs down to his knees. As he rested on his back, his erection bobbed tall and proud in the dim light.

"Can I?" With a slender finger, she reached toward him.

"Sure, go ahead. It doesn't bite." Shifting his hips into a more comfortable position, he relaxed, basking in the warmth from the fire and the soft heat from her hand as she grasped his shaft.

"Do you like it when I touch you here?" Her finger had trailed up to his tip, where she settled into the tiny slit on top, gently swirling the pre-cum.

"Yes." Willie closed his eyes and tried to keep his hips on the floor. "That's a very sensitive area, Lou, and when you touch me like that …"

"That sets you off?" She stroked up and down his shaft for several minutes, tracing the swollen veins underneath his skin. At last she gave his cockhead a tiny squeeze, smiling as he let out a light moan.

"Give my balls a squeeze, won't you?"

She stopped a moment, blinking in surprise as he guided her hand to his plump sac. With a smile, she cupped him with her other hand and rolled the spongy flesh between her fingers, tugging lightly at intervals.

"That's it, Lou, just keep going. You see, if you keep up what you're doing, I'll show you something."

"Show me." Louise, her voice barely a whisper, kept at him, hard and fast.

The touch of her hand had riled up the ache in his cock. He'd only last a few more seconds. "Get ready, 'cause here I come." With a light groan, he released himself, thick jets of lust bursting from his shaft.

With a soft gasp, Louise jerked her hand away, keeping her eyes on the area between his thighs. Out of curiosity, she dipped a slender finger into the milky puddle and rubbed her fingers together. "What an unusual texture. Thick and slick."

"Have you never seen a man spend before? As a matter of fact, have you ever seen a man at all?" He viewed the awe in her face.

"I've never seen a man do what you just did, but when I was younger I saw one of my brothers coming out of the bathroom one night. He'd just finished a bath and had a towel wrapped around him, as best he could, anyway. It was a little too small. As he ran into his room, I happened to catch a quick peek at him. That's all I've ever seen."

"So you've never been with anyone before?" He reached out for her hand.

She shook her head. "Don't think men haven't tried, though."

Willie grinned back, keeping a steady gaze on her. "What's kept you from tossing all caution to the wind? You're a pretty girl, Lou."

The gleam in her eyes brightened. "I believe in waiting for the right person. I'm not one to give myself over easily."

"Have you ever done what we just did?"

Glancing down, she shook her head. "Not even that far."

A long silence came between them. Willie pulled her close. She snuggled next to him, resting her head on his chest. For the first time he felt a sense of contentment and security as he held her in his arms. Just as he'd hoped, he was her first choice for any semblance of sexual contact. Fresh, ripe, willing, she had offered herself up to him first for the taking. For just a moment, the thoughts of engaging in moments like this overwhelmed him. What if he could have this forever, anytime he wished?

Louise popped her head up and smiled at him. "I hear your heart beating, so alive, so strong, just like you are." Edging herself nearly on top of him, she gazed down, a thoughtful look in her eyes. "Tell me, Willie, where did you go for so long? What really happened while you were there?"

CHAPTER 9

This was the day, the big showdown. Willie's restraint had been whittled away to such a point, he almost considered himself painted into a proverbial corner. Not that this was a bad thing. The whole prospect actually excited him, relieved some of the tension he couldn't control anymore.

Hand in hand, ascending each step together in silence, Willie led Louise to the top of the landing and pulled her on down the hall to his bedroom, the tension between them pulsing with anticipation. Once they entered, her eyes roamed the spacious room, but her quick dismissal of the ambiance reflected an entirely different interest at the moment. He locked the door shut, even though they were alone. With a light push, he guided her next to the bed and turned her facing him.

"Okay, Lou, I invited you over today because I wanted to bring you up here. Ever since that first night we became intimate with each other, you've been hard at me all this time to tell you where I went for such a long time." His eyes burned into hers, long and hard. She made no answer, but merely gave him a light nod of her head. "But the truth is I simply can't tell you what you want to know, not right now, and you probably wouldn't believe me anyway." As he cupped her head in his hands, his voice became more intense. "After giving this issue a lot of thought, I think you're ready for the next step. So what I want to do now is start showing you what happened while I was away, some things I learned, tricks of a trade, so to speak."

She nodded again, eyes sparkling, her breathing more rapid.

"But here's the deal: if you want me to give you a glimpse into the world I visited, you have to promise you'll do everything I say, without question, and without giving me speeches on the subject, either."

"What kinds of things are you going to do, Willie?" Her words, barely a whisper, rung with excitement. She clenched her hands as if to keep them from trembling. "You still haven't told me that. Don't you think you should give me a few hints, so I know what I'm agreeing to? I think that would only be fair if—"

"Quiet!" His voice split the quiet air with sharp authority, a tone Louise had never heard from him until this moment. Surprised at how easy he found himself sliding quickly back into his old character, the one he'd learned from his stay at The House, he continued asserting control. "Louise, are you in on this deal or not? When I say I don't want any speeches or questions, I mean just that." Running his finger over her blouse, he grazed over one of her breasts, ending with a firm squeeze on the nipple. She blushed a bright pink.

"Willie, what's gotten into you all of a sudden?" She started to reach up and grab his hand, but he stopped her.

"Don't even think of moving unless I tell you to."

"Is this part of the deal you're talking—?"

He squeezed her nipple harder. She gasped, tensing her body. Gazing down at his hand, she swallowed and turned her face up to his again.

"Shall I take that as a yes, then? We're in agreement?"

In silent affirmation, she gave him a nod of her head.

"Good, then let's begin now. And remember, this is just between us, our dirty little secret, you might say."

He stepped back and smiled. "Now, I need you remove everything. I don't want to see one stitch of clothing on you."

The shock on Louise's face dissipated as quickly as it had come, and Willie viewed a new eagerness burning in her eyes; he almost believed he detected a faint whiff of her lust, and imagined a thick pool gathering in the cleft between her legs. He liked her willing nature, which had grown stronger with the passing of time. Within seconds, her blouse hit the floor with a soft swoosh. He continued watching as she stripped off each piece of clothing until she was only a vulnerable, naked form standing before him. Between his thighs, the ache throbbed stronger.

"Now I need you to get on the bed, and lie down on your back."

With nimble, light moves, she did as he requested. In the golden afternoon sunlight stealing through the windows, he marveled at the muscular curvature of her buttocks and thighs, strong, yet delicate. Louise made a pretty picture as she reclined, posing as if an artist had painted her to perfection on a wine-colored canvas. Willie beamed at her slender white body stretched out on the satin covering on the bed.

"Very good, Lou." He smiled in approval. "Now one more thing. I want you to open up those pretty legs of yours. That's it. A little wider, please. Good."

As she breathed, her soft breasts moved in tandem with each gentle rise and fall of her chest. The fleshy nipples on top matched the rosy blush she wore on her face.

"That's it, just keep your arms above your head. Like that. Yes, much better." He studied her for a second, admiring the way the moist flesh between her legs teased him. Was he right? Had that thick, feminine pool he'd imagined a few seconds ago materialized? He slipped a finger inside her and smiled, noting the tiny jerk of her hips as he touched her. Just as he'd guessed, her fluids bubbled over him, hot and wet. "I have a deal for you, Lou, if you think we're ready."

She didn't answer, but Willie knew he had her full attention, as the snapping sparkle in her eyes said everything. "We're no strangers to fooling around because we've done it a lot lately, but we haven't gone all the way, yet." He turned around and made his way over to a bureau and opened a drawer. After rustling around he returned to the bed, carrying a small mechanical device and a long string of luminous pearls. "What I have here is a vibrator. I know you've seen these before."

Turning her head to face him, she smiled. "Yes, as a matter of fact I—"

"Quiet, not another word, Lou. Don't look at me or speak until I tell you to. If you become too uncomfortable, say 'stop' and I'll do as you wish. This is the way we'll conduct ourselves during these special moments together. Do you understand?"

Louise turned her face back up, viewing the underside of the canopy.

"Good, much better." Moving closer to her side, he took up the pearls and dangled them over her. "These pearls are old. They belonged to my great-grandmother. When Grandmother died, she left them directly to me, indicating that she wanted me to give them to my future wife. What do you think about that?"

Silence.

To his satisfaction, her eyes had widened at his last statement, and the struggle to keep from speaking showed on the pursed lips. As her chest rose and fell with each heavy breath, the nipples on top looked tastier than ever. Thoughts of plunging into that dripping slit of hers nearly caused the erection in his trousers to burst with passion. He took a deep breath. "Though I don't have a wife, I can still find a good use for them for the time being. I'm going to wrap these pearls around your wrists. If you strain hard enough to break the strand, I get to go all the way with you. If you don't break the strand, I'll give you a choice on what you want to do next." Willie now dropped his face close to hers. "Tell, me, are you ready for this next step?"

She gave him a light nod of her head, but he detected a troubled look on her face.

"You have something else on your mind, what is it?"

Her words came out in barely a whisper. "If I lose, just be gentle."

With a nod, he wrapped the strand around her wrists. "There, now for the real fun." He reached for the device on the bed and plugged it into the nearest wall outlet. With a flick of a switch, a small hum filled the air. "You know, Lou, I bet you never dreamt that a simple vibrator could be used for more than just making aching muscles feel better, did you? Tell me, what do you know about these things, and have you ever used one?"

"I admit, I've used one over my back. Like you said, it's great for relaxing areas of the body."

"Have you ever used one on that sweet twat of yours?"

"Huh?" Her cheeks turn a light scarlet. "I don't know what you mean."

"Here, let me do you the honor of a quick demonstration. Remember, you break my pearls, and I get to have my way with you."

Taking aim, he placed the end of the machine against the most sensitive area between her legs. Louise let out a whimper, dug her heels into the bed, and fought for self-control. "You like that? Makes that little clit of yours fairly hum, doesn't it?" Willie paused, inserting his finger inside her. "Oh, yeah, even wetter now." He placed the vibrator back in the same place, smiling as Louise struggled to keep her hips on the bed. She craned her neck and rolled her eyes back, trying in vain to get a view of her wrists, but finally gave up, sinking back into the pillow.

The hum from the vibrator seemed to grow louder. Her eyes snapped shut, and she clenched her jaws together, undulating her hips, digging her buttocks into the bed. Another whimper sounded from her throat. Willie watched and held his breath, noting that she'd begun to strain against the strand of pearls. His heart pounded; he just might be getting what he'd wished for. In silence, he watched as a hard orgasm overtook her body, hips rolling in quick, pumping motions.

Snap!

Louise let out a small shout, fluttering her eyes wide open.

Willie beamed in triumph. He switched off the machine and tossed it on the other side of the bed. "I win, Lou, fair and square. You know that, don't you?"

She barely nodded, eyes glued to the canopy, trying to catch her breath.

"Here, let me take these." Reaching for the pearls, he began unwinding them from her wrists, making sure he retrieved a couple of stray beads that had fallen off the string. "Good thing these were knotted. I've been meaning to have them restrung anyway." Once he deposited the pearls on the nightstand, he stood there a moment, watching her, hardly believing his good fortune.

He climbed on the bed and straddled Louise's body. "Tell me, are you sure you're ready?"

"I'm ready, Willie." She stroked his hair, trailing her fingers down over his chest. "I've been waiting for this moment just like you."

Without another word, he got off the bed and walked over to his bureau where he stored some lubrication. This was it, their big moment about to unfold. She hadn't told him no, and she could have done so. She knew it; he knew it. Did she break the strand on purpose? It didn't matter. The moment he'd been dreaming about had finally arrived, and she had not told him no. At this point, all he cared about now was making her first time as pleasant as possible.

'... *with fresh ladies, be gentle.*' Delores's words rang out loud and clear in his memory, and he vowed to pay attention.

He returned to the bed and stood beside her. With a stroke of his finger, he brushed over her cheek. "Are you scared, baby?"

"A little." She gave him a breathless smile.

"Look, for right now I want you as comfortable as possible, so try to relax yourself. I'll be as easy as I can. " He kicked off his shoes and socks. Within seconds, his clothes lay in a heap on the floor. Glancing down, he viewed his huge erection. He felt the heat of Louise's eyes on him.

"Again, I'll try to be easy, Lou. I just need you to lie back and let me do what I need to do." He pulled himself onto the bed, situating himself between her legs.

She wriggled a little, trying to get more comfortable. He wanted her back in the mood again, relaxed as much as possible. Should he offer her some wine to help things along? Never! His first initiation into manhood had passed under the spell of alcohol. He vowed she would complete her initiation into womanhood with a clear mind. With eyes on her chest, he aimed for the peak of one of her breasts. Touching the flesh with his lips, he began with light kisses, graduating to soft licking, and finished with light sucking. As she wrapped her hands around his head, he fought the urge to take her right then. He mimicked his previous movements on the other breast, delighting in the sound of a light moan from her lips.

Every time he moved, his thick shaft hit against her flesh, raising the question of how much longer he'd last. Trying to contain himself, he focused on grazing his tongue over her abdomen and down to her pubic area, lighting on her clit. With one last round, he showered the sensitive bundle of nerves with firm strokes of his tongue, sending her convulsing with spasms. She was ready now. He sat up, grabbed the lubricant, and smothered his length with a hearty layer. Placing his hands on either side of her shoulders, he pressed her thighs further apart with his knees before lodging himself inside her cleft.

"Here I go, Lou. Here we go!" He looked down at her and smiled, taking a few seconds to give her a small kiss on the lips. With a deep breath, he pushed against tight, virginal walls. Her face lost all expression of excitement.

"Oh, god, Willie!" She tensed under him and closed her eyes, stifling a groan.

"Take some deep breaths for me, Lou." As she inhaled, he pushed, forcing her interior to yield to his advances. With every breath she took, he inched forward, pausing at times to place a reassuring kiss on her lips. His emotions ran wild, a mixture of liking the power of possessing her, yet wanting to keep this first moment of complete union a tender one. Most of all, he wanted to ensure the experience was just as special for her as it was for him. They had remained true to the promise they made in the garden: to play straight, no teasing, and no hurting. Louise had submitted herself to him, agreeing to join him in an adventure he'd been planning at length for both of them.

With an eager heart, he looked forward to the future, with no fear, no doubts, only sharing a deep sense of connection with one he'd been wanting for so long. He closed his eyes, as the strong hug of her walls around his flesh instigated a series of tingles through his body. The inside of his sac fairly hummed with the anticipation of release. He remained still for a bit so she could acclimate to his presence.

"You okay?" He kissed her again.

"Yeah, I'm fine." She blinked her eyes a few times and adjusted her head on the pillow. "Okay, Willie, your turn." With a smile, she pulled his face over hers. The passionate kiss she gave him, hot and wet, encouraged him to start moving in and out, slowly. When she appeared more comfortable, he moved a little bit faster, the pressure building inside his loins. The ache had grown more intense, and his rhythm succeeded in an eruption, bringing him instant relief. He caught his breath, focused his eyes, and allowed himself a slow return to the present moment.

"Oh, so that's what you feel like when you …" She let out a light giggle.

"Good?"

"Good, like little fluttery kisses inside."

Instead of pulling out, he cradled her firmly in his arms and rolled on his back, carrying her with him. She let out a small shout of surprise, followed by laughter. "Here, let's stay like this for just a bit, let you get used to everything some more."

She sat up and ground her hips against his. "Hey, I kind of like it up here on top, Willie! Not bad at all."

"Doesn't surprise me, coming from you." He grinned, matching her hip movements with his. Hidden deep inside her body, his erection bloomed again.

"I feel you now, hard and strong." She smiled and rolled her pelvis, switching out with a few sliding motions up and down his cock.

Willie reached up and latched his fingers on to her nipples, squeezing in time to a new cadence. Louise threw her head back, eyes closed, lips parted enough to show the hint of glistening teeth, creating a look so seductive the total image of her held him spellbound. Not breaking her rhythm, she kept riding, accepting each upward thrust of his hips as he impaled her harder, deeper. "Nice. Yeah, Lou, that's it!"

Her rocking motions made him groan as the pressure strummed away inside his loins. Within seconds, his sac would discharge a new load. His mind wandered back in time, back to The House, a place where sexual freedom ran amok, and all words of passion, whether coarse or gentle, signaled pleasure. Carried away by their synchronicity, words came tumbling from his lips, strange due to the passage of time, yet not forgotten. "Harder, Lou … I like it when you fuck me hard!" He let out another groan. "Admit it, you like my fat cock in that tight little pussy of yours! I bet you'll be begging for it from now on, won't you?" His hips moved in circular motions, followed by a round of staccato thrusts. "Tell me you like being pegged hard and good!"

Louise opened her eyes and peered down at him, a sly grin twitching at the corners of her mouth. Without a word, she leaned down and delivered a sharp bite on each of his nipples.

Her hot breath and the hard clench of her teeth set him on fire. In fervent motions, she worked her hips again. Willie writhed. "I'm coming. Keep going. Don't stop. YES!" The clench and release of her walls around his cock worked its magic, effecting sweet release. She settled herself into his arms. The two remained motionless for several moments.

"We finally did it, Willie." She lifted her head and popped a kiss on his lips.

He said nothing, but hugged her warm body, moist with perspiration, close to his. "Yeah," he whispered in her ear, "we finally did it." For another hour, they remained together, just holding each other, and making light conversation. Their relationship had progressed to the next stage, and Willie saw his life with greater clarity, filled with a great sense of purpose, promise—and happiness.

CHAPTER 10

Your suit is pressed and clean, ready for you to wear tonight, Mr. Strumpkin." Judith had entered the study where Willie spent some of his spare time poring over his clients' books.

He glanced up at his loyal housekeeper and gave her a grateful smile. "Thanks, Judith. I know I can always depend on you to get things done."

She gave him a polite nod of the head, but lingered in the doorway.

"Is there something else? You seem worried, preoccupied about something." He turned away from the ledger and faced her. "Come on over here, it's okay."

Clearing her throat, she walked over to the fine antique desk where he sat.

"I know that look on your face, Judith, something's bothering you. So tell me, what is it?"

The housekeeper, arms by her side, kept her eyes on the floor a moment. When she found the nerve, she began her questioning. "Mr. Strumpkin, I know you and Miss Carnwell have been … how shall I say it … involved for a while now …"

"Yes, go on." Willie gave her an intent look. He knew she still hadn't warmed up to the fact that Louise had become a large part of his life, though Louise always managed cordial exchanges with her.

"I-I just wanted to ask you, on an informal note, how things are going. Quite good, doubt?"

"Yes, but somehow I think there's more to this than just wanting to know how Miss Carnwell, um, Louise, and I are getting along."

Judith cleared her throat and began again. "Mr. Strumpkin, I don't know if you've noticed or not, or given any thought to the matter, but I'd be wary of Mr. Carnwell. Don't think he isn't keeping an account of how much time you and she spend together, especially if that time lingers into the night, even on the weekends."

Willie's face clouded over. He'd tried hard to put George Carnwell out of his mind, but he'd also learned to pay attention when Judith spoke. Whether he liked it or not, she was usually right. "Have you heard him say anything? Is there something I need to know?"

"I just know that when a man and woman start spending time together, it's expected that they will most likely get … well …" She shifted from one foot to the other. "Are things becoming serious between the two of you?"

"That's a rather personal question, Judith, but coming from you, I'll allow it, because I do respect you and the care you've given to me and my home. In answer to your question, yes, I think quite highly of Louise, and we seem to get along well for the time being. That's really all I can say for right now." He felt his cheeks flush. What business was it of anybody's what he and Louise did? They were adults who could make their own decisions, and people meddling in his personal affairs always tried his patience.

"Sir, I must confess something to you."

"And what sin do I need to absolve?" Willie smiled, making the Catholic sign of the cross with one of his hands.

Her face remained grim. "When I did laundry the other day, I couldn't help but notice light stains of a woman's lipstick on the sheets and covers, and also … well, you know."

He bolted upright in his seat, managing to keep his rising anxiety in check. "What did you notice? And may I remind you that part of your contract in working with me is that you'll keep any information you learn here confidential."

"I know that, sir, and I wouldn't dream of sharing anything I discovered, but that's why I'm just warning you about Louise's father. Please don't do anything to endanger your good standing with him or anyone else. You've always been an honorable man, and I just felt it my duty to remind you, that's all."

"And I thank you for that. Louise and I can handle ourselves against dear old George just fine." He sat back in his chair, hoping his smugness masked his uneasiness.

"That's all, sir." With a light nod, she turned around and left the room.

Willie spent the next several minutes cursing and fuming in silence at this unfortunate discovery, never dreaming simple bed linens might shine a glaring light on his private life. Judith always aimed for perfection in all her duties, but inspecting sheets to such a degree seemed a bit overboard, even for her, in his opinion. The last thing he needed was to give anyone any reason to talk, including her. He turned back to his ledger to give the figures on the page one last quick review before slamming the book shut.

He sank back in his chair and tapped his fingers together, trying to concentrate on the evening he'd planned with Louise. Try as he may, the discussion with Judith held his mind in a vice-like grip. This little incident proved more than ever why he needed a private place to conduct his special times with Louise—a place so hidden, only he knew about it, where only he held the key to access.

A whirlwind of thoughts took root as he considered every room, alcove, and space in his house. Nothing suitable came up. He walked over to his bar and poured himself a scotch on the rocks. Maybe the burn of alcohol would help his creative juices. Thinking on this subject a while longer, he snapped his fingers when the "Ah-ha" moment hit full force. He reached inside his desk for pen and paper and jotted down a list of items, furniture, toys, iron screen, wet bar. One item already lay hidden under his bed because he hadn't selected the perfect place for it. Other services ended on the list, drywall, paint, carpentry, plumbing, electrical. Estimating the cost and running the numbers quickly on the adding machine, he noted the final approximate figure. The cost to create this room would take a small bite out of his coffers, but he could still do it. He had the connections to get the work done. And the best part, he remembered the most perfect place.

The idea set, he checked his calendar, noting the dates when he'd give Judith a long overdue vacation. He sat back in his chair and smiled. He loved it when he had a plan, one that would get him what he wanted.

§§§

With one last tweak of his tie, he preened in the mirror, admiring his own image. Narcissism didn't suit him, normally, but since his return home, he couldn't help but pay closer attention to his appearance. Not only Delores, but other females at The House had acknowledged his striking face and build.

"You look very handsome, sir." Judith rustled in the doorway, standing with her hands on her hips.

"Thank you, Judith. You still here? I thought you'd left already." He turned around and smiled.

"I had one last chore to do before I left for the day. Before I leave, is there anything else you need from me?"

"No, I think you've done quite enough. Um, you've done quite enough for everything I need for the weekend, that is." He smiled at her from the mirror. "I should be fine until you come next Monday."

"Very well, sir." She nodded and started to leave. "I hope you and Miss Carnwell enjoy your time together tonight."

"Louise and I will have a wonderful time tonight, you can bet on that. I know how to treat a lady to a good time."

"Just mind what we discussed earlier, sir, that's all I request."

"I'm well aware of what we discussed." Willie chuckled, trying to hide his growing annoyance. "You don't have to worry, I'll mind my manners."

"Yes, sir, I'm sure you will."

The reflection in the mirror showed an empty doorway; alone once again, he gave himself once last once-over. Yes, Louise was in for a good time. He'd see to that. With a flick of a switch, he turned off the lights, headed out of his room, and made his way downstairs.

His heart raced with excitement as he settled inside his car and sped away toward Louise's home. Beside him, tucked inside an envelope, resided two tickets to a special party, actually a private showing of the most unique collection of art, a collection not shown to the public. He reached over and patted the envelope, rounding a curve as he headed on down the street.

Situated in one of the older, rich neighborhoods, the home and surrounding magnificent lawn rivaled his parents'. As Willie followed the drive toward the house, he became aware of an overwhelming sense of gratitude, thankful that he'd been blessed with the good fortune to receive money. Unlike the blue bloods who owned it, money didn't judge; his money had the same buying power as theirs. Money, whether he wanted to admit it or not, allowed him into social circles and attain things he'd never have been able to do otherwise. And his stay at The House, with all its wonderful, yet twisted, unconventional teachings, had added the ultimate resource to his personal arsenal.

He parked the car, whistling a light tune as he walked to the front door. To his dismay, George answered his knock."Well, well, come in, Willie." The gentleman glared back at him. "I'm happy to see you too."

Willie caught himself with a start and forced a light smile on his face.

"Louise is still getting ready." He ushered Willie into the house and led him to the living room. "Can I get you a drink while we wait? You know how these women are. They say they'll be down in a minute, but it takes them forever." He strode to the back of the room to a small wet bar, where he proceeded to pour them both a small snifter of brandy. "Go on and have a seat. We'll at least have a little while to talk." Though the older man tried to sound pleasant enough, Willie caught the smoldering tone in his voice.

Willie smiled, but cursed silently inside. Where was Helen, their housekeeper? Had Louise's father answered the door just to rattle his nerves?

He reached for the snifter held out to him. "Thank you, sir."

"This is a fine brandy. Smooth, and easy over the tongue." Mr. Carnwell seated himself in a wingback chair across from the sofa where Willie sat. "I'm sure you like the taste of something hot, wet and smooth over your tongue, don't you, son?"

Willie nearly choked on his drink. "Excuse me?"

"A fine drink." The gentleman held up his glass. "There's nothing like the taste of it. I don't know about you, but the taste of a fine alcoholic beverage is a lot like a fine woman. Makes you a little heady and orgasmic, don't you think?"

"Um, I-I guess I'd never thought about drinks in that way, sir."

"Oh, I'm sorry. Did I embarrass you?" Mr. Carnwell shifted in his chair a little, the first inkling of a smile twitching at the corner of his mouth. "I don't know where I got this urge, but I thought tonight seemed like a special time to crack open the bottle and share it with someone who at least appreciates the same things I do."

"Yes, sir. We do seem to appreciate a lot of the same things, don't we?"

"We do, one of these being my daughter."

Willie's eyes narrowed, viewing the furrowing brows of the man sitting across from him. He licked his lips, suddenly feeling a rising heat inside his chest.

Mr. Carnwell raised his glass and took a quick sip. "I'll just get right to the point, if you don't mind. You and Louise have been spending lots of time together, and, lately, I've seen a change in her, something I can't quite put my finger on. She seems to have an extra spring in her step, if you know what I mean."

"An extra spring in her step? But I always thought she had that, Mr. Carnwell." Willie smiled as his uneasiness grew with every passing second.

"Oh, it's like I can sense a new awareness in her since she's started spending time with you, like she's suddenly coming into her own. She has a certain way she carries herself now, like a true woman for the first time." George flashed Willie a small wink. "And you do know what I mean, don't you?"

"Sir, I'm not really sure I understand." Willie dropped his head and concentrated on his glass, feeling the first twinges of numbness. Was it fear or the brandy kicking in?

"Let's not mince words anymore, Willie. I know you two have been keeping some late hours at times, and though I might be an old codger to you, I haven't forgotten what it's like to be young."

Willie nodded in silence. The heat building up inside threatened to suffocate the life out of him. Where was Louise, and why didn't she hurry up?

"But I'll tell you this one thing, and don't you forget it." The man's gray eyes flashed with intensity. "You do anything to dishonor my daughter or sully her reputation, and I'll have your head as my personal trophy. I have friends in high places, and make no mistake, I'll have no problem settling the score."

Willie lifted his glass and took a long draw. The relaxing effects of the alcohol had worked their way throughout his system, and Mr. Carnwell's new challenge had somehow ignited something in him he found strangely enticing, a throwing down of a gauntlet of some sort; lately he seemed inclined to take on challenges such as these.

"You know, Mr. Carnwell,"—he began, with more confidence in his voice than he would have suspected—"when I become a father, I'm sure I'll be as protective of my daughter as you are of Louise. I can promise you she's safe with me. And let's be honest, we both know she can take care of herself. After all, she's a grown woman who could probably teach *me* a thing or two."

Mr. Carnwell remained quiet a moment, tapping his fingers on the rim of an empty glass. He finally gave Willie a soft smile. "You know what, son, as much as I hate to admit it, I admire your nerve. You've changed since you've come home from your travels. You seemed so shy and quiet before you left, but now, I think I almost sense you mocking me."

"Oh no, sir, I'd never do such a thing as that. That would be quite rude of me." Willie, overcome with a new wave of bravery, returned his stare, equal in stony intensity. "Let's just say that I understand and respect what you're saying, and perhaps we can leave it at that."

Instead of a retort, the gentleman beamed, his face showing a warmth that Willie recognized whenever Louise came near. "Well, here she is at last, the lady of the hour."

"So have you two been having a nice time together?" She smiled, but quickly cast Willie a doubtful glance.

"Your father and I have been comparing all the things we enjoy in life, and he even brought out his best brandy to start the evening off just right. Isn't that right, sir?" He raised an empty snifter in a mock toast.

"I was telling Willie, just as you came down, that he seems to have become a rather bold individual since his return from the country. I guess the fresh air and smell of wild flowers in the fields tend to perk up one's disposition."

Louise's eyes widened in alarm. "Willie, I think we're ready to go." With a nervous smile, she offered her hand, gesturing they needed to make a run for the door.

Willie accepted her hand and stood up, taking a moment to place the snifter on an end table. "Sir, I thank you for sharing your best drink and indulging me in some fascinating conversation. It was a pleasure."

Mr. Carnwell stood up in silence. He gave Louise a small kiss on her forehead. "You have a nice time tonight." He gave Willie a cold nod of his head and exited the room.

Louise grabbed Willie's hand and pulled him toward the front door. When they stepped outside, she breathed a sigh of relief. "Good god, won't you two ever find peace with each other?"

"What, you don't think we had a pleasant conversation?" He wrapped his arm around her waist and gave her a soft, quick kiss on the ear. The smell of lilac perfume filled his nose, and tonight she wore a straight-fitting coral dress with a series of large, ornate buttons down one side, a striking representation of the latest fashion. Around her head she wore a matching headband with a sparkling floral brooch as a decoration, all of which framed a face that resembled an angel's. She always presented the perfect picture of loveliness, with her slender shoulders and soft, ivory skin. But the sight of a matching pearl-bead necklace, tied into a knot near the end, created an ache in his loins.

"You two will be the death of me." She slid onto the leather seat inside the car. Willie closed her door and headed to the driver's side.

Seated behind the wheel, he started the ignition and sped away from the house, dismissing further talk about her father. The event awaiting them this evening took center stage in his mind.

"So where are we going, Willie?" Louise primped a little, checking her lipstick in the small mirror of a tiny compact she pulled from her beaded handbag.

He flashed her a bright smile. "I have here in this envelope two tickets to an exclusive art show." He picked up the envelope and tapped it against the seat for emphasis.

"So what's so exclusive about this show? And where did you get such tickets, anyway?"

"I was in my study at home one evening, and some delivery person handed them to me when I answered the door. They didn't tell me who the owner of the collection was, only that it contained a sensual theme."

"A sensual theme?" She gave him a quizzical look. "Are you sure it's not a burlesque show of some kind? Art collection, indeed."

"All I know is that this event is not open to the public. It's actually being held downtown in an abandoned warehouse. I recognized the address on the card. It's only my best guess, but I'd wager he's showing his art there because he's trying to keep the moralists at bay."

Louise rolled her eyes. "Oh, yeah, too many people these days want to impose their puritanical beliefs on anybody who'll listen." She frowned a little. "There seems to be a movement to rid the community of any and all moral depravity, leaving us all spiritually sterile. God forbid we have any desire for earthly pleasures, carnal or otherwise."

Willie shook his head and chuckled at such a notion. "Don't you find it interesting, Lou, that every effort to suppress man's so-called wickedness only causes some group or individual to lash out by setting up an outlet for relief, whether it be for sex or indulging in forbidden drink?"

"You know something, you're right about that. It does seem that way." She turned to him and smiled. "I don't know about you, but I plan on having a sinfully good time tonight."

He kept his eyes steadfast on the road in front of them. "You and me both, baby. You and me both."

CHAPTER 11

They left behind the quiet, orderly neighborhoods and found themselves on the streets of downtown, where large office buildings and department stores dominated the landscape. As the sun began to set, the first twinkling of streetlights and various business signs lit up the night. Willie followed the main boulevard before turning left at an intersection and onto another street. Within minutes, the scenery changed to an industrial motif, cold and hard, almost isolated and lonely, featuring large factories with their uniform windows lined up in neat rows.

A few more blocks down, a foundry appeared, with its blackened pipes and chimneys billowing smoke into the air. Inside these buildings, humming with activity, hot and sweaty workers toiled nonstop, oblivious to life outside those brick walls. As they drove by, Willie whispered another prayer of thanks for his good fortune in life.

He slowed down, easing the car over some railroad tracks, and drove another half mile down the road to a lonely building that sat on the left-hand side of the street. He pulled into a parking lot and stopped the car in an available spot. "I think this is the place. From the looks of all the cars, several people got invites to this event."

Louise turned her head, taking in the view from all directions. "You weren't kidding, this place does look abandoned." She smiled at him. "But you're right, no moralist in their right mind would ever think of coming here, would they?" She patted him on the thigh.

"Let's just hope we've come, seen, and left by the time any moralist wises up. Good news travels fast these days." He chucked her under the chin, leaning in to give her a soft kiss on the lips. Willie grabbed up the envelope and stuffed it in a pocket inside his jacket.

They walked, hand in hand, toward a door that looked like a probable entrance. This place looked as if it hadn't been used in several years, and now he couldn't even imagine its original purpose. The only windows allowing in light happened to be situated near the top, prohibiting any peeking inside. How handy. Willie smiled. Maybe the owner of the art collection really knew how to put on a show such as this; he seemed to know how to keep it a secret.

"Here, let me get that for you." Willie tugged on the handle of a large metal door. The door swung open, slamming behind them as He and Louise entered a small hallway. Several feet down, a gentleman sat at a small table next to the main doors leading into the heart of the building. "I think we head on down that way." Wrapping his arm around her waist, he walked toward the table.

"Welcome. Thank you for coming tonight." The older gentleman at the table showed impeccable taste in clothing. His salt and pepper hair rested neatly against his head, and the warmth of his smile equaled the sparkle in his eyes. "May I have your tickets, please?" He eyed Louise up and down, while Willie fumbled in his pockets. "And I see you've brought along a lovely lady."

"Yes, I thought this might be something we'd both like to see." Willie smiled and handed the man the tickets. "Do you happen to know who the owner is? No one has been able to say."

"No, sir, I don't." The gentleman took the tickets and placed them in a box.

"So how did the guests get on an invitation list? And I still don't understand the secrecy."

The man frowned a little. "Unfortunately, I don't have an answer for that, either. I just volunteered to help out with tonight's event, sort of like a friend helping a friend. You know what I mean." He smiled again.

"I see." Willie gave a polite nod.

The man smiled at the couple. "I'm so sorry I'm not much help, but the collection is quite amazing, as you'll soon see." He motioned toward the door. "So please, go on and enjoy the show. There's a bar for drinks too. He turned his attention to the new guests who had just come up to the table, ignoring Willie and Louise altogether.

Willie turned around to quickly see if he recognized anyone. All were strangers. He turned toward Louise. "I guess we're ready."

"I'm more than ready. This sounds too good to miss." She squeezed his hand and passed through the door he'd just pushed open, and they found themselves in the main interior of the building.

Willie glanced around the room, and when his eyes fell on a series of paintings on the wall, his heart nearly stopped. He immediately recognized the style. He closed his eyes and took in a deep breath, before letting it out slowly. He turned his attention to the middle of the room. On a large glass table stood a crystal vase of roses. But somewhere deep inside, his intuition suggested these were no ordinary rosebuds.

"Hello, and welcome to the show." An attractive woman in a light green gown walked over and greeted them. Over her short hair she wore a matching head-covering studded with a flashy pin. She extended a slender hand, first to Willie and then to Louise. "If you two would like to start the evening off with a cocktail, the bar is over there." She pointed off to her right, back near the entrance. "We have an excellent bartender, and as a special thank you to our guests, the drinks are on the house."

Willie, grateful for the momentary distraction, raised an eyebrow to Louise. "We sure can't pass that up, can we, dear?"

"Definitely not." She smiled back, linking her arm through his.

"But first, madam, can you tell us anything about this art collection, what it entails or who owns it?"

The lady grinned. "Unfortunately I can't tell you who owns the pieces, but you're in for a treat tonight. Not only will you be viewing the most prized collection of erotic art, you'll also be treated to a special live show, which will be held in the back of the building."

"A special live show? You mean someone will be doing a performance for us?" Louise glanced from the woman to Willie.

"Oh, yes." The lady's cheeks turned a soft pink. She angled her head closer to Willie and Louise. "You see, this show is one the general public is not allowed to see. So consider yourselves privileged." Stepping back, she placed her hand on Willie's elbow and guided him toward the bar. "Please, go treat yourself to a good cocktail. This tour is self-guided. All the exhibits have cards explaining what they are."

"How do we know when the live show starts?" Louise said.

"We'll announce it over the loudspeaker. Until then, have a wonderful evening." The lady turned around and walked over to greet the others who'd just come in. Willie kept walking toward the bar. His eyes trailed over to the wall once again to view the portraits in more detail. Yes, he knew this work.

"What'll it be for you and the pretty lady?" The bartender, a dapper young man dressed in a smart tuxedo, smiled as he finished wiping up the counter.

"I think I'll have a Southside, and my lady here will have a Mary Pickford."

"Excellent choices, both of them." He turned around and pulled out a couple of glasses, mixing up the tasty concoctions with amazing speed.

"Hey, pal, I have a question that I've been dying to get an answer to. If I, you know, sweeten the pot a little, do you think you could tell me what I want to know?"

"And what would that be, buddy?" The man stopped momentarily to look up at Willie, and turned back to slicing a lime.

"Just who, exactly, owns this collection of art we're about to see? Nobody will tell me. They all claim they don't know. And can you tell me a little about those paintings over there? They seem somewhat familiar. I think I've seen them somewhere before."

The bartender smiled and gave him a wink. "Oh, I'm sure you have, buddy. You don't have to be coy with me. You see, the reason you and everyone else are here tonight is because you've purchased one from the artist."

"Oh?" Willie's eyes narrowed, his gaze meeting the bartender's.

"Look here," the young man said, leaning closer to Willie's ear, "here's another thing about those paintings. There's only one place you'll find them—the entrance hall at The House."

Willie felt himself go pale. "The House?" He staggered a little, grasping for Louise's arm to help steady himself. He didn't fail to catch the flash of surprise on her face. Yes, he had purchased one of these, and it figured into the plan he'd concocted earlier.

He tried to keep his face straight. He knew at this point he trod on dangerous ground, already feeling the heat from Louise's eyes.

"Yeah, The House, the crazy house." The bartender went back to mixing the drinks. "You don't exactly look like the nutty type to me, so how did you come to learn about these paintings in the first place?"

Willie swallowed hard, trying to think of an answer fast. "Um, I have a friend who has one, and I saw his. I thought they were rather unique, and decided I wanted one for my own art collection."

"That's usually how it goes." The bartender nodded and smiled. "Here you go, buddy, a Southside and a Mary Pickford. Hope you enjoy them, and if you need anything else this evening, I'll be right here."

Willie took a quick sip of his drink, slid the bartender three dollars, and left. Saying nothing, Louise pulled him immediately to the wall of portraits. In silence, they sipped their cocktails while studying each painting. The information on the card only shared how the artist loved art and the human body, and how he liked to add a humorous element to catch the viewer off guard. Louise smiled, and let out a giggle.

"Well, darling, I can't wait 'til you show me yours." With a wink and a quick turn on her heel, she pulled him toward the direction of the table of roses. "I'm dying to see these buds."

"M-m-m, yes, I agree." Her not pressuring him more about the paintings made him uneasy. He took another sip of his drink, grateful for the relaxing effect of the alcohol. Was her curiosity satisfied now? Did she finally realize where he'd been for so long? Did it even matter anymore?

"Oh, Willie, look!" She tugged on his hand. "Get a load of these, would you?"

He shook his head in disbelief. Upon closer inspection, the rosebuds were penile tips, with the scrotum mimicking the leaves one might find on a stem. "You have to appreciate the creativity, don't you?" he said, as innocently as possible.

"I think you're creative at keeping secrets." With a flutter of her lashes, she blew him a kiss and headed through a curtain to see the next section of exhibits.

His pulse quickened. Clearly he wasn't getting out of this trap, and he knew she'd eventually settle the score. The big question was when? He needed to act on his plan as soon as possible. Monday he'd make some phone calls.

"Willie, are you coming or are you going to stand there all night?" Louise tugged on his arm and pulled him forward. "I thought you were behind me."

"Sorry, hon." He gave her a quick kiss and wrapped his arm around her.

§§§

The next section of the building held the majority of the exhibit. In the middle of the floor, a pool had been constructed, with benches placed on either side for those who wanted to sit and relax—or make out, as Willie saw one couple engaged in a passionate kiss.

"Looks like this show gets people going, you think?" Louise ran her fingers over one of Willie's buttocks. He gave a little jump.

"You're full of yourself tonight, aren't you? I think that drink has gone more to your hands than your head." He flashed Louise a light frown.

"Look at these." Her eyes had landed on one of the statues situated around the edge of the pool. She tugged on his arm, leading him over for closer inspection. "Ugh, what an unusual piece. I can't believe it. I mean, it looks like he's peeing on her." The statue depicted a male straddling a female, and created in the style of a fountain, water fell from the male's cock onto the space between the woman's thighs.

Willie stooped down for a closer look, feigning interest. This statue showed him nothing new; he'd seen this activity at The House on numerous occasions. "Maybe I ought to purchase one of these for my garden." He winked at Louise and stood back up.

"You're awful." She wrinkled her nose and popped him on the rear.

"You seem awfully interested in my ass tonight. What's gotten into you?"

"What's gotten into them?" Ignoring his question, she pulled him toward another statue, one showing a female impaling the male from behind. "And how, exactly, is she doing that?"

"Hm-m-m, interesting. Not sure." Willie stifled a grin. Teaching Louise how to use a strap-on just made it high on his "to do" list. "Enough of these crazy statues, let's go look at the others along the walls." Taking her hand, he pulled her to one side of the room where a collection of ten statues stood, each one showing a unique position from the Kama Sutra. Along the opposite wall stood the other ten statues, showing more unique positions.

"I think we've done some of these." Louise nuzzled his ear, delivering a quick lick on his earlobe. The touch of her wet tongue shot a jolt of lust straight to loins. She turned around, her smile fading. "Come to think of it, just where would you have learned these positions?" She snapped her fingers. "I think I've got it, but I can't tell. You understand how that goes." With a whirl she turned her attention back on the row of statues.

Sassy! Somehow her boldness had crept out again. Time to put her in her place, like he'd been doing ever since their first session together in his bedroom. The more she pushed, the swifter he established control. Her insistent pokes and prods for personal information usually ended up with pokes from him, right into that hot snatch of hers, leaving her breathless and abandoning questions for the time being. He pressed hard against her backside as she gazed at the row of statues.

"Oh!" She turned her head and started to pull away.

He encircled his arm around her waist with lightning speed, pulling her closer, grinding his hips harder. "Don't even think of acting out here." With a smile, his lips brushed against her ear. "You're getting yourself in hot water, gal, so you best be on good behavior."

"I'll be good, Willie, really I will." She loosened his arm and faced him. "You wouldn't be too hard on a poor girl who's just having an innocent good time, would you?" Her face flushed, and her eyes danced with excitement.

"I have no problem showing you what hard is." His smile widened.

Louise grinned. With a light sniff of her nose, she walked toward the glass cases next to the back of the building. "I wonder when that show's going to start."

"Maybe it'll be a kinky burlesque show like you've been dying to see." Willie gave her a light pat on the rump. In his mind, nothing would set this show off with a flourish like a hot striptease act.

"These are interesting." With a slender finger, Louise pointed to the assortment of fetishes. "Wow, I didn't know frogs had big … you know." She stifled a giggle. A jade statue of a frog bearing a huge phallus rested on the shelf.

"Could be a fertility symbol of some kind. Just because we don't use symbols like these in our culture doesn't mean others don't." His eyes scanned the collection of brass, clay, and jade pieces, all depicting carnal acts. One shelf displayed a bronze statue of a young girl, legs spread open, pleasuring herself through clitoral stimulation. "So tell me something, doll, is this what you do when you're alone, thinking of me?"

Her cheeks flamed red while she viewed the sculpture. "You are absolutely horrible. Have you no decency?"

"I'm sure you have no decency when you're alone at night."

She stifled a laugh. "I'd never tell you, anyway."

He rested his head against hers. "Trust me, I'd never make you just tell." He smiled as her face became sober; hot lust blazed in her eyes.

Just then a loud crackling came from the loudspeaker. *"Ladies and gentlemen, if you'll turn your attention to the back of the building, we're presenting a special performance. Please make your way to the back. Once again, on behalf of the artist, thank you for your patronage of the arts, and we hope you enjoy our show."*

Louise's face beamed. "This is it, the moment I've been waiting for!"

She and Willie made their way back to the curtained space separating the show area from the remainder of the building. The young lady in green who greeted them earlier smiled as they approached.

"So you decided to stay and see the show."

"My naughty little gal here has been talking about it all night." Willie chuckled, delivering a soft pinch to Louise's cheek.

"Sir, I'm sure you're more anxious to see it than she is. I think you're the naughty one."

He gave the lady an ingratiating nod of the head. "Touché, my dear." Without a doubt, he knew no burlesque show here could trump what he'd seen during his stay at The House, but he looked forward to watching Louise enjoy the show.

The lady pointed to a set of tables and chairs in front of the stage. "These are the best seats in the house."

Willie pulled out a seat for Louise first before situating himself beside her. No sooner had the lady left, than another person edged up to the table. When he turned, his eyes fell directly on a pair of smooth, long legs. The new lady, wearing nothing but a beaded brassiere and tight, silky short bottoms to match, stood next to him, holding a silver tray with an assortment of drinks. "What'll it be, sir?"

"Excuse me?"

"You and your lovely companion look like you could use another round of cocktails made by our talented bartender."

"What've you got?" Willie gave her a lusty smile, surveying the lithe body standing close to him. "And I must say, what a wonderful breastplate you're wearing."

"Well, that's an interesting term. Hardly the way I'd describe it, though." The young lady looked down at her chest and smiled, shimmying just enough to make her breasts jiggle. "You have to admit, it suits the evening, doesn't it?"

"I think you'd be suitable for any evening." He flashed her another smile. "Any man would be a fool to pass you up."

"Flattery gets you everywhere." She cocked her head toward the tray. "We have gin and tonic, a Sidecar, a French 75, and The Last Word."

Willie turned toward Louise. "What'll it be, doll?"

"I'll take the French 75." Louise's eyes sparkled.

"And for you, sir?"

"I'll have The Last Word." He grinned, patting Louise on the cheek. "Although we both know you like having the last word, don't you, dear?"

"You know us gals, Willie, we end up getting in the last word, whether you like to admit it or not." She offered a mock kiss with her lips and patted him back.

"Just so you know, these are all made with quality gin, not the bathtub brand, if you know what I mean." The lady winked and removed the drinks from the tray, placing them on the table. "Hope you enjoy the show."

"Oh, Miss, before you go, I have a little something for you, to support the arts, you know." He reached in his pocket, pulled out two dollars and slid it into her brassiere. The lady gave her foot a tiny flirtatious lift behind her and blew him a kiss before whirling around to leave.

"You're such a flirt tonight." Louise gave his arm a light slap. "Are you sure you need another drink?"

"Just as much as you do." He chuckled and took a sip from his glass, impressed with the way she didn't seem jealous when he carried on with other women. This self-confidence elevated his love for her even more. "Ah, she's right, good quality gin. And you know I can tell quality when I see it, or taste it." He enunciated the last two words for her benefit, staring straight into her eyes. She lowered her lashes and reached for her drink.

Within moments, the seats were filled, cocktails distributed, and the house lights began to dim while another set of lights illuminated the stage. A voice spoke over the loudspeaker. *"Ladies and gentlemen, we now begin our show. I'd like to introduce to you the talented, sensual Sylvia Noire."* A drum roll sounded, followed by the flair of a trumpet.

The music changed from a crisp trumpet prelude to a style most often used by belly dancers. Sure enough, Sylvia Noire came out from behind the curtain, twirling her way to the center of the stage. The audience clapped, while some of the men, including Willie, let out whistles of approval. Sylvia glided without effort, waving her arms, gyrating her hips in seductive movements that held her audience spellbound. The red veils swayed back and forth. Her matching brassiere, red like the veils, dripped with beaded fringe along the bottom and flashed with silver-studded rhinestones. Her auburn hair fell in ringlets around her face, which glistened with a skillful application of cosmetics.

As the music changed tempo, so did the shaking of her hips, swaying with a slow, tantalizing speed at first, before exploding into a series of swift shakes, sending the veils scattering in a frenzied red cloud around her. Her breasts seemed to have a mind of their own, pumping up and down, performing an independent flirty dance, rivaling her hips in every way.

With a few quick turns, she stood in front of Willie, seductive, fiery, undulating her hips with almost lightning speed. She whirled around and wagged her rump nearly in his face, making him almost dizzy with her frantic movements, like one fluttering a feather in rapid succession. Willie clapped and let out another whistle. Out of the corner of his eye, he caught Louise gaping in amazement.

Sylvia leaned in closer, rattling her breasts before him, the fringe vibrating in unison with her movements, so fast he could barely see it all. With a seductive smile, she backed off slightly, only to lunge her chest at him one last time, sending her breasts into a series of choreographed twitches before she spun back to the middle of the stage. Willie sat back in his seat, blinking hard. He'd definitely underestimated this show. Even at The House, he'd never witnessed anyone with this type of talent. Sylvia's sexy dance intoxicated him more than the cocktail before him. His cock stiffened, creating an ache so hard he considered making a quick bathroom run to jerk himself off.

Whistles and clapping filled the room, and before all eyes, Sylvia began methodically snatching off each veil, tossing one piece at a time to the floor. The more she removed, the more rhythmic the clapping from the audience. Oblivious to her nakedness, she plucked off the fabric without a thought until she'd stripped down to nothing but a G-string and her top. With a cue from the drumroll, she jerked off her brassiere, showing a set of firm breasts, topped with ripe, red nipples. In a daring move, she pumped her breasts up and down a few times, sending the men into a roar of catcalls.

With one last flourish, she ended the act by reaching down and giving the G-string between her thighs a good, hard yank, revealing a neatly trimmed mons in the shape of a triangle. At that moment, time stood still, with everyone stunned into silence. All the lights turned off without warning, leaving the room in total darkness. When the lights came on again, the stage was empty. A crescendo of clapping filled the room. People filed out of the area, chatting in animated conversations about what had just transpired.

"Wow!" Louise beamed at Willie, eyes sparkling, cheeks flushed. "What a show."

After helping her out of her chair, he put an arm around her waist. "I agree, what a show."

CHAPTER 12

Willie pulled into his driveway and turned off the ignition. He walked around to the passenger side, opening the door for Louise. Even after all this time, he still liked playing the role of the gentleman, a sharp contrast to their intimate moments, where he let the coarser side of his nature run free. He'd been riddled with excitement all evening, hardly able to concentrate on dinner. If anyone had asked him about the movie he and Louise had just seen, he'd have no idea what to say. Judith would be back Monday. She'd put up such a fuss when she found out about her thirty-day vacation.

"And just what will you do during all that time without my help?" He remembered how she'd stood, hands on her hips, ready to challenge him every step of the way. "You're trying to slowly get rid of me, aren't you?" She'd eyed him with horror. "It's Miss Carnwell, isn't it? She's making you get rid of me."

"Now, now, don't be silly, Judith. I can take care of myself. And no, Miss Carnwell has nothing to do with this." He'd tried desperately to reassure her, hoping she wouldn't catch the flush on his cheeks as he escorted her out the back door. "You can call and check in. If I'm down and out on my luck and need a helping hand, you can come straight back. Sound like a deal?"

Grumbling, she'd turned on her heel at the end of the day, threatening to call him daily. Luckily for him, she had called once.

The next day after her departure, his pet project slowly emerged, ending with its completion two days ago. All the accouterments for this special secret had been installed with planning and care. Always one with an eye for detail, he'd added a finishing touch by including the object under his bed, the painting he'd been salivating over for a quite some time. Tonight, he planned to introduce Louise to his new creation, their special hideaway.

"Don't you think it's a little late? My dad's probably waiting up for me."

"It's Saturday night. Surely he's not keeping time, is he? After all, he should know our routine by now." He slipped his key into the lock and opened the kitchen door.

"That's the thing, I think our late-night hours still bother him."

"I'll get you back at a decent hour, so don't worry." They passed into the kitchen, and Willie closed the door behind them. "So did you enjoy the evening?" He slipped up from behind and pulled her into his arms, holding her close.

"I loved it. What a treat!" She leaned her head back, fitting it snugly beneath his chin. "But there's still one question I've been wanting ask since that art show a while back. Where did you really go?" Wriggling from his grip, she stared into his eyes. "I agree with the bartender. You don't seem crazy, but I think you're hiding something. And where is that painting you purchased? Somehow, if my hunch is right, I doubt there's a real friend involved in any of this."

"You just don't let up, do you, Lou?" He sighed, smoothing his fingers through his hair. "Tell you what, let me pour us some wine, and I'll show you something, painting included."

§§§

Louise turned slowly, round and round. "So this is your wine cellar. What an amazing collection!" Shelves lined all four walls. Racks of bottles covered with colorful labels rested neatly beside each other. A certain musty odor lingered in the air, accompanied by peaceful silence. Louise held Willie's hand as he led her toward the back of the room.

"Nobody, not my parents or even Judith, comes down here. It's like this place is an afterthought, forgotten. When I get new bottles in, I simply bring them down here myself." He stopped for a moment and lifted Louise's chin with his finger. "Look at me, Lou. There's an even bigger secret that nobody knows about. I discovered it soon after I moved in this house. I'd nearly forgotten about myself, but it's this right here." Tucked away in the corner stood a simple wooden door, almost disappearing into the dimness.

"A secret room?" Her eyes widened. "And why would you have a painting hidden down here where you can't see it all the time?"

"If you'll remember, it's not your ordinary painting." Willie pursed his lips. "But what I'm about to show you is not your ordinary room, either. While Judith has been gone, I've fixed it up into something very different."

"So what's 'not ordinary' about it?" Her eyes narrowed in their customary manner when she was about to challenge him. "And again, all these secrets, these hush-hush, I-can't-tell-you secrets."

"Come on in here." Willie slipped the key into the lock and gave a small twist. A click sounded, and he opened the door. "After you, my dear."

Louise crossed the threshold into a new, hidden world. When she saw the room, her mouth dropped open in surprise. "Good lord, you scrambled to get this done." She walked further inside and scanned the contents. The far left corner of the room held a bed, complete with a narrow bench at the foot and a nightstand at the head, holding a lamp. Over the iron headboard of the bed hung the infamous naughty painting. "Ah, now I see it!" She walked over to give the work a closer look. "Yes, this couple has the same bulges in all the right places like the other ones did at the art show. Perfect for this room."

She turned and viewed the chest of drawers on the right-hand wall opposite the bed, but her eyes strayed to another oddity a few feet further down. "And what on earth is this?" A few short steps landed her in front of a large, imposing iron screen, situated on a small section of tiled flooring. Grasping one of the iron bars, she gave the screen a light tug. "Boy, this thing doesn't budge, does it?" In the corner, down from the screen, an attractive settee had been placed. A liquor cabinet next to the left wall, a few feet down from the door, showcased a fine collection of spirits. "And I've got to see this." Louise made her way to the middle of the room. "This is the largest rocking horse I've ever seen. An adult could ride it!" She glanced at him. "Why would you have a huge rocking horse in here?" She ran her fingers over the glossy wood, smacking her hand over her mouth when she viewed the saddle. In the center, rose a richly carved phallus, depicting the male shaft and head, accurate in every detail. "You've got to be kidding! How on earth does anyone ride a horse like this?"

Willie smiled. "You like it? You're right. I scrambled like crazy, and Judith gave me hell too. I didn't think I'd ever get her out." He pulled Louise into his arms. "When I put my mind to something, I get it done."

"But why did you need to go to this extreme?"

"I love Judith to death, but I suspected she was getting a little too nosy. Finally told me she'd seen stuff on the sheets."

Louise covered her cheeks, stunned. "You can't be serious. You mean we …?"

"I guess so, hon." He kissed her. "But I think this place will be fun. It reminds me of …"

"Reminds you of what, Willie?" The look she gave him bore straight through his soul, her breathing growing more rapid with excitement. "Does it remind you of The House? Is that where you were? I heard the bartender." Her eyes narrowed again. "You can't keep me in the dark forever, I'll get to the bottom of this, one way or the other. You can show me what you've learned all you want."

His pulse quickened; panic and irritation rolled inside of him, each vying for first place on his scale of emotions. The fact that something as innocent as an art show could blow his cover unnerved him to the fullest. He grabbed her wrists. "Enough! You know what, you're a persistent little thing, aren't you? Ever since I've come home, you've been pestering me with this. You don't ever seem to know when to quit, do you?" He gripped her tighter. "Why does it matter where I spent my time? Who cares? Does our time together mean anything to you, or not?"

"Yes, of course it does." She pouted.

"Then why do you keep at me like this?" He'd hoped to squelch her curiosity with their sexual escapades, but apparently he'd failed. The conversation with the bartender inflamed everything all over again.

She lowered her head, sullen. "I want to hear the truth from your lips. Why do you insist on keeping secrets from me, Willie? You're just as persistent and stubborn as I am."

His voice softened, her words sounding in his ears like a slap on the wrist, but he still refused to give in, not just yet. A new wave of boldness set in, and he desperately made his last stand. "What if I ended all this right now, found another gal, one who won't be questioning me all the time?"

She jerked her head up, lips trembling, eyes filled with an anger he'd never seen before. "You'd do that?" She swallowed hard, squaring her shoulders up in defiance. "Well, then, maybe you just might want to find another gal, because I've been patient long enough. I thought with some time and trust between us, you'd come clean with me at some point." With a huff, she pulled herself free from his grasp and left the room.

Willie stood rooted to the floor, dumbfounded. He'd finally crossed the line, and in doing so, risked losing the one he loved most. Did his guarded secret mean more to him than Louise? If he let her walk out now, what kind of life remained ahead of him without her? Flashing before his eyes, images of loneliness and isolation fluttered by, flaunting a dull existence even alcohol wouldn't be able to soothe. He heard the door rustle open and caught sight of her leaving the wine cellar.

"No, Lou, wait!" He charged after her, the pounding in his ears nearly deafening, panic weighing him down. "Please … I'm sorry … Please don't leave me!" With urgency, he grabbed her hand and pulled her back down the stairs. "Don't go. You win."

"I win?" She glared at him. "Is this some kind of competition or something?" Her jaw tightened. "I trusted you, Willie. I gave myself to you totally and completely because I wanted you. I've put up with you testing me and hiding stuff." She stamped her foot. "I'm done!"

Struggling to fight back tears, something he'd never done until now, Willie held her tighter. "Lou, listen to me. I'm going to come clean right now, I promise." He took a deep breath, fighting to stop the stinging in his eyes. "Here, come back and let's sit down and talk." With a gentle tug, he led her back through the cellar, into the room, and over toward the sofa. "Now, sweetheart, we'll talk here." Patting the seat with a nervous smile, he guided her down. The scowl on her face gave him little hope of forgiveness, but he prayed his confession might soothe her ruffled spirit.

When he sat down, he reached out to smooth her hair back, and to his dismay, she flinched a little at his touch. "Just get to the point!" The tone in her voice rattled his nerves, raining down on his courage, merciless, unrelenting.

"Lou, you're right, my parents sent me to The House because they were concerned about my being so down and out of sorts. I tried not to tell you for several reasons. One thing, I really didn't want you to think there was something wrong with me, and the other reason is because I signed an agreement with them to keep my experience there to myself." He paused a few seconds, waiting for a response, anything. No emotion showed in her eyes, though the expression on her face had changed from a scowl to one of light intrigue.

Clearing his throat, he continued. "Again, I signed a confidentiality agreement. If I do anything to stir up trouble with what I experienced there, they'll send people to come get me and take me back there again. And this time, I won't end up on the side I started off with."

"Confidentiality agreement … the side you started off with?" Louise shook her head. "I'm not sure I get what you're saying."

Relieved to hear some kind of response, he continued his explanation. "Here's the thing, Lou, The House has two sides. On one side, they house the crazy people, the ones who are truly a danger to themselves or to others. It's the other side that's more unusual, the side they want to keep from the general public. That's where I somehow ended up."

Louise reached for his hand, squeezing hard. "Willie, I'd never rat on you or do anything to get you in trouble, and I sure don't want any men in white coats coming here to take you away from me. I missed you so much when you were gone!" She looked him directly in the eyes, and seemed to be at least beginning to understand the issue at hand.

"Well, they want to keep their operation quiet," he continued, "because they believe they offer a valuable service, though I must say their treatment methods would make most people cringe. As for me, once I got over the shock, I enjoyed myself to the fullest!" He smiled, grateful for the thaw in her attitude.

"So tell me, Willie, what was so unusual about the side you were on? What did they do to you there, because you've never been the same since you've come home. You've been more bold, much more a take-charge kind of guy. I liked you before and all, but I have to admit I like you even better now!" She reached over and kissed his lips. "You're also a terrific lover. Is that what you learned there, how to act with women?"

"Lou, the intimate moments we've spent together show a little of what I learned there. Again, I haven't even begun to show you all of it. Like I said earlier, that's why I created this room, so I could teach you, and we can have some unbridled fun together." He grinned. "And to keep Judith from being so snoopy."

"But what about your getting into trouble?"

"They don't mind me practicing what I've learned. I simply can't go around telling everyone so the authorities get stirred up. I have to use some discretion. You know what I mean, those moralists we talked about before we got to the show."

"Oh, you're right." She smiled and snuggled in his arms. "Again, I'll never tell a soul. Why, we can let this be our dirty little secret, nobody knowing anything but you and me!"

He popped a kiss on the tip of her nose and gave her chin a light nip. "Yeah, Lou, just you and me." She seemed so delicate, her slender form resting in his arms. He marveled at the contrast, the strength and determination in her that he loved yet tried to tame. The warmth between them now encouraged an erection in his trousers. He trailed one of his fingers over the top of her dress, tracing the outline of a nipple. "What about another quick drink to get us back in the mood."

She giggled. "That'd be terrific. Yeah, I guess we did spoil the mood a bit, but that was my fault for being so pushy. I never suspected you'd been sworn to secrecy."

He got up and headed toward the small bar across the room. "Oh, you have been naughty tonight, pestering me and then walking out, so you owe me big."

Louise kicked off her shoes and settled back against the arm of the sofa. "I'll pay back everything I owe you, I promise." Within a few moments, she took the glass he handed her and swallowed a sip. "I'll even try not to talk so much."

"Do you think you'll be able do that, Lou? Just keep quiet and give yourself over to the thrill of the moment? I've sometimes had the devil of a time getting you to pipe down, but now, I'm going to step it up a notch." He sat down on the opposite side, and no sooner than he had taken a drink from his highball, a tiny foot rubbed over his crotch, sending him nearly swooning.

Resting her head back, Louise remained silent for few moments. "I liked Sylvia Noire's dance. Have you ever seen anything like it?"

"I have to honestly say I haven't, not even you-know-where."

Louise took another sip, her eyes glossing over just a little. He smiled. He'd made her drink extra strong, hoping to get her in a more willing frame of mind. The teasing of her foot hadn't stopped, and he thought in terms of how he wanted the rest of the evening to go. Glancing at his watch, he knew he had only a little time left before he needed to get her home at some semblance of a decent hour.

Willie finished off his drink, and leaned over Louise. "Here, drink the rest of this because I want to get down to business. You owe me, remember?" As he held the glass to her lips, she swallowed the remainder of the drink.

"Whew, I don't know about you, but I think this dress is rather tight." She took up the pearl beads in her hands and toyed with them, running her fingers up and down the strand, shaking the beads just to hear them rattle against each other. "I wonder if I could dance like Sylvia." Her eyes glistened, her lips parting in a light smile.

"Well now, doll, you'll never know 'til you try." He brought his face close over hers. "Are you going to dance for me?" His hand slipped under her dress, crawling up her thigh until he hooked his fingers around her undergarments.

"Yeah, I'll dance for you. I can shake it with the best of them." Her words floated into his ear like sweet, seductive music. With an upward lift of her hips, she allowed him to strip off her panties. After he tossed them to the floor, her legs worked their way around his waist. "Come give me a kiss, and I'll give you a show too, just like hers." She let out a soft laugh.

"I'll give you a kiss, all right!" Willie pushed up her dress and landed his lips on top of her slit. Her feminine essence had already made its way out, and greeted his tongue, filling his mouth with the unique, sweet taste that was hers.

She writhed a little at his touch, but quickly pushed him off of her. "It's show time, honey!" With a light stretch of her arms, she pulled herself off the couch.

"You're such a tease, just the way I like you." He chuckled and sat back.

Louise whipped off the strand of beads, tossing them in his lap, wiggling her hips and taking a few awkward twirls. She smiled and waved her arms, imitating Sylvia's movements. With a quick motion, she grabbed the hem of her dress, whisking it off. She sent the garment sailing across Willie's head, laughing as it landed in a heap next to the sofa. "Oh, I seem to have forgotten the veils." Glancing down at herself, she smiled and caught hold of her bra. "But I do have this." Her hips gyrated and pumped, while she waved her arms over her head. With a few light swirls, she stood in front of Willie and, imitating Sylvia Noire, yanked her bra loose, leaving herself completely naked.

"Who-o-ho-o-o!" He clapped and whistled. "That's it, keep on, baby. Show me what ya got!" She turned around, wagging her rear from side to side, pumping her hips at intervals. She finished her routine by facing him again, giving her breasts one last shake.

"All I have as a reward is this." He reached out and tweaked one of her nipples. "Sorry, babe, I have nowhere to tuck a twenty."

"Is that all I'm worth to you, a twenty? For being completely nude, I think I deserve more." She hiked up a foot and laughed before heading toward the rocking horse. "It's time to ride."

"Oh, careful there." Willie jumped up and strode to the horse. "I'll help you. You don't want to come down hard on this thing, you know."

"I wonder who's harder and better, you or this horse?" She stepped into one of the stirrups and climbed onto the saddle."

"Sassy girl!" He gave her bare buttock a firm swat, something he'd never done until now.

She opened her mouth, letting out a piercing shriek. "Ow!"

When she turned around to face him, he saw a blaze of lust in her eyes brighter than he'd ever witnessed.

"Oh, you've got a naughty girl." She swung her leg over the saddle, poising herself over the phallus. With a last, quick wiggle of her rump, she whooped with glee. "Swat that pony, this gal's gonna ride."

Willie obliged. "Yah-h-h, git on, there." Down came the palm of his hand on her backside. She squealed and bucked with delight.

"Oh-h-h, yeah. M-m-m." Louise settled onto the saddle, the phallus disappearing, inch by inch, until her bottom made full contact. She sucked in her breath through clenched teeth and snapped her eyes shut, swirling her hips, the horse rocking beneath her. A smile lit her face; a light hum floated from her throat.

He rubbed his hand over her back. "Does it hit you in all the right places?"

She swayed a little, undulating her hips to enhance the bulk of the phallus inside her. "Yeah, you're right, I like a holding a fat cock inside." The rocking of the horse increase. Louise glided back and forth with an animated speed.

"Whoa there, girl, I think this ride's over!" Willie grabbed the head of the horse, bringing Louise to a screeching halt. "There are plenty of things this horse can't do, and one of those is filling you up with all my love."

"Love?" Her lashes fluttered. "You've never used that word before."

Heat flared throughout his body, and he knew his cheeks, no doubt, flushed a bright pink. The word 'love' had never escaped his lips for any reason, except when he talked about his prized car. Was the drink making him careless? He helped her off the horse and led her to the bench at the foot of the bed. His cock had grown so stiff he thought he'd burst. The only thing he cared about right now was getting relief.

Willie stripped himself free from each piece of clothing, sending the items flying off in different corners of the room. He and Louise stood facing each other. "It's time for you to ride again." He stretched out on the bench and guided her over him. With slow upward thrusts he sank himself deep inside. She moaned with satisfaction. "So who's better, me or the horse?" He bucked hard, plunging hard enough to make her whimper. "Ride it, Lou! Ride me like you did that horse." The crack of his palm against her backside spurred her into gyrating her hips.

Every clench of his shaft, every gliding motion stroking his head sent him deeper into bliss. He closed his eyes, sensing a sharp sting in his nipples. Louise had delivered her usual firm bite, a customary nip given during their lovemaking. She latched on to his wrists for more support and rocked her hips faster. The flirty bouncing of her breasts pushed him to the limit. With a groan, he lifted his hips, pressing them hard against her mound. In a series of spasms, he emptied himself and sank back down on the bench with relief.

Louise cupped his head in her hands, plunging her tongue into his mouth. This particular kiss somehow contained a passion he'd never felt before, each stroke of her tongue against his, each soft brush against the roof of his mouth, performed with deliberate care and attention. Running his fingers over her moist flesh, he breathed in her scent, the heat from her body nearly setting him on fire. As they remained locked in total union, with no secrets between them any longer, a new vibrational essence bound them together, seeping into every crevice of soul and spirit.

He gently pushed her back, and slid off the bench. "We're not done yet, Lou. Just a few more things to help wind down the evening before I get you home. I just need a few items in here." He walked over to the chest of drawers where he gathered up his supplies. With a wave of his arm, he motioned for her to follow him to the iron screen. "I need you to lie down."

"What are we going to do next, Willie?" She bounced up and down a little with excitement. "Are we going to do some things you learned at The House?"

"Not another word out of you. Get down, now." With a gentle push, he guided her to the floor. "You really leave me no choice but to use this." He waved a ball gag before her eyes. "Just a little something to keep you quiet."

"What's that? You've never—"

Willie popped the gag in her mouth and tightened the strap. "Now lie down, like I told you." A sharp crack filled the room as he smacked one of her buttocks. Wide-eyed, she did as he instructed. "Excellent. Now, for this." He placed a blindfold over her eyes and, after slipping the strap in place, slipped some towels under her hips. From beneath the gag, her cries tumbled out muffled, yet determined. "Quiet!" *Swat* went his palm, followed by a louder squeak from her throat. "Open your legs, Lou," he commanded her.

She lay still, with only the frantic rise and fall of her chest revealing her emotions. Her cheeks flushed a bright pink, and with each force of his hands between her knees, she strained against him. "I said, open up." His lips fell against her ear. "Don't make me pop you again. You know I'll do it." In nanoseconds, her legs opened wide. "That's it, Lou, you dirty girl, you know you want this." He jangled a pair of cuffs, smiling as the noise of clanking metal created a trace of panic on her face. "Raise your arms above your head." One by one, he fastened her wrists to the iron bars of the screen. "There, you're all set now." With a loud whistle of approval, he stared down at her lithe form, bound, gagged, and blindfolded. The dark red of her nipples enticed him, plump and irresistible. With the tip of his finger, he grazed over the top of one breast. She jumped at the touch. When he reached over and bit down, he delighted in hearing her stifled shout. "You like that, dirty girl?"

The cuffs knocked against the iron bars as Louise strained hard to move her arms. Her hips rose and fell; Willie kept his tongue rooted to her flesh, trailing over her abdomen and landing inside her nether regions. Another blocked cry forced itself against the ball gag. Inside her slit, the contents of his lust had drained from her dark interior and pooled, thick and white, at her entrance, some remnants already streaming down the inside of her thigh.

A salty taste hit his mouth as the wet tip of his tongue remained steadfast on her clit, teasing the bud of hot nerves into a frenzied state of excitement. Just watching her buck and writhe incited a hard ache in his cock and balls. "Is all my work on that sweet little stump of yours making you want another drink, Lou?" He let out a chuckle. "From the looks of you, I think another quick refreshment might liven you up a bit." He quickly removed the gag and positioned himself over her head. "Don't say a word, or I'll send you home with an ache in your crotch so bad, you won't have a decent night's sleep for thinking about it." Bending his knees a little, he aimed his stiff length so the tip touched her lips.

She let out a gasp, which suddenly came to a halt as he pushed himself inside. "Open your mouth, Lou. I want you to hold all of me." Inching his way in, he sighed as her oral walls hugged his near-bursting shaft. Overcome by instinct, she flicked her tongue over his head, prying open the slit at the top. "Oh, Lou, you naughty girl, you know how that gets to me." He groaned as he grabbed hold of the metal bars for support. "Okay, I'm going to give you that drink right now, and I want you to swallow, you hear me? No thinking, no questioning, just swallow."

The movements of her tongue over his head and the sucking sensations brought out a series of spasmodic waves. His smile grew wider, and the sounds from her throat gave him greater satisfaction. "That's a good girl, Lou, just drink it all in. It won't hurt you." He pulled out and gave her a few moments to catch her breath. "Speaking of drinks, mine have caught up with me, and if I remember correctly that little twat of yours could use a little rinsing off, if you know what I mean." His pelvic region burned, and no traditional carnal release would ever make it go away. Positioning his hands on either side of her shoulders, he lowered his hips over hers, the silky tip of his shaft teasing the inside of her sex. She started to speak, but he stopped her with a kiss. "Sh-h-h, open up wide for me down there." He gazed at her and smiled, pushing her legs wider apart. "Remember the fountain at the art show tonight?"

She nodded in silence.

"You liked that fountain, didn't you?"

She nodded again.

"Would you like to pretend we're the fountain, Lou, just you and me, doing what they did?"

"Yes." Her voice sounded timid.

"Would you like for me to remove the blindfold now?"

"That would be nice." She smiled.

"Yes, but on second thought, I think I'll let you wear it a few moments longer."

She pursed her lips, catching herself in time before letting out an expression of dissatisfaction.

"That's good, doll, you're learning how to hold your tongue." He wriggled his hips, teasing her crotch again. "Let's play statue, Lou." His words fell in a whisper against her ear. Closing his eyes with concentration, he relaxed his muscles and let his golden fluids course over her. Feeling the fire in his loins subside, he gave a little internal push, rinsing off all traces of his passion. "How was that?" He slid off the blindfold and gazed down at her.

In silence, she blinked several times, her eyes glued to his, stunned beyond words.

"Well, well, for once you don't have something to say. Imagine that!" He reached down and bit one of the peaks of her breasts again. "Don't worry, you don't have to shower me with words. Sorry, no pun intended." He got up and headed to the chest of drawers, where he pulled out a large brass bowl. When he returned to the screen, he unfastened the cuffs and guided her to her knees. "Now it's your turn. You can't tell me the alcohol hasn't affected you by now." With a light push, he wedged the bowl between her knees.

"What do you want me to do?" She looked at him, her eyes bright with anticipation.

"You'll pee in this bowl."

"I'll what? You can't be …" With a frown, she started scrambling away.

He caught her. "Oh, no you don't. You'll go now, right this minute, or I'll make that sweet bottom of yours sting like you won't believe." On a whim, he caught the flesh of one of her buttocks and gave a firm pinch. She winced and cried out.

Defeated, Louise placed her hands on the floor and lowered her hips over the bowl. The sounds of water tinkling filled the room, and she closed her eyes and smiled. After a few seconds, she raised to a kneeling position. "There, are you satisfied?"

"I am, and from that grin on your face, so are you." He winked at her with approval and picked up an extra towel to dry her off. "Here, let's rest on the bed for a moment before we head on out."

"How late is it, Willie?" Louise reached for his wrist to glance at the time.

"Not too late, only ten-thirty."

"Well, let's not let time get away from us." She stretched her arms and yawned.

Willie strode over to the bed and sprawled out. "Come on!" He patted the covers. Louise crawled on beside him and cuddled into his arm. Her fingers tickled over his chest, and her warm breath filled his ear, lulling him into feelings of peace and contentment. He closed his eyes.

CHAPTER 13

With a flutter, his eyes opened with a start. Confused, he blinked several times and glanced over to see Louise curled up in a heap beside him. The events of the day came flooding back into his memory. Panic-stricken, he scrambled off the bed, remembering he needed to get her home fast. When he looked at his watch, his heart almost stopped. The time showed eight o'clock. Was he dreaming? Did the time on his watch suggest a new day had dawned? Deep under the house, tucked away inside the cellar, there were no windows to let light in, and time seemed stood still, holding no meaning.

She didn't stir, her even breathing showing signs of a deep sleep. Willie cursed under his breath, trying to come up with some quick story he'd be telling her father. He snatched up his clothes and dressed, his trembling fingers barely able to push the buttons through his shirt. After zipping up his pants and putting on his socks and shoes, he slipped out of the room, passed through the cellar, and made his way up the stairs, taking great care to not disturb Louise.

Thank god it was the weekend, and he didn't have Judith nipping at his heels. He opened the door and passed into the living room. The sound of the doorbell jarred him. Who would be coming to his house at this hour of the morning? Filled with an unexplained sense of dread, he reached the door and jerked it open. For a brief moment, his blood ran cold, and he staggered a little to keep his balance. The world seem to spin in front of his eyes.

"Where's my daughter?" George Carnwell, waiting for no invitation, pushed his way into the house.

Willie stood staring outside, dazed, trying to regain his bearings.

"Are you going to stand there like a fool, or are you going to tell me what you've done with Louise?"

Willie, numb with fear, scrambled to concoct a story her father might believe. He licked his lips, trying to smile. "You know what, Mr. Carnwell, I dropped Louise off at a friend's house after our date last night." Stepping back inside the house and closing the door, he swallowed hard and hoped he sounded convincing enough.

The gentleman squinted, looking him up and down. "Getting ready for church, I assume?" With bony fingers, he reached out and plucked at the collar on Willie's shirt. "Your clothes look a little rumpled to me, son, a little unkempt for Sunday meeting, wouldn't you say? And wasn't that the same suit you wore last night?"

"I …" Willie cleared his throat, knowing all too well he may have been beaten at this game. Meanwhile, the invasion by this man into his home, challenging him like a child, set off a sudden surge of indignation. "I wasn't exactly out making mud pies last night, so I felt my suit was still clean enough to wear again, thank you very much for asking."

The older man, his face twitching, clenched his fists and lunged forward. Bolts of rage flared up in his eyes, giving him the look of a cornered animal. "Well, you are one brassy son-of-a-bitch, aren't you?" Aghast, Willie stepped back. He knew one more fiery remark paved the way to a physical altercation, and the thoughts of coming to blows didn't suit him, not today, not ever.

Willie held up his hands. "Look, Mr. Carnwell, I'm sorry. I guess I thought Louise would have called you. We didn't mean to worry you or anything."

"Willie …?" A faint voice came from the cellar door.

Willie felt the blood drain from his face. Mr. Carnwell jerked his head around in the direction of the voice. "I'll be right there, Judith, just a minute, please." Willie's voice nearly cracked as he shouted in response. Seized with another round of panic, he grasped the man's elbow, opened the door, and rushed to pull him outside. "Look, sir, I need you to leave. I'm still trying to get dressed, and I don't have much time." He gave Louise's father a light push, all the while praying in earnest for Louise to stay put.

"I always thought Judith had Sundays off. She working today?" The smirk on the man's face, along with his persistence, set Willie off on a path of rage he'd never experienced before.

Filled with a burst of inner strength, he lashed out with bravado. "Look here, George. I can understand your concern for your daughter." He moved forward, nearly touching the man's face with his. "But let me just say this once and for all. Don't you ever think of coming to this house again, barging your way inside my home, asking me questions about my personal business, and acting like you're going to knock me out! This is my house, my property, and you'll do me the decency to respect that, whether you like it or not. Do I make myself clear? George?"

For what seemed like an eternity, silence fell between them. Total silence, with no vehicles on the streets, no chirping of birds, or any other sounds hinting at life. Willie quickly glanced down to see his own hands balled up in fists. Inside his chest, his heart nearly burst.

Mr. Carnwell's face softened, the corners of his mouth hinting at a light grin. Finally he found his voice. "You know what, son, you do have a set of balls on you!" He lifted his chin higher, his eyes shining. "I respect any man who can stand up for himself, and you've just proven yourself in my book." He turned to leave. "But the next time, do an old man a favor, and please tell me when you … drop Louise off somewhere else. When you're a father someday, you'll understand." With a wink, he waved and walked toward his car.

Willie stood at the door and watched Mr. Carnwell speed out of sight. The door opened behind him.

"What are you doing out here?" Louise pulled him inside. "And why did you call me Judith? I thought she had Sundays off." She stood before him, wearing her wrinkled dress. Her hair, tousled from sleep, gave her a rather comical appearance.

He laughed and put his arm around her. "Apparently your father knows that too."

"My father?" She went pale. "He was here?" She started to pace. "Oh, this is bad news. Willie, what will I tell him?"

"Do you have a friend who'll vouch for you?" He smiled, leading her into the kitchen. "That's what I told him. I dropped you off at a friend's house after the show."

"But, didn't he hear me call out?"

"He did, but luckily he couldn't see you. Anyway, your voice was too soft to make out."

With a grimace she headed toward the kitchen, where she pulled out some eggs and butter from the refrigerator. "I'm sure he suspected something."

"Oh, I wouldn't worry, doll, I think I made everything perfectly clear." He kissed her and sat down at the table, watching her as she moved about the kitchen, collecting everything from more food to pots and pans, laying each item out in her usual methodical order. She seemed to own the place and everything hidden away in all the cabinets and drawers. His house had somehow morphed into their house, with her feeling more at home as time passed.

Sitting back in his chair, visions of the future flashed before his eyes. What would it be like to have her here with him every day, someone to come home to, someone to sleep with, and no suspicious housekeepers and fathers prying into his affairs? He'd played the scenes over in his mind so many times at night while trying to fall asleep. The incident with her father only served as a strong reminder to make a decision and get on with his life before it got away from him.

"Willie, what are you thinking about? You seem like you're miles away from here."

"Oh, nothing really. Hey, Lou, when we finish breakfast, can we go back downstairs for a while? I have a feeling I might be in the mood for, well, you know."

She said nothing, but smiled.

§§§

After breakfast, Willie and Louise headed back to the cellar. "Your father won't be looking for you for a while, yet." Willie pulled her onto the bed. "Do you like our secret room down here?"

Louise stretched out and smiled. "I love our secret room down here." She rolled over and rubbed her hand between his thighs. "Are you sure you'll keep this room just for us? I don't think I want to share it with anyone else."

He pulled her close, positioning his chin so it rested against the top of her head. "Interesting question, Lou, the stuff about sharing and all. Do you think I'd want to share all this with someone else?"

"Oh, I don't know, Willie, but I know how you men are. You like variety." Her fingers found the way to his zipper and began pulling at the tab.

"You don't think this room will give us all the variety we need?" He closed his eyes, silencing a groan as she slipped her hand in beneath his briefs and fondled his flesh.

"I think you'll give us all the variety we'll need." She flicked out her tongue and licked around the edge of his ear. "I love the way you come to life in my hands."

"And I love the way you've come into my life!" They lay together in silence, the only movement coming from Louise's fingers caressing over his swollen length. He took a deep breath. Should he ask, or did a better time await? No. He'd learned at The House to live each day to the fullest. Love hard, love well; be naughty, play nice. The warmth of her body wrapped him in comfort and security, making moments like these so perfect. As he lay next to her, his heart pounded faster, knowing the next question would seal his fate forever. "Hey, Lou, I need you to stop for a minute and look at me."

She sat up. "What is it?"

"How would you like it if I promised to share this room, my whole house, and all my possessions with you, and only you?"

"Nobody but me?" Her lashes fluttered a little in disbelief. "What are you talking about?"

He reached up and stroked her hair. "I want you here when I come home. I want you in my bed at night when I go to sleep. I want us to make love anytime we want to, and let our passions run wild whenever we want to." He grinned at her, rubbing his finger against her cheek while she sat next to him, stunned. "So what do you say, Lou? Will you be my gal 'til death do us part?"

Her answer, a hot wet kiss on his lips, engaging her tongue in a playful dance with his. She ended the kiss and beamed down at him. "Oh, Willie, I couldn't imagine being anybody else's gal but yours. I love you, but I guess you knew that already."

"I love you, too, babe, but it's always nice to hear you say it."

"Hey, Willie?" She wiggled around a little, gyrating her shoulders. "What, Lou."

With a few twists, her dress came off and flew through the air, landing in a heap in front of the liquor cabinet. She hooked her fingers around the top of his pants and yanked them off, followed by his underwear. Between his legs, a full cock stood tall and proud, bearing a ripe pink head on top.

She grinned and cupped her breasts in her hands, giving her nipples a light tweak. Within seconds, she straddled his hips. "I have a feeling I might be in the mood for … well, you know."

MISTRESS OF THE HOUSE

CHAPTER 1

Thelma Starnsby slipped the brown leather bag over her shoulder and turned around to give The House one last, hard stare. The ornate building seemed to stare back as its methodical chevron-shaped architecture sprawled across a massive expanse of velvety green grass. Most people tried to avoid thinking about the local asylum, viewing it with horror. But for the past few months, her stay here had provided the opportunity to learn one other truth about this place; one the public would shudder even to think about. Unlike them, however, she had quickly embraced the treatment, reveling in their methods to help in her healing.

She turned around to open the car door, settling herself in the front passenger seat of a handsome 1926 Chrysler Imperial E-80. Once she had adjusted herself, placing the bag beside her feet, she pulled her cloche hat lower over her eyes, wishing to remain inconspicuous during the drive home. The driver, provided as a courtesy of The House, shut the door and returned to the other side, sliding into the driver's seat.

"Where to, lady?" A broad smile lit up his handsome face as he started the car.

She smiled back, not without some wistfulness, knowing this might be the last time she'd ever find herself surrounded by the most handsome people on earth, all collected in one place. "6969 Chastity Lane."

The young man's smile faded, his expression turning into one of disbelief. "Chastity Lane, is it? Is that a real address, or are you just toying with me?"

"Oh, no, it's my real address." She lifted her hand to her mouth and stifled a snicker. "Not so fitting after a stay here, don't you think?"

"I should say so." He chuckled, slowly pulling out of the drive. "But I'm sure you'll be able to make it live up to its name now, won't you?"

"Trust me, I already have a plan to make that happen." Thelma grinned and closed her eyes.

Yes, she had concocted a plan, all right, using all the wisdom garnered from her stay at The House. The plan incorporated her intense training in pleasures of the flesh, along with a last-ditch effort to get Harry Wisenburg to marry her. After a little over a year of their having spent time with each other, she'd grown tired of waiting; something had to give. Many would consider her method most unorthodox, even damning to her soul; but secretly, she damned society for quashing sexuality, man's most basic nature. Worse yet, she damned them for placing women in a status not much above that of animals: mere property. But she rested a little easier these days, aware of the new crusade young women had lately begun to lead, trying in desperation to rid themselves of the shackles wielded by old, patriarchal domination.

"So what's a dame like you gonna do once you're home? And I must admit, for an older broad, you sure are a looker: nice hair, slender figure, not to mention some great fronts." The driver whistled, giving her a quick, approving wink, and then turned his attention back to the road.

With a wrinkle of her nose, she sniffed in disgust. "Yes, what to do once I'm home? I'll be trying to get my life going forward again, instead of stalling out like it did before." She shook her head a little. "Geez, I thought life was about over for me, at my age, but it's not. Why it's just beginning, really!"

Before her admission to The House, her last statement would have rung in her ears as a loud lie. In fact, the miserable, helpless feeling of life passing her by had almost become the final nail in the coffin of her lonely existence, causing her to spiral out of control into an emotional breakdown.

"You don't say so! Really?"

"Trust me, most of you think life is for the young, but, as I've just learned during my stay at The House, it's just not so."

"Tell me something, if you don't mind me being so bold to ask." The driver's face now showed sincere interest, and he wiggled a little to get more comfortable in the seat as he drove the distance from the countryside where The House stood, hidden from public view, to the populated town where Thelma lived. "What brought a pretty little thing like you to The House? You know, once everybody finds out where you've been, they'll think you're just a crazy old bat!"

"Will you please stop calling me old!" She reached over and swatted him on the thigh. "If we weren't driving, and in another location, I'd strip those breeches off you and swat that mighty fine rump of yours."

"Ah, my rump couldn't be swatted by any finer a lady than yourself." The warm grin filled his face, while a light flush colored his cheeks.

"As for being called crazy, I think it's funny most people think The House is just the loony bin."

"Well, it is, at least one side of it, anyway." He patted her on the knee. "But from the sound of you, the staff on the naughty side taught you a lot, didn't they?"

Thelma stretched her shapely legs as best she could. The car began to feel a bit cramped, and the road to her house still stretched out several more miles. "Yes, they did, lucky me!"

"You were lucky. Better for you to end up on the naughty side, after all. They have lots of wicked fun over there." He turned his head toward her and lowered his voice. "I know, because I've walked through those halls and peeked in the rooms."

She laughed. "I'm sure you have, given the fact there are no doors to those rooms. You got yourself quite an eyeful, didn't you?"

"Oh, baby, what I'd give to …" He shook his head. "Enough about my being a Peeping Tom. So how'd you get to the good side, that's what I wanna know?"

She shrugged. "I was feeling out of sorts, frustrated at life to the point I nearly lost my mind, so my doctor recommended it. He's a good friend of Dr. James, the House's physician."

"You don't say!" The driver stared straight ahead, tapping his fingers on the wheel. "They must be some mighty interesting cohorts, Dr. James working at The House and his friend recommending you to come. Makes you kind of think, you know."

"Good point. As a matter of fact, I never would have described Dr. McGuiness as a sensual type, now that I think about it. He's always so stuffy and straight-laced when I see him. I wonder if, behind closed doors, he's anything like his buddy."

Thelma's mind flashed back to her first encounter with the handsome Dr. James. Rules of The House dictated that every patient, or "admit" as they were called, undergo a physical exam before participating in The House program. And yes, Dr. James knew how to perform a thorough physical exam, in every sense of the word, using his fingers to rub, explore, and tweak all the right, sensitive places. She took in a gulp of air, then exhaled little by little, trying to dull the beginnings of a new ache looming between her thighs.

The driver shifted in his seat. "I know you want this kept secret and all, but what are you going to tell everyone when you get home? People are nosy, you know."

"I have that story planned too." She threw back her head and laughed. "I'm a teacher by occupation, and before I left I made up this story about going off to do some temporary teaching in another city. They'll just think I've come back, that's all."

He nodded and clicked his tongue. "Good way to do it. Keeps 'em minding their own business, and it's a believable story."

Yes, even Harry had believed her. She smiled, remembering the sadness in his eyes when she told him of her leaving. He seemed heartbroken, wanting to know the address where he could send letters, reminding her of his undying devotion. But she managed to make enough excuses, and finally convinced him he didn't need to engage in letter writing, since she'd only be gone for a short while.

Thelma closed her eyes for a moment, feeling the hum of the car as it moved on down the road. All this nervous-breakdown nonsense she blamed on Harry, for dragging his feet on popping the question, all the while flirting with her nonstop. How he'd carried on, crooning away about how her eyes lit him on fire, how her smile made his heart flutter, how her very presence filled him with purpose, giving him every reason in the world to get out of bed every morning.

She pursed her lips and reached to pat the leather bag, nearly laughing out loud. How quick he'd be willing to get out of bed once she'd had her way with him remained the big question. Yes, he might have every reason to stay in bed!

After a few moments of driving in silence, the driver tapped her on the knee. "You got a special someone in your life you can practice on when you get back?"

"Um, I think I do, and if this doesn't do the trick to get him to propose marriage, then I guess I'll be doomed to spend the rest of my life alone."

"You ever been married?"

Thelma winced. She didn't talk to a lot of people about her past, which was, frankly, a humiliating one. "Only for a brief time. I was eighteen, and we were married just a few months before he suddenly left: no word, no warning, just up and left. I finally got a letter from him telling me that he just wasn't ready for marriage." She took a deep breath and continued. "I never saw him again, and in order to not seem like used goods, I've always told everyone that my spouse died of an illness."

"Yeah, like I said before, keeps 'em minding their own business." The driver turned and smiled at her. "But I just know a bewitching dame like yourself won't be alone much longer, I just feel it. And with what you know about men, you'll bring any one of 'em down to their knees, begging you to never let 'em go!"

"I'm hoping so … I'm hoping so." Though she felt armed and ready for her next set of battles, a twinge of doubt still tugged at her. What if Harry wasn't the type to fall to his knees … for anybody? After all, his wife's death several years ago had to hit him hard; he'd never seemed inclined to marry again.

The car sped through town, and after some longer roads and a few turns, they headed into an old neighborhood filled with ornate, well-maintained Victorian homes. He nodded and gave a light whistle. "You live in a nice place, gal." His head moved back and forth, surveying the fine houses, each perched on a neatly manicured lawn. "You got money or something?"

"Just what I inherited from my parents. I live in the same house I grew up in."

"I see. Nothing wrong with that." He turned the car to the right. "I bet the man you have your eye on has money too? I mean, you people seem to stick together, you know."

Thelma smiled. "Yes, we do, don't we? And yes, he's done quite well for himself." She turned her head toward the driver. "You know, he only lives a couple of blocks from me, and walks over to my house a lot if he's out and about or just wants to drop by."

"You don't say. Well, now that's pretty handy, especially if both of you are wanting a quick little something-something." He clicked his tongue again a few times and nodded, smiling. "Hey, lady, I think we're almost at your place."

"Yes, turn right there, the road on the left."

"So this is Chastity Lane … which will soon be known as Lover's Lane, yeah?"

"I'm praying so. Oh, please drive on around the house. I'll go in through the back door, just in case. I don't feel like getting any of my neighbors stirred up. They're nice, but I just want some time to get used to being back home again."

"I understand." He brought the car to a halt next to the back door.

"Hang on, I'll help you out." He climbed out of the car and headed toward Thelma's side.

She picked up the leather bag and swung her legs out of the car.

"I see they fixed you a goodie bag." He smiled and quirked an eyebrow.

"Yes, and I intend to use everything in here." As her feet hit the stone drive, she pulled herself out of the vehicle and threw the bag over her shoulder. "I've got it from here. I don't have anything else with me. My doctor told me to leave everything at home."

"The House provided everything you needed and then some." The driver tipped his hat and made his way around the car. Before he got in, he turned around to face Thelma one last time. "Hey, doll, just remember one thing, a girl who is chaste will never be chased. I really suggest you use everything in that bag. And if you want my advice, I'd be quick about it too!" He gave her a farewell salute, slipped inside the car, and slammed the door shut. With a few maneuvers, he turned around and headed back down the driveway before he sped out of sight, taking away with him her last tangible connection with The House.

Thelma smiled and reached in her pocket for the key. With a quick twist, she opened the door and stepped inside her home, her world, the real world, where life didn't flow with any predictable routine with adoring attendants who cared only for your comfort … and pleasure. With a breath of relief, she found the house had remained the same as she'd left it, with everything in neat order and all furniture covered in large sheets to keep out some of the dust.

She'd chosen not to have anyone check on her place, which might have proven a foolhardy decision, but considering where she'd spent her time away, this choice had seemed the most prudent for privacy. One by one, she began lifting off the sheets, uncovering a magnificent collection of Victorian furniture. A stale odor reached her nostrils, and to freshen up the air, she moved around the room, opening up the windows. Within minutes, the scent of gardenias and fresh-cut grass filled the downstairs area.

After moving through the kitchen and dining room, she crossed over the hallway to the large living room where she removed more sheets and opened up windows. The dark, cold fireplace still smelled of burned wood, yet in her mind's eye, she beheld a future of roaring fires and intimate moments she planned to have with Harry. But a wooden door on the opposite side of the room sent a smile to her face. On the other side of the wall was a room, one that might have been used by others as a private study or office. Thelma, however, had decided long ago her home had needed another bedroom on the lower level instead.

After much daydreaming during her time at The House, she'd already determined how this room might figure in her plans to win over her beloved Harry. Giving the leather bag a fond pat, she walked over to the door and slipped into the room. Perfect! She'd even had a small bathroom added for convenience. Her eyes scanned over the simple iron bed, a small nightstand and lamp resting beside it. On the opposite wall, in one corner, stood a chest of drawers.

Other than a dainty overhead light, the room, almost coincidentally, reminded her of the one she and her attendant had shared at The House. A simple room, but one where a lusty couple could indulge in pleasures of the flesh. She let out a laugh. At least this room included a door for privacy, a stark contrast to the doorless rooms at The House.

She walked over to the chest of drawers. From her "goodie bag," as the driver had called it, she pulled out containers of lubricant and vials of scented oils. After placing these inside the drawers, she pulled out a strap-on phallus, some cuffs, a blindfold, and a ball-gag, which were her favorite items. She kissed each one, remembering fondly how her attendant had introduced each one to her, and placed them in their own special drawer.

Once the room met her final approval, Thelma turned out and headed to the hallway, where she climbed the stairs to her own bedroom. At the top of the steps, she turned right into a large master bedroom. The spaciousness took her breath away, after having spent time in a much smaller and modest room at The House; but the feeling of isolation and loneliness hit her the hardest.

As she stood in her own bedroom, silence came crashing down against her ears. No lusty moans, no flirtatious giggles, and no clinking of metal cuffs against iron bars filled the air. The other three remaining bedrooms, meanwhile, were devoid of naked bodies entwined in passionate embraces, or tongues and fingers of the occupants exploring moist nether regions or stimulating sensitive areas of the flesh.

She slipped out of her clothes and changed into a comfortable robe before heading off downstairs to make some tea. Tomorrow, she'd uncover the furniture in the other upstairs rooms, and give her whole house a good, general airing out. In the coming week, she'd have her house back to its former beauty. As she sat at the table, sipping from her cup, all thoughts turned to thinking of ways to get Harry to propose. At thirty-eight years of age, Thelma knew little time remained before spinsterhood might be her lot in life. At forty-three years of age, Harry still looked good, and he'd been widowed long enough, in her opinion. The intense sexual training she'd received during her stay at The House gave her a strong advantage over most women, who merely played a passive role during lovemaking sessions with their husbands.

Passivity remained a thing of the past for Thelma, and she knew from this point forward, if Harry spent any time with her, he was about to learn a thing or two; no woman around stood a chance against her. Swallowing the last drop of tea, she got up from the table and made her way to the living room again. Along the right side of the wall, opposite the fireplace, stood a studio upright piano, which had been her mother's. She sat on the stool, opened up the lid, and stroked the keys. Music relieved her of stress, and for quite a while she played, stopping at times to think about Harry, imagining how his soft flesh, instead of these hard, ivory keys, might feel beneath her fingers.

He'd be surprised to see her. Or would he? Had he forgotten her already? A chill ran up and down her spine. Out of sight, out of mind, she'd always heard. Perhaps her absence made his heart grow fonder? One thing remained certain, she'd find out soon.

The afternoon sun faded away to darkness of night. Tired and weary, Thelma returned upstairs, slipped on a nightgown, and crawled into bed, settling under the sheets. Wearing a nightgown felt strange after an extended period of sleeping nude. For a while she tossed and turned, thinking just how to spend her first day home tomorrow.

The bed felt cold; how odd to spend a night alone, and not in the company of an attractive man. Bedtime at The House had given everyone an even greater excuse for cuddling, fondling, and checking out dark, sensitive areas with flicking tongues and sly fingers. Finally she rolled over and closed her eyes. If she played her cards right, she'd never have to sleep another night alone.

CHAPTER 2

The chirping of birds and early strands of sunlight flashing through the curtains caused Thelma to awaken with a start. Confused, she sat up, rubbed her eyes, and looked around before remembering she wasn't at The House anymore. The clock on the mantle over the fireplace in her room showed only eight thirty, but her eyes simply refused to close again for more sleep.

She threw off the covers and got out of bed. Today showed the promise of sunshine, a perfect day for working in the flowerbeds surrounding her house. They desperately needed attention, having been left to the whims of Mother Nature since her departure. With a few steps, she padded over to her closet and threw open the door.

Smart, fashionable dresses hung in a neat row, and though some of them reflected the new, shorter hemlines, nothing at all in her closet compared to the form-fitting, sexy red attire she'd worn as an admit, The House term for "patient." At this moment, all the clothing hanging on the racks confused her, none of them striking her fancy. A neat array of hatboxes lined a shelf above the clothes. Thelma reached up and whisked one of them down, pulling off the top. Yes, a trip to Matilda, her prized milliner, was definitely in order. Maybe she'd have Raul, her tailor, create some new, fresh clothing.

At the very end of the closet hung a couple of dresses used for outdoor work. Selecting one of them from a rack, she slipped it over her head. From the hat shelf, she grabbed an old straw hat, the one she always wore when she worked outside. Should she apply some cosmetics to even out her complexion? A little powder, rouge? Giving the matter some thought, she decided against it and left to go downstairs. Nobody knew she'd arrived, and who would see her, anyway?

Though her stomach rumbled, food didn't mean anything to her at the moment. She entered the kitchen and walked over to a closet near the back door to retrieve some cutters and a burlap bag for weeds and cuttings. Where to start, the front or the back? The back gardens needed clearing up as much as the front. If she wanted privacy a while longer, that was the best place to start.

Fresh air and sunshine hit her face the moment she opened the back door and stepped out. Squinting up at the sky, the vision of a blazing sun foretold a hot day ahead. With the worn straw hat perched on top of her head, she stepped over the stone path to the far end of the garden. Though the greenery showed signs of neglect, with weeds and gangly overgrowth running amok, the sight of the landscape still stirred up memories of The House's lawns and gardens, with fountains at every turn, sculpted shrubs, and cascades of colorful flowers in all varieties imaginable. This modest garden, though quite attractive before she left, paled in comparison, even on the best of days.

Across the distance, in the far right-hand corner, stood a monstrous weeping willow, raining down its branches in graceful arcs. Thelma smiled. What naughty things she could do to Harry, resting beside the flowing tendrils, basking under silvery moonlight and twinkling stars.

Dropping her bag down beside some wilted hydrangeas, she stood, hands on hips, surveying the large bush. The blooming season had just ended, signaling the right time for pruning. She gripped the cutters and removed the old foliage. Time seemed to stand still, while she concentrated on nothing but running the cutters over all the right places, old blooms sprinkling the ground.

"Well, well, if it isn't my sweet little hen come home to roost!"

Thelma jumped with a start, dropping her cutters to the ground. Her heart pounded so hard she thought it might explode. She whirled around at the sound of a strong, familiar voice. "Harry!"

He smiled, stepping forward, arms opened wide. Not waiting for an answer, he took her in his arms and held her close. "Oh, I've missed you so much!" Through a whirlwind of emotions, she threw her arms around him, taking in the scent of Bois 1920 when her face nestled against the side of his neck. Harry hugged her a few seconds longer before stepping back. "Look at you. Even in your gardening dress, you're as pretty as a picture."

Her cheeks grew warm, and silently she cursed her decision to forego the cosmetics. "Oh, you're just saying that, Harry. You always do." She rearranged her hat, reviewing him up and down. He'd always struck her as handsome. Today he stood before her, neatly dressed in casual khaki slacks and shirt, wearing just enough pomade to ensure his coffee-brown hair remained neatly in place. Even for an older man, he still sported a strong frame, with well-muscled thighs and arms. Unfortunately, though, the loose-fitting slacks gave no hint of the flesh underneath. "I've missed you too. But what made you come over here? How did you even know I was home?"

He gave her a broad smile. "I saw you coming home yesterday." His eyes widened. "That sure was a mighty fancy ride home from the train station. Whose was it?"

"You saw me yesterday?" Thelma frowned.

"Have you forgotten? I always take my walks in the late afternoon. I was just coming around the block when I saw the car. You were already in the drive and heading to the back. You wouldn't have seen me." He reached out and took her in his arms again. "It was all I could do to keep from running over here the moment I saw you, but I didn't want to intrude, at least not right away. I've missed you so much, Thelma!" He hugged her even tighter, lifting her off her feet while turning from side to side. "I've dreamt about you every night since you've been gone." He whispered in her ear. "I've hardly slept much, thinking of you all the time."

"You look pretty rested to me," she chuckled, patting him on the back. Yes, he'd remained the same old Harry; nothing had changed … so far.

A mock frown covered his face. "And why, oh why, didn't you let me write to you? You've nearly killed me by not allowing me to keep in touch!"

"Oh, Harry, I knew I'd be busy, teaching the students and all."

"Bah, teaching students. And you couldn't find the time to write me at least once or twice?"

She lowered her head, staring at the ground. "I'm sorry, I just thought I'd be home sooner."

"So who learned more, you or the students? I hear students can sometimes teach the teacher." He reached over to give her left cheek a soft pinch.

A faint smile crept over her face. "Come to think of it, I did learn some things while I was away."

"Did you really miss me, or did you forget about me completely while you were gone?"

"Don't be silly, Harry, I'd never forget about you."

"And just when did you plan to tell me you were home?"

She gave his arm a playful swat. "I only got here yesterday. Can't you give a poor girl some time to get settled in?"

"No, as a matter of fact, I can't." He chuckled, leaning in to give her a light kiss on the lips.

The touch of him nearly sent her swooning, but she didn't let on. "Listen, I don't know about you, but I could use a cup of coffee. Why don't you come on in the house and join me?"

Thelma ushered him into the kitchen and motioned for him to sit down at a small table. "I'll make us some coffee. I'd offer you something to eat, but I haven't had a chance to get to the market yet."

"I couldn't eat, anyway." He smiled and stretched his legs out from the chair. "Just feasting my eyes on you makes me forget all about being hungry."

"Harry, just listen to how you carry on." She turned around to admonish him further, but resisted when she caught the twinkle in his eye and grin playing across his lips.

"So how did your teaching stint go, really? Did you do anything else while you were away? Any fun sightseeing tours or fancy soirees?"

"Now that you mention it, I did see some pretty interesting things." Thelma tried to appear casual, knowing no one in the community most likely contained enough imagination or the open mind to understand what she'd just recently experienced. And the most interesting aspect was the fact she'd enjoyed herself immensely, not wanting to trade the time at The House for anything in the world.

"Well, 'fess up, woman, what kind of things did you do?"

"I met some well-rounded people, you might say. We ate together, and spent much of our spare time outside."

"The great outdoors, huh?" Harry now sipped some of his coffee while he held Thelma's hand. "You always like being outside, don't you?"

"I got to soak in a real natural hot spring, and I also explored the inside of a cave."

"Ah, so you turned into a spelunker, eh?" He squeezed her hand, gazing at her with interest.

"You could say that." She smiled, knowing the real truth about what she'd done with her attendant when they'd spent time together in these places. The property surrounding The House contained just as many exciting places on the outside, all of which served as a means for enjoying carnal pleasure to the fullest, whether under a brilliant sun or beneath the glow of moon and stars by night.

She swallowed down some coffee and rubbed her hand over his. The mere sight of his thick, soft fingers quickened her loins. As she gazed at them, she imagined how they might feel buried deep inside her, probing, exploring, gliding over her receptive flesh. The very thoughts sent a roaring ache to top of her sex.

"It's Friday, Thelma, so what do you have planned for tonight?"

She set her coffee down and thought a moment. "I haven't thought about it. Why?"

"Let's go out, just you and me. Maybe we can dine at Rolando's. I just love the food there." He pulled her hand to his lips and kissed her fingers. "We could sneak a drink of wine in the back room. Maybe go for a walk at Willow Pointe when we're done."

Dining, wine, a walk at Willow Pointe. Thelma's mind raced. "*... a girl who is chaste will never be chased ... use everything in that bag ... be quick about it too ...*"

"How about this as an idea, Harry, why don't I cook a special meal for you tonight, complete with candlelight, and who knows? We can always figure out the rest later."

Harry beamed at her. "Are you really up to it, my girl?" His face became more sober. "That's a lot of work, you just coming home and all. Don't you think it would be more fun to go out?"

"You know what, handsome? I'm rested well enough, and like I said, I've missed you too. It'd be great fun to cook for you again."

He tapped a hand on the table in approval. "Then I'll come back here tonight. It's a date, and I'll bring the wine. I have a special bottle hidden away."

"And I'll make sure everything's even more special than dinner at Rolando's." She gave him a flirty flutter of her eyelashes before taking another sip of coffee.

"Just being with you is special, Thelma." He got up from the table and stooped to kiss her cheek. "I'll see you tonight, but what time?"

"Six thirty will be good. I'll have everything ready." She followed him to the door. With one last hug, he slipped outside and disappeared around the corner of the house.

With a racing heart, Thelma found her mind swirling in a flurry of thoughts: what to buy, how to set everything up, dine inside or outside under the willow tree. So much to get ready! She glanced up at the clock on the kitchen wall. The day had several hours to go before six thirty arrived.

A few more beds needed weeding, and then she'd head out to the market to buy everything for tonight's meal. As for everything else, her "special" room held those items safe and sound. But how far she might venture with Harry tonight remained a mystery. Clapping the straw hat on her head, she made her way back outside, where immersing herself in pruning and cutting gave her ample time to think.

CHAPTER 3

Thelma slid out of her 1919 Chevrolet 490. Seven years old, and the car still ran well. Maybe one day she'd try to purchase a car of similar quality to Harry's handsome Rolls-Royce Silver Ghost. Little had anyone ever suspected her admiration for cars, and though her family pedigree had left her with ample income, Harry's monetary stash left her financial coffers reeling.

After pulling out her bags of groceries, she headed toward the back door to the kitchen and began preparing everything for the night's meal. While the memories of mealtimes at The House made her smile, others would have cringed. On the side where she'd resided, House directors had one strange rule: no nudity, except for certain designated activities—and mealtimes. Memories of decadent behavior, admits and attendants using each other as serving vessels, feeding each other in the most arousing ways, sped up her pulse. At the time, she'd enjoyed herself immensely, thinking nothing of serving pieces of fruit or tidbits of select food from her loins, with her attendant flicking his tongue and sucking hard.

She chuckled and shook her head, knowing such behavior would not be suitable tonight. There had to be a better way to approach intimacy. Maybe preparing the food so they could eat with their fingers might make for a sensual evening. For the next two hours, pans, knives, and spatulas clattered against each other while she created dipping sauces, and carved meat, vegetables, and fruit into tiny, bite-sized pieces. Each item of food found its way onto a large glass platter, placed in neat, colorful piles. In a round, wire basket, she tucked away some thinly sliced bread.

With forty-five minutes left on the clock, Thelma ran upstairs to bathe and dress, engaging in her toiletry rituals. Jerking open the closet door, the red shift dress caught her eyes. It was the closest reminder of her House attire. Just how she'd be able to maintain some decency sitting on the ground in a shorter dress remained a little concerning, but she'd decided to start working on Harry right away, and this dress appeared sexy enough. He definitely hadn't changed in his attitude toward her, but a new bold nature had changed her.

She grabbed the dress out of the closet and dropped it over her head, where it fell neatly into place over her slender frame. Thelma smiled as she gazed down at her chest, admiring her ample bosom. Many women these days tried to minimize their breasts for the sake of fashion, but she wanted to accent hers, especially around Harry.

Not a moment too soon. At the sharp ring of the doorbell, Thelma scrambled for some simple matching pumps with ankle straps, slipping them on while heading to the door.

Giving her hair one last once-over with her fingers, she answered the door. Harry, looking dapper in his fawn Oxford bags trousers, white collared shirt, and matching canvas shoes, nearly took her breath away. Under his arm he held a small burlap bag.

"Come in, come in!" Thelma opened the door wider, stepping aside as he passed into the entrance hall.

"Oh, look at you. Love the dress!" He leaned over and gave her a kiss on the lips. "I brought us a special treat. A bottle of 1921 Chateau Cheval Blanc. I've had it a few years, but it's a premium wine."

"Everything with you is always premium, Harry." She'd spied the Silver Ghost in the drive, and from the looks of his clothing, his outfit appeared brand new.

"Nothing's too good for my woman, and I've been saving this vintage for a special occasion." He took the bottle out of the bag. "Wanted to hide this, just in case anyone saw me getting out."

Thelma shook her head. "Wouldn't want to get into that kind of trouble." She took the bottle and led him to the kitchen. "When will everyone wizen up and understand there's no way to stop people from enjoying a drink every now and then?" The ice bucket sat up high in a corner cabinet. She reached up and pulled it down, aware of his eyes on her legs as the short dress rose.

"I'm with you, my dear, but that's just how it is now." He stepped behind her and put his arms around her waist as she placed the wine in the bucket.

"I-I'll need to get some ice from the trays." She lingered in his arms. The hardness between his thighs as he pressed against her incited a dull ache between her legs. For a second she closed her eyes, picturing herself with her face between his thighs, pleasuring him with her mouth. Thelma wiggled out of his grasp.

"So what's the plan for tonight? I can see from the dining room we're not eating in there."

"You're right. I have a special idea. We're eating outside under the willow tree. It's a nice evening, and I want to take advantage of the fresh air."

"What a fantastic idea, hon!" He followed her to the refrigerator. Taking her in his arms, he pressed his lips against her ear. "I just love the way you get so creative sometimes, thinking of fun things for us to do."

"Really? I never thought I was that creative. As a matter of fact, you seem to make most of the decisions on what we do."

Harry chuckled. "Well, come to think of it, I do, don't I? Maybe I need to turn over the reins to you, and we'll see what you can come up with now that you're back home."

Thelma felt her face flush. "H-m-m." She rubbed her chin in pretense. "You sure you want me to do that? You trust me so much, that you'll do anything I suggest?"

"My little primrose, I'll do anything with you, go anywhere with you." He gave the tip of her nose a soft nip. "I'm sure you'll surprise me. Now I'm leaving all the planning and ideas in your tender hands."

She grinned at his willingness, as she stroked his hair. Harry didn't have the faintest idea how she planned to wield her power over him. "Yeah, well, I'll take you up on that, Mister."

"Now that we have that settled, what do you need me to do next in the way of getting ready to eat? I'm starving, and I can't wait to see what you've fixed."

"Go over there to that closet and pull out a tablecloth. I'll get everything out of the oven. I've been keeping it warm."

"Do I need to get us some silverware? Wine glasses?" Harry pulled a green tablecloth out of the closet and headed back toward the row of drawers along the opposite wall.

"The wine glasses are in the upper cabinet there on the right."

"And silverware?"

Pulling out the glass platter and basket, she laughed. "We're not using utensils tonight."

"Oh?" He blinked in amazement. "Why not? How will we eat?"

"The same way man did in early times." She smiled back at him and trotted over to the door, balancing the platter and basket on one arm. "Come help me over here."

Harry did as instructed, with glasses, cloth, and wine in tow, and followed her out across the garden to the willow tree. "The garden looks like it's shaping up a bit, now that you've taken the pruning shears to everything. It's grown up so thick, everything blooming."

"You think so?" She passed him a grateful smile, winking at him. "I still have a ways to go before I get this place back in shape, but I can do it hard and fast when I get the notion."

He flushed, nearly stumbling with the food.

Thelma stifled a smile. *Thick … Hard … Fast … Blooming.* What was wrong with her? Every word conjured visions of Harry settled neatly between her thighs. Pent-up energy? The fact that she'd now gone for a little over a day without a man's hands on her or inside her? She placed the food on the ground and shook out the cloth. "Grab a corner and let's spread this open."

He picked up the glasses and wine, placing them in the middle of the tablecloth. "I'll get the food over here too." She didn't fail to notice his eyes lingering on her a little longer, especially staring at her crotch. Yes, she'd picked the perfect dress. With a light tug on the hem, she sat down next to Harry, using every means to maintain some pretense of modesty.

"Good thing you've got lots of property and all kinds of hedges and plants to give you some privacy back here." Harry pulled a corkscrew out of his pocket and began removing the cork. "Luckily I remembered we'd need this thing." He gave her a wink and turned the device. Thelma watched the corkscrew sink into the cork, imagining Harry's cock sinking into her. She shook her head, blinking her eyes a few times.

"What's the matter, babe? You seem mighty intent and interested in my getting a cork out of a wine bottle. How about unwrapping the food." He laughed and gave the top a hard pull, twisting and turning. Pop! "I think we have it now. Hand me your glass and I'll fill you up."

"Yes, I can't wait until you do … all the way now." Her heart nearly caught in her throat.

"Thirsty little thing, aren't you, girl?" Harry shot her a bright smile.

"You really wouldn't believe how thirsty I really am, Harry."

"Long day in the hot sun wears a body out, doesn't it?" He finished pouring himself a glass, and took a sip. "Ah, that's the spirit! Now for a toast to new beginnings."

Harry clinked his glass with Thelma's. "Mmm, nice, wet, and smooth over the tongue."

Thelma took a sip, running her tongue over the rim of the glass— nice, slow, and seductive—while Harry gave her a concentrated stare.

"Good? Nice vintage, I think." He took another sip, rubbing a finger over her hand, his gaze never leaving her.

The sun faded just a little from the sky, leaving behind a soft, pink cast. "Now I want you to try this and see if you like it."

Harry took the glass from her as she unwrapped the platter and basket.

"What have we here?" He eyed the food, grinning. "What neat little piles. I've never seen a spread quite like this before."

"Open your mouth." She'd picked up a tiny slice of bread, gathered up a bit of spiced meat, and placed the morsel in his mouth."

"This is very good. I like it!" He chewed, savoring the flavors until he swallowed. "How interesting. I've never tasted these spices before."

"It's a dish I learned to prepare while I was away." She smiled and picked up another slice of bread, this time gathering up some seasoned shredded vegetables. "Try this." As she placed the bite into his mouth, the food started dripping. He lifted his hand to push everything into his mouth, leaving his finger covered with remnants of food. Not wasting any time, she grabbed his hand and placed his whole finger in her mouth. With soft, licking and sucking movements, she cleaned off the remainder of the food.

Harry's eyes widened as he swallowed. He blinked a few moments and grinned. "Well, that felt …"

"Strange, yes?"

"I must say, that's quite a way to eat, now." He threw his head back and laughed. "Now it's my turn." Mimicking her former movements, he offered her a tasty tidbit.

"You're right, this does taste good!" A tiny bit of food stuck to her upper lip, and before she licked it off, Harry leaned forward, flicking his tongue lightly over her lips.

"You learn fast, darling!" She let out a giggle, and gave her lips a light rub with her finger.

He settled back down beside her, propped up on one elbow. After taking a sip of wine, he treated himself to another slice of bread and a vegetable from a new, colorful pile. "The food is so good, Thelma. Remind me why we haven't eaten like this before."

"I don't know." She sipped slowly from her wine glass. "I guess I just wanted to try something a little different, see if you'd like it."

"I like it." He offered her another bite. "It's a … How should I say it? A romantic way to dine, feeding each other like this. You see it in films, but I've never done it in real life."

She considered his words. Had he not engaged in tender moments when he used to date? Did he and his wife not enjoy each other to the fullest while they were married? At least her plan seemed to be working. Thelma sniffed the breeze and gazed around her. The air had grown cooler, with the sky fading from rosy pink to light lavender to charcoal gray. With each passing minute, the darkness and sounds of night deepened, and a bright moon lit the sky. Harry stretched out and reclined back.

Thelma, stretched out beside him, and began running her finger over his lips, finally taking the opportunity to kiss him. His lips felt so soft under hers, and his tongue wet and warm as it flirted with hers in a playful dance. She traced around the outside of his ear, and ran her tongue over his earlobe. The wine had kicked in, full-force, decreasing her inhibitions. Her fingers played over his chest, feeling the tips of his nipples under the shirt. Round and round her fingers moved, over one, then the other. He reached out and guided her face toward his so their lips met again. While they explored each other's mouths in another fiery round of play, her hand flowed over his abdomen, landing softly between his thighs.

His thigh twitched. He let out a sigh. Her heart pounded. Closing her eyes, she let herself drown in his kiss. Her fingers gently caressed the mound of flesh, which became more prominent, despite the loose clothing. Just when he hardened a bit more, she slowed down, and propped up on one elbow again.

"Harry, how long has it been since you've indulged in a moment like this?"

He cleared his throat, bending up one knee as he tried to relieve his discomfort. "Mmm, about five years, I believe. Why?"

"Do you miss it, being able to enjoy a woman anytime you want? You were married for such a long time."

"It was okay."

"Just okay?" Thelma thought for a moment, not wanting to sound too intrusive. "I know this is a little personal, but why was it just okay?"

A few seconds of silence seemed like an eternity as Thelma waited for an answer, while the sound of crickets filled the evening air with a rhythmic melody.

"Believe it or not, we really didn't enjoy intimacy all that much." He turned his head in her direction. In the moonlight she detected a grim expression on his lips. "Anne was actually rather frigid. Didn't like for anyone to touch her. So given that issue, we didn't spend too much time in the bedroom."

"Did you ever try to remedy that—make her feel special, try a different approach?"

He let out a long, deep breath. "You know, I don't remember exactly." He grasped her hand in his and gave a light squeeze. "Most likely not, now that I think about it. I think I just finally gave up."

"That's too bad. Do you wish you'd never married at all then?"

"I don't know, Thelma. That's a good question." He sat up suddenly. "As far as the bedroom goes, it's my experience and understanding that women simply aren't that active, or even interested, during those, you know, special moments. And Anne seemed to drive that point home."

"Do you ever have fantasies of what it might have been like if your marriage had been different, or if you'd been with someone else?"

"Good lord, woman, what questions!" By the tone of his voice, his patience level appeared a little stressed, so she backed down. He continued. "We've never really had these kinds of talks before. Why are you so interested in them now?"

"Oh, Harry, we've been friends for a little over a year now. It's part of getting to know someone, becoming closer, understanding them better. Nothing more, and I definitely didn't mean to upset you." She sat up, too, and gave him a soft, quick kiss, while her other hand pushed him lightly back down on the ground. "If it's too unpleasant for you, we don't have to talk about this anymore."

For the next few moments, they said nothing. Thelma spent this quiet time rubbing her hand in light circles over his abdomen, hoping to make him feel comfortable again, while collecting her wits in the meantime.

Her thoughts raced. Do I dare test him now? He didn't seem to mind her touching his most private area, and had even sounded a little exasperated when she'd removed her hand. Anne's cold, reluctant nature had not squelched his desire for a woman's hand touching him in all the right places, allowing his body to enjoy a good, hard release.

What the hell? Enough stalling. Her hand crept slowly back down to his crotch, and this time, she threw all caution to the wind. Taking in a deep breath, she slid her hand slowly inside his pants, running her fingers over the soft pubic hair, until she'd grasped what she so desperately sought.

He let out a soft gasp, and lifted his hips a little, but said nothing. The sound from the crickets had reached full crescendo, and the light scent of lilacs perfumed the air. Thelma rested her cheek on his chest for just a moment, so she could hear the rapid beating of his heart. His breathing had grown a little faster. With eager fingers, she toyed with a plump tip on top of a stiff shaft. Thick pre-cum in his slit oozed its way out and over her fingertip. She pressed a little deeper into his soft flesh, but not so much as to cause pain. His hips shifted ever so slightly. With gliding movements, her hand ran up and down his full length. Under a blossoming cock rested a set of balls waiting for her to squeeze, which she did, gently. He let out a soft groan.

"Thelma." Her name came out of his mouth as a light whisper, but an earnest one.

She remained silent, but her fingers spoke volumes to his flesh, commanding him in ways she was certain his wife had never ventured to attempt. Stopping again seemed a cruel thing to do to a man she cared so much about. They'd never been physically intimate until now, and whether or not he'd been with other women since his wife's death, she couldn't hazard a guess.

The cock between her fingers had reached its full size, and she knew by the sound of his breathing and the intermittent moans, he didn't have much longer to go. Rubbing around the ridge of his tip finally became too much, and with one last, soft grunt from him, he covered her fingers with his lust.

His breathing softened, and at that moment, she sensed a relief from him so profound, so calm. She whispered in his ear. "Good?"

"Yeah, very good." On his face, a light grin played at the corners of his mouth.

Her hands didn't move, but stayed right where they were, just holding him. She laid her head on his chest again, and both of them remained together for several minutes before they disengaged and spent the remainder of the evening in light conversation, picking up where they'd left off before her trip to The House. Later in the evening, Harry kissed her good-bye, climbed into his prized Silver Ghost, and made his way back home.

Thelma closed the door behind him, and leaned against it to get her breath. He hadn't let on, acting like they fondled each other every day, but had she gone too far? Suddenly a twinge of panic set in. Did she now seem like a common trollop? The smile on his face after his lusty release indicated otherwise, but then again, she knew how weak men became anytime sex figured into the equation. For the moment, they thought you were the most wonderful creature in the world, but afterward, you became a mere slut. Would he call her again? Should she call him next?

With a doubtful heart, she made her way back upstairs to her room, where she proceeded to slip off her dress and shoes. Not bothering to throw on a nightgown, she pulled the covers back and crawled beneath the sheets, feeling the cool fabric against her skin. No matter how hard she tried, her eyes refused to close. The grin on Harry's face still popped up in her head, and the touch of her fingers over his flesh made her tingle all over again.

He hadn't reciprocated her advances, but perhaps their conversation had told her all she needed to know about his stance in the bedroom. Did Anne really suffer from frigidity, or was poor, dear Harry merely a lousy lover? Thelma smiled. Oh, she possessed the means to make any man melt at her touch. House staff had seen to that. But would she be able to get him to pop the question? Only time held the answer. Tonight was a big start; tomorrow she'd give some more thought on a specific plan. At last, her eyes closed, and she fell fast asleep.

CHAPTER 4

Thelma held the cup under her nose and took another whiff, savoring the aroma of hot, fresh coffee. Mornings like this, in her robe, sitting in her kitchen and gazing out the back window, usually filled her with a sense of contentment. Outside the sun promised another hot, bright day, giving her more time to work on her gardens. But at the moment thoughts of her garden became peppered with visions of Harry and their romantic interlude the night before. She lifted her cup for another sip, hoping to push aside memories of him long enough to decide what area of the back lawn needed the most work. The hydrangeas had shaped up beautifully under her skilled hand, and after much thought, she determined the rose bushes needed the most immediate attention.

The tendrils of the willow tree flowing in the wind caught her attention, flooding her brain with images of the previous evening. *Damn!* She shook her head, swallowing some more coffee as she struggled to make them go away. No matter how much she fought them off, they returned with a vengeance, the smile of relief on his face still just as clear as if he were with her now.

A loud knock at the door made her jump. With a light frown, she padded toward the door. Who on earth wanted to see her this morning? Surely not one of the neighbors, most of whom didn't even know she'd returned yet. Had one of them seen her car yesterday?

When she opened the door, her eyes fell on Harry, leaning against the doorframe, his face covered with a boyish grin. His tan newsboy cap rested easily on his head, and the matching slacks and light sweater brought out the deep, rich pecan-brown of his eyes.

"There's my angel!" The grin on his face widened.

"Harry!" Thelma blushed, and stepped back, clutching her robe tighter around her. "I-I wasn't expecting anyone today, this early. I know I look a sight!"

He lingered in the doorway a few seconds longer before following her motions to come on inside the house. "You always look beautiful to me, Thelma."

"You've never seen me in my … looking like this." She ran her fingers though her hair, pushing some scraggly locks back into place.

"Tut, tut, my dear." He chucked her under the chin before giving her lips a light kiss. "Again, you're my angel, and I think you're a vision no matter what."

"How generous of you." A faint smile lit her lips. Hopefully he didn't detect too much nervousness. The pounding of her heart triggered a fear of fainting, but she took a deep breath and regained some composure. "How about some coffee? I made a fresh pot."

"Nothing would be better than sharing some coffee with you." He followed her into the kitchen and sat down in the chair across from hers.

"What brings you out this morning, pray tell?" Thelma gave him a quizzical glance and poured him a fresh cup of coffee.

"I don't know. The day was so pretty, and I did get some good sleep last night. I don't know about you, but I haven't rested that good in I don't know how long."

"Good to know." She sat the cup down in front of him before dropping back down in her own chair.

The smile left his face, and his voice took on a more serious tone. "To tell you the truth, Thelma, once I got up this morning, my first thoughts were of you. I couldn't wait to get over here and ask you to come to dinner with me tonight, at Rolando's."

"You couldn't wait to get over here to ask me that?" She kicked him lightly under the table. "Couldn't you have just telephoned? It would have been much easier, you know, instead of walking two blocks over here."

He grasped her hand in his, entwining his thick fingers through her delicate ones, giving her a light squeeze. She grew wet at the sight of him.

"Don't scold me, angel! I'd much rather see you than speak on the phone, where I can't see your smile, or drown in your eyes."

"Harry, you do carry on!" She shook her head laughing. "If I go with you to Rolando's, can we still go to Willow Pointe, like we'd originally planned?" Everyone knew the best places to make out with a lover resided at Willow Pointe, filled with thick willow trees, as well as a secret hideaway or two.

"Our night wouldn't be complete without that. And from the looks of the weather today, tonight will be a perfect evening to go to Willow Pointe, walk by the water, rest under the trees."

Let me have my way with you, or perhaps you have your way with me. Thelma kept a light grin on her face, pretending to listen.

"… and as you know Rolando's has that special back room where we can indulge our palates with not only good food, but some of the best wine around."

"It's been a while, now, since we've enjoyed that back room." She placed her hand on his arm. "But I'm quite sure his vintages are no better than yours."

"You flatter me, dear girl. Yes, I have to admit, though, I do manage to get my hands on some pretty rare bottles when my luck is running high."

Hopefully luck will be running high and hot for both of us tonight at Willow Pointe. She returned his smile. "Maybe I'll even try something different on the menu, instead of my usual veal cutlet."

"I think the duck terrine might be a wise choice."

"Yes, something refreshing and new." She leaned over in his direction, grinning. "Might be something we can both nibble on."

"I'd be happy just nibbling on those sweet fingers of yours." He lifted her hand to his lips, tenderly kissing her fingers.

She closed her eyes a moment, imagining how he might nibble other parts of her.

Harry lifted his cup and drained off the last of the coffee. "So how about I pick you up tonight at six o'clock? I'll call Rolando's for reservations when I get back home."

"That would be great." She patted his arm and finished off her own cup.

"Excellent, then it's a date!" He got up from the chair and headed toward the hallway.

Thelma followed him to the door. He turned around and caught her in his arms, landing a soft, lingering kiss on her lips. His tongue still tasted of coffee as he slipped it into her mouth and showered her with wet, warm caresses. "I'll be antsy all day, just waiting for six o'clock to roll around." He held her head between his large hands and stood still, staring hard into her eyes.

She cleared her throat, and tried to retain a casual demeanor, hoping he wouldn't detect the hard beating of her heart beneath her robe. "I'm sure you'll find something to occupy your time." She opened the door and ushered him out, watching until he'd made it to the end of the drive, at which point he threw up his hand in one last wave.

Excellent! Thrilled he'd made the next move after her bold attempt the night before, she felt her confidence climb once again. Though the upcoming meal at Rolando's filled her with excitement, going to Willow Pointe afterward made her all the more eager. Would he be as bold with her tonight as she'd been with him last night? As she turned to walk back to the kitchen, enslaved in lustful thoughts, thick moisture had already seeped down to her cleft.

Unable to take her mind off Harry and their upcoming date, she turned around and headed upstairs to check out her wardrobe again. Thoughts of what she'd wear became an obsession. What other dresses did she have in her closet—ones well-suited for teasing an eager man's imagination?

After rummaging through the rack of clothes, she spied an appropriate outfit for the evening. This dress was similar in length and style to the previous one she wore, and might get darling Harry in the mood more quickly tonight. Since the ice had been broken regarding their physical intimacy, she hoped the shortness of it would only entice his fingers to start roaming once they rested together, snuggled in each other's arms, somewhere at Willow Pointe. In her opinion, the sooner the better. She smiled, changing into her gardening clothes before heading downstairs to the kitchen to pick up her tools. At least gardening solved the issue of making time pass more quickly.

Around four o'clock, she returned to the kitchen and replaced her tools on one low shelf in the closet. She scurried up the steps, two at a time, and entered the bathroom, spending extra time to bathe and pamper her skin before fixing her hair. At last she swung open the closet door, grabbed the dress she'd decided on earlier, and slid into a spectacular satin sheath of burgundy, complete with elegant beadwork and a daring hemline. With great care, she applied face powder, rouge, eye makeup, and mascara, ending with a matching shade of lipstick. Digging through her jewelry box, she pulled out a set of earrings and necklace.

Just as she'd slipped into a pair of matching pumps, the doorbell rang. The clock on the mantel showed exactly six o'clock. Whisking up a bottle of tea-rose cologne on her dressing table, she poured out some fragrance and rubbed it into her cleavage. She grabbed a matching handbag from her chest of drawers and headed out of her room.

CHAPTER 5

Harry stood, leaning in the doorway, dressed in a pristine pair of gray slacks, a white, collared shirt, and a coordinating sports jacket. The masculine scent of his Knize Ten cologne filled the space between them. Thelma used every ounce of restraint to not pull him inside and ravage his body, right then and there, in the middle of the hallway. He gave her a succulent kiss on the lips, before slipping in his tongue to flirt with hers. The taste of him nearly sent her swooning. Luckily his strong embrace held her tight, keeping her erect instead of letting her slump down to the floor.

He stood back a moment, inspecting her dress. "Well, I see you're wearing another fashionable beauty on that sweet frame of yours." With a light touch, he ran his fingers through some of the beadwork near the top, grazing the tops of her breasts as he moved from one side of the dress to the other. A hot flash of heat ricocheted down between her thighs, and Thelma felt her cheeks flush. Had he meant to touch her that way? He'd never seemed too interested in the details of her clothing before—not so much that it made him reach out and caress her the way he just did.

His smile seemed amiable enough. However, she swore a lusty gleam peeked through his warm, brown eyes. Maybe he was warming up after all, testing the waters as he began to tear down his own wall of reserve. Thelma had always detected a steadfast politeness at the root of all his flirty gestures, somehow keeping him in check. Perhaps he needed permission to let the more sensual side of himself take root and blossom, and her awakening of his most lusty urges the night before appeared to be working. Yes, tonight may be promising after all.

"So I take it we're ready to head over to Rolando's?" He indicated toward his car.

"You bet. I've been looking forward to it all day."

"You and me both, my girl." Harry opened the door, and they made their way to his treasured Silver Ghost.

Little did he know how much she loved that car, too, and riding in it with him whenever they went out had made their times together even better. Being seen with Harry, in general, had given her a smug sensation, viewing the longing glances from other women as they wandered through quaint shops, hand in hand, or sat across from one another in restaurants. Harry, handsome in every way, managed an air of quiet authority and a distinguished nature, while at the same time showering her with warm affection.

The car hummed down the street, leaving behind the majestic Victorian neighborhood, toward the hustle and bustle of downtown. He glanced over at her for just a moment as they drove. "So, hon, what exactly are you planning to do with yourself, now that your teaching job is over, and you're back here now?"

"Huh?" His question startled her, catching her off guard. "Oh, you know, I hadn't really given it much thought." In her mind, her intentions surrounded one thing, and one thing only: giving her relationship with Harry a good jolt forward.

He nodded and squeezed her hand a little before rubbing his thumb lightly over her fingers. "Let me know if you need any help with finding something you'd like to do."

Thelma clutched her handbag with a frown. His words rang with a sour note. The fact that his words hadn't alluded to a future together bothered her most of all. Filled with a sense of panic, she struggled for an answer. At last she came up with a mild excuse. "It's true, my teaching stint is over now, and since I resigned from my position at the high school, I guess I'm free to make an occupational change if I want to."

"True enough." He smiled at her. "You know what, sweetheart? I won't burden you with any more questions about this tonight. I just want us to have fun … like we did last night."

His fingers wiggled their way through hers, filling her with a small glimmer of hope. So her first attentions to his hidden male urges had not been totally lost on him, after all. From their brief discussion, she really needed to come up with a hard and fast plan to get him seeing things her way—and that didn't include taking jobs or making career choices.

Thelma tried to calm her nerves by thinking about the night ahead. At least Harry seemed sensitive enough to honor their Saturday night treks to the city, which had become almost a ritual before she'd slipped off to The House. She rested her head against the back of the seat, thinking how weekend nights always buzzed with people coming downtown after a long, hard workweek, seeking solace in fine dining and jazzy music. Under the spell of a heady Charleston dance, slender girls in sleek, fringed dresses put their cares aside for a brief moment and kicked up their heels with giddy excitement.

As the classy Silver Ghost carried them to the heart of the city, Thelma surveyed her surroundings and took a deep breath, feeling an almost electrical tingle from the frenetic energy of passing cars, people on the sidewalks, and the twinkling lights from merchant establishments. The anticipation of it all heightened her excitement, soaring her carnal desire for Harry higher than ever.

He turned to her and smiled. "Seems like we're in for a crowd tonight, from the look of things."

"Seems like it." She reached over and clasped his hand resting on the seat beside her. "But it's always fun to see everyone so happy. I don't know about you, but I get a charge out of watching everybody and just being a part of it all."

"I agree. Nothing like immersing yourself into the moment, letting it carry you away for a while."

Finally they pulled up to a vacant parking space in front of a row of storefronts. The name "Rolando's" covered the large picture window of the restaurant, and through the large wooden doors, people had already started filing in. Giani Rolando had established this upscale eatery forty years ago, when his family had emigrated from Europe. Since old Giani's death ten years earlier, his son Frank had taken over the business, along with his uncles. They still held true to the restaurant's original mission: to showcase fine food and drink for customers who could pay the money.

Harry opened his door and stepped around to assist Thelma from the passenger's side of the car. "After you, my dear." With some awkward moves, she managed to slide her legs out of the car. This dress, like the one last night, presented both good and challenging points. The good point, it seemed to entice Harry. The bad point—well, there was no bad point, especially when she spied him trying to catch a fast peek between her legs as he offered his arm for assistance. He grinned and, lacing his arm through hers, led her into Rolando's.

The aroma of fresh-cooked veal and savory sauces wafted from the kitchen, filling her nose, and making her hungrier than ever. Rows of tables with white linen tablecloths filled the main room, and wrought-iron chandeliers with pale, golden globes lit up the room in a soft light, adding a romantic ambience. Lovers, tucked away at tables in the far corners, whispered to each other in hushed tones, while families taking up the larger tables in the middle of the room shared jokes and fun tidbits, breaking out in loud laughter.

Harry seemed oblivious to the activity going on around him, head up, eyes straight ahead, moving forward until they reached a small wooden door located off to the right side of the bar. He opened the door, gently propelling Thelma through. This was the back room, which hummed with just as much activity as the front side, except the patrons here enjoyed all kinds of alcoholic beverages with their savory meals.

After pulling out a chair for Thelma at one of the tables in the back corner, Harry seated himself across from her. Within seconds, a server arrived to take their order.

"Good evening, and what can I get for you wonderful guests tonight?" The gentleman, dressed in a smart uniform, smiled graciously.

"I'll have the gnocchi with the meat sauce, and do you mind if we break from Italian tradition and serve my angel here your infamous duck terrine, if you still have any available?"

"Sir, we'd be delighted. As you know, Rolando's is known for all kinds of cuisine, not just Italian."

"Wonderful!" Harry gave the server a broad smile. "My lady and I are feeling a little adventurous tonight, and wanted to try something different." He gave Thelma a quick wink and turned back to the server. "Can you bring us the best vintage you have in the house? One that will go well with our meal? Money is no object."

The server's eyes twinkled. "We'll be only too happy to make sure you get the best bottle. I'm sure from your experience with us before, you know we don't skimp when it comes to quality."

"I know it well." Harry kept his eyes on the server, while finding Thelma's hand, enveloping it with his own.

"Very good, sir. I'll get your request in to our chefs and bring out your wine." With a humble nod of his head, he turned around, heading toward the kitchen.

Harry focused his full attention on Thelma, eyes glowing. "You are such a vision of loveliness tonight. I can hardly take my eyes off you." He leaned over closer to her face. "I thought about you all day long. Did you know that?" Again, he ruffled through the beaded fringe dangling at the top of the dress.

The warm, tickling touch of his fingers hardened her nipples. On a wicked impulse, Thelma slipped off her shoe, and stretched out her leg hidden underneath the tablecloth. The lights had been dimmed for dinner hours, and being seated at the farthest corner of the room afforded some semblance of privacy. She lifted her foot, landing the tips of her toes right in the center of Harry's tempting crotch.

The astounded expression on his face rewarded her gesture, and she fought back the urge to laugh, lightly glossing her tongue over her lips. With slow, gentle rotations of her ankle, she pressed her toes against him, grinding lightly over his most sensitive area. The gradual coloration of his face from normal flesh tones to a light scarlet sent a smile across her lips.

"And I've been thinking about you all day, too, Harry." She puckered her lips and blew him an imaginary kiss from across the table.

He craned his neck around, scanning the rest of the room from right to left. Comfortable that all the other diners seemed engrossed in their own personal affairs, he flashed Thelma a smug grin. "I also thought about you all night long … all night long." With a deep chuckle, he blew her an airy kiss.

She straightened up, the smile fading as quickly as it had come. Confused, Harry gave her a puzzled look.

"Your wine, my friends." Their server stood close and placed two wine glasses on the table before reaching in his pocket for a corkscrew. He glanced at the pair, first one then the other. "Am I interrupting anything? If I have, I'm so sorry." With a quick flourish of the wrist, he applied the sharp tip of the corkscrew into the top of the cork, and began twisting the tool until he had buried the whole shaft inside. Meanwhile, Thelma and Harry kept their eyes glued to the top of the bottle, the color rising in both their cheeks. With a sharp *pop,* the server removed the cork and filled the glasses with a rich, burgundy vintage.

Harry picked up one of the glasses, placing it in front of Thelma. "Thank you." He glanced up at the server. "You were mighty handy with that that corkscrew, the way you just plunged that tip right in and began screwing, um, unscrewing." He sighed in defeat, tapping his fingers on the table, lost for words.

The server narrowed his eyes as his gaze bore into a confused

Harry. "Well, sir, let's just say I have lots of practice, um, screwing or unscrewing." He let out a light laugh. His expression turned into one of solemnity. "Your meals should be out shortly." He gave Harry a light pat on the shoulder and left the table.

Thelma took a sip of her wine, not forgetting where her foot had remained rooted. She rotated her ankle again. "Do you think he knew what we were doing?"

Harry nearly choked on his wine. He rubbed his finger over the rim of the glass for a moment. "Oh, probably not. Anyway, he's most likely seen worse back here than what we were doing." In an uncharacteristic move, he dipped his index finger in the glass, swirling the wine around. Before he could place his finger in his mouth, Thelma intercepted with lightning speed, encasing it in her own mouth, giving the wet tip a teasing wash with her tongue.

"Thelma, you naughty …!" He closed his eyes and stifled a light laugh.

Within minutes, their meals came out, artfully displayed on china plates. The server placed napkins and silverware beside each one. "Will there be anything else?" He gave them a pleasant grin.

"Um, no, I don't think so." Harry smiled up at him and turned back to face Thelma. "Well, darling, are you going to let me taste a tiny nibble of that luscious looking duck terrine you have there?"

She eyed the pâté resting on a bed of bright green spinach leaves. Tiny, thin-cut slices of sourdough bread surrounded the plate. "This looks interesting. I didn't know it came prepared this way."

"Go on and try some. Or do you want me to taste it first?" Harry reached for his knife.

"I'll let you try some first." She picked up the knife and loaded some of the spiced meat on a slice of bread and held the bite in front of his lips.

He leaned forward, consuming everything between her fingers. Just as they'd done the previous night, he grasped her fingers and began suckling the tips. Thelma laughed, enjoying Harry's frisky side.

"I tasted yours, now I'll let you taste mine." She arched her eyebrow in surprise as Harry dipped his spoon into his dish of gnocchi, ladling up a small sample. He brought the spoon to her mouth.

She turned her gaze to the ceiling and grinned. "M-m-m, this is good."

"My darling, the only thing I can say is let's enjoy our meal here for a bit, and then head on out to Willow Pointe before it gets too dark."

"I agree." Thelma nodded, feigning a serious expression.

Teasing Harry, she lifted up her foot, stroking the space between his thighs one last time. Harry winked, and turned his attention back to his own plate, concentrating with mock interest on his gnocchi. After an hour of light conversation, the two finished up their meal at Rolando's, and drove off to Willow Pointe, trading the bustle of city nightlife for a serene country atmosphere. The pale orange-pink sky and a soft breeze created a romantic atmosphere, one suitable for flirting and light fondling.

The car wound around country roads until Harry turned right on a narrow dirt trail, made wider by the use of more cars than bikes. The lake on the left twinkled in the dusky light, with water lapping at the edge of the land. True to its name, large willow trees dotted the landscape of Willow Pointe. Thelma gazed all around, determining how much privacy she and Harry might have.

Memories of her time outdoors at The House came flooding back. Even when she and her attendant had engaged themselves in naughty acts outside, no one had cared or paid much attention. After all, The House directors had created those grounds for such carnal merry-making. Unfortunately, Willow Pointe didn't have House staff permitting such behavior, so she and Harry would need to use discretion. He wound the car around one last turn, bringing the vehicle to a stop in front of an enormous willow tree, full and thick, with its tendrils dipping into the lake.

"You like this spot?" He turned to her, smiling.

"From what I can see, it looks like we're pretty much alone right now." She nodded with approval.

"I think we hit it here at the right time. Everyone's still in town whooping it up with a band and some hidden drink." With a final squeeze of her hand, he got out of the car. Not waiting for formalities, Thelma opened the door and slipped out too. In just a few moments, she and Harry made their way to the large, old tree. In one arm, he carried a thick quilt. When they reached the tree, they spread the quilt over the ground and settled down.

"These branches are thicker than what I have in my garden at home." Thelma sat in awe of the tree, marveling at how much the branches sheltered them from view.

He sniffed the air. "I'm sure being around water doesn't hurt matters, either."

"I loved the meal tonight. Thanks for taking me there." She rested her head on his shoulder.

He patted his tummy, smiling. "Rolando's is always my favorite spot to go. Never had a bad meal there—ever."

They sat together in silence for a long while, each one looking out over the water. The sky had lost its warm colors, having changed into a cool, silvery gray. In another hour or so, they'd find themselves steeped in darkness. Thelma's mind turned to thoughts of doing more than just sitting on a quilt, gazing at the water like silly school kids. Had their special interlude made any impact on him at all? He'd seemed receptive to her bold, flirty footwork under the tablecloth. Now she craved some flirty finger-work he might shower on her sensitive clit, which now thrummed with an intolerable ache. Nice and easy, she rubbed his back lightly with her fingers, sensing him relax with every stroke.

Her lips brushed against his ear. "So tell me, Harry, and be honest, which meal did you like best? The one we ate last night under my willow tree, or the one tonight at Rolando's?"

A light breeze blew, ruffling is hair. His eyes narrowed a moment as he thought. Turning to her, he answered, "The thing I really like best, Thelma, is spending time with you. The meals are only a small part of the equation." He ran his finger softly up and down against her cheek. "I think the real question should be, what have I enjoyed most about the meals?"

She sensed the heat flaring up in her cheeks, and her stomach lurched for a quick second. But she played dumb just a little in order to hear what he might say next. "I don't know. What have you enjoyed the most about them? I mean, was there something that made them special or stand out in some way, their texture, their flavors?" Her eyes strayed off his and trailed back to the lake again. Out of the corner of her eye, she caught a glimpse of his face, with only the faintest hint of a grin to soften his otherwise intense expression.

"Textures and flavors—bah!" He clicked his tongue, pretending to chastise her. "I think you know exactly what I mean, Thelma. Let's just say our time together last night did something to me, something I haven't felt in a long time."

"Oh?" Her heart raced.

Without another word, he reached out and held her face between his hands, delivering a soft kiss on her forehead, her cheek, her lips. With a force and power she'd never seen from him before, he kissed her with greedy, desperation, plunging in his tongue for a teasing swim in her mouth. All of a sudden, he wrapped both arms around her, pressing her lightly down on the ground, never taking his lips from hers.

The very heat of him set her on fire as his hands stroked her hair, all the way down her neck. She let out a soft breath, heart beating with anticipation. Just as she'd hoped, he seemed intent on taking the lead tonight, and she possessed no mind to stop him. His fingers had found their way to her breasts, rubbing the nipples underneath her dress. A tingling sensation ignited her whole body, and deep within her slit, the tiny bundle of nerves at the top continued tapping out a silent rhythm, driving her mad.

The touch of his hands running up and down her right thigh gave her a jolt. He'd ventured close to the spot where she wanted him most. She let out a soft whimper. For a split second he stopped. The evening contained just enough light for her to see the lusty glint in his eye and the passionate look on his face. Luckily, they still had no other intruders tonight to disrupt their tender moment under the tree.

Not a word left his lips, and ever so softly, he slid his hand underneath her dress. Little by little he worked his way inside her panties, reaching behind and cupping her buttock. He delivered a light squeeze. She smiled to herself. He didn't have far to go; the short dress had indeed come in handy tonight.

"My turn, darling." He whispered the words in her ear. His hand moved away from her rear, making its way across her hip. In what seemed like an eternity, his fingers trekked over her soft mound and rested inside her slit.

Thelma stifled the urge to cry out. His soft, thick fingers coursed over her wet flesh, gently massaging her small lips, before sliding over and rubbing her large lips. Without thinking, she parted her thighs a bit wider. Just as she'd imagined during her fantasies of him at night, alone in her room, his touch shot her arousal level to the highest degree.

She closed her eyes and swallowed hard. Through the breeze, the sound of her own wetness met her ears as he explored her nether regions like one fascinated by a new toy. With utmost tenderness, he slipped in a finger deep inside her, smiling as her whimpers grew louder. The gentle gliding of his finger, back and forth, encouraged her to lift her hips in hopes of satisfying the carnal hunger.

"Oh, Harry … my God!" Her words came out raspy, panting.

"Good?" He slid out his finger, using her fluids as a lubricant, slipping over her clit, nice and easy, creating a heaviness that threatened to erupt in a series of spasms. "It's your moment tonight, sweetheart. Just relax and let go."

Another light cry came out of her mouth, and within seconds, the familiar tidal wave of release came crashing down over her, washing her away in a sea of pure bliss. The last few days of being home, free from the arms of her sensual House attendant, had plunged her body into erotic withdrawals. A gnawing emptiness inside had turned into torture, creating a desperate desire for someone to simply ravage her. As it turned out, dear Harry wasn't bad with those fingers, after all. His burst of confidence, with gentle, sure-handed moves, succeeded in morphing her fantasies into a new reality beyond her wildest dreams. The light kiss from his lips on her forehead did little to cool the storm still swirling in her body, but by this time, he'd slid his hand away from her pubic area.

"That's how you made me feel last night, Thelma. First, you filled me with tension, a pain that hurt so bad it felt good. Then, like a snake, your fingers struck, and I totally gave way." He smothered her with another round of kisses. "Did I make you feel the same way?" His eyes burned down on her, earnest, but tinted with a faint glimmer of uncertainty.

Recovering her breath, swept away by his bold move, she smiled up at him. "Let me say this, Harry, my own fantasies of us like this didn't compare to this moment."

"Your fantasies?" He moved his face close to hers. "You mean you've thought about moments like the one we just had?"

Didn't he? She sat up a moment, not sure whether to be amused or disappointed. "Like you said last night, we've never really talked about things like this before, so I know it's a little awkward. But now that we're on the subject, I'll just be honest with you. Yes, I've been fantasizing about us in this way for quite some time now."

"Why didn't you tell me this sooner?"

"Oh, for the love of God, Harry, that wouldn't have been proper at all!"

"Then do you think what you did last night was proper?"

Thelma opened up her mouth to answer, but stopped, suddenly at a loss for what to say. Any confidence she had up to this point vanished in an instant. She just stared at him, speechless.

A smile lit his face, and he kissed her again. "I didn't think you were improper at all, my dear." He wrapped his arms around her and held her close. "As a matter of fact, I'm glad you did what you did. It was liberating."

"Really?" Her words barely came out in a squeak. "I thought you'd taken me for a common harlot, but I just couldn't resist anymore."

"You awakened something in me, Thelma." He gazed toward the lake. "Like I said yesterday, Anne and I had no intimacy between us. It was just never there, and I'm not sure why."

"I'm not sure, either, because those hands of yours were pretty darn good." She whispered, "Harry, have you been with other women after Anne or even before her?"

He answered, "There were a couple of women before her but, I must admit, no one after her."

His voice became more intense. "How can I say this? You see, Anne's continued refusals, denying me, made me wonder about myself. As her husband, I guess I could have forced the issue, but something in me didn't feel right about that, either. Oddly enough, she almost made me feel ashamed for having any sexual desires at all. So several months after our marriage, our physical relations pretty much ended.

"After Anne died, I didn't know how to react to having sexual freedom at that point. I'd been in such a habit of going without, I still put any search for physical union out of my mind, choosing to shut myself off. I guess I thought it would just be easier that way. In the meantime, I felt like not only my body, but my soul was shriveling away and dying. I didn't dare let myself think about sex, even with you. I wouldn't do it, that's all." He hugged her tighter. "But last night you made me feel alive again, and showed me everything was okay."

Thelma didn't say anything. The full moon bathed the night in a gentle glow as they sat under the tree, shrouded by a cloak of weeping branches. Did those branches weep for his spousal alienation all those years, or did they weep for joy at his reacquaintance with the most basic of human nature, one he'd been forced to deny?

She knew Harry had struggled to tell her these things, secrets he'd no doubt hoped to hide away in the black recesses of his mind forever. Now her mission took on another dimension, one mirroring just what she'd learned during her stay at The House: to assist another in attaining strength and peace through sexual liberation.

Every admit experienced personal growth as each attendant revealed different exercises, all with the goal of showing the admit how to surrender and trust sexually. During those moments, she'd also learned to dominate and be dominated. She knew, beyond a doubt, the need to share her knowledge with Harry—all with the hope of his wanting her as a new, lifelong mate, one who understood his masculine cravings, and one who would never deny him.

"I think it's getting a little late. Let's get you home." He glanced at his watch before standing and offering Thelma his hands to help her up. In silence they gathered up the blanket and made their way back to the car.

Once inside, Harry started the engine, and the vehicle sped through the streets, winding the couple back to their stately, ornate Victorian neighborhood until they pulled up to Thelma's back door.

"I've had a wonderful time tonight." She plastered a quick kiss on his lips. "Your mouth tastes so good. I love kissing you."

"I love kissing *you*." He held her head in place, locking his mouth with hers, finishing off with a playful spar with her tongue. "Can I see you again soon? If not tomorrow, when?"

"How about we talk about it tomorrow and make some plans?" Her fingers played through his hair, smoothing back a few stray locks.

"I'll call you." He gave her a wink.

With one last smile, she got out of the car, walked to the door, and waved him off. With a quick turn of the key, she let herself inside.

The clicking of her heels on the hardwood floors shattered the silence in the house, but inside her head, memories of the evening clamored even louder. She headed up the stairs, thinking about her sensual evening with Harry. Once inside the bedroom, she whisked off her clothing, dropping everything into a laundry basket inside her closet. The clock in her room showed ten thirty, a decent enough time for a woman to be arriving home from an outing with a gentleman. She slipped off her earrings and necklace, replacing them back in their special compartment in her jewelry box before heading to the bed.

Standing there for a moment, she gazed all around, feeling the solitude more acutely than she had the previous nights. How she wished for Harry's presence. What she'd give to have him snuggled up, warm and close, feeling the heat from his body and the touch of his groin next to hers. Without warning, her sex quickened. Maybe once she got in bed and tried to sleep, she'd settle down.

She threw back the sheets and slid into bed, closing her eyes and adjusting her head on the pillow, trying with desperation to get comfortable. But try as she might, sleep avoided her like one with a disease. Continued thoughts of Harry heightened the ache between her thighs as she relived their moment under the willow tree, replaying each touch of his soft, thick fingers as they had spread her apart and coursed over her flesh with the gentlest touches of the most adept lover.

With her eyes closed, she bent her knees and separated her thighs, mimicking the action she'd done with him earlier, trying to recapture the exact sensation she'd felt as his finger had filled her darkest, hidden place. But imagination alone didn't satisfy her internal craving, and in Harry's absence, only one other alternative remained. She threw off the covers and, not bothering to put on a robe, crawled out of bed and headed downstairs to her special hideaway behind the living room walls.

The door gave a little creak as she turned the knob and stepped into the private world she'd created. She reached out and switched on the main overhead light to the room. The space paled in comparison to her large room upstairs, with the smallness creating a type of intimacy that immediately put her at ease and made her feel secure. She headed over to the chest of drawers and retrieved the strap-on phallus. Holding it up to the light, she examined the sleek, ebony surface, tracing around the well-pronounced ridge of the shapely tip. Even the top sported an indentation in the likeness of a man's slit. The more she rubbed over the glossy phallus, the wetter she became.

Going back upstairs didn't enter her mind at this point. Why wait? With a little jump, she landed on the bed and wriggled herself into a more comfortable position. No need for the oils, as her own fluids would do quite nicely. She held up the phallus closer to her face one last time, inspecting the girth before encircling her hand around it. If memory served her correctly, she almost swore Harry's cock was just as ample as the one she held. Now to see what he might feel like, buried deep inside her.

She closed her eyes and lifted her hips a little to get into a more receptive position. At last, she opened her thighs as wide as she could, inserted the tip of the phallus in her slit, and gave a gentle push. A light groan from her throat broke the silence in the room. The wine seemed to have caught up with her, too, creating a light ache in her pubic area. Nothing better than a good hard orgasm with a full bladder. Thelma smiled, sliding the thick phallus back and forth, using the finger of her other hand to work her clit.

Her hips writhed with each passing movement of the phallus between her legs, and the work of her finger over her slick button of nerves brought up thoughts of Harry's tongue teasing her, tasting every bit of her. In just a few moments, the area between her thighs erupted in a torrent of hard, rhythmic spasms. She cried out hard and loud. The burning sensation, which had started out as a light, pleasurable ache, stung so strong, she feared losing control and wetting herself.

Thelma quickly slid out the phallus and tiptoed to the bathroom, where she placed herself on the toilet and promptly relieved herself. The tinkling of water on water reminded her of some of the exercises her attendant had put her through, such as making her experience humiliation by relieving herself right before his eyes. As a reward for pleasing him, he'd graciously used his tongue to wipe her off, paying special attention to the top of her sex. Thoughts of his warm tongue, strong and wet, nearly drove her to another orgasm.

But lessons in pleasure with her attendant hadn't stopped at what most couples would call "ordinary pleasure." He'd taught her how to raise a man's lust to the boiling point, by permitting her to insert a small, heavy, perfectly smooth steel ball into the slit at the top of his penis. She'd maintained control with an attached chain, raising and lowering the ball, taking care to avoid its entrance into the bladder. When the ball slid up and down, over and over, the glassy look of sheer bliss in his eyes had given her a sense of power she'd never experienced before.

Just how far she'd ever go with Harry, using some of these techniques, she had no idea; for the moment, she knew it was time to turn up the heat on their new intimate trysts. He'd taken her out to a fine dinner, now she must reciprocate by preparing him just as good a meal—with an unusual dessert at the end. She wiped herself clean, cleansed and sanitized the phallus, and returned it to a special resting spot inside the chest of drawers. After straightening up the cover on the bed, she turned out the light and began the trek back to her bedroom. This time, sleep came easier than it had before.

CHAPTER 6

True to his word, Harry called the next day, arousing Thelma out of her sleep. The clock indicated ten o'clock. Had she slept that long? She tumbled out of bed, eyes half closed with sleep, and shuffled toward the phone in the hallway. Her hand fumbled for the receiver.

"Um, hello?" Her words came out in a tiny croak.

"Thelma, you little puss, did I get you out of bed?"

She rubbed her eyes with her other hand, trying to wake herself up more. "Oh, I was awake. I just hadn't gotten up yet." Clapping a hand over her mouth, she barely stifled a yawn.

"I think you're telling me stories, dear. I got you out of bed." He gave a light chuckle. "But I bet I can just imagine why you slept so well last night."

"Oh, you can, huh?" Her eyes popped wide open at his last comment.

"Well, darling, I promised I'd get in touch with you to see when we could get together again. I'm dying to see you, so let's get something planned."

Thelma said nothing, rousing her groggy mind.

"How about Friday night? I've got several things I need to do this week, and nights after work just won't work, I'm afraid."

"Yeah, Harry, that'd be fine. I understand … about during the week and all … yeah, this Friday'll be good."

"I'll miss you terribly in the meantime, you know."

She chuckled. "That's okay. I'll miss you too."

His tone changed, and he cleared his throat. "Hey, honey, remember us talking about you finding a new job soon?"

At this question, she straightened up, her body tense. Damn! Couldn't he just stop worrying about her and a new career path? "Yes, I think I do remember us talking about it briefly." The blood rushed to her temples as her irritation level rose higher. "What about it?"

"I just thought, in case you might start looking this week, I'm here to help you if you need me. You know that, my little sweet."

Out of sheer desperation to change the direction of the conversation, an idea hit her. "You know what, Harry, the more I think about waiting all the way 'til Friday night, the more I don't like it. Can't you make an exception, and let's maybe have dinner here on Wednesday? At least seeing each other during the middle of the week might help break things up, if you know what I mean."

She heard nothing but silence on the other end of the line.

Finally he spoke up. "Hmm, Wednesday? Darn it, I just remembered I had a meeting planned that evening. I'm not sure if I can reschedule it or not. Let's see."

She heard him rustling through some papers on the other end of the line. "C'mon, Harry, won't you at least consider it for me, just this once? Surely you can put the meeting off for another time. Maybe you can make it earlier in the day?"

"Does this mean that much to you, sweetheart?"

"It would mean the world to me. If you want, maybe we can see each other on Tuesday if Wednesday can't work." She tried to sound a little over desperate, hoping she'd convince him. "You're the boss, so you can always schedule meetings to suit yourself. No matter what, though, I promise I'll more than make it worth your while." There, that ought to get him thinking.

Except for some light breathing, she heard no response.

"Harry?"

"You know what, precious, if it means that much to you, I'll make sure I'll see you Wednesday. Why, you're right, I can always have the meeting on another day or at a different time. Besides, I do remember promising you could have more input on what we did together, didn't I?"

"You did, and I haven't forgotten." What a lie. She'd forgotten that much already, never intending to take him too seriously on such a suggestion.

"Very well, then, it's a date."

"Good. Can you come around six o'clock, then?"

"Well, I think I can make that time. No, I will make it, no question about it."

"Wonderful. I'll see you Wednesday."

"You most certainly will, doll. You take care in the meantime, and don't forget what we just talked about, now."

"Oh, I won't forget, with the way you keep reminding me and all." She let out light laugh, hoping irritation hadn't leaked into her tone too much.

After they hung up, Thelma trudged back across the hall to her bedroom again. She plopped herself on the bed and pulled the covers over her. For the moment, she felt a little tired. Trying to convince Harry to cancel a meeting to see her had stirred up uneasiness again. As she gazed up at the ceiling, keeping her eyes fixed on the small crystal chandelier dangling above, she took several deep, controlled breaths, trying desperately to think about her situation with him a little more. Without a doubt, she knew she possessed the ability to capture Harry's attention, but what about the capacity to capture his heart?

Could a heart—his heart—be captured? After all he'd experienced with Anne? With all his talk about finding a job, was he politely letting her know he preferred to remain a bachelor so he wouldn't have to endure another bad relationship, or worse yet, avoid permanent commitment for fear of losing the terrific sex between them? She knew one thing for sure, Wednesday's meal required a special touch. It needed to be simple, with the after-dinner activity as the main course—one he wouldn't forget easily. A plan to lure him into the room behind the living room still needed fleshing out, so for the next hour, one thought after another spun through her head as she mulled over the arts of seduction, especially the ones she'd learned at The House. Finally, she calmed her mind and decided to just let the evening unfold naturally. After all, she'd succeeded in seducing him in the garden, and he'd reciprocated the gesture out at Willow Pointe. Giving a chuckle, she slipped out of bed, put on her gardening clothes, and headed on downstairs to gather up her tools for a long day in the yard.

§§§

Wednesday came faster than she'd bargained for. Earlier that day, Thelma had purchased the items for dinner. After returning home, she decided to finish some more work on her plants before preparing dinner and getting ready for Harry's arrival.

Once in the kitchen, she busied herself with seasoning everything to perfection. The savory smell of cooking food restored her confidence. While she chopped lettuce, sliced radishes, and cut up the remainder of the vegetables for a salad, she suddenly realized Harry hadn't contacted her since their first conversation, leaving her wondering if he'd remember to come.

What if he forgot to show up? Should she have given him a quick call for a reminder? No, he'd always been as good as his word, never having stood her up or left her in a compromised situation. He'd be here. She shook off her worries, placing the last finishing touches on the meal before heading off to the "love room." This was the name she'd attached to the space that housed all her toys. Her eyes absorbed the sight of the room, the neat bed, dusted furniture, and she wandered to the chest of drawers, ensuring every toy rested in its spot. Tonight the plan included going all the way with Harry—without the use of toys; she'd save them for another time.

Upstairs in her room, she finished bathing and dressing. No need for a short dress tonight, but she did choose a smart blouse and skirt ensemble, in which the blouse showed a little more cleavage than normal. After applying the tea-rose fragrance between her breasts, she slipped on her shoes and made her way back down the stairs to check on dinner. Just as her feet hit the bottom step, the doorbell rang. Six o'clock sharp, as good as his word, Harry had arrived.

He stood in the doorway, casually dressed in a pair of khaki slacks and a pale argyle sweater, holding a bouquet of roses. In his other hand, he held a burlap bag, which obviously contained a bottle of wine. She breathed a sigh of relief. In all her hurrying about to get ready for the evening, she'd forgotten to chill some wine.

"You remembered!" Thelma smiled and rubbed his back with the palm of her hand as he passed into the entrance hall.

"Now, what makes you think I'd ever forget I'm supposed to spend an evening with you?" He chuckled, delivering a light kiss on the lips.

"Well, you could have gotten busy and simply forgotten about little ol' me." Thelma fluttered her eyelashes and flashed him a wide smile.

"Bah! Listen to you." He followed her into the kitchen. "As if you didn't know already, I've thought about nothing else but this evening, my dear."

"Oh?" She only hoped that, after tonight, his thoughts held nothing else but the vision of their bodies intertwined, locked together, with nothing between them but intense heat and the pounding of their hearts.

"Mmm, something smells good!" He took in a deep breath, closed his eyes, and smiled. "So what's the wonderfulness I have to look forward to tonight?"

"Fresh salmon, seasoned fried potatoes, and a refreshing green salad." She turned to him and rubbed his back again. "I hope that's enough."

"I should say so." He'd placed the bottle of wine and the roses on the counter. "Just feasting my eyes on you fills me up—to my very soul!" Reaching out, he caught her arm and pulled her into his embrace, smothering her lips with a flurry of kisses. The longer his mouth engaged hers in a playful, flirty round of lovemaking, the closer and harder he pulled her into him, until they both united, bodies pressed tightly against each other.

Thelma found herself taking in every breath he exhaled, letting his heat course through her, igniting every nerve, consuming every muscular fiber. Through his slacks, she felt the fullness of him teasing the inside of her cleft as their thighs made complete contact. For a moment, time stood still and the world, in that moment, seemed so perfect, glowing rosy and golden in a strong love, enfolding both of them in a strong embrace.

When his kisses stopped, she found herself staring up into his eyes, those rich, pecan-brown eyes, smiling and glowing with affection. Or was it just plain lust? At any rate, she didn't mind right now. If this interlude foreshadowed the later events of the evening, they were right on track.

"Can I help you set the table, and can you get me a vase to put the roses in?" His words fell soft and warm against her ears.

"Sure, I'll get everything out, and if you don't mind, just place the dishes, glasses, and silverware on the table. I have a beautiful crystal vase in the china cabinet in the dining room." She pulled away, with some reluctance, and trotted off to get the vase. Within minutes, the table held a complete setting for two, gleaming with fine china, crystal goblets, and sterling silver. The silver candlesticks winked at her from the side stand across the room. She placed them on the table, inserted cream-colored tapers, and lit the wicks. Nothing created a mood for a romantic evening like the soft, golden glow of candlelight. Harry helped carry the food to the dining room.

"I'm sorry, Harry, I should have set all this out beforehand, but I wanted to keep the food fresh and warm, and time just got away from me. I feel like I don't have enough time to get everything done."

"I sometimes feel that way, too, hon. Not to worry." He gave her a reassuring kiss before making his way across to the other side of the table, where he sat down in his chair.

Thelma placed some salmon, potatoes, and salad on Harry's plates before filling her own. In the meantime, he poured wine into the goblets. Between them, the candle flames danced and twitched with a life of their own. She gazed over at Harry as he loaded his fork with some of his salmon. In the golden light filling up the room, his strong jawline stood out, proud and strong, framing the curves of his face into a handsome picture. Just the sight of him sitting across the table made her weak in the knees, igniting her lust.

She took a bite of her salad, enjoying the fresh, cool, earthy taste of lettuce and tomatoes hitting her palate. "I appreciate you coming here on a night during the week. I know we usually save our times for the weekend." Her lips brightened into a smile.

"I wouldn't have missed this for anything, and you know what, I think I like seeing you during the week, so I don't have to wait so long for the weekends." He grinned back and raised his goblet to his mouth, taking a quick sip.

For a few moments they ate in silence, with only the sound of silverware breaking out in a soft musical tinkle against their plates. The depths of her mind swirled in confusion as she tried to set the mood for their planned interlude after dinner. So far he'd been easy to seduce, but moving their relationship toward the wedding chapel seemed a bit more daunting.

"I enjoyed our time at Willow Pointe, Harry. The evening couldn't have been more perfect. Good food, good company, good …"

His face flushed a light pink, which she managed to glimpse, even in the dimly lit dining room, and his eyes brightened with a new sparkle. "Yeah, it was a perfect evening, wasn't it?" After popping a bite of salad in his mouth, he leaned forward a little, swallowing his food before speaking again. "You know what, Thelma, I have to confess something to you. I haven't said anything, but I just have to say it now."

Her pulse quickened. She placed her goblet back down on the table, never removing her eyes from him. "Oh, what's that, then?"

With a wink of his right eye, he reached out across the table and stroked the top of her hand. "You seem different since you've come home. I don't know what else you did while you were away, but I suspect you were doing far more than just teaching students." The flush had left his face, and in its place, a solemn expression. "I can't quite put my finger on it, but something is different about you now, and I can't, for the life of me, figure it out."

Thelma stared at him. His suspicion caught her off guard; the heat rose in her face. Just how she'd address his observations, she didn't have a clue, but she knew he wanted an answer. "I've changed? In what way?"

He grinned at her. "You really have to ask me that? You don't know?"

She sat there stunned, and somewhat panic-stricken. The House had strict rules about admits sharing where they had learned their sexual skills. House directors permitted one to practice the art on someone else; but new admits signed a confidentiality agreement to remain silent about other details. If she and Harry were to be—married—perhaps she might break down and share anyway. But at this point in time, she decided against it.

"Harry, don't you think I've probably been the same all along? We're not exactly strangers anymore, and I don't know. I just thought …"

"Don't think I'm complaining one bit, my dear." He gave her fingers a light squeeze. "I'm just surprised by it all, I guess."

From what she'd learned about his life with Anne, and from what she knew about most men and their stuffy notions of what women should or should not do in the bedroom, no wonder he was confused by her moves on him. But this was exactly what he needed. Harry deserved to feel alive, vibrant, vital, allowing his male urges to course through every part of his body. The thought of him being denied by some cold, selfish woman, who seemed to care for no one but herself, set off a surge of indignation in Thelma's heart. If the truth be known, the whole ordeal simply angered her. "I think, at this point in my life, I want to live a little, make some changes, maybe …" She caught herself before getting too carried away and sharing a little too much of her private thoughts. This was a conversation for another day.

He removed his hand from hers, tapping his fingers lightly on the table. "You're definitely right about that." With a sigh, he shook his head. "We're not getting any younger, you know, but somehow I still feel there's a lot more life left in both of us."

She gave him a broad smile. Yes, this was exactly the path he needed to go down. "Good! I'm glad I'm not the only one who thinks that way."

They both turned their attention toward their plates, and finished off the meal, making light conversation in the meantime. While they ate, she spent time admiring his body, the broadness of his chest, and the musculature of his arms, which showed strength for a man his age. The image of the nice roundness of his rear end blazed up in her mind. A moist pool formed between her legs as she remembered how he'd squeezed hers during their time at Willow Pointe. When they finished eating, they placed the dishes in the kitchen, and Thelma led the way to the living room.

CHAPTER 7

I'd love to hear you play something Thelma. You don't do it for me often enough." Harry had wrapped his arm around her waist, holding her close as they walked. She truly wished they could simply forego the piano recital and head straight for the bedroom. As much as playing her piano had always filled her with happiness, nothing made her happier right now than the thoughts of running her fingers all over Harry.

He moved toward the settee and sat down while Thelma sat on the piano stool and reached for some sheet music. Giving a little run of her fingers up the keyboard and back down again, she finished off with a white-key glissando, flipped open "Deep Purple," and played to her heart's content. When the end came, she segued into "Three O'Clock In The Morning," "The Cat's Pajamas," and ended with "I'm Sorry Sally."

There, that should be enough to suit him. It had been hard enough getting through those pieces, and she prayed to God above he'd be ready for something else.

"Good enough for you?" She spun around on the stool and gave him a wink.

"Bravo!" He stood up clapping and walked over to the piano. He wound his arms around her neck and covered her with kisses. "Absolutely divine. I could listen to you every night."

Oh, I'm sure that could be arranged, if you'd only ask the right question. All she did was let out a giggle and lean back into his strong arms. "I'm not that good, but I do try."

"Bah, you're always so modest, but that's what I like about you, sweet and charming, with a pinch of naughtiness when the mood hits." He emphasized "naughtiness" with a soft whisper.

Thelma pushed herself up off the stool and snuggled in his arms. Their lips met in another round of tender kisses, with Harry slipping in his tongue to seek refuge in the warmth of her mouth. She embraced the warm flesh with soft, gentle sucking motions, ending the kiss with a small nip to his lower lip.

"You are a naughty little minx, aren't you, girl?" He let out a light chuckle.

Overcome with desperation—or overheating lust—she whispered in his ear, "Do you really want to see what naughty is?"

"I'd love to see what naughty is. Are you going to show me?" He tried to appear serious, but his eyes brimmed over with a flood of excitement.

"Follow me." She cocked her head in the direction of the bedroom door and pulled him to the threshold where they passed through. She shut the door, locking it behind her. A thin stream of light through the window lit the way to the nightstand, where she flipped a switch, turning on the light.

"Are you holding me captive by locking us in here?" His lips broadened into a wide smile.

"Just in case you try to escape." She moved in close, licking the rim of his ear.

He pulled her into is arms, smothering her cheek, her lips, and her neck with a series of light kisses. "I don't think you'll have to worry about me trying to escape." He stopped and stared into her eyes. "You do strange things to me, Thelma, things I haven't felt in a long time."

"Do I, Harry?" She smiled up at him, while her hands slid down the small of his back, landing on his bum. Yes, even the shape and feel of them against her palms was as nice as the way he looked from behind. As their thighs pressed together, his hardened cock signaled he was primed and ready. She worked one hand away from his backside and around to the front, where she slipped her fingers inside his slacks.

He closed his eyes and threw back his head a moment, allowing her fingers to explore his slit, which oozed pre-cum. "God, I love it when you touch me like that!" His hips twitched a little as she touched him with more determination.

"Let's get undressed, Harry!" She whispered in his ear. "No more shy play. I think it's time we go all the way. What do you say to that?"

"Do you mean it?" He pulled her hand away and stepped back, his eyes searching, almost imploring. "You're not just teasing me, are you?"

"Darling, I'd never tease you about something as important and special as this. That would be so insensitive." Her voice grew more emphatic. "For the love of God, Harry, you're a man, and you deserve to enjoy all male pleasures." She grasped his arms, giving them a firm squeeze. "It's time for you to cast all cares aside and explore your sensual side. Let's do it together!"

His face broke into a warm smile. "Let's do it, then, you and me."

Without another word, she removed his sweater and shirt, revealing a strong chest. Grabbing the fly of his slacks, she gave the zipper a firm, steady tug. The slacks dropped to the floor, revealing his briefs, which showed the prominent bulge between his legs. Her heart caught in her throat at the sight of him, nearly naked and vulnerable. "I'll let you remove the rest of your clothing." She gave his rear cheeks a soft pinch, watching as he slipped off his socks and underwear. In the soft light, the view of his erect phallus nearly made her climax right then and there. He proved more physically beautiful than she'd ever imagined. She wanted to view him a little longer, but time ticked on. Grabbing up one corner of the bedspread, she threw it back to reveal a set of clean, starched linen sheets.

"Come on, get in." She took his hand and pulled him toward the bed.

"But I want to undress you, too." He ran a soft finger against her cheek.

"Not this time. You just watch me." Though soft, the tone in her voice rang out with authority.

Before he could answer her, she gave him a gentle push. Once on the crisp sheets, he stretched out on his back, focusing his gaze on her. Thelma slipped out of her shoes, unfastened her garters, and loosened her stockings. With a few tugs, she unfastened her skirt, followed by her blouse. She stood there a moment, nude, wearing only a smile and sparkling eyes. Harry's eyes grew wider, and a soft pink flush crept up his cheeks.

"You're absolutely beautiful." He propped up on one elbow as she slid next to him. "Let me look at you for a moment."

She stretched out, striking a seductive pose, bending her right knee to open herself up to him. The placement of her arms behind her head showed off the curvature of her breasts, allowing them to flirt a moment with his eyes. For several seconds, neither said a word, and Thelma allowed him to take in all of her. He reached out to touch her with his finger, but still determined to keep an upper hand, she stopped him. "No touching, darling. Just touch with your eyes only."

"Thelma, you little tease!" With an intent look, he leaned over to kiss her, but she objected again.

"No kissing, not just yet." She put out her hand to stop him.

He dropped back down with a chuckle. "You playing hard to get? Is that it?" Wagging a finger, he squinted at her. "Or maybe you want to call the shots."

"Maybe I do want to call the shots. You have a problem with that, big boy?"

"Then have at it, milady!" This time he stretched out, waiting for her next move in silence.

Thelma took swift action now, flipping herself over and taking hold of his wrists. In a sleek move, she straddled his hips, allowing his cock to rest snugly against her slit.

Her eyes closed, and she gritted her teeth, fighting to contain herself. How nice it would have been to just glide on and bring them both to a climax, but then again, taking things slowly made the bargain sweeter for both. "I'm sorry, dear, I don't mean to be a tease. Well maybe just a little." She dove down and gave his earlobe a sharp nip. This time she didn't stop him when he wrenched his hands free and aimed for her breasts.

The touch of his fingers grasping her nipples nearly drove her over the edge again, and with every tweak, curbing the urge to impale herself on his length became more challenging. To contain herself, she feasted her lips on his, plunging her tongue into the soft, warm depths of his mouth. Between her legs, his erection raged harder. Her kisses became more passionate, and the working of his fingers instigated a raging throb in her nipples.

She moved her lips away from his mouth, licking a path, hot and wet, over his neck, down his chest—taking time to deliver a sharp bite to his nipples—and dipping the tip of her tongue into the slit of his cock. The soft groan from his throat filled her ears like sweet music. The salty taste of his essence seeping its way out soared her lust. She wanted more of him. Opening her mouth, she encased all of him, savoring the sensation of his tip hitting the back of her throat. At The House, she'd learned how to handle all sizes of cocks, enjoying the variety, feel, and taste of each one, while learning to control certain physical reflexes that threatened to ruin a good mood or experience—or, worse yet, make the other partner feel undesirable.

Harry bucked a little, encouraging her to suck harder. The hard, full veins along his cock pushed back in defiance against her tongue, and as she traced over them, he groaned a little louder. From the sound and feel of him, he wouldn't last much longer, so she stopped long enough to encircle her fingers around the top of his balls and give a gentle, but firm squeeze.

He writhed beneath her. "God, Thelma, I don't know if you're an angel or a succubus." He gasped and swallowed as the tip of her tongue went back to tickling and probing his cockhead once again. "I don't think I can last." She gripped him harder, then stopped. His breathing, rapid at first, slowed down enough for him to speak coherently. "You really know how to torture a guy, don't you?"

"Just a little, but on second thought, I have a sneaking suspicion you've got lots of spunk in you just dying to come out. I'll give you a little relief." Giving him a sultry smile, she dipped her head down again, teasing and savoring him to the fullest, enjoying the dose of fluids coating her mouth as he resigned himself to the hand of nature. Thelma swallowed his lust without batting an eyelash, as he watched her with surprise and wonder.

"No one has ever done that before." Smiling, he reached up and stroked her cheek.

"What's that? Taste every bit of you?" Thelma lowered herself into his arms, basking in the silence and total unity of the moment. The sound of his beating heart thrummed against her ear as she rested her head on his chest.

Harry moved his hands over the smoothness of her backside, palms first, before grazing her skin with the tips of his fingers. When he dug into her flesh lightly with his fingernails and trailed them across her buttocks and over her back, she shuddered. This was a sensation she loved, the touch giving her cold chills while radiating sheer bliss throughout her body.

"I want you, Thelma. I want to take you like you took me, and more."

She said nothing, but obliged him by crawling off and moving to a supine position. His eyes danced in anticipation while she bent her knees outward, opening up her cleft just enough to tease. "Good enough for you?"

"Perfect." He positioned himself between her legs.

"Have you ever done this before, Harry?" Her eyes searched his as he glanced up at her.

He pursed his lips and shook his head. "Not in a very long time. Shouldn't be too hard to remember, should it?" The corners of his lips turned into an easy grin.

"No, dear, not hard at all. Just do what you feel, what feels natural to you, that's all." Thelma repositioned her head on the pillow and closed her eyes, ready to lose herself in his touch.

Using his thumb and forefinger, he spread her lips apart and landed his tongue near the top of her slit, hitting her clit spot on. Digging her buttocks into the sheets, she clenched her teeth, struggling to keep from crying out. "That's it darling. Just keep it up. Like that. Yes."

He cast his eyes up toward hers for a moment. With a smile, he dipped his tongue down again, sweeping over the soft wetness of her folds, sinking into her entrance, sliding up once again to the hot bundle of nerves pulsing out a strong rhythm. He toyed with her sensitive flesh, delivering soft caressing licks and flicks of his tongue, alternating with light sucking. Thelma rolled her hips in time to the rhythmic spasms of pleasure breaking out in waves throughout her pelvic region.

She reached down and caught his head between her hands, anchoring him in place. "Keep going," she whispered. In a final climax, she let out a cry, tossing her head from side to side. Before she could gather up a new breath, Harry repositioned himself over her, hands on either side of her shoulders. He lodged his cock inside her sex, pushing himself in, little by little.

"Open up good for me, sweet one, I want in. Now!"

With a smile, she shifted a little, opening her thighs more to accommodate him. She'd been waiting for this moment for a long time, even thinking about it during her time at The House. Even though her adored attendant had filled her up most admirably, she'd often found herself pretending it was Harry who pounded at her with sweet determination. Taking a deep breath, she reclined in complete relaxation, swallowing his fullness with ease. Just as his fingers and tongue had tantalized her earlier, rocketing her pleasure into orbit, his fat length filled her better than anyone she'd previously experienced—even at The House.

Again, he'd exceeded her expectations. She especially liked the way he closed his eyes and smiled as he buried himself deep inside, only to pull out and plunge back in again. Over and over, he kept at her, sinking himself into wet darkness, settling into his own rhythm. He took his time, moving in slow thrusts for a few minutes, speeding up a little, then slowing down again. A new vitality seemed to flow through him with each movement of his hips, which seemed to crash through the emotional wall he'd created from his own fear and hesitation all these years.

His face changed from a smile filled with anticipation to the look of rapture a man shows when he experiences a good, hard release. He opened his eyes and smiled down at her. She'd done it. She'd given him his manhood back, totally and completely, with no cause for shame or disgrace. And he'd acknowledged her womanhood, never holding back, tasting all of her and penetrating her with the eagerness of one who'd been starved, left alone and forgotten. Harry spent a few moments sucking on each of her nipples, before removing himself from between her thighs, dropping lightly down beside her.

Thelma smoothed his hair back, wiping away a trickle of perspiration from his forehead. Harry took her in his arms and held her close. She remained silent, allowing him to just be, to digest everything that had just happened. Nestled close, her head resting easily against his neck, she caught the lingering scent of Acqua Di Parma. For the first time since they'd begun seeing each other, she truly appreciated him— all of him, from the easy, practical side of his nature to the lusty side he'd repressed for so long.

She ran her fingers over his chest, paying close attention to the hardness of bone, each muscular contour, and the softness of his skin. If only every night could be like this one. If only he didn't have to leave her and get dressed, to head home to his own world. How she wished more than ever for a world where they shared everything, every waking and sleeping hour.

"Well, I hate to say this, but I do think it's getting late." Harry broke the silence, kissing her on the forehead and sliding off the bed to retrieve his clothes.

Thelma nodded, feasting her eyes on his physique as he got dressed, salivating again over the curves of his arms, chest, and thighs, and enjoying a last peek at the flaccid cock now resting neatly against his sac. God, how she'd love nothing better than to drop down on her knees and suck him back to his full, hard length again. But after this night, given his openness, she knew their relationship had changed forever. She slid off the bed and slipped quickly into her clothes.

"I'm glad you suggested getting together tonight." He pulled her in his arms and kissed her. "I'm especially glad you brought me here."

Thelma, wrapping her arms around him, grinned back and rested her head on his chest. "Me too."

They stood together, holding each other in a silent embrace until Harry gently pulled away and led her to the door, where they passed through and headed toward the entrance hall. Standing at the front door, she waved him off as he drove away in his Silver Ghost.

She closed the door behind her and walked back into the kitchen to pour herself a glass of wine to commemorate the evening. Nothing suited her better right now than taking a little more time to sip some wine and relive again in her mind each moment of their first intercourse, from the touch of his fingers against her flesh, to the slippery warmth of his tongue, down to the fullness of him inside her. This time, no doubts lingered with regard to appropriate behavior. Everything had gone according to plan. From the vision of his eyes simmering with lust, to the smile of deep pleasure radiating across his face as they'd made love, it seemed he had wanted everything this evening just as much as she had, and he'd proved a willing and adept lover.

Lifting the wine to her lips, she drained the glass. She winced at the sight of dishes piled high in the sink. Cleaning up the kitchen topped her list of chores, along with changing the sheets on the bed in the bedroom where she and Harry had finally consummated their relationship. At least all this work might provide some time to plot out the next escapade with Harry. With a smile, she cut out the kitchen light and headed upstairs to bed, where she promptly fell into a peaceful, happy sleep.

CHAPTER 8

W hew, I think I need a good, hot bath!" Harry wiped his forehead on his sleeve, taking a brief moment to inhale his own scent. "Yes, I do need a hot bath."

Thelma opened the back door to the kitchen and ushered him inside. "I'm just as drippy as you are. Look at me!"

He smiled and plucked up a lock of her hair, damp with perspiration, and placed it behind her ear. "Nothing like a heavy-duty trek through the park to get the old blood pumping, eh?" With a chuckle, he landed a quick kiss on her lips.

Everyone had always talked about the hiking trails dotting the Sorrel Mountains, located about an hour's drive from their neighborhood. At the top of one of the trails was the famous Mount Majestic Falls, which people came from miles around to see. No paved roads led to the falls, so one had to make the trip by foot, stepping over four miles of rugged trails to see this wonder of Mother Nature.

"A trek through the park, you call it?" She gave him a light frown. "You mean a hike up a mountainside, don't you? You told me we were going for a nice walk through the woods."

"But you have to admit it was worth it, wasn't it?" Dampness and all, he took her into his arms and held her tight.

She smiled, taking in the body heat radiating through his damp clothing. "Yes, darling, it was worth it, and the waterfall was gorgeous. I'd never seen it before, so now I guess I can count myself as one of the lucky few who has seen it."

"Absolutely, and we both had the stamina to do it."

"Oh-h-h!" She shivered a little. "All this talk about waterfalls is making me cold." With a gleaming gaze turned up to his sparkling brown eyes, she said, "Hey, don't forget there's a tub in our room."

"Hm-m-m." Harry buried his face in her hair, kissing the top of her head. "Yes, there is. How silly of me to forget that." He gave her a few light pats on the rump, before kissing her again. "I'll bet there's plenty of hot water in there. And you know what, I just remembered something. I happened to bring a spare change of clothes."

Her eyes gleamed up at him. "You did?"

"I try to come prepared. I didn't know what the day would bring." He patted her arm and turned toward the door. "Let me get them from the car, and I'll be right back."

After their first get-together in Thelma's "love room," they'd made use of the space quite often during the last few months, with Harry coming over a couple of nights a week now; weekends, as always, remained sacrosanct. Thelma had succeeded in bringing his comfort level, not to mention his self-esteem, up several notches. And the fact he'd brought extra clothes this time only confirmed her thoughts. They'd never bathed together, and the prospect of this, coupled with her naughty plans for some new activities after the bath, instilled a certain giddy excitement. In a few minutes, he returned to the kitchen.

"Harry, let me pour us some wine, and then I'll fill up the tub."

"I've got a better idea. Let me pour the wine while you fill the tub." He dropped a flannel bag down by the door and walked over to a small wine cabinet where Thelma kept a few bottles of some of her favorite labels, compliments of his generosity when he'd had some extra vintages to share. "I know where you keep the wine glasses and corkscrew, so just run along and get everything else ready." He turned back to her and smiled. "I'm more than ready to get out of these wet clothes and …"

"Oh, I'm sure you are!" She squeezed his rear. "You know where to find me when you're finished."

Once she'd stepped out of her shoes and into the bathroom, she inserted the drain plug and turned on the hot and warm spouts to let the water run. An antique cabinet held a small assortment of fresh, fluffy towels; she grabbed a couple of them and placed them in a small chair beside the tub. This was the first bath she and Harry would be sharing. To make the experience more relaxing, she opened the medicine cabinet to retrieve a small bottle of bath oil for the water. A soft scent filled her nose as she inhaled, breathing in one of the new unisex scents of the day. Thelma poured a little of the liquid into the tub, knowing all too well how the power of certain aromas heightened the libido.

Her stomach clenched with excitement on hearing the rustle of footsteps at the door. Harry came in with two glasses of burgundy wine; he'd already slipped off his shoes. "Where do you want me to put these?"

Thelma took the glasses from him. "Let's rest them on the floor beside us."

Once she'd rid herself of the glasses, his hands reached to unfasten her tweed knickers. Breaking from their usual tradition of her undressing him first, she let him continue. They'd started this ritual from the first night, so why ruin a good thing? He sometimes tried to see if he could slip in and change things up a bit, but Thelma usually stood her ground. For the moment, she deferred to his wishes; she'd stand her ground later.

He unbuttoned her blouse, feasting on a set of plump nipples. The touch of his tongue, warm and tantalizing, ignited an ache between her legs, and when he gently bit down and grazed his teeth over her flesh, she fought to stifle a cry catching in her throat. With eager fingers, she unbuttoned his slacks and shirt. Just like her, he loved the attention she gave his chest, and she eagerly returned the favor, licking and biting at his nipples, ending with a kiss on his navel.

"Come on, let's get in!" Thelma slid his underwear down, waiting until he'd pulled off his socks before stepping into the warm water. She turned off the spouts and stretched out in the water. Harry stood there a moment watching her. "Come on, what are you waiting for?"

"You think we'll fit in there?" He gave her a look of uncertainty.

"Without a doubt. We'll be snug, and that's all that matters." With a playful splash, she motioned for him to join her. She reached over the edge for one of the wine glasses. "Hmm, good year. Thank you for bringing these bottles over. I don't know if I've thanked you enough."

Harry had settled himself between her legs. "Trust me, at this point you've done more than given me adequate thanks. In fact, I should be thanking you."

With a light chuckle, she pulled him back so his head rested against her chest. "Here, sweetheart, won't you have a sip?"

"I'd love nothing better." He reached out and took the other glass of wine, bringing the rim to his lips for a quick sip. "You're right, this isn't bad at all."

"Do you find this to your taste as well?" She placed her glass down. Her fingers encircled his tip, working him until a firm erection formed between his thighs.

"God, I love that!" He lifted his hips a little as she pressed gently into his slit, caressing the sensitive flesh. He sucked in his breath at the sensation.

"What about this?" Thelma reached down a little further, gently slipping her middle finger inside his anus.

His body tensed for a moment. Neither said a word while her finger slid in deeper. A smile crept over her face, loving these times when he became speechless with surprise.

"I think you are the devil, after all." He pressed his head harder against her, and gulped down some wine. "This vintage seems a bit strong, don't you think?"

"No, I think it's good, just like all the others you've given me." She ran a forefinger over his left nipple, ending with a soft pinch. He let out a sigh. "Is the wine going to your head or something?"

"Let's just say I'm feeling, well, a little light-headed." He stroked the outside of her leg.

"Just relax, Harry." Thelma continued working her finger inside him, while her other hand grasped his cock. Up and down she ran her hand, smoothing over the swollen flesh, massaging the ridge area under his tip. Against her palm his length strained until she felt him shudder, covering her hand with his thick emissions. She slipped out her finger, but kept a softer grasp around him with her other hand. By this time, he'd finished his glass of wine. "Here, let me take that before you drop it." Thelma repositioned herself a little, and helped Harry settle back down again.

"Something smells so nice in here. What is it?" He scooped some of the warm, scented water over his abdomen.

"You like that? It's one of these new-fangled scents they're pushing now, one where a man or woman can use it."

"Clever that you added some of it here." He rubbed her leg some more, sending a flurry of shivers up her spine, despite the warm water. "That's what I've enjoyed most about you since you've come home. You're free, and more daring."

Thelma ran a finger over his chest, toying with one of his nipples. Grasping his flaccid shaft between her fingers, she gently fondled the silky tip between her thumb and forefinger. After twenty more minutes in the tub, the water had cooled. "I think we're ready to get out of here, Harry. Can you go ahead and step out first, and I'll be right behind you?"

He pulled himself up and climbed out of the tub, grabbing the rim to steady himself.

"Easy there, don't fall."

"I think the warm water and drink have given me a full-fledged buzz." He let out a light chuckle as he offered his hand.

"Thanks." Thelma stood up, letting the water drain off of her before stepping out onto the bath mat beside the tub.

"You are absolutely beautiful, Thelma. There's not a more heavenly vision for my eyes than seeing you as nature intended for you to look."

"I feel the same about you. Personally, I think Anne was a fool, if you want to know how I really feel." Suddenly she regretted saying those words, but he gave her a rueful smile. "I'm sorry, I never should have said that. How thoughtless of me."

"Don't think anything of it, dear." Harry pulled her into his arms and gave her a quick kiss on the forehead.

Wanting to change the subject fast, she glanced down to the floor. "Oh, there's still some more of my wine. Why don't you have it? I'm kind of done for the moment." He took the glass and swallowed down some more. Thelma had taken a towel from the chair and quickly dried herself off first. She dried Harry off with the other towel as he polished off the rest of her wine. He stood against the bed, steadying himself. Perfect! Getting him relaxed was just what she'd hoped for, because tonight she planned on using some of the toys in the chest.

"Sweetheart, you just get your bearings for just a moment, and I'm going to get some things we can enjoy tonight."

"Get some things for us to enjoy? Gosh, just ravishing you is enough for me." He popped her lightly on the rear as she moved toward the chest of drawers.

From one of the drawers, she pulled out the blindfold, the handcuffs, a bottle of oil, and the strap-on phallus.

"Good lord, what have you got there, girl?" He stared at her with hard curiosity. "What's with all that? And what is it?"

She sidled up beside him, placing the items on the bed. "I want you to play along with me, Harry." Her mouth rested close to his ear. She gave his earlobe a light lick. "Let me surprise you in the most pleasant way, how 'bout that?" A glazed look filled his eyes. Relaxed with the alcohol in his system, she knew he'd be more receptive, while still being able to perform.

"You wicked little wench, just what have you got up your sleeve?"

His eyes twinkled as his lips turned up into a boyish grin.

"Go along with me here." Thelma picked up the blindfold and popped it over his eyes.

"Now I can't see anything." His lips turned into a light pout.

"That's just it, sweetie, you're not supposed to. It's more fun that way." She turned him around to face the bed, steadying him as he moved. "Nice and easy, Harry. Don't panic. Now hold out your arms." He held out his arms. With a snap, she placed the cuffs around his wrists. "What on earth?" Before he uttered another word, she'd pushed him down on the bed, barely giving him a chance to catch himself.

"There, that's much better, darling. Are you comfortable?" She gave his rump a soft pat, before delivering a sharp pinch on each butt cheek.

"I feel silly, that's what."

"Trust me, dear one, you won't feel silly much longer. Just relax."

Thelma slipped on the phallus, admiring how smooth it felt against her fingertips. She remembered all too well how nicely it slipped back and forth inside her own hidden center. But Harry's frequent visitations had made its use mostly unnecessary for the time being. Now, she'd give Harry his moment, one where he'd experience something truly unique. Taking up the small bottle of oil, she tipped some of the liquid onto her finger and lightly entered his anus. With slow, smooth strokes, she glided her finger back and forth, applying a light pressure, hitting the area near his prostate. He gave a small grunt, wriggling a little. She removed her finger and applied a larger amount of oil on to the phallus.

"Are you ready?"

He hesitate a moment. "If it feels as good as what you were doing, then I guess I'm game."

Spreading his buttocks apart, she aimed the tip of the phallus at his anal entrance and gave a light push, working in the tip nice and easy as she pushed through the initial resistance. Harry gave a small shout, struggling against her.

"Stay down!" Thelma's authoritative voice filled the room. With a light whimper, Harry settled back down onto the bed. "I'm not going to hurt you, dear. I just don't want to injure you. Stay still, and most of all, enjoy." Her words ended in a softer, sultry tone, while her hands rubbed over his rear and over his hips. Little by little, she pushed the phallus in deeper. As she penetrated his dark space, his whimpering turned into soft moans. His muscles relaxed beneath her hands as she buried the phallus to the hilt. She glided in and out, nice and slow.

"Oh, God, Thelma. I've never …" He strained against the cuffs, grinding his hips into the bed.

"Stop that!" She gave a rear cheek a sharp smack.

"What?" He jerked a little. "I wasn't doing—"

"No moving."

"Come on, you think I can hold still while—?"

She popped him again, glad he couldn't see her smiling face. "I told you to stay down." Her hips moved faster, slipping the phallus back and forth with ease. For a few moments, neither spoke. In the meantime she knew an erection raged between his legs, just by the way he pushed against the bed, trying in vain to subdue his own movements. Thelma slipped out the phallus for a few seconds, long enough to direct him to wriggle onto all fours.

This time, he didn't object, but followed her commands. Just as she suspected, his cock had hardened with each of her thrusts. She lightly touched his cockhead, dipping into the pre-cum forming on top.

"You wouldn't." He let out a groan.

"I just might, Harry. So get ready!" She inserted the phallus inside him once again, and regained her prior rhythm. She reached around and encircled his length with her hands, paying special attention to his tip.

"Thelma, you're the devil, for sure." He panted as her fingers stroked him, pushing back against his swollen flesh. Driven to the point of no return, Harry released his lust in dripping streams onto the bed, before dropping his head to catch his breath.

"That's a good boy." Thelma rubbed his back, spooning herself around him, soothing him back into a state of calm. She cooed in his ear, "So how does it feel to have it up the bum, Harry? Ever had it that way before?"

"Can't say that I have." He sucked in his breath long and hard as she pulled out of him. She unsnapped the handcuffs and pulled off the blindfold. "And where on earth did you get such contraptions?" She smiled and slid off the bed. Harry's eyes widened when he turned around and saw her standing with the phallus between her legs. "You look so strange with that thing on." He shook his head. "Where did you get all this? Thelma, I swear you're not telling me the whole truth about what happened while you were away." His eyes narrowed, but she caught a playful spark lurking behind them. "I think you're a little sneak, that's what!"

Oh, no, this was a conversation she still didn't want to pursue. Off came the phallus, and all the rest of the toys found a place at one corner of the foot of the bed. Diversions came in handy, and she knew how to help focus his attention elsewhere. She dropped down on her back, resting her head in her hands. Like she'd done previously, she bent one knee up and let her leg fall open. Harry eyed her groin and smiled.

"I love nothing better than prowling in that little cooch of yours." He glanced back at her. "You know that, don't you?"

"Tell you what, big boy, I have another idea." She toyed with one of her nipples, clutching the plump flesh, tugging a little. He watched with eager eyes as the thick nub sprang back into place.

"God, now what, you wicked, wonderful woman?" Harry's eyes blazed, his erection growing again.

"Come here. Straddle your hips over my head and place your lips between my thighs."

Obeying her instructions, he cradled her head between his legs. Thelma reached around his buttocks and pulled him toward her, guiding his swollen flesh into her mouth. To her satisfaction, he let out a soft moan of approval. On instinct, his lips settled over her mound, and he flicked out his tongue, burying it inside her nether regions.

Thelma let out a soft, muffled cry as he teased the hot bundle of nerves pounding away at the top of her sex. She stopped her sucking motions on Harry for just a few seconds, allowing herself to savor the touch of his tongue playing inside her entrance. The sounds of him gliding over her own wetness created a stronger ache inside her pelvic region. In response, the tip of her tongue wiggled around in tiny circles inside his slit, and the salty taste of his new essence excited her more.

On a whim, she stopped, slipping him out of her mouth. "Hey, hon, let's switch positions."

Harry gave her nether regions one more go-around with his tongue before settling back down on the bed. "I was having fun just like this."

"Oh, you!" She kicked lightly at his foot and laughed. "You'll have fun any old way we do this, so don't give me any lip about it."

"You're right about that, my dear girl." He grinned. "So how do you want to do this?"

"You lie down on your back, and we'll go from there." Once he'd repositioned himself on his back, Thelma straddled him, with her head looming over his swollen cock. "There, I think we have it even better this time." To start of their new round of lovemaking, she dipped her head down, encasing him. She took her time, licking over his cock, and sucking his balls, before massaging the spongy contents inside with her thumb and forefingers.

Her hips lurched when he pulled her down over his mouth and explored her folds and clit with his tongue. In a surprise move, she felt him work a thick finger inside her anus, and the sensation of him moving back and forth inside nearly sent her over the edge. This interlude became a contest of who'd come first, with Thelma being the winner.

To be honest, she'd stopped sucking on Harry so her body could enjoy a good, hard climax brought on by the insistent flicking of his tongue against her sensitive fun-button. When she'd calmed down, she focused on him, tormenting his cock until he came in a torrent of pleasure, filling her mouth with his salt-laden treat. Together, they enjoyed the afterglow, curled up in each other's arms.

"You're never without a surprise, are you?" Harry kissed her, holding her tighter.

"I must admit, Harry, for someone who's been kept back from enjoying sex so much, I'm surprised that you're such a willing and wonderful lover." She reached over and stroked his cheek. "You really are, you know, absolutely wonderful." Her last words came out in a soft whisper.

"Does that surprise you?"

"Yes, it does. I'm glad we can enjoy spending time together doing all kinds of things, even this."

"Me too. I think it's made getting together even more fun than before." He gave her a warm stare. "I could do this with you forever," he whispered in her ear.

Thelma's pulse quickened. What did this mean? He'd never mentioned doing anything with her "forever" before.

To her disappointment, Harry stretched out a little and stifled a yawn. "You know what? I'm hungry. No wonder the wine went to my head. We haven't eaten in a while."

She sat up, struck with another idea. "Tell you what, I'll cook us up something eat. Why don't you rest here, and I'll get you when everything is ready."

"Great idea. I'd like that. It won't be too much of an imposition on you, will it?"

"Not at all. I'd be glad to."

Secretly, she hoped her tender ministrations might move him to think about how he might get this kind of care for the rest of his life. After all, he'd just admitted for the first time that he didn't want it to stop, even if he had only alluded to their lovemaking. Didn't he harbor some kind of yearning for them to stay together as a couple—permanently?

But damn it, he hadn't seemed inclined to talk much about the future, and definitely not a future containing the two of them.

She'd never brought up the subject first because she wanted the suggestion of marriage to come from him. Her sexual skills may have put her a notch above most women when it came to boudoir activities, but her traditional side still maintained that the man must do the proposing. At this point, she started to believe a different approach might be needed.

She crawled out of bed, threw on a robe, and headed toward the kitchen. Thirty minutes later, some salad and pan-fried chicken rested on two china plates. Wanting to keep everything to a minimum, Thelma placed the food on the small kitchen table where she and Harry had often shared coffee together, or a nice round of tea. The small, informal coziness of eating in the kitchen struck her fancy more often than spending time in the stiff, formal dining room. Once she'd filled up two glasses with water and set out the silverware and napkins, she grabbed up his flannel bag and strode back to the bedroom. It was time to get Harry.

CHAPTER 9

When Thelma entered the room, she smiled and stood in the doorway, watching Harry sleep. Yeah, nothing like a warm bath and some good naughty fun to make a guy sleep like a baby. And he hadn't even bothered to dive under the covers after she left the room. Between his thighs, the soft, button-like tip of his flaccid shaft rested nice and easy, cupped by an ample set of balls. His chest rose and fell lightly with each breath he took. She hated to wake him, preferring to crawl on the bed and settle beside his naked, warm body and fall into pleasant dreams.

"Harry." She tiptoed to him, lightly placing her fingers on his chest. "Harry."

The sound of her voice awakened him with a start. He fluttered his eyes open in confusion. "Was I that out of it?" He stretched and gave a little yawn as Thelma kissed him.

"Like a baby." She stroked his hair and smiled down at him. "I hated to wake you, but dinner is ready. I have your clothes here too."

"Okay, give me a minute, and I'll meet you in …" Giving another yawn, he sat up for a moment, collected his thoughts, and picked up his bag. "Where are we eating, by the way?"

"In the kitchen. I just wanted to keep it simple, if that's okay with you."

He looked up at her and smiled. "Fine with me. I'm game for anything you want." With a wink, he snatched up his bag and started dressing.

Thelma sat on the bed, admiring the way his muscles flexed as he put on a new, clean shirt. She especially admired the way the flesh between his thighs swayed with each side step he took as he slid into his slacks.

"Here, let me put your socks on for you." She patted the empty space beside her. "Come, sit here by me."

Tossing his socks in her direction, he walked over and sat down beside her. "I love it when you take care of me, Thelma." He gave her a penetrating stare. "Have I ever told you that? You make me feel happy and secure."

"No, darling, I don't think you have, to tell you the truth." She gave him a demure smile and lowered her eyes. The blood rushing to her head created a woozy sensation. She struggled to contain her excitement. *Play it cool, don't let him see how eager you are.*

Harry settled back on the bed, stroking her cheek. "Maybe I need to do that more often. Sometimes I'm not the greatest at talking about these things."

"That's okay, but I do like hearing you say it." She put on his socks and reached down for his shoes, placing them on his feet. "Come on, handsome, dinner's getting cold."

Together they walked to the kitchen and sat down to eat. Harry cut a slice of his chicken and popped it into his mouth, closing his eyes, savoring the flavor. She took a bite of salad, watching him while he ate.

"I love your cooking, Thelma. You seem to add the nicest spices to make things taste so good." He opened his eyes and smiled. "I could eat every night with you."

She nearly choked when she heard him say this. Was he having any thoughts at all of having someone in his life with him? He'd been making occasional tender comments lately, which gave her some glimmer of hope of his wanting to spend the future with someone, with her. Feeling a little bold, she finally asked him, "Harry, I can't help but wonder, do you ever get lonely going home to an empty house?"

He swallowed his food and blinked a few seconds, at a loss for words. "Well, that's a good question." His brow furrowed in thought.

"I mean, I enjoy my home, my garden, playing the piano, things like that. But I agree with what you just said, that it's fun to share meals together, make love together." She quickly took a bite of chicken, chewing while waiting for his response, which seemed to take forever in coming.

With a light shrug, he finally said, "Oh, I guess I have ways to entertain myself." Clearing his throat, he concentrated on loading his fork with some salad, before taking a sip of water.

Thelma felt a twinge of panic burning in her gut. "Me, too, but sometimes I wonder what my future will hold. Do I want things to stay as they are forever, or would a change be nice?"

"I see." He nodded and kept eating, his eyes burning through her.

She swallowed some water, trying to keep her impatience in check. Why did he seem intent on backing down with his feelings now? "Yeah, I know I'm not getting any younger, and sometimes I just feel like life's passing me by. Do you ever feel that way, too, Harry?"

He swallowed and slowly dipped his fork back into his chicken. "Hmm, I guess I'm mostly okay with everything. I haven't really thought much about things like that."

Her heart sank. "Oh, yeah. Well, I was just wondering, that's all."

"I tell you, what keeps me occupied and my mind off worries is working, that's what."

"Mmm, yeah, I guess so." She stabbed at her food, frustrated. Damn it! This conversation had turned south. Maybe she'd gone too far; maybe she shouldn't have gone down this road with him—maybe she had moved too fast with him after all.

They finished the rest of the meal in light conversation, mainly with Harry conversing while she struggled to keep her tone polite. The lump in her throat and the nausea kept her from enjoying the remainder of her dinner. The sound of his voice had become like a gnat buzzing around her ear, creating a growing fear, rather than mere annoyance.

When they finished, Harry kissed her cheek and went back to the bedroom, returning with his flannel bag filled with damp clothing. "I'm heading on back home. Oh, and one thing I wanted to give you before I left." He handed her a small slip of paper.

She read the name and phone number, and turned her eyes toward him. "What's this?" New dread raged even stronger now, and she tried to keep from shaking.

"It's the name of my good friend, Bill. He told me he was in need of a competent secretary. If you aren't interested in teaching anymore, I thought you might consider a different type of work." He patted her on the arm. "Bill also has a teenage son who would benefit from a good tutor to help him with his writing and spelling. You'd be good for that, too, Thelma. If I were you I'd put my teaching skills to use. There's plenty of families around here who'd love to have a private tutor for their kids." Harry gave her a wink. "Something to think about, old girl." He headed for the kitchen door, but stopped for a second, turning back to her. "By the way, are you feeling all right? Somehow you seemed to lose some steam during our meal."

"How do you mean?" Thelma sensed her cheeks coloring a bright pink.

"I don't know, exactly. You just seemed a little preoccupied." He shook his head and chuckled. "Maybe it was just my imagination. But again, don't forget about Bill."

Stunned didn't even begin to describe Thelma's feelings. She gave him a weak smile. "Um, thanks, Harry, I'll be sure to get in touch with, um, Bill."

"He might get in touch with you first, but either way, I think you'd do a great job for him." Harry leaned forward and kissed her on the lips. "I'll call you so we can make plans to get together again. And I enjoyed dinner, and the whole day with you." He walked to his car and drove toward his house.

When the car rolled out of sight, she slammed the door, the glass rattling when it shut. For a moment, she considered ramming her fist through one of the panes. But she pulled back and paced through the kitchen, from the kitchen to the entrance hall, from the hall through the living room, and all over again. Her blood ran cold, and a dull ache pounded in her head. A glass of wine might do the trick and soothe her. She trotted back to the kitchen, reached for a new wine glass, and emptied the open bottle sitting on the counter, catching every last drop.

The green bottle gleamed back at her in the dim light, mocking her. The small row of bottles lining her wine cabinet seemed to jeer at her just a much. Never mind Harry's generosity in presenting her with a fine, tiny collection of some tasty vintages. So what more did he want—and why didn't it include her—for the long term?

She stood there several minutes, deep in dark thought, brooding over life's unfairness. She'd done everything right in life, been an honorable, kind person, with her only fault being the desire to have a lifelong mate. Her sensual skills were better than average, and she'd brought old Harry back from the brink of what she felt was his own inner denial and self-destruction. And what did he want? Work! In a surge of anger, she picked up the bottle and slammed it against the kitchen floor, sending shards of glass scattering in all directions.

Dodging the broken remnants, she picked up her wine glass and turned toward the living room, where she made her way to the room where all their special times together had taken place. She climbed onto the bed, and sipped her wine, letting her dark, hateful thoughts smolder.

"I guess I'm mostly okay with everything." His words rang in her mind. Why was he okay? And was he? Had Anne done this to him, killing his very spirit? Making him afraid to commit to another woman ever again? The more her thoughts focused on Anne, the more she hated her. Selfish bitch, that's what she was! And now Thelma had to pay the price, being denied the only man she had ever truly loved! She lay there on the bed, staring on occasion at the empty space where Harry

had lain only a short while ago, resting in comfort, while all she had to do was lavish all her love, all her heart and soul on him.

She lifted the glass to her lips and drained off the remaining wine. The alcohol had begun to numb her just a little. Her eyes burned with fatigue. Anger had worn her out, but being at a loss on how to snare the love of her life forever filled her with deep, inconsolable grief. Settling back on the pillow, Thelma closed her eyes and fell into a deep sleep.

CHAPTER 10

The sound of birds chirping outside the window woke her up, and she sat up, confused for a moment, wondering how she'd ended up downstairs in this bed—her and Harry's bed—and not in her own upstairs. A new heaviness filled her heart. Yes, she remembered now. She dropped back down on her pillow and rubbed her eyes. What on earth was she going to do now? Just blurting out how she felt about him or what she wanted from him didn't seem right. Women, of late, had started taking more active roles in relationships. Though her skills in the bedroom beat out any other woman Harry might date, she still believed in the man taking the lead in some things. And one of those areas was matrimony. Women always seemed to come to conclusions as to what they wanted much faster than men did. At least Thelma held this notion near and dear to her heart.

She'd tried to woo him with food, drink, and fun romps in the bedroom, but his armor seemed a little too hard for her to pierce. What would be the worst thing to happen as a result of her telling him how she felt? If he said no, then they could still continue to see each other, or simply part ways. But did the risk seem worth it? Thelma thought long and hard about her dilemma, reviewing the pros and cons of how to move forward in the relationship. After much thought, she'd come to the conclusion that Harry might also be taking her for granted. He didn't like to talk about his emotions too much, but at some point, she needed to force his hand, and now the time had come.

"Cut him off." She said the words out loud, feeling them roll off her tongue with ease, though part of her cringed a little at the idea.

But continuing the dating process without the prospect of marriage bothered her most of all. If it meant giving Harry up, then she'd have to do just that to avoid spending the rest of her life alone. And she'd start today. She planned to avoid him entirely for a while, just to see what might happen, though scheduling her gardening work might prove the most challenging. If he became suspicious, he might try to catch her outside at odd hours. Early mornings or late evenings might be the only times for her to work. Pretending to have a busy schedule made for a good excuse if he happened to catch her unawares. There, she had created a plan for most scenarios, with no need for rudeness.

She'd still be nice, while deciding against being a man's play-toy. Why, she might even call Bill about the secretarial position. After all, if Harry wanted her to work, then work she would, but no more lively naughtiness in her playroom—no more for him.

With her mind straight on her new game plan, all the emotional turmoil faded, and a new light-heartedness took over. She yawned and stretched, and decided on a nice long bath to start the day. A couple of hours later found her dressed and ready to finish out the day.

Over the next couple of weeks, Thelma busied herself cleaning, re-arranging shelves in her pantry, going through her old clothes, select-ing pieces for her church's charity projects. She focused on her garden work, sneaking outside at times when Harry was at work, and during the weekends, only at odd hours when she just knew he surely wouldn't come by. The phone had rung several times during the week. The urge to pick up the receiver was the hardest to resist. She put her fingers in her ears at times to drown out the ringing until the sound stopped. If she decided after all to call Bill, she'd make the move, instead of tak-ing the risk of answering Harry's call by mistake. Weekends, however, seemed to drone on and on. She dreaded them altogether. She'd played almost all of her music collection on the piano, took up some needle-work, and spent the remainder of the time reading to pass the time away.

At the end of the third week, on a Saturday evening, Thelma jumped when a knock sounded at the door, followed by the buzzing of the doorbell. Could it be Harry? No one else usually called on her at this time. She'd been upstairs in her room reading, and the thoughts of him being so close tempted her to forget everything and run down-stairs. Regaining her resolve once again, she remained rooted to the bed.

If she peeked out one of the bedroom or main bathroom windows, she'd catch a good glimpse of the caller. Thelma put down her book, got up, and tiptoed out of the room. She scurried across the hallway to the main bathroom, where the window offered a nice view of the front yard and entrance to the driveway. If Harry had walked over here, she'd see him when he turned around to go back home. Hardly able to control her rapid breathing, she pulled the curtain back, just enough to give her a small view outside.

On the sidewalk, a lone male figure was making its way back to the main street. Sure enough, Harry had come knocking. Thelma didn't know whether to cry or laugh. Part of her wanted to tear off running and catch up to him, but she headed back to her room, settled back down on the bed, and tried to read again. Leaning her head back against the headboard, she thought about all the fun times with Harry. True enough, she missed having someone to take her places, someone who enjoyed her cooking, and most of all the sexual companionship. But thinking about their last meal together stirred up the anger once again, reminding her why she'd decided to keep her distance for three whole weeks. Maybe holding out a few more days might not be bad, and then she'd answer his calls. She definitely couldn't keep this up forever. In all fairness, though, Harry needed to know what was going on at some point, meaning a face-to-face meeting loomed in the near future. Just a few more days to muster up some nerve, and then she'd talk to him, but not any sooner.

Later that night, after a light dinner and a few more hours of reading, she undressed for bed and slid in between the sheets. The chirping of crickets outside broke the silence in the room, offering Thelma some companionship, even if this came about only in the way of sound. Everything reminded her of Harry, the outdoors, sounds of nature, the smell of good food cooking on the stove. Between her thighs, a new ache raged. *Damn it!* She'd done a pretty good job of stifling her urges for the time being, but now they came back to pay a call—just like Harry. She giggled in the dark. Who'd hold out the longest, her or Harry? From calling on the phone to finally knocking on the door today, he appeared to need relief a little quicker than she did. After taking a few deep breaths to calm her mind and body, she rolled over and fell asleep.

CHAPTER 11

Thelma bolted upright out of a deep sleep. What was that sound downstairs? She heard it again, the sound of loud pounding at the door, followed by the doorbell buzzing. Within seconds, the furious banging and buzzing came again, forcing her out of bed. This time she knew it was futile to simply roll over and ignore the caller. She flung the covers back, ran to her closet and grabbed up a robe, wrapping herself up to gain some semblance of modesty.

All kinds of thoughts raced around in her mind, and a sudden attack of fear sent a chill through her body. Who on earth needed her at this hour? Had there been an accident? Did someone need help in an emergency situation? Her feet sped over the steps until she reached the bottom of the staircase. She ran to the door and flung it wide open.

"Harry!" Her mouth dropped open and her eyes, wide with surprise, fixated on a forlorn man leaning against the doorjamb. "For the love of—come on in here." In exasperation, she grasped his sleeve and pulled him inside the house. "What on earth are you doing out this time of night? And good lord, look at you!" She stood back examining him closer. The stubble on his face showed he hadn't shaved recently, his eyes contained a glassy stare, and the fatigue on his face suggested a lack of sleep. "Are you okay?"

"I don't know, Thelma, but tell me one thing, please." His voice rung with a melancholy tone she'd never heard before. "Are you okay? I've been trying to call you for the past several days now, and I can't understand why you won't talk to me."

She backed away a little more, almost ashamed. "Well, Harry, I've been out and about, busy doing things, you know?"

"Out and about? Really?" His voice flashed with irritation, and he move toward her. "How come I've seen your car here most of the time, then?"

"What?" The blood rushed from her face, and dizziness started to set in. "What do you mean?"

"You can't fool me. I know your car's been here, because I've walked around the house to see it parked in the driveway."

"You've been …?"

"Yeah, I've also peeked through the windows. You've been prancing around, tidying up here, tidying up there."

Thelma stepped toward him and sniffed. "Have you been drinking, Harry?" You're carrying on like a raving lunatic!" Anger took the place of fear. "And why, for the love of God, have you been spying on me, peeping through the windows like some silly schoolboy?"

He lunged forward and grabbed her arm, holding on so tight she cried out. "I want to know why you've been avoiding me." His eyes narrowed. "You're nothing but a tease, you know that?"

"How dare you!" She jerked her arm free. For just a moment, she wanted to slap him, but held back. He spoke the truth. After all, she had been the one to make the first move, arousing him in ways he hadn't experienced in a long time. A dragon had been awakened, and the blame fell on her. Rubbing her eyes, she turned away and walked to the living room, with Harry close on her heels.

"So you're just going to ignore me, is that it?" His voice rang out.

She dropped down on the settee, staring off in silence. He sat down beside her, taking her hand in his. Her heart swelled with emotion. Apparently the time apart had had an impact on both of them. She'd missed his touch and the sound of his voice, as well as the security she felt whenever they were together. Thelma drew in a long breath, letting the air out of her lungs slowly.

"I'm sorry, Harry. I didn't mean to come across as a tease, really I didn't." She turned her head and made full eye contact with his. "It's just that I think I'm wanting more out of life, and when you told me last time that you were mostly okay with things being the way they were, I guess I just snapped."

He didn't say anything, but sat there, rubbing his finger over the top of her hand, listening to every word without judgment.

"To be honest with you, I want a husband, someone who comes home to me every night, someone I can eat dinner with, someone who comes to bed with me every night."

She turned her head away for a few moments before gathering up the nerve to speak again. "All this talk about me finding a job and working made me think you didn't care about us as anything more than friends. After last time, I decided I wouldn't be some man's toy any longer, so I decided to cut everything off, to see if you even cared or not!"

Harry swallowed and cleared his throat. "So that's what this is all about?"

Though relieved to have finished her confession, Thelma hung her head in embarrassment.

"I don't know what to say, really." He shook his head in disbelief. "Let me ask you one thing, did you do all these things to trick me or lure me into marriage?"

A heated flush colored her face, and his questions pierced her soul. If she loved this man, telling the truth led the way out of the predicament she'd created. She faced him. "Harry, I did all these things with you because I wanted to. And, yes, I want marriage out of the deal, but I wouldn't have dared gone so far if I didn't … love you so much."

"You love me?" His hand tightened around hers.

"Of course I do." Thelma thought for a second, struggling to find the right words. "We've been together going on two years now, and I'm just ready for something more. But I'm also prepared to let you go, too, if you're not ready." She sighed and rubbed his arm. "And if you walked out of here right now, I'd understand. But please, don't think I don't care about you."

They sat together in silence for several minutes, Harry with his eyes on Thelma, and her eyes back to focusing on the floor.

He spoke first. "I don't what to say, hon. I really don't." He sat closer to her and put his arm around her. "I think after Anne died, I let that be my clean way out of marriage, and part of me hoped I'd never have to do it again."

"And I'll say this, Harry. I blame Anne for turning you against relationships." Thelma's courage had returned, and with it, a looser tongue. "I never thought I'd share this with you, but honestly, I hate her for what she did to you. No man should ever be shunned like that, especially not someone as fine as you are. You deserve much better than that." She gave him a light smile, patting him on the thigh.

"Since you're into sharing so much right now, there's something else I need you to share with me." He looked her straight in the eyes. "I think you can pretty much guess what that might be."

Thelma paled at this last comment. "What do you mean?" His face wore an intensity she hadn't seen often, but it signaled the seriousness of their conversation at this point; coming clean with whatever he wanted to know was the only way out.

"I haven't pushed too much on this issue, but I've made a few comments—I even asked you a couple of times about it. But you distracted me and change the conversation to something else." He took her head in his hands and placed his face close to hers, his eyes burning straight through her, so much she almost swore for a moment he saw into her soul and every thought she'd ever possessed. "Where did you learn your skills in the bedroom?"

She pulled away a little. "Harry, really, I can't tell you that."

"You can't tell me? Why's that?" He pulled her back toward him.

"I promised I wouldn't, that's why." A light scowl covered her face as she flinched, wishing hard he hadn't pursued this topic of conversation. Talking about Anne was easier.

Now his eyes seemed to glow with a fierce intensity, a mix of irritation and a twinge of despair. "I'll say this, Thelma, if you can't tell me certain secrets, after all we've been through, then you won't be able to tell me as a spouse or anything else, for that matter."

Her eyes widened. She said nothing. Where did he plan to go with this line of questioning? Did her answer really matter that much? Would the answer determine her future?

He continued. "This may come as a surprise to you, but I've actually been doing some thinking about us lately, especially since we've begun to share some more intimate moments. In doing so, I realized what was missing between Anne and myself was a good solid friendship." His fingers stroked her hair, straightening out some small locks, watching as they fell back into place. "Do you understand what I'm saying?"

"Maybe," she answered with caution. *Do I dare tell him the truth, after all, or let him walk?* She'd never had any reason not to trust him before. He'd always seemed like a discreet man, one who honored secrets if the need called for it.

"To me, it's just as important to be good friends as lovers, and if you care about me as much as you say you do, then put your money where your mouth is."

She sat up straight and inhaled a deep breath, filling her lungs to their full capacity, before exhaling again. Looking him in the eyes, she unburdened herself of her great secret. "Harry, when I tell you I was sworn to secrecy, I'm not kidding about that. If certain people find out, or if trouble comes up because I told, I can be punished."

Harry nodded. "Go on."

"When I went away, I really didn't go on a teaching job."

His eyebrows shot up on hearing this. "So where did you go?"

"I went to The House."

Silence.

"You see, our relationship, even then, had me in such a state that I simply broke down. Nothing was happening, nothing was moving forward, and I just snapped one day."

"So it's my fault?"

Thelma gave a little shrug. "I could blame you. As a matter of fact, I did blame you at first, right when I came home. But I thought if I could entice you more, do something special to make you pay attention, then you'd come around on your own and see it my way."

Harry's cheeks turned pink. "So you did have something up your sleeve, after all, didn't you?"

"Good lord, I guess so." She sunk into his arms, exhausted at this conversation, and equally surprised he didn't push her away. "But just remember, I want to be with you, and not anyone else."

He sat back, eyes closed, thinking for a moment. "The more I think about it, seems like I've heard some stories about The House. It's just been so long, I can't remember right offhand. So what did they teach you there that's so much of a secret they threaten you with bad things if you tell?"

"They taught me skills on how to love well, how to enjoy the body and sexual pleasure." Her mood livened up a little. "The more you told me about Anne, the more I believed I might be able to help you get your vitality back. And Harry, you have to believe me when I say you're a terrific lover. Crazy old Anne didn't know what she was missing, so too bad for her."

Her voice became urgent. "But please don't make me pay the price for her mistake or foolishness. And most of all, you can't tell anyone what I've told you, because the staff at The House could come after me and take me back there again. They'll say I'm insane, not to believe anything I'm saying, and put me on the crazy side next time."

"The crazy side? You mean to tell me there's different parts of The House?"

"Oh, yes, the one for treating the insane, and the other side that's a whole different world." She whispered, almost to herself. "It's a world of complete, unadulterated hedonism."

"You don't say." Harry grinned at her. "Well, I must admit they taught you well!" He rubbed his fingers over her shoulders.

"And you, you're a natural. You feel so good, and ..." She caught herself just in time to ward off the new ache looming between her thighs. Intense conversation or not, thinking about him lodged deep inside her always enticed her.

Smiling, he sat for a few seconds, staring at her.

She took a deep breath before asking the question, one she had feared the answer to most of all: "Are we through, now?"

The smile had left Harry's face, and the former look of intent had taken its place. "I think we're finished with this particular conversation, now that I know what's been going on. But I'm not through with you, if that's what you're concerned about."

Thelma closed her eyes, relieved, and said a silent prayer of thanks. Resting her head on his shoulder, she ran her fingers over his thighs, feeling the strong muscles underneath. "So where do we go from here?"

He paused for what seemed like an eternity, rubbing his lower lip lightly with his finger. "Well, it's too late to go to the justice of the peace, so we can't do that. But come Monday, we can decide what we want, a wedding or to go to the courthouse. Either way is fine with me."

She lifted her head up, gazing at him with disbelief. Did she hear "wedding" and "justice of the peace" come out of his mouth? "What are you saying, Harry?"

With a chuckle, he kissed the tip of her nose and slipped down on one knee, taking her hand in his. "Will you marry me, Thelma, and love me, even if I am slow at taking hints? I promise I'll pay closer attention, and I'll take care of you, love you, and treasure you forever." He grinned.

"Are you really ready to take this big step? I don't want you feeling forced into this."

"Silly girl, I told you I've been thinking about us more ever since you've been home from The House, and you making the moves you did actually worked. I began toying with the idea of giving love another chance. You gave me permission to love again."

"Or at least lust. You have to admit, Harry, you won't find another woman who can or will do what I do."

He let out a hearty laugh, pulling her into his arms. "That much I agree with. And, Thelma, I do want sex this time around, and lots of it. I don't want a cold marriage ever again."

"You won't have one, darling, I promise." She pulled his head toward her, landing a kiss on his lips. "You're much too good to go to waste." Her eyelashes fluttered a little as she spoke. "And I won't be naughty again and keep secrets from you, either."

"There won't be any need for secrecy, but naughty? Well …" His eyes shined, and his lips met hers again. He offered her his tongue, which she flirted with, sucking lightly, taking in every breath of his as her own. When they finished, he whispered in her ear. "I'm feeling naughty, Thelma. It's been way too long for me."

She didn't say anything, but got up from the settee and pulled him up after her. They walked to the bedroom and closed the door. This time she let him undress her, savoring the moment, enjoying every touch from his nimble fingers. When he finished, she reclined on the bed and watched him undress, thrilling at the sight of him when his slacks and underwear came off. In the glow of the soft lamplight, he looked so strong and handsome, with muscles showing off their curves under his skin.

His smile and sparkling eyes warmed her heart, and his body heat sent her lust soaring to new heights. This time, when she opened her thighs and let him in, she wasn't merging with just a friend now, but with her lifelong lover, soon to become her husband, the one she'd wanted, cared about, and loved for so long. She closed her eyes, letting her senses feel every bit of him as he penetrated not only her most hidden place, but her soul. Yes, they'd pulled each other from the brink of despair, saving each other from their own demons, and now the future looked good. Very good.

TAMING BAD

CHAPTER 1

Dr. James, The House physician, rested back in a broad leather chair, nodding occasionally at the attractive, dark-haired lady in front of him. From behind a large mahogany desk, he held a Manila folder, filing through papers, narrating various lines.

"This guy will be a handful, I warn you."

Daria shifted forward in her seat, craning her neck toward the folder. "How so? And why would you trust me with him?"

"You've recently been treated here at The House. You're now an attendant. You know how to treat and care for patients, whom we call admits. With all your rave reviews and splendid performance, of course I thought of you first for this case." The doctor dropped the file on the desk and smiled. "Thomas is a worthy attendant, and though he wasn't assigned to you, times with him meshed well with what you learned from your personal attendant. You've got a strong personality, believe in our treatment methods, and can hold your own in any situation. I think you can handle this man, but it's important you keep a few things in mind as you go along."

She inched forward in her chair. "Is there something special about him, something different from most admits we receive?"

"As you know most admits who are admitted to this side of The House have issues surrounding their sexual nature. Some don't feel comfortable with it; don't understand it. Because they shy away and repress their natural urges, other problems arise. Others are curious and want to explore it more. When they do, family members or the community try to stifle their progress. This guy is no different as far as experiencing those same urges. However, the difference I suspect is that he's out of balance, and doesn't know how to control himself well enough to create an enjoyable moment with someone.

"Doesn't know how to connect with someone, you mean?" Daria tilted her head, narrowing her eyes.

"Our gentleman is smooth, charming, but contains an arrogant streak. I hear he can be a bit hard around the edges, too, especially when he gets impatient. He simply wants to enjoy the contact of another like we all do, but he blows it because he comes on too strong. His family brought him here because they want him cured of his deep infatuation with women once and for all, and I already have a plan. But first, you're going to have to put him in his place."

Her ears perked up at this prospect already. She loved a challenge, putting men in their place.

Dr. James got up from his chair and joined Daria on the other side of the desk. "Look, from what I understand, his dad's already a lothario in the community. Chases anything in a skirt. I've known of him for a while. Most likely old pops doesn't want sonny boy for competition, but he surely doesn't want his son's forward behavior sullying his own reputation. The only difference between father and son, dad knows how to handle himself with discretion, finesse, and good timing, while his son tends toward over asserting himself—and not in the most positive way. Newton needs a … how shall I say it? A transformation, if you will."

"Newton? Transformation?" Daria furrowed her brow.

"His name's Newton Grenfield, and like I said before, I've already decided how to treat this guy. Your role in his treatment will be no different from anyone else's, for the most part. But my task in this deal is more radical and permanent."

Shrinking back, she eyed the doctor, and frowned. "Radical and permanent? Like how?"

Dr. James's expression turned grim. "I don't even like sharing this with you, but you need to know so you can determine your treatment plan. Newton will be surgically altered before he leaves here."

The doctor's eyes bore into her, sad and sympathetic, and for a moment she stifled a wave of nausea. "Is that necessary? I mean if we can teach him control and proper behavior, I don't see the need for going to such extremes."

He sighed. "Daria, I don't like stripping a man with what nature gave him, but sometimes, it's the best solution."

"How on earth can that be a best solution? If you do this, he won't enjoy sex anymore. This whole idea is crazy, and I'm not buying it." The sound of her own voice inching up in volume alarmed her, and she glanced away, taking a few deep breaths.

The doctor placed a hand gently on her shoulder. "Look, sometimes men have an extra strong drive, which goes much more beyond liking a particular activity a lot. And let me share this. If I don't perform this surgery his father wants, he'll take his son to another place, and Newton will leave with nothing to help him enjoy physical pleasure in his new condition. In my opinion, this would be a tragedy. He needs our help so he can enjoy life in the best way possible.

"Let's face it, in this day and age, most women are looking for husbands. They're not figuring the need for a compatible sex partner into the equation. A good relationship has two people who also enjoy each other physically. Our friend Newton is putting the cart before the horse. He's going straight for the sex, when he should be concentrating first on helping the woman feel comfortable and earning her trust so she sees other good traits in him as a potential spouse. That's where we come in.

"So right now you need to concentrate on gearing his mind toward appealing to women first and pleasuring them later, all because it makes them happy. Teach him the art of persuasion for a positive outcome so the fairer sex finds him irresistible and wants him. Teach him how to pleasure himself and ways to stimulate pleasure. Just because he'll be toned down doesn't mean he won't be able to enjoy physical contact and still use what nature gave him." Dr. James smiled and squeezed Daria's hand. "Are you still in on this? This man needs you, and he'll learn it sooner or later."

"I think so, Dr. James. I don't want him going somewhere else where he'll be neglected and not cared for." Daria gave him a resigned smile.

He patted her hand. "I want you learning about Newton and how he thinks, how he functions, what drives him. Let him open up, and I guarantee you'll have a better understanding of this man and see things my way." He winked at her and stood up. "You'll find him on the third floor in room 168 at the end of the hall. We quickly processed him. He's been settling in for the last hour. If he's really the kind of guy I think he is, he'll be at the end of his rope by the time you get there. Use that to your advantage. Try him out and see what he's made of. Don't give him the upper hand until you want him to have it. Use different rewards and punishments. See what works, what doesn't. He's not here for only *his* pleasure, but for learning how to pleasure every woman he meets from this point forward. Right now, the only thing standing between an overeager man and a great lover and husband is you, Daria. You can help make this change, because he can't do it on his own. If he gets out of line, show him who's running the show."

"Got it." Daria grinned and nodded.

As she walked the long hallways back to the room, she remembered her first time coming to The House, viewing its castle-like facade as it stretched over a large, manicured lawn. Apprehension had reached a peak as she passed through the doors with her parents. After speaking with the steward in his office, her parents had said their good-byes and promised they'd come back for her.

Bitterness dissipated once she'd ended up in Dr. James's office for a required thorough physical exam. His asking her to strip ignited a surge of curiosity, as she'd not been given a gown or other means to cover herself. Instead of shame, his request only stirred up lust. She'd liked the look of him immediately—his strong build and handsome face outlined by a strong jawline. His piercing eyes mesmerized her, and she adored his warm smile.

When he assisted her to the exam table and asked her to spread her thighs, she did so willingly, thrilled when he inserted his finger inside her and continued the remainder of the time exploring her nether regions, running his fingers through her folds and teasing her clit, all with the simple explanation that he wanted to make sure she was fit for participation in the House's program. And the rest had been history. She'd taken to the treatment regimen with no reluctance, relishing every opportunity to explore sensual pleasure in all its unadulterated glory.

Would Newton feel the same? Would he be as willing to submit, or would he fight her every step of the way?

§§§

Daria stood back from the doorway, gazing at the nude man on the bed. One of his hands had been cuffed to the iron headboard. The other remained free. Since he was in a room, staff had wasted no time stripping him of his street clothes, according to House protocol. The cuffed wrist was unusual. Admits and cuffs went hand in hand with attendants deciding when and if to use them. Finding her new charge already tethered held an allure, nonetheless.

His brawny chest displayed strong ripples in the soft bedroom light, and from what she surmised, his face showed extraordinarily good looks—chiseled jaw line, and what looked like a succulent set of lips. Stretched out, he appeared at least six feet in height, with muscular thighs and equally developed arms. No wonder he radiated sex appeal.

Putting the conversation with Dr. James behind her, Daria turned her attention fully on Newton. With eager fascination, she watched as he toyed with his cockhead, fingering the tip. Apparently his trek through the halls had put him in the mood, and he'd wasted no time in imitating many of the inhabitants. He took special delight in stretching out his shaft and releasing, shifting his hips in pleasure when the flesh sprang back into place. Daria licked her lips, her loins heating up. Time to learn more about this bad boy and what made him so bad that his dad wanted him fixed once and for all.

No matter how sensual the interactions between attendant and admit, there remained one rule: no falling in love. Unbridled lust and sex were permitted. Attendants fully treated and cared for their admits, with everything from stern discipline to tender nurturing to basic physical needs, while offering their body for the admit's learning purposes. Both enjoyed equal satisfaction in the process, engaging in domination and submission roles.

She took a deep breath, strolled into the room, and stood by the bed, gazing down at Newton with lusty eyes. His beauty came through equally well up close. Short cropped sandy hair, taut skin, lips turned into a faint grin. His bright gray eyes held a sullen irreverence, a look that burned through her when he turned his face. A paradox of hot lust mingled with a sting of uneasiness crept slowly through her body.

"Hi, Newton. I'm Daria. I'll be your attendant during your stay here."

"My attendant?" His eyes roamed over her. "The whole time I'm here?" He chuckled, and went back to playing with his cock. "Since everybody else seems to be going at it, I thought what the hell. Might as well have fun too. What is this place? Some kind of goddamned twisted hotel, where men run around half-dressed and the gals priss around in tight, short dresses up to their asses?"

"It's dress protocol for The House. Men wear nothing but black trousers, and the ladies wear these dresses. You'll soon see why."

"Hell, I've seen why. Did the men building this place forget to put the doors up? Got an eyeful when I came down the hall, women getting felt up, men humping ass." His face brightened into a wider smile. "I even saw a lady humping a man's ass. Those man pants are handy, the way the front unsnaps, and the whole crotch panel can be pulled out of the way. With your cock and ass exposed, no wonder it's easy to get some on both sides."

"Then you've had a brief introduction to The House." Daria smiled and joined him on the bed.

"Hey." Newton angled his head, motioning for her to come closer. "Do I get a chance to run my tongue through that sweet pussy of yours, like I saw some of the other men doing to those women?" He shot out his tongue and flicked it up and down in rapid succession. "You're pretty, and a smoking hot chick like you …" He let out a light whistle. "Bet I could make you howl."

Daria's gut clenched and her slit moistened. She'd love nothing better than to settle over that luscious mouth and let his hot, eager tongue wash over her clit and slide in and out of her hole.

"Are you always this charming, Newton? Talking to a girl like that after you've barely met?" She ran a finger against his cheek.

The smile left his face. He remained silent a few seconds. "No, I usually keep my nasty mouth to myself, but from the looks of this place, I figured I could let my hair down for a minute."

"So you have two sides, a nice side and maybe a naughty side?" She whispered the words in his ear.

He grinned. "You're a tease, aren't you? What are you talking about, two sides?"

She propped up on her elbow beside him. "Most of us have different sides to our personality, one we use in public, the other we use when we're with different company."

"You may have a point there. Never gave it much thought." He frowned. "If I had my way about it, I'd probably show my naughty side more."

"Why is that?" Daria studied his expression: the tight jaw, a quick lick of his lips, a distant look in the eyes. A struggle brewed. It held him captive.

Newton shrugged. "It'd be so much easier to just cut to the chase and get on with it. Formalities wear my ass out. Besides, this place seems to have ditched the formalities and hopped right into the sack. I kind of like that." He glanced up at her and grinned.

"Sometimes things aren't what they seem." Daria kept a straight face.

He grimaced. "Then tell me why I'm in what looks like a fancy whorehouse, and why I have an arm cuffed to the bed like a god-damned criminal?" His face clouded with irritation. "Why am I here buck naked with a hot gal, and what's with all the carousing I see?"

Running a few fingers through his hair, she continued, "Why don't you tell me why you're here, Newton?"

His jaw tightened. "Are you playing games with me?"

"We may look like we play games here, but we don't."

"And why the hell are you touching me like that?" His eyes trailed down to his chest. Daria continued smoothing over his nipple with her finger.

"What's the matter? Don't you ever have women running their hands all over you? You're mighty handsome."

Newton swallowed hard. Daria pulled her hand away and propped back up on her elbow.

"I don't normally have women touch me like you just did." He turned his face away and stared up at the ceiling. "Women, they bat their eyes, smile, act like they're interested, but when you go in for a little more, they shut you down."

"Why?" She kept her voice soft and calm. This approach seemed effective so far—test him, feel him out, get a sense of what was going on in his head.

"I don't know. Maybe because they're teases? You don't lead a guy on and then back out. That hurts, you know what I mean? It hurts right down to the crotch." He turned and gave Daria a steely look. "Let me tell you something. You get this guy's motor running, I want to be in for the finish. I don't appreciate a gal getting my cock stirred up and ditching me at the last minute."

"They ditch you? How so?" She pursed her lips and waited.

"We're together, alone, enjoying the scenery. We're out on some nice date, you know." His voice lightened a little. "I put my arm around her, start with a kiss, and by the time it's all over, she's trying to push me away. Says we're moving too fast. Yeah, that's the bunk they give you."

"Do you stop?" Alarmed, she sat up and stared down at him.

"Hell, yeah. What choice do I have? I don't need a slap on the face or their old man coming after me with a shotgun. They've cut and run. Well, that usually means I take them straight home. I never hear from them again, and when I try to talk to them or be nice afterward, they give me the cold shoulder."

Daria nodded. "So you feel like they've led you on."

He glared at her. "Pretty much. You don't know what a struggle it is to keep my cool. Sometimes I wonder if they're just telling me no but they really want it. They're just too prim and proper to admit it. You know, sometimes I have fantasies of tying them down, yanking off those panties, and when I spread those legs apart, showing them what a real man is. I bet once they had a shot of me, they wouldn't be all up in arms. They'd see it was okay. For the life of me I can't figure out why gals get so flustered when it comes to holding a stiff one in their cunt. I'm just tired of the bullshit, that's all. No more. I've had it."

Daria considered his words, studying the man next to her. Handsome, yet women pulled away at the last minute. From his animated accounts, she understood perfectly. Though his fantasies might work quite well at The House, they'd never work outside these walls unless he managed to find a willing partner. Oversexed, testosterone-laden? Most likely. And that's what Dr. James had tried to point out.

"You like sex, don't you, Newton? I can tell it's a passion of yours, the way your voice heats up when you talk about it." She nodded toward his genital region. "Just thinking about it stirs up that magnificent cock of yours."

Newton reached down and encircled an erect, fat shaft. "Hell yeah. I think about sex a lot. Most men do, and how to get the girl." He grinned, rubbing his thumb round and round his cockhead while she watched with interest.

She grabbed his wrist, pulling his hand away.

"I got you going too. I saw your eyes light up when you saw what I got." He nodded, licking his lips.

She maintained composure, making a mental note of concealing emotions from this man. Her clit ached. For a moment she wanted to throw caution to the wind, mount him, and ride him like no other, let that beautiful cock grind inside her and give both of them some relief. But all in good time. For now, she wanted to know him a little better.

"Has a woman ever let you have your way with her?" Daria's voice softened, hoping he'd talk more.

"I've had a couple of them wanting me to hump them, but they were loose anyway, women who'd do it with anybody. I don't want someone like that. I want a nice girl like every other man."

Daria gave him light smile. "What if I told you I could teach you how to get the girl? While you're here, you'll learn control and the difference between when to keep going and when no means no."

He narrowed his eyes. Without another word, he reached for his cock. With a few jerking motions and a rub on the tip, he shot out thick streams of lust. His lips turned into a triumphant smile. "There, I decided it was good to keep going."

She grasped his hand and fastened it to the bed with the remaining cuff. "Tell you what, for now I'll be the judge of when you'll keep going."

Newton chuckled. "Anyone ever tell you you're a feisty little thing?"

"Anyone ever tell you why you're here?"

Exasperated, he answered, "You still want to talk about that? I just want to do what everyone else is doing here. Hell, looks like you have a big time. And you still haven't answered my questions, Miss Smarty Pants."

Yes, a handful. Dr. James pegged this guy fair and square, and if she'd not been trained and so intrigued by this man, with his arrogance and saucy talk, she'd have slipped a gag in his mouth—and still impaled herself on him. He pursued sex, was driven by sex, consumed by sex. His story held something deeper, a victim of the body and its workings. Either way, she'd teach this man whatever the doctor said he needed, and Dr. James always did what was best for the admit.

"Your father brought you here because of your enthusiastic fascination for women, which we've discussed a little already. Your treatment here will help you deal with that better." Daria settled down beside him again.

"My old man." Newton paused in thought. "Now that's the irony of it all. Everything I learned, I learned from watching him. But the thing that chaps my ass is that I get thrown in here, and he runs around scot-free, dipping his wick in anything that'll let him."

She placed her face over his, staring deep into his eyes. "And do you think that's the key difference between you and your father? Women really want him? He knows how to handle them so they'll say yes. They never tell him no."

Newton gazed back at her. "When I was in high school, I caught my old man with another woman. Mama had gone somewhere, and he thought he'd sneak a fast one with someone else. I came home from school and heard giggling down the hall. Curious, I slipped up to the bedroom door, not even breathing because I didn't want anyone hearing me. But I saw them on the bed, him with arms all around her, though she tried to push him away. She wasn't really fighting him off, but I didn't think she was totally keen on whatever it was he was trying to do, either.

"Every time she stalled, he backed off a little, talking all nice and sweet, telling her that he'd take it slow, everything was all right. He smoothed his hand over her thighs. Of course he'd managed to get her dress above her waist. He whispered god knows what in her ear." Newton glanced up at Daria. "She calmed down a bit. And by damn, if the old coot didn't slip his fingers nice and easy around her panties and pull them down. When she started to flinch, he cooed some more, saying it was okay. Then he went for it before she knew what hit her.

"His face went down on her, and she wasn't squeamish anymore. When he touched her, she bloomed like a flower, those thighs spreading even wider. Matter of fact, she laid back quiet as a mouse while he licked and flicked that tongue of his all over her." Newton's gaze focused on the ceiling again. "I just never had a knack like he did. When I get heated up, I just want to go for it. And why would that lady have wanted to stop? She went home with him. What did she expect, Sunday dinner?"

"Newton, whatever it is you're lacking, we'll help you develop the charm you need, make you a better lover. Right now it seems like you're probably a little pushy, and I'm here to help you get control."

"I thought I was in control, going after what I wanted, making the first move, taking the lead."

"Going after something doesn't mean you're really in control. Control is using discretion, judging a situation and when it's okay or not okay to make a move. Despite what you think, your dad has mastered that technique on some small level. You, not so much."

"Yeah, tell me about it." He moved to run his fingers through his hair, but the cuffs stopped him, clanking against the iron headboard. "Can you take these damn things off?"

She wrapped her fingers under his chin and gave him a firm squeeze, enunciating her words nearly into his mouth. "I'll tell you when they'll come off, and no time sooner."

He slid his jaw around after her fingers released him. "Damn, you sure know how to get your point across."

"Let me tell you a little secret. No matter what happens, no matter how tough it may get, we're here to help you. You're lucky we took you in on this side of The House, because there's another side where you wouldn't have gotten out. You'd have been trapped forever, no pretty women, no cozy comforts you see here. Just filthy, ugly bodies and decaying souls."

"Another side? You mean there's two sides to this place?" He looked at her in amazement. "I've never heard of a nut house having two sides."

"Well, we have that here, and no one who leaves this side ever discusses it in the community, or they risk being brought back here if they're caught. And if you're brought back here, you won't be with me."

"So does that have something to do with all the fucking I saw in the rooms? And will we be doing any of that, or do I have to stay here cuffed to this damn bed?"

Daria caressed his nipple again. "Listen to me. If you want to enjoy what you've seen in these rooms and get out of The House, you'll need to do everything I say, learn everything I teach you. You'll actually be learning how to enjoy sex in a proper way where it's not only enjoyable for you, but for the lady you're with. By the time you're done here, you'll out-best your dad and any man where women are concerned."

He eyed her, squinting as she spoke. "Let me get this straight. The only way I'll be able to get some pussy is to have you boss me around?"

"Pretty much. When I tell you to do something, you do it. When I tell you not to do something, you stop."

"Or what?" The insolent gleam played in Newton's eyes.

"You'll be punished." Daria's gaze deadlocked with his. Not only had her professional side kicked in full force, her lusty side ran right beside it. She liked a challenge. Newton, so far, rated number one on her list.

"Ooh, should I be scared?" He chuckled.

Without warning, she delivered a sharp swat on the outside of his thigh.

He glared at her. "Son of a bitch!"

Grasping the underside of his chin again, she lowered her face over his. "And you'll not talk like that to me again. Ever."

Daria stared into his eyes. "Every time you step out of line, I'll whip that ass of yours into shape. Or I might have some other punishment up my sleeve. Regardless, you'll do what I say. Play nice, and I'll give you more tits and pussy than you ever dreamed of. I'll wear that cock of yours out so much, you'll be begging me to stop."

With a loud laugh, he said, "You're on sister. You'll never wear this man out." He laughed some more.

CHAPTER 2

There, at least you're cleaned up a little before we have dinner." Daria swiped a hot washcloth over Newton's thighs and pelvic area where his cum had dried, taking extra time with his cock and balls.

"I shoot hard, don't I?" A set of fine white teeth gleamed from his mouth.

"What did I tell you about keeping quiet for the next hour?" She smacked his thigh and shot him a warning glare. "You'll speak when I ask you a question."

He pursed his lips and turned his eyes to the ceiling, stifling a grin. Daria knew he wanted her fondling his cock and rolling his balls between her fingers. Each time she pressed firmly and let the spongy contents in his sac spring back against the pads of her fingers, he sucked in his breath.

"Has a woman ever given these trinkets of yours a good squeeze?"

"No, ma'am."

She rubbed the side of his thigh with approval. "Good, and that's it, keep those eyes glued on the ceiling while you're lying here."

One cloth remained in a brass bowl filled with hot water. Earlier Daria had used the others, wiping her charge from top to bottom, taking precious time in examining him everywhere. The startled yet aroused look on Newton's face set her clit on fire as she remembered inserting a finger inside his rectum, all with the explanation that she wanted him extra clean. He'd been tight, hot, squirming when she rimmed his ass. From the contortions on his face, he struggled to keep quiet, but no doubt found her touch pleasant.

A revved-up man like this one, though, needed frequent rewards. If he played his cards right, minding her until bedtime, she'd decided on an extra special treat. She needed to know what he was like unleashed, at full capacity, letting his passions run amok and unchecked. Besides, she'd checked in with staff at the desk, requesting that they pay special attention to this room at the end of the hall, listening and looking out for anything that might signal trouble.

If other women had run away nervous, unwilling, what would he be like in the arms of a willing woman, one who wanted his tongue slipping eagerly over a hot clit, one whose core ached for a well-endowed cock like his? Were his hands really gentle, glossing over soft flesh and thumbing nipples until an ache settled in the chest? Or was he a pure beast, an animal with no thought or care?

Yes, if he'd settle down long enough, they'd both enjoy a lusty reward. She'd told staff to serve dinner in the their room tonight. As eager as he'd presented himself, dining in the main room with everyone else risked sending him overboard, and she didn't want the shock value at such an early time in his treatment.

He lifted his neck as she ran a cloth over the taut flesh. Even the muscles there bulged a little when he turned his head. He let out a little sigh. Switching out arms, she unfastened the cuffs so he could flex, stretch, and release tension. When he finished, Daria replaced the cuffs, ignoring the scowl on his face. With firm pressure, she massaged the muscles pressing hard inside his skin. A strong man, for sure.

Taking his fingers in her hands, she massaged each one, followed by pressing certain points in the hand and wrist. She admired the long length of his fingers, but marveled even more at the thickness of them, fleshy, soft, and how delicious they'd feel fondling her nether regions. Her loins quickened as she imagined him spreading her apart, sinking his middle finger deep inside, grazing slick walls wet with thick fluid. She pressed on the inside of his wrist; his face drew up in pleasure.

"Do you like this, Newton? Does it make you feel good?"

"Yes, ma'am. I like it more when you play with my cock and—"

"Enough! I don't need detailed explanations. A simple yes will do."

She turned her attention back to his hands, taking in a quick view of his cock, which had stiffened a little. It didn't take much to fire Newton up, but the act of bathing and caring for him told her much about his immediate personal likes and dislikes.

He definitely struggled with her taking the lead. The back massage she'd given him earlier seemed the most effective in calming him down, but caressing his nipples took the prize, the way his face went blank, the way his eyes nearly glazed over. Pinching the tiny nub of flesh, bad. That move only stirred him up, with him sucking in his breath and arching his hips ever so slightly. Better to save it for when she wanted him hotter.

One more push against a pulse point, and she stopped. "I think we're done now." Daria carried the bowl to the door, placing it in a designated pickup spot. A staff member would be along soon to remove any used items. Another beauty of The House was efficiency and creativity. Things got done as if by magic. Anything you wanted—food, supplies, toys—could be obtained day or night. All these activities occurred in a setting filled with opulent beauty. Eye-catching glass sconces lit up artfully, tiled hallways, and the common room held luscious thick-piled carpet topped with cushioned couches and chairs. However, the most beautiful place was the magnificent marbled entrance hall filled with cunning naughty paintings, scantily clad statues on the stair landing, all topped with an enormous, glittering crystal chandelier. Daria loved The House. Her admit couldn't comprehend his luck now, but he'd soon learn.

Daria settled on the bed next to Newton. "Let me tell you a little about the rooms. First, they're all designed the same as this one we're in: bed, nightstand with lamp, chest of drawers, and sink. It's small, but it's safe and cozy. Most important of all, it's our sacred space. And you've already learned that anyone can see or be seen at any time.

Much of the time we'll be too engrossed in our own activities to care much what others are doing."

Newton blinked and nodded.

"The only time we can be nude is during meals in the main dining room and in our own room. Staff stripped you of your clothing because most of us like being undressed when we're in our rooms. To a newcomer, that can be startling, make you feel vulnerable. Sometimes we have special activities requiring nudity, but that's not every day. Otherwise, you'll wear trousers like you've seen on the men, and I wear a dress like this. From what you can see, it's all well thought out and efficient when it comes to getting down to business." She grinned at him.

He returned the smile, a sincere one without any hint of a smirk or indication of testing limits. Too bad his nature held a rebellious streak. When he smiled in the purest sense, he hinted at some kind of charm, which must have been hidden below the surface of arrogance and stubbornness.

"I've decided that tonight, we'll eat dinner here in the privacy of our own room. You'll have plenty of time for the ruckus that goes on at mealtimes. Do you have any questions for me?"

"If we can be buck naked in our rooms, why haven't you taken that dress off?" The question actually came out without suggesting a hidden agenda, but one of genuine inquiry.

"Of all the things I've been telling you, and seeing some of the activities on your way to this room, all you can think of is why I'm wearing House attire?"

"It's an honest question." He blinked at her like an innocent child. "I mean, I asked you based on what I saw and what you've told me. We're in our room, and I'm not wearing anything. So why haven't you removed that dress of yours?"

"Don't you want to know about more about The House, consequences if rules are broken, anything like that?" Daria tapped her fingers on the bed, amazed at such a one-track mind.

"You told me the basics and what would happen if I stepped out of line. You told me what I needed to do to get what I want. That's good enough for me."

She sat up and stared down at him. "Is that all you think about, Newton? Seeing a woman naked, wondering if this will be the time you can finally get inside her panties? Is that it?"

He shrugged. "Pretty much, and if you tell me how to catch a woman and keep her, then I'll be set." Again, that silly grin.

"Tell you what, you stop worrying about your next hot moment, and let me worry about that. To answer your question, I'll take this dress off whenever I like."

Newton turned his face away and stared up at the ceiling, irritated.

"We have two more hours before dinner. Rest here. Take a nap. Count sheep. I don't care, but you need to cool off. Trust me, it'll be to your advantage."

Silence.

Daria stepped out of the room and strolled down the hall to the attendant's station.

"Well, how is our fine gentleman?" Dr. James put his arm around her as she strolled up to the desk. "I couldn't end the day without checking on you first."

"He's full of energy, and I'll leave it at that." She grinned, shaking her head.

"An interesting fellow."

"I know we all have high amorous drives here, but there's something about him, almost animal."

Dr. James nodded. "Men like him are driven by high testosterone, and he's a classic case. You have to keep on them, if you haven't guessed that already."

"I'll get control of him. I've already set some limits, and he's trying awfully hard." She gave the doctor a sad expression. "Part of me feels a little sorry for him, but god, how he carries on."

The doctor nodded in sympathy. His eyes took on a distant look as though Daria's comment about feeling sorry for Newton seemed like a shared emotion.

"Are you sure he'll need such drastic measures as the one we discussed earlier?"

The gentleman moved to leave. "Daria, you just do the wonderful job you do, and we'll do what we have to do. In the meantime, you have any problems, come straight to me." He gave her a quick hug and left.

§§§

Newton turned in Daria's direction as she entered the bedroom. His face lit up when she settled next to him. "Glad you're back. It's lonely in here by myself."

"Who told you to talk?" She frowned down at him.

He scowled back. "Aw hell, my hour's surely been up. You said for an hour."

Laughing in spite of herself, she ran her fingers through his hair. "And you've tried to be good."

"I have. Don't I get something for that, a little treat? I'm not picky, really I'm not."

His lips begged for a kiss, and Daria wanted to kiss him, and sink her tongue into his mouth and taste him. This man had witnessed unusual scenes as he'd walked down the halls of The House, a strange place unlike any other. He'd been forced to lay cuffed to a bed, naked and exposed for all eyes to see when they passed by the room. Yes, those lips deserved kissing.

She landed her mouth over his, enjoying the way he kissed back, boldly taking in her tongue and sucking it. He extended his tongue deeper, brushing over the roof of her mouth, teeth and walls. He tasted sweet. Though he moved with urgency, an underlying tenderness pervaded the whole kiss. The sound of cuffs crying out in protest against the iron headboard disrupted her thoughts, and she caught desperation flooding his eyes.

He wanted to hold her, feel her. She knew it. His knees raised and lowered, sometimes bending out before settling on the bed again. His body echoed frustration a kiss couldn't settle. She whispered in his ear. "Newton, you can hold out a while longer."

"It's so hard. I don't think I can do it. Please get me out of these cuffs. They're killing me." The words came out raspy, urgent, yet sincere.

Someone this wayward hated the locked-in feeling of cuffs. No doubt their secure grip rendered him claustrophobic in some manner. Somewhere deep inside, she wondered what might happen to him once he returned home. "Just a little longer. You'll be okay. This is your first step in training, learning to follow direction." The pained expression on his face bit into her heart, and again she considered unfastening the cuffs and freeing him. "I'll stay right beside you until dinner comes, and that won't be long at all now."

Daria snuggled up against him, resting her head on his chest. How his heart pounded in her ear, screaming at her for such injustice as having him wait for what his body craved. Out of the corner of her eye, she caught sight of a new erection and stifled the urge to take it in her mouth. Too early for giving in. His taming had only begun.

"Newton, tell me a little bit more about yourself. What do you do?"

"There's not much to tell. I'm a simple person, though I get a wild hair and do crazy things every now and then, like sneak into one of the blind tigers, the hidden saloons, where you hope you can sip a drink or two without anyone carting you off. I like hanging with the guys and trying to meet chicks. Sometimes I'll take my car and head out to the woods and just camp by myself, enjoy the stars, maybe hunt something and eat it for dinner. I've caught animals with my bare hands." He shook his head. "I can catch a wild rabbit, but I can't seem to get my hands on a woman."

"Do you work?" Daria massaged his arm, concentrating around the wrist.

"My dad owns a car lot. I help him sell sometimes, but my real job is fixing cars."

"So you'll have a job when you return home."

"Oh, yeah. My old man sees to it that I don't go hungry, but I work for everything I have. I'm saving up my money to get my own place." His eyes lit up. "I plan on having a nice place a woman can be proud of."

She didn't dare broach the subject of children. If he looked around hard enough, he'd surely find a woman who didn't care for traditional roles of motherhood and housewife, or at least motherhood.

Her fingers trailed back over one of his nipples. "Looks like you've already made some plans for yourself and perhaps someone else, if you ever find her."

For the next twenty minutes they conversed until a staff member entered the room with two trays covered with silver domes. Newton flinched in embarrassment. A strong need for sex didn't always equate with total body comfort when it came to nudity in front of others. The attractive man carrying the trays kept a straight face, eyes focused on Daria.

"Your dinner is served, my friends. Hope you enjoy it." He placed the trays on the bed, according to Daria's instructions, and left.

"Are you going to let me loose so I can eat, or are you going to starve me, too?" He seemed dejected, barely looking at her at this point.

"I'd never starve you." She fluffed pillows under his head so he could eat; the cuffs remained intact.

"And what's with the change in personality? First you're smacking me around, barking orders, now you're all nice like you give a damn." His tone reeked of new hostility, and Daria's muscles and gut tightened. *Here we go again.*

"Newton, you really know how to kill a mood, don't you? We've finished a nice conversation, and now you get nasty. You'll learn trust and kindness while you're here. Those are some mighty powerful tools for winning someone over." She removed the tops from the trays, revealing a succulent meal of cubed vegetables, bite-sized chunks of meat, and strawberries for dessert. Cut-glass beverage glasses held iced tea. Newton eyed the trays.

She picked up the fork, spearing a piece of the meat, and held it in front of Newton's mouth. His brow wrinkled, but he obediently took the food, chewing and savoring the flavors before swallowing.

"Damn, this is good." He licked his lips. "Can't I eat on my own? I'm not a baby."

After swallowing a bite of her own meal, Daria studied the man before her, viewing his hair and the way it shined in the evening light beaming through the bedroom window. His eyes gleamed with passionate beauty, whether smiling, sullen, or downright angry.

Inside a dark cleft, her clit hammered away. Any other gentle action or words from him may have wreaked havoc with her own self-control. That's the way it usually went between attendant and admit. Holding back the urge, only to cut loose and ravish each other later.

"Are you going to answer me, or have I broken some other rule I didn't know about?" Clank went the cuffs.

Remaining calm, she locked her gaze on his. "There's great tenderness and beauty in caring for someone, meeting their needs, ensuring they're safe. Most of all, enjoying the happiness you feel knowing they like it." She propelled another fork load of food, a rich orange carrot coin, toward his mouth. "Has no one ever taken care of you?"

He ate the morsel she gently placed in his mouth. Meanwhile, his eyes squinted in thought. "I don't know, now that you mention it. My parents weren't ones for coddling anybody, and the old man did it for one thing only."

"It's more than just getting one thing only, Newton. There are acts of love, trust, and respect that go on long after intercourse is over. It's understanding someone's needs."

"Are you kidding me?" His eyes widened in surprise. "You talk a lot of bullshit. Just craziness." He accepted another bite of food after swallowing down some of his drink, which she held to his lips, maneuvering the glass carefully so he didn't choke.

"Do me a favor. Let's not talk for the rest of the meal. You can think about what I just told you and maybe with time, you'll understand better. It's a little unusual for people to grasp at first."

Newton shook his head, fixing his eyes on her. They ate the rest of the meal in silence. When it came time for dessert, Daria fed him the strawberries, and with the last one, took the delectable piece between her teeth and guided it into Newton's mouth.

"You're cute, you know that?" He said, after accepting and swallowing the fruit.

Daria gave him a warning glance. He grinned, eating the rest of the meal in silence.

Golden hues of evening lapsed into grey shades of twilight, deepening into dark of night. The beauty of darkness had settled over The House. Most attendants and their tantalizing admits had retired to their rooms. They may not have slept, but used the time for indulging lust and kinkier fancies.

The noise in the hallway had quietened to hushed whispers and the occasional soft footsteps as people traveled back to rooms or on their way to other wings. Daria had determined that this was the hour for releasing the cuffs, giving him free reign. She needed to see what he'd be like acting as the dominant one, with no instructions, no guidance. This exercise remained the last test for determining his skill in the bedroom, which equaled in importance for determining a well-rounded treatment plan. She turned down the covers of the bed. In the glow of the lamplight shining from the nightstand, he presented a more seductive figure.

From a pure physical aspect, she'd waited just as much as he for this moment. She'd gladly accept the entrance of the beast as it devoured her, welcoming it with open arms and a willing spirit. She had ached as much as he. Like all wild animals, he needed moments to exercise the wildest parts of himself, to explore, pursue, and finally pounce on his prey with a voracious appetite.

He had a deep hunger that gnawed in the pit of his belly, all the way down to the depths of his loins, burning, unyielding, nearly unstoppable. She knew, saw it from the glimmer in his eyes to the irascible nature and raw hostility in his voice. He'd watched everything she did with keen interest, most likely waiting with bated breath for her dress to hit the floor.

Her heart pounded inside her chest. The dampness between her thighs had nearly driven her insane. He'd have an easy time sliding into her. She caught the hem of the dress, whisking it off. As she ran her fingers through her hair, she stretched and twisted her body, showing off a set of firm breasts with each nipple holding a steel ring. Daria plucked at them, moving them gently up and down before resting them neatly against her skin. In silence he watched, eyes widening, mouth slowly turning up into a greedy smile.

"You're beautiful." For the first time his voice floated out in hushed tones.

"Thank you. We'll be sleeping together, in case you haven't figured that out by now." She reached for the cuffs and worked the fasteners. "There, you're free."

Newton stood by the bed, flexed his arms and fingers, and massaged each wrist. He stretched, arching his back before taking some steps around the room. For a few seconds, he entertained himself with sticking his head outside the door, stealing a few peeks up and down the hallway. He ran his toes against the softness of the carpet, and drank some water from one of the glasses on the sink. After a few gentle twists of his torso from side to side, he ended with a quick squeeze of his buttocks as he bobbed up and down on the balls of his feet. Between his thighs raged a new erection. Daria watched him with greedy eyes, admiring his muscles as they strained against smooth skin. He'd be delicious, inside and out. After several minutes, he returned to the bed and snuggled down.

"These are nice little rooms for a place like this. Just enough for what you'd need, I guess. And I like the idea of sleeping next to someone. I've never done that before."

"It's different here than out in the community, where people shame sensual pleasure, making others believe they've done something wrong." She ran her finger over his chest.

"What are those rings in your tits? I've never seen anything like those before." Without asking, he reached over and gently rubbed his finger over one of the rings, grazing her nipple. She caught her breath. "Oh, I didn't even think to ask. I'm sorry." He removed his hand.

"Newton, I promised you a treat, so I'm yours for the rest of the night. You can touch or do anything that you want with me. You can't be destructive or harm me in any way, but other than those simple rules, anything goes. If either of us feels pain or needs the other to stop, then we do."

He chuckled. "Oh, yeah! I wanted to fuck you the minute I saw you." The smile left his lips. "You've thought about it too. I've seen it in your face and the way you look at me. Women give me that look all the time, but I don't get my way with them, not like you're letting me do now."

Daria reached out and smoothed a stray lock of hair away from his forehead. "You just learn what I teach you, and you'll have just about any woman you want. That's my promise to you. Now do you want the light on or off?"

"I want it on. I want to see everything about you. If you're saying I can do what I want, then I want to see it all."

"Fair enough." She reclined back and waited.

Newton gazed at her through lust-filled eyes, pulling the covers all the way off. Like a hungry person before a feast, his gaze glossed over all of her. He hesitated.

"Go ahead. Don't be afraid." She urged him, a little surprised he hadn't ravished her all at once.

His finger trailed over her breasts, toying gently with the nipple rings. He moved them up, and delivered a series of soft squeezes to each peak. She smiled, closing her eyes.

"Your tits are gorgeous." He dipped his head down to her chest, flicking out his tongue over the rings, moving them up and down, ending with a gentle suck. When he took a nipple in his mouth and bit down gently, she let out a cry. His hands had landed on either side of her waist, where he caressed up and down her sides. He kissed over her abdomen and navel. "You're so soft too."

His mouth suckling her had already served as kindling for this interlude, and she ground her hips into the bed, wishing he'd just pry her open and fuck her hard. For once he kept his mouth shut and spoke only with his eyes, mouth, and fingers.

But she knew there would be more. This man who spewed rough talk and presented an equally rough facade was nothing more than a tender beast who didn't want a full-fledged attack all at once, but wanted to circle, tease, and torture her with moving slowly and deliberately. He kissed her neck and trailed his tongue down the same path his finger had traveled. Once he reached the top of her pubic bone, he stopped briefly and stared hard into her eyes.

His fingers roved over her thighs, sending her senses reeling. She felt the juices pouring out. With the greatest care, he nudged her thighs apart. Not caring if she seemed too eager, she opened them wider, offering herself. He spread her nether lips apart, eyes shining, an intent look on his face. She lay open before him, wet and throbbing, breathing fast. She didn't care. She'd be a sacrificial lamb. As he lowered his face, his hot breath flared across her skin.

Flicking out his tongue, he teased her, moving inside her cleft and pushing the tip of his tongue as far into her as he could. When he moved over her clit, she nearly screamed. A heated ache roared between her legs, painful and pleasant at the same time. He prodded harder at the little knot of nerves and ended with lowering his lips and suckling it like he'd done her nipples. Lick and suck, alternating between one delicious movement and another.

Her core clamped down with a splitting ache. She squeezed her eyes shut until she recovered her breath. She'd never wanted to be filled as badly as she did right now. As if reading her mind, he slipped in one of his fingers, sinking it deep inside her, swirling it round and round, slipping over her walls. Daria gasped. Her nipples tingled. The orgasm was coming, a slow pressure leading up to a dull ache, which would end in an explosion of sheer internal bliss.

Inside her center, his finger moved in slow gentle circles while another finger stroked her clit. The licking and sucking at intervals drove her to delicious madness. She closed her eyes and tightened her jaw, stifling a cry. One last suck, and the tidal wave came in a series of hard, sweet contractions. Her ass clenched, and when he ran a finger over her asshole, she whimpered.

Newton positioned himself over her, sliding easily between her legs. A rigid cock bobbed against her open pussy, and she counted the seconds it would take for him to slide that wonderful flesh inside her willing core. He aimed himself against her entrance, staring into her eyes with a brilliant, lusty gleam. With a smooth push, he slid inside her, piling himself in until he reached her back wall. She shuddered.

Daria sucked in her breath, reveling in the impalement, slick, fast, determined. His ample cock filled her beautifully, sliding against her walls. His eyes burned with greed before he closed them, concentrating, his mind wandering off to sacred places men often sought when caught in the paradox of swelling pain and baptism of release. He pumped his hips with ease, with purpose, grunting at intervals. As the seconds passed he moved faster, moaning louder. When he took her in his arms, the weight of him nearly suffocated her.

The movement of him built up a heady vibration within her loins, setting off another quick, hard climax. Her pussy clenched his cock; her spasms and his motions created the final eruption. He let out a loud growl and emptied himself.

Out of breath, he pulled her close and rolled over on the bed, landing with her on top. Beads of sweat on his forehead glistened in the light. He reached up and thumbed her nipples, relief reflected in his smile and touch. Daria grinned down at him. Like other attendants, her lessons included control of self and others while incorporating the last goal tantamount to treatment at The House: sexual pleasure.

Newton let out a soft, beautiful laugh. His teeth gleamed in the lamplight. He spent a few seconds flicking the rings in her nipples, taking utmost care, moving easily without jerking or hurting her. "Damn! That was the best ever."

CHAPTER 3

At least an hour had gone by. The hallways of The House looked the way they always did, admits and attendants walking arm-in-arm over the tiled floors to their next point of interest. She turned the corner, unlatched the door leading to the next wing, and paused, studying the wooden molding. Smiling, she remembered her reaction the first time viewing such remarkable artwork. The frame displayed carved scenes of people in various sexual acts, from anal intercourse and fellatio to cunnilingus and traditional missionary position. Leave it to The House for coming up with clever ways to keep the internal fires stoked.

She walked through the door, carefully shutting it behind her. Each floor housed people with different tastes and persuasions, and the aesthetic surroundings and comfort never wavered. Daria liked this about The House, its acceptance of lifestyles shunned by the community, embracing sensual pleasure in all its glory. The House catered to carnality with an almost worshipful attitude.

Those who entered here, perplexed by their own urges and required to repress them, received a profound healing not found anywhere else. They returned home with greater understanding, freedom, and a sharpened sense of self and others. Their relationships formed with purpose and greater selectivity, with personal needs and desires in mind.

These thoughts passed in quick succession as she roamed the halls, peeking in doorways, searching for someone lost. She finally gave up, as no one could give assistance. With growing irritation, she threw up her hands and headed back to her room. Surely he'd return at some point. No reason to continue on a fruitless chase. When she returned, her frustration hit full force as she viewed Newton casually standing at the sink, finishing up his morning activities, preening in the mirror with a comb in his hand.

"You're finally up. I guess last night wore you out?" He turned around, flashing her a huge smile.

She frowned back. "Where in the hell have you been, and how long have you been up?"

"I'm not sure about the time, but I've been all over this place, seen all kinds of weird shenanigans." He turned around and finished combing his hair.

"You've disobeyed me again. Why didn't you wake me up if you wanted to go somewhere? I've told you more than once to never leave without me."

"Maybe I just forgot. It happens. You looked like you needed the sleep, and I wanted to get moving, see what this place was like. And I guess I don't need to tell you the shit I saw going on."

Daria snatched the comb from his hand and tossed it back on the counter by the sink. "I would have gladly given you a tour. Actually that was my plan today." She pulled him back toward the bed and motioned for him to get on it.

"Tell me about the eyeful you got on your self-guided tour."

Newton propped up on one arm, eyeing her with curiosity. "So you let queers stay here too? Do you fix them so they're all right by the time they leave?"

Her eyes widened. "Excuse me, but we help them with their lifestyle, give them freedom to explore and feel comfortable in their own skin. And we definitely don't fix them, as you say. They're not broken. They prefer being with someone of their own sex."

"You do know they run the risk of getting their asses kicked or probably killed if anyone finds out." He turned his eyes up to hers, his face solemn.

"That's an unfortunate truth here in the late 1920s. The most we hope is that one day these people can love openly and without fear. Teaching them to love themselves and enjoy their partner is a big step for us."

"Let's just say it was really weird for me to see two girls kissing and fooling around with each other's pussies. And the men were worse, humping each other in the ass or tied to the bed, spread eagle, electrocuting themselves with strange contraptions attached to whatever it was up their asses or on their dicks. But they seemed to like the feeling once their buddies flipped a switch. They sure had big goofy smiles on their faces. And what's with men all dolled up in fancy party dresses, with their faces painted up like women? Hell, I hate to admit it, but some of them were prettier than a lot of girls I've seen." He grinned up at Daria with his last sentence.

She kept a straight face. "Just so you know, some of those pretty men still like women."

"Well, they apparently like their clothes too. Do you think they'll ever try on their girlfriend's undies or slip on their wife's dress once they leave here?"

With a sigh, Daria shook her head and studied him. "Newton, we can't control what people do once they leave, but we do try to heal."

"Through sexual healing? Is that what all this is?" He gave her an incredulous look.

"More people would benefit from sexual healing." She sat up and stared him straight in the eye. "Do you know that if you drew an imaginary line straight up through the human body and circled each gland or organ at certain critical areas, you'd have a spiritual or psychic counterpart to the actual physical part?" She placed her hand on his genital region. "This area is called the root, and it's the seat of all creation in the physical sense. On a spiritual level, if this area is blocked or not freely acknowledged, if you can't fully immerse yourself in the pleasures associated with it, you don't grow and develop. You can't continue in your own spiritual growth. If you can't satisfy your basic urges, you're stuck. And I'd wager a good solid bet that you're as blocked as the next person."

Newton narrowed his eyes, waving her away. "I've never heard such craziness in my life, and every church I've been to has taught that this place is anything but good." He reciprocated by placing his hand between her legs. "That no good comes from it unless you're in a married relationship. And don't get me started on the other crazies I saw on those floors."

Scowling, Daria replied, "Let me just say again that once you're unblocked, you'll experience freedom. But this won't be learned in one day. In the meantime, you went out roaming the halls without permission, you didn't wake me up when you needed or wanted something, and you need an attitude adjustment, so your punishment will be a writing assignment."

He frowned. "A punishment? A writing assignment?"

"Yes." Daria got up from the bed and moved to the chest of drawers, retrieving a notebook and pen. "You'll write five hundred times, 'I will obey Daria.' The next five hundred times, you'll write 'I will not judge others.' She tossed him the notebook and pen. "Get to work, because this will take you a while."

"You're serious, aren't you?" He glanced back and forth from the notebook to Daria.

"I'm dead serious. I don't play around. While you're here, you'll respect me, the rules, and others, whether you like it or not. And if you want a shot at my "root" area today, you best jump through the hoops."

"All righty, then." He pursed his lips and jerked up the notebook, positioning himself to write. Taking up the pen, he studied the blank page before applying the first stroke of ink.

§§§

Daria sat on the bed fuming. He'd done it again, slipped off as soon as she'd turned her attention elsewhere. Did her trip to the front desk or a quick run to another attendant's room signal time for a quick get-away? Apparently Newton thought so. After his writing spree, which she forced him to do over again because he cheated on the number of assigned lines, he'd behaved somewhat better during these past three days. "I didn't think you'd really count all those lines," he'd said, giving her that insolent look when frustrations seemed to get the better of him.

She sprang up from the bed in a huff, determined she'd win this war, or die trying. From the chest of drawers, she pulled out a collar and leash. Every dog had his day, and she hoped hers was next in line. As for Newton, wherever he was, she'd bring him back crawling on all fours, with his proverbial tail tucked between his legs. And once she got him back, another device awaited him in the drawers, and she couldn't wait to see the look on his face once he saw it.

Along the way, she approached attendants and staff mingling in the hallway and resting in their rooms, urgently seeking information on Newton's whereabouts and if anyone had seen him. Everyone shared what they knew without hesitation, suggesting he'd traveled to the main staircase of The House. There could only be one place he'd most likely go: to the front door where he'd head on out and enjoy a sunny after-noon. Maybe some of the gardeners could offer information on where to find him next. Every path turned up nothing. Each alcove contained other people enjoying each other without a care in the world. Daria turned and faced the forest line. Surely he wouldn't go that far alone. She kept walking, collar and leash dangling from her hand.

Several yards of wandering through different paths ended in frus-tration, so she headed to one of the three ponds. Many an attendant and their admit found their way to these ponds where they engaged in passionate lovemaking under the trees, or simply enjoyed the after-noon dipping their toes into the water. Would Newton be doing the same, basking in the sun, using his charm on a stray beauty who'd be willing to have a lusty rumble in the grass?

And there she saw him, in the first one, apparently in a struggle. As she neared, her eyes widened. Newton stood, twisting his hips, grunting, and grasping something between his legs—and it didn't look like he was pleasuring himself, either. She ran until she reached the edge of the pond. Newton looked up.

"Hey, come here and help me." He muttered a few swear words, turning back to the space between his legs.

"What the hell is going on?" Daria stepped into the water and let out a scream.

"Don't just stand there screeching, help me get this thing off." Panting, he grasped the fish which had latched onto the head of his cock, and tried prying it loose with the other hand. "Damn, these things have sharp teeth."

He let out a yell. Daria stepped closer, but when the fish thrashed its tail, she screamed again and stepped back.

With a few more maneuvers, Newton freed himself and held the fish out to Daria, a triumphant smile on his face. "Isn't she a beauty? Do you think the cooks can fry her up for me?"

Pursing her lips, she took a couple of steps forward, smacking the fish out of his hand. With a plop, the fish landed in the water and swam away.

He clenched his fists. "Why did you do that? I spent a good twenty minutes trying catch it."

"With yourself as the worm?" She glanced down at a reddened cockhead. "Good, god, please tell me I'm dreaming." Pushing the hair back out of her face, she squeezed her eyes shut and tried to get her breath. Nothing like stifling a dual urge to yell and laugh.

Newton took her hand for support, and both stepped back onto the grass.

"Please tell me what possessed you to do such a stupid thing as this?" Daria glowered at him, jingling the leash and collar at her side.

"I'd heard men could do that. My buddy Jimmy claimed he'd tried it once. I just thought, while you were busy, I'd step out for a bit. I saw these ponds had fish, so I thought I'd try and see if Jimmy was telling me a tall tale or not." He leaned forward to Daria's ear. "I think old Jimmy was telling the truth, don't you?" He grinned down at her.

"Get down on all fours, right now." Daria barked out the orders, swatting his backside with a swift stroke.

"Ow! Damn, that stung." He glared.

"And get your pants back in order."

Newton reached for the panel of his trousers, pulling it back between his legs and fastening it in front.

"Now, down on the ground." She jangled the collar and leash in front of him.

"What? Are you for real? And what's with all that shit?" He stood and crossed his arms. "I'm not your dog, and I'm not about to start acting like one."

A flash of heat crossed Daria's face, and she touched her nose to his. "Acting like a dog is no worse than acting like a silly worm to catch fish. Since you want to practice your acting skills today, just look at this as another role."

"Not gonna." He didn't budge.

Neither did she. "You will, or I'll lock your sweet ass up in isolation, cuff those fidgety hands of yours behind your back, and let you spend a night or two, alone, with an aching cock."

He blinked, uncrossing his arms. "You wouldn't do that, would you? I was just wanting to have a little fun, maybe try out some life survival skills."

Daria's face kept the same cold stare. "Want tits and pussy? Then time to act like man's best friend."

"Aw, hell!" He sucked in his breath and stared at the ground before dropping down to his hands and knees.

She wrapped the collar around his neck, buckling it in place. Using the steel ring on top, she attached the leash. "Let's go."

Newton followed Daria over the grass to the entrance of The House, where she walked him up to their ward. He crawled down the hall, head down, eyes focused on the floor. Ignoring grins and winks of approval from her fellow attendants, and giggles from admits, she led her charge back to their room. Part of her felt sorry for her admit, but mostly she enjoyed the endorphins kicking in from the display of power. She just about had this guy where she wanted him.

They arrived at their room, where Daria removed the leash, but not the collar. "I want you to stand up and don't move."

"Aren't you going to take this infernal collar off? I didn't get mouthy with you once while you made me crawl back here."

"And I suggest you don't get mouthy now, or you'll get your mouth washed out with soap." She strode over to the chest of drawers and removed a small, cage-like device.

"What the hell is that thing?" Newton cast a wary glance at Daria's hand.

"Come over here." She opened another drawer and removed a bottle of liquid and some gauze wipes. "Undo your trousers. I need to see just how much damage you caused yourself."

He did as instructed. She spent a few seconds inspecting the tip of his shaft. "It's a little red. Does it feel sore?" She applied light pressure, watching as he squinted.

"It's … it's a little sore. But it'll be all right."

"Here, I need to clean it a little. It doesn't look like your skin was broken, which is a good thing, or I'd be taking you to see Dr. James." She picked up a couple of gauze pads and dampened them with the liquid. "This is just a general antiseptic, something that will help soothe and ward off anything too nasty. Whatever you do, don't you dare do something like that again, at least not while you're here." Gently she swabbed his tip. When she finished, she picked up the metal device, slipped it over his cock, and secured it in place by slipping a metal ring around his sac. With one final move, she locked the ring to the cage.

Newton stared down in horror, viewing his sac neatly sandwiched by the ring and the cage. He turned his eyes to Daria.

"There, you won't be getting it up until you're out of this thing. It's a chastity device, and the whole idea is to keep you in place—really in place."

"I thought you said I'd get some tits and pussy if I acted like a dog. You lied." His eyes flashed with indignation.

"I didn't tell you when you'd get it. And I'll give it to you when I say so. Besides, you already got your dick-fondling today. Isn't that enough?"

"You—"

"Don't say it, Newton." Daria picked up the bar of soap. "I won't think twice about using this."

He cast his gaze briefly to the ceiling and back to her face. "People will laugh at me in this thing. I sure got enough grins when we came back in here."

She placed her face inches in front of his. "If anybody saw what I did, you'd be the laughing stock of The House."

His face went pale, and fear crept into his eyes. "You won't tell anybody about that will you? Can't you at least spare a man some dignity?"

"You need to start acting with some dignity and stop your foolishness. When you start behaving with some respect, you might get some in return."

He hung his head.

"Now I want you to sit down here and do another writing assignment. This time you'll write, 'I will behave with dignity' a thousand times."

Without a word, he took up the notebook and pen she handed him and began writing.

§§§

He couldn't help himself. He'd been warned, but didn't care at the moment. The restlessness had set in, drawing him out of the confines of his tiny room, no matter how comfortable the bed or beautiful the lady sleeping next to him. But something's hotter burned inside him, a heat he couldn't kick back or shake off no matter how hard he'd tried. The saving grace was nighttimes with Daria, but sometimes, it wasn't enough for him.

Justifying his reasoning, he'd be gone only a minute or two, check out the nightlife on the floor, and sneak back into bed. She'd never know. Newton slipped out of bed, into his trousers, and tiptoed down the hall. With a polite nod to the staff at the desk, he wandered on, catching sight of a female walking his direction. He perked up. She was alone. Whether she'd suffered an attack of wanderlust or was returning from an assignment, it didn't matter. As he neared, she flashed a smile his direction.

"Hi there." She stopped, waiting for Newton.

"Well, hi there, yourself." He returned the smile, heart racing. He adored the look of this woman immediately. "Don't know about you, but I couldn't sleep."

"I'm Vivian. It's really nice to meet you ..."

"Newton. Nice to meet you too, Vivian." Instead of a formal handshake, he took the liberty of placing a light, friendly pat on her back, as if he'd known her forever.

"I've seen you around. How do you like it here?" Vivian settled easily against the wall, appearing in no hurry to return to her room.

"It's the strangest place I've ever seen. Odd that someone hasn't opened their mouth about this place." His expression sobered up, but his vision drilled through her dress, imagining the beauty and softness of her breasts. Should he suggest they go off somewhere? He'd love nothing better than to have a shot at suckling and playing with her nipples.

She shook her head. "I don't think that'll happen. They make it clear you'll be in big trouble if you say anything."

"Do you like your attendant? He's lucky to have someone as

gorgeous as you." Newton ran a finger through her hair. She didn't flinch, but stared him straight in the eye.

"He's a tough one, but he feels good, inside and out, if you know what I mean." She winked.

"Know what you mean. Mine's a beaut, but she's one tough cookie." Newton leaned in closer. "Do you ever get into trouble for things?"

Vivian gave him a coy smile, turning her eyes toward the ceiling and back to him. "Sometimes."

Newton grinned. "I bet you do things just to egg your attendant on, yeah?"

"That's my secret." She pushed herself off the wall, edging closer to him.

"I gotcha." Newton continued, "So where's your room?"

"Just three doors down from here. Yours?"

"At the end of the hall." He angled his head toward the room where Daria slept, keeping his eyes locked on the woman in front of him.

She continued chatting. "I think this place is so interesting, and so pretty. Have you seen the woods? One day my attendant took me to a hot spring. I'd never been in one of those before. And the gardens, how gorgeous they are? There're some frisky things going on in them. I've seen some of the ponds. They're so pretty. Maybe you've been to one?"

Newton paled at the mention of the ponds, but the sudden expression of concern on her face took center stage. Her eyes widened; her mouth opened. He turned around and stood face-to-face with Daria, who indicated she didn't aim to trifle with him tonight. Cringing, he grimaced, turning to Vivian. "Sorry, hon, but I better get going. Nice to meet you."

Vivian offered a weak smile, giving a light flutter of her fingers as a good-bye wave.

Daria and Newton returned to the room in silence. She threw the covers back, allowing Newton to crawl in first. Neither said a word. He'd disobeyed again; he knew it. Transgressions didn't matter at the time he thought about doing them. Getting caught was always the down side. He prayed a good night's sleep might soften her by morning.

§§§

Newton struggled against the cuffs, sending out clanking sounds echoing through the tub room. He glared at Daria. "Why in hell do you have to cuff me to this damn screen?"

"Because you keep wanting to do things your way. You don't mind what I tell you, and I don't need you running off anywhere else—again, for the umpteenth time." Daria gave him a cool stare.

"Look just because I got up in the middle of the night doesn't mean you have to get so hard-nosed about everything. I couldn't sleep. Besides, I thought we could move around and check things out. Hell, everyone else does." He tugged again, wincing against the metal restraints.

"You don't get up and wander off without my permission. How many times do we have to go over this? No admit does that without a damn good reason, and so far, you've not given me one." Daria rustled through the cabinets aligning the wall, pulling out various supplies for the morning bath.

"I wanted to check things out, and I was doing good with that girl, until you came along. Damn, she was cute as hell, blonde fluffy hair, hot tits. Really sweet. And she was into me, too. All smiles. What was she doing walking the halls if she didn't want some action? I see people in and out of rooms, trying other people out. Why can't I?"

"Listen to me. I don't know why that admit was out of her room, but I'm responsible for you. And just because she acted polite didn't mean you could have your way with her. Besides, 'trying other people out' is not grabbing the first stray you see. Intimate meetings are supervised by attendants or created through House activities, and again, an attendant is always involved."

"Oh, save it, sister. You wear my ass out." Scowling, he shot her the middle finger.

Daria, catching the hand gesture, strode over, supplies in tow, and stared her admit square in the eye. "I'll wear your ass out for that." With a quick, smooth stroke, she turned him enough to deliver a sharp smack on his buttock. "Is that good enough for you? Maybe you need another."

Newton tried turning away, dodging the blow, but too late. *Smack* went her hand across his flesh.

He drew in his breath and winced again, lifting himself on his toes. She watched him, noting the irritation on his face.

"You misbehave, your ass gets it, plain and simple. I'm still fighting you on the most basic rules." She loomed next to his ear. "Does a good ass-swatting calm your dick down?"

Silence.

And that's how it had been, this badgering back and forth between the two of them. He tried following her lead most days, but his patience ran on a short fuse. Though the idea of playing by her rules to get what he wanted interested him in the beginning, the actual follow-through had fallen through. Of all the admits Daria had taught since her promotion, Newton was the most challenging. Withholding sex for an extended time may have worked as punishment for other admits, but forcing this approach had proven counterproductive to his spirit and temperament, setting her progress back whenever she tried it.

At night, she put the struggles of the day aside and let him ravish her. Lions needed the hunt; cheetahs needed the chase. Newton needed unbridled sex. As much as she liked power, continued domination wearied her after a while, and she gladly switched roles when they bedded down together. Nothing struck her as more delicious than Newton awakening in the middle of the night and fingering her nether regions, slipping in his beautiful fingers, stirring inside her darkest passage. When her juices flowed, he positioned himself over her and sank his cock deep inside, thrusting with piston-like speed and equal smoothness. Sometimes he pulled her on top and let her ride him while he bucked underneath, strong and steady.

The more Daria understood him, the more she sensed his incapacity for curbing an animal appetite; thus he jumped without thinking, trying to satisfy his lust at all cost. She gazed at the sullen face, his clenched fists. His whole body seemed charged with an energy prodding him mercilessly, creating inner torment.

"Hey, I gotta pee." His voice rang out. "I forgot to tell you that."

"You went right after we woke up. You can wait a few seconds longer and let me finish what I'm doing."

"I drank a lot at breakfast. I gotta go." He rattled the cuffs again, shifting from one foot to the other.

Daria didn't move, but stood with her arms crossed, watching and waiting a few more seconds. With any luck she'd head back to the cabinets for the towels and soap in the hopes of scoring a decent morning without too much hassle. So far, the situation didn't look positive.

His scorching gaze displayed pure defiance, and in true fashion, he shot out a hot stream of urine. Daria jumped aside, watching his fluids hit the floor. She smacked the side of his thigh, the sting of the impact searing through her hand.

"Stop it! Her voice echoed off the tile walls. Newton paused, the golden stream dribbling to a brief halt. "Why do you do this? What's wrong with you?"

"I'm an animal!" He screamed back. Squeezing his eyes shut, he clenched his teeth and strained himself, sending out another heavy stream.

Stunned, she watched with twisted fascination until he heaved out his last drops. When he finished his eyes deadlocked on her, face void of emotion. "I don't have to go, now."

His words kept ringing in her head. An animal? Examining the puddle on the floor, she nodded and said, "Nice piss job." She strode across the room back to the cabinets for some additional towels. "You'll clean up your own mess." Daria uncuffed him and handed him the towels.

"I thought it was your job to take care of me, sister. You didn't do your job and take me to the toilet like I asked. So *you* clean it up." Newton kept his eyes on her, his face filled with a trace of satisfaction.

"You have a choice. Clean this mess up, or we go straight to the isolation rooms where you'll stay, stripped with your hands cuffed. We've talked about this before, and I'm not joking." Daria gave him a quick look.

Silence.

"I'm counting to three. What happens after that is your choice. I'll find somebody else to sleep with. You won't."

He crossed his arms, narrowing his eyes.

"One … two …" She stepped forward, reaching for the cuffs.

"Fine, damn it. Just give me a minute." Pouting, he cleaned up the puddle, placing the soiled towels in a bin for contaminated linen.

"Good." She spread out the other towels neatly on the floor. "Now lie down." Her words came out calm, matching a casual demeanor on the outside. On the inside, a twinge of frustration fluttered.

"Why? You haven't asked me to do this before." He stamped a foot. "Can't we get inside that tub over there and take a bath together? I've seen other admits and their attendants do it."

"Newton, we shower here together every day. We have our playtime like the other admits and attendants." Daria knew the allure of the tub rooms on this side of The House, with mosaic-tiled floors, cabinets full of lush towels, herbs, aromatics, and other seductive supplies. The white porcelain, claw-footed tubs had been fashioned to hold at least two people comfortably, and many an attendant and admit snuggled together under warm sudsy water, enjoying a sensual or relaxing soak.

"Yes we do, but I want to suck your tits and play with your pussy in a tub of warm water. I think a nice long soak would …" His face showed sudden defeat, as if he'd at once grown tired.

"Do you think a tub bath would relax you? Is that what it is?"

"It couldn't hurt to try."

His longing gaze bothered her on a deeper level. Maybe she needed to change their routine a little.

The decision made, she continued, "Tell you what, I'll cut a deal with you. Lie down on these towels, let me do what I need to do first, and we'll enjoy a tub bath this morning."

"First, tell me why I have to get on the towels. What trick do you have up your sleeve?" He eyed her warily.

"Do you want that bath or not? If you do, then don't ask questions and do what I say. Regardless, I'll have my way with you. It's your choice if you want to place nicely and have tub time." She tapped her foot against the tiles.

"Fine." He grimaced and slumped down to the floor, where he wriggled into position. "Now what?"

She arched an eyebrow, before cuffing his hands to the screen again. "You need a lesson on control and following directions. First, you spoke to me in a disrespectful manner, and then you urinated when I didn't give you permission."

"Aw, hell. Do you really have to give me permission for everything? All this is bullshit after a while."

"None of what we do here at The House is bullshit. Nothing. And don't ever refer to anything I ask you to do or any treatment as bullshit. Everything we do has a purpose, and you'll understand this. Your job while in treatment is to obey me, listen, and don't talk back."

He closed his eyes in disgust, growing more sullen.

Daria had already planned how she'd teach Newton his lesson, how she could teach control, punishment—definitely not in the traditional sense—and throw in pleasure as a small reward all in one fantastic, easy manner. The whole plan fit with her style: punish, but reward the attendant for having participated. With Newton, this method worked in small doses. In the cabinets, she retrieved a small bag of fluid, tubing, syringe and sterile water. From another drawer, cleanser, rubber gloves, tape, lubrication, and a catheter. After washing her hands, she settled on the floor at Newton's side and arranged all the supplies in a neat row for easy access.

"What the hell is all that for?" He squirmed and pulled on the cuffs. "Look, I promise I won't give you any more trouble. I'll be good. Just don't use that stuff on me."

"What's the matter? Do these little things scare you? You, a strong, brazen man with enough sexual energy for a whole town? A man who's hell-bent on doing things his way?" She clucked her tongue and shook her head. "My goodness, how you've changed your tune. And why?"

"Don't fuck with me!" His jaw clenched and his eyes blazed.

She chuckled. "It won't hurt that much. I'll be easy. I suggest you think about fun in the tub."

For once she saw his face pale with fear, which sweetened this scene even more. Some of the more unusual approaches to control and pleasure made new admits nervous, creating even more fun for attendants who had no intention of harming. True harm was totally against House protocol, and could get you banished from the premises. Fear, on the other hand, was all in the mind.

Newton let out a deafening yell. Daria clapped her hand over his mouth. "Stop! Remember what we talked about a few minutes ago if you don't behave?"

He stopped, eyes bulging, chest heaving.

"If I take my hand off, will you hush? You still want that bath?" She'd rested the tip of her nose on his. "Good, I thought so." Daria sprang up and ran to a drawer in the cabinet. "For good measure, I'm using this."

With a few quick maneuvers, she popped a ball gag in his mouth and secured the straps. When his cries came out muffled, he finally gave up and stared blankly at the ceiling.

"Now I can get down to business so we can be one step closer to making tub time into fun playtime." She flashed him a warm smile.

Taking a deep breath, she calmed her mind and seated herself next to his thighs. From the array of supplies, she prepared each piece for its role in her lesson. She took up the rubber gloves, unwrapped them carefully, and snapped them on. Newton jumped at the sensation of her cleansing his cockhead.

"We haven't done this before. But don't worry. I'll be gentle. I'm doing this because you disobeyed."

His breaths came faster, and he tried pulling away.

"Stop it, or I'll call another attendant to hold you down. Then they can watch a big boy cry."

He frowned.

"Thought that would settle your ass down." With a few more preparatory steps, everything was ready for the big moment. "Here I go."

No protests.

"Take some nice, deep breaths for me." For the next few seconds, Daria concentrated on nothing else but his face and the well-lubricated catheter she passed slowly into his bladder.

Newton strained at the cuffs holding him fast.

"You like the sensation? Most find it pleasant." She attached the bag, lifting it so the fluid filled him. "Feel a little full? This is sterile water, and what I'm doing won't harm you." His face didn't indicate pain, but when she pressed above his pubic bone, he winced. "Good. I'm clamping this catheter off. You won't be able to pee until I let you. Around the tip that's inside you is a tiny balloon. I'll inflate it from here." She rubbed her finger over a small tube branching off the main one. "That balloon will hold the catheter in place." Daria performed all the steps she'd discussed, smiling when she'd finished. "Rest while I clean everything up." She gathered all the empty wrappings, disposing them in a receptacle next to the cabinets.

Newton's eyes glazed over. A look of despair covered his face. He groaned.

"I'll start getting our bath ready. I'm sure the sound of water running will help get you in the mood."

For the next several minutes, Daria pulled towels, washcloths, shampoo, and soap from the cabinets. One last thing she wanted was a relaxant for the bath water. She and her former attendant enjoyed these when they'd bathed together. Sometimes attendants slipped in aphrodisiac blends, but she highly doubted Newton needed these. From the jars marked Catnip, Clary Sage, and Neroli Flowers, she concocted a generous blend, pouring the mixture into a cotton drawstring bag. Out of the corner of her eye, she watched Newton continually. He appeared composed, but she knew the urge to urinate trumped other urges, including the desire to fuck. If catheter use worked as a small control over his animal urge, even for a few moments, the lesson succeeded.

While the water ran and the bag of herbs steeped, she returned to Newton. "I think you're ready." A shift of the small clamp, and the urine drained back into the empty fluid bag, which Daria had left attached to the catheter for ease and cleanliness. "Feel better?"

He blinked a few times in acknowledgement.

"I'll remove this gag, too."

She deflated the balloon of the catheter, pulling it out slowly. As the tube grazed his walls, he closed his eyes. "You like that? I told you it wasn't all bad." Daria ran a finger against his cheek. "I hope you learned a lesson in this little activity. I'm not afraid to use it again if you act out."

"Are you satisfied now?" The cold tone in his voice matched the cloudy expression covering his face.

"I'm very satisfied. You were good once everything got started."

He didn't answer. She didn't push him at this point. He'd liked the sensations of the catheter kissing him internally. Some things even he couldn't hide very well, and erogenous zones were one of them.

"When I undo these cuffs, I want you in that tub."

The cuffs unsnapped, and Newton moved to an upright position, rubbing his wrist a few seconds before he pulled himself up and headed toward the tub. He tested the temperature with his fingers, stepped in, and stretched out. Daria slipped off her dress, indicating for him to move up while she seated herself behind him, cradling his body between her legs.

"What's that tiny bag for?" Newton settled against her chest.

"Just an herbal potion for relaxing, that's all. Do you like it?" She splashed a little water over his abdomen, stroking over his skin.

"I like it, I suppose." He let out a soft groan.

They spent several minutes soaking, resting, saying only a few words in idle conversation.

Before long, he'd stiffened a little, and his hand had reached out for his own cock, grasping it securely. She didn't intervene, but let him tug and pull until a fine erection bobbed between his legs. Her fingers caressed his nipples, and the more she worked the nubs of flesh between her thumb and forefinger, the faster he worked himself.

"Those balls of yours full again?" She licked an earlobe.

"I don't think these ball are ever empty." His breathing became more intense, and the weight of his head rested heavier against her breasts.

Part of her wanted to push his hands aside and finish him off herself in grand fashion, but a larger part of her liked watching him, the way he touched himself, fingering his favorite hot spots, moving slower, moving faster. Her clit ached, and she wanted to rub herself and climax when he did. She shifted a little and wedged her hand behind him just enough to reach the throbbing bundle of nerves at the top of her slit.

Now they felt the same bliss, apart yet together. His fingers worked faster and hers did to, creating an ache and fullness inside her loins that matched his. She rested back against the porcelain and enjoyed the warm water, his weight, and the pleasure-pain between her legs. He let out a soft grunt. As she watched the cum spouting in thick streams from his cock, her own fingers brought out a hard climax and she bucked against him.

"Let's stand up." Daria pulled the stopper out of the tub drain. She refilled the tub with fresh water, and they snuggled down again. "We'll finish cleaning up." She splashed some water over Newton's hair, and reached for the shampoo bottle.

"Your hands feel so good." He lifted up his head while she worked up a thick lather.

"You like massages, don't you, Newton?" She plucked up one of the washcloths, rubbed some soap over it, and washed all of him, paying special attention to the space between his thighs.

"I get to wash you next. It's only fair." He rubbed her shin.

When she finished, he reciprocated. Daria drained the tub again, using the sprayer for rinsing off the extra soap. Newton grabbed the sprayer, placing it back in its holder. He suckled her nipples, before kneeling down and focusing on her clit, bringing her to another orgasm. When she pumped her hips, he glanced up, smiling.

He climbed out of the tub. "See, I knew we'd have a nice time. How come we had to wait so long?" He manipulated one of her nipple rings.

"You've only been here a week. It hasn't been that long."

"I guess I've lost track of time. With everything going on, I've not thought as much about home."

"I understand." Daria cocked her head toward the door. "We'll head on back to our room and get dressed. I want us to go outside and enjoy some fresh air and sunshine."

Wrapped in towels, the pair headed out of the tub room. More admits and attendants passed up and down the hallways. A handsome, dark-haired attendant and his blonde admit walked toward them. The gentleman smiled.

Daria stopped, waiting for them to approach. "Hey, Thomas! Headed for a bath?"

"We are. Can't wait to enjoy a good soak with this jewel." He hugged his admit close.

"Newton, I guess you remember Vivian from the other night." She patted Thomas on the back. "But you haven't met her attendant."

Thomas grinned. "So you're the rascal Vivian keeps telling me about. Said she'd met some guy the other night, but she didn't tell me who."

Daria inched closer to Thomas. "Newton has a way of bolting off without me. I've scolded him for that."

"We love our admits, but some are hard to keep in line." Thomas gave Newton a friendly smile.

Newton announced, "I give her a run for her money, but she tries." He reached out and rubbed Vivian's shoulder. "For someone who's tumbled out of bed, you look fresh as a daisy."

Vivian laughed. "Thanks, and you still look …" Her face sobered up. "You look good, even in towels."

Daria and Thomas exchanged uneasy glances. Newton and Vivian surveyed each other up and down, and the way their eyes locked suggested they'd briefly lost themselves in another world.

"Thomas, you and Vivian have a great bath. I have to take care of my man." Daria grinned, pulling Newton along down the hall. More attendants and admits walked up and down, some having already bathed and dressed, others heading toward the hall where the tub rooms were located.

"Turn around and stop ogling her." Daria gave him a light swat on the backside.

Newton shook his head. "Didn't I tell you she was the cutest thing? I'll say it again, I think she likes me."

"You still need to do what I tell you to do, no matter what."

"Oh, come on. Can't she and I do something together, eat, go for a romp outside? Is that Thomas guy as strict as you are?"

"He's wonderful, and very protective of his admits." Daria ushered her admit into their room. "Get dressed, Newton. Let's get out of here and head on outside."

CHAPTER 4

The path led to a secluded part of the gardens, situated several yards behind The House. Flanked by colorful pansies, it scrolled around until it reached a high wall of box hedges with an ivy archway. The smell of flowers lingered in the air, along with woodsy scents of leaves and grass.

"What is this place?" Newton viewed the surroundings, turning in all directions.

Floral beds and elegant fountains slowly gave way to an enormous arbor, so large the dimensions were difficult to discern from where the entrance began. Vines of wisteria created a sweet-scented floral curtain, winding around domed trellises above. Throughout the garden, maze-like paths led to rooms squared off by box hedges for privacy. The intoxicating smell of flowers and greenery enveloped the pair in a perfume as alluring as any young lady may wear to greet her lover. As they passed through the archway and wound deeper into the arbor, Daria showed Newton how to determine if a space was occupied or available.

"See these flowers on the outside of each space?"

Newton angled his head toward one of them for closer inspection. "It looks like someone pulled out the stalk."

"Yes, these are the variety of calla lilies with the long golden stalk centers. House directors created these imitation ones for use here in this arbor. If the stalk is resting by the flower, the space is vacant. New occupants place the stalk inside the petals, and a whole flower means others should stay away."

"Hmm, I get the meaning. Pretty damn clever, if you ask me." He grinned at Daria. "These House folks know how to put on a spread, don't they?"

"They think of just about everything. Come on, let's take ours." Taking his hand, she made one more turn and selected a vacant spot. Newton placed the stalk in the flower and followed Daria.

"The hedges make you feel like you're in a small room, don't they? I imagine someone could easily peek through these hedges and do some spying, though." He grinned over at Daria, who pulled him down next to her on the cool grassy carpet. The breeze blew, and she immersed herself in the moment, into the freedom of nature, where inhibitions slipped off like a wispy scarf carried by the wind, and lusty imagination ran as wildly as the vines covering the arbors and trellises. The House had created gardens for beauty and pleasure, and the surrounding grounds led from one hot adventure to the next.

Newton wasted no time in stretching himself out on his back, squinting when the sunlight struck his eyes. Daria gazed down at him. How grey those eyes, how thick his hair. A stiff cock already made itself known through the trousers, and it took every ounce of willpower to keep her fingers off him. A part of her wanted to rip open the front panel of the trousers and suck him off, but she needed some answers to questions that had bothered her. Talk first, suck later.

After taking a few deep, calming breaths, she snuggled up to Newton and rubbed over his abdomen. "I want to talk to you about a few things, if you don't mind."

"Will we get to fuck or are we just going to talk, because sometimes we've had moments of just talking and no fucking afterwards. You know that hurts a guy like me?" He shaded his eyes a second and glanced over at her.

"That's not fair, Newton. I've made nighttimes your time for having your way with me, which you use to your advantage quite well. I've worked in rewards for you in ways I don't normally do with other admits because I know your needs are unique. The whole point of your treatment is to help you enjoy sex within the balance of healthy relationships, and most of all, to regain mastery of yourself."

He took her hand in his. "I'm sorry. That was totally out of line on my part. I know you've done your damndest to help. So what's got you so bumfuzzled?"

"While we were in the tub room this morning, what did you mean by saying you were an animal?"

Newton didn't say anything for several seconds, but swallowed hard. "I don't talk much about what I'm going to tell you, mainly because I don't know how or even where to start. You people here whoop it up until the cows come home. You never seem to stop, never want to stop. In my sane mind, I know a body can't keep going forever, and I know all these people don't keep it up constantly. But think for a minute if something inside forced you to keep going. Think of a lion always on the prowl for food, filled for just a little while, only to search all over again because he's hungry." He opened his eyes and the intensity of his gaze mesmerized her. "My constant fear is I'll never have enough, and the continual urge to search scares me most."

Daria said nothing, but his words confirmed Dr. James' earlier suspicions. Thinking a moment, she tried imagining what it would be like if her body didn't allow her to shut off physical urges? What if she wanted to, but couldn't? The mere thought of this reality stunned her.

He continued. "I think I try to win women over out of sheer desperation so that hunger will be satisfied, and when I move too fast, what I was counting on to satisfy me runs away, like the gazelle that gets away from the lion. I'm left starved and frustrated." Newton squeezed Daria's hand. "As much as you love being with people, I bet you've never been scared of yourself, have you?"

"Quite honestly, I've never thought about it, Newton, but I'm so sorry you go through this every day."

"Maybe I should have brought up this issue sooner. It's not like we don't talk, but I'm not sure I really understood some of it until I got here and saw all this." He smiled at her. "You may think of me as a big asshole, but since I've been here, which is the strangest place on earth, I'm watching all the time, watching everybody, how they act, how they look. I consider how I'm different, and it scares me."

For the first time, a sense of protectiveness overwhelmed her, so strong the realization of it made her swoon. Whatever he carried inside him, whatever upset him, she wanted it banished forever. She sat up, taking both his hands in hers.

"Let me remind you again: I care very much what happens to my admits. I want treatment here to serve them well when they leave. Just know that I don't treat you the way I do to be mean. Coming into The House is a shocking initiation in and of itself. I'm hoping you'll learn self-control and how to view women differently, not as objects for use, and definitely not as a means of feeding an internal appetite you'll never fully satisfy.

"I'm not trying to be a dick, Daria. I swear I'm not. I know I carried on when I first got here, and still do. Now you know why. The truth is, I never really intend to hurt anyone, especially women. I hope you can help me be a better person, someone they'll like."

"I know deep down you're not a mean person. Stubborn as they come, but not intentionally cruel. I can see why women are initially attracted. You're a physically beautiful man and one hell of a tiger in bed. It's okay to tell me when something upsets you, when you're frustrated, and even when you're scared. You may be a big man, but that doesn't mean you don't feel the same emotions women feel. We're people, Newton, not men versus women. It's so important that you learn this, or you'll be doomed for more problems than just physical urges. Your relationships will starve; your life will starve."

He grimaced. "Tell that to people out there in town, people you see and run into every day. Everyone has certain expectations, and you know in these times, women are used for cooking, cleaning, having babies, and sex."

Daria stretched out beside him again, rubbing her fingers over his chest. "You're about to learn some different things, Newton. You'll take these skills with you and have a more fulfilled life, one where you're not afraid anymore; one where you'll have a special someone to cherish. You'll want to make her happy. Does that sound like something you'd like?"

"Yes, but you know what else I'd like?" He grinned. With one smooth move, he flipped her on top of him. "Enough talk."

The sparkle in his eye enhanced his boyish charm, and his hard cock pressing against her fired off an uncontrollable lust in her loins. His hands had slithered over her buttocks, ending in a firm squeeze. She cinched his hips between her thighs, and leaning over his chest, licked at his nipples. Her fingers curled over the top of his trousers. Repositioning herself lower, she unsnapped the front panel. Bobbing before her stood a rigid cock, which she encased inside her mouth.

His skin smelled clean, a mingled scent of soap and masculinity. A light hint of salt teased her tongue as she swirled the pre-cum pooling in his slit. She sucked hard, flicking around the ridge of his cockhead.

"Oh, damn, I love it when you suck me off." He let out a groan, tensed his thighs, and raised his hips. He'd encased her head between determined hands, and the firmer he gripped, the faster she lashed her tongue against his swollen veins and cockhead. Opening her mouth and relaxing her throat, she took him in deeper, loving the way he lodged in her throat, nice and tight. When she swallowed, he let out a loud growl. She toyed with him, relentless and teasing.

His rapid breathing hit her ears as pleasing and refreshing as the breeze swirling around them. From the sound and feel of him, she'd soon consume his release. Newton held his breath and pressed against her; Daria swallowed.

Newton raised up and slipped off her dress. Within seconds she lay naked in the sunshine. Each time she found herself in this garden, she still buzzed with giddiness when the air tickled her wet slit. He positioned himself over her, flicking his tongue at her clit, tormenting her to distraction, a strong pleasure-ache centering itself in the space between her legs. She inhaled the fresh scent of flowers and grass, and closed her eyes while his tongue trailed over the folds in her pussy, taking her smaller nether lips in his mouth and releasing them slowly. Two of his fingers slid in easily, and he moved against her walls.

She reached up and fingered her nipple rings, squeezing her flesh between thumb and index finger. For each sucking sensation down below, she matched with a firm squeeze on top. The ache grew with steady speed, her clit throbbing harder. The sound of him swirling her fluids sent her reeling, more so because she knew his cock was also on the rebound. One hard draw on her clit, and she writhed, spreading her thighs open wider. Would he just fuck her now and set off the climax?

No, he liked tormenting her, fingering deep and creating a vibration inside her that threatened to send her over the edge. Breaths tumbled out ragged and hard, and she cried out his name. Then it happened, a series of spasms rippling between her legs, so hard the sharp clenching in her pussy nearly blinded her. When she'd caught her breath, he positioned himself between her open thighs.

Newton plunged in, nearly taking her breath away. A groan escaped her lips, and for a moment she didn't see anything but the vines above her and snatches of golden sunlight. He moved with beautiful speed, sliding in and out, eyes shining with each thrust. His breathing trailed out faster, and his face contorted with desperation. She contracted around him, milking his cock. Each time she tightened, he smiled a little, a light moan spilling out of his mouth.

Pausing a moment, he caught his breath and kissed her, slipping in his tongue. Daria liked sucking his soft, wet tongue as much as his stiff, plump cockhead—a pleasing duo of soft and hard. He probed and ran the tip of his tongue over the top of her teeth, and ended with a long kissing tug of her lower lip. Just as the throbbing settled a bit, he revved up and resumed thrusting earnestly, not slowing down until his cock shot out a warm, thick load of cum.

She repositioned herself on top of him, and went to work on his nipples, licking and sucking on the nubs of flesh. For every tiny bite she delivered, she sucked and ran her tongue over the tips, enjoying the sighs as he rubbed his fingers over her back. The interlude ended with a kiss. The pair lay together for several minutes in silence, with nothing but the call of birds piercing the air.

"I've never done it outside, buck naked in broad daylight." Newton chuckled, stroking a lock of hair out of Daria's eyes. "Secretly, I was hoping someone would find us by accident. We'd have given 'em a show."

She laughed. "That's true."

§§§

Daria lay on the floor of Thomas's room, having slipped out while Newton napped. Vivian was spending time with another attendant for the afternoon, leaving Thomas with some free time. With her thighs stretched apart, Daria had settled back, enjoying the motions of Thomas's finger deep inside her pussy, as he slowly rubbed in and out while they conversed. This little act had been a favorite during their lusty times together when she'd been an admit, and they'd managed to find time together. After her promotion, they'd simply continued as before.

"He keeps going on about Vivian. He slips out at night and comes down here. I don't know if letting them get together would be a good idea or not. What if it didn't work out? I'd hate for him to have a bad experience or get his heart broken, or he breaks hers." She smiled and closed her eyes at the sensation inside her.

"Interesting. Vivian keeps hinting about wanting to see Newton." Thomas swirled his finger a few times and switched back to moving it in and out.

"So what do we do?"

"First, tell me how Bad Boy is working out. I take it from what you've told me, he's giving you a run for your money."

"Little by little he's coming around. We had a talk the other day,

• 375 •

and I've changed my game-plan with him." She grinned at Thomas. "The *Jardin d'Amour*, garden of love, fascinated him. Nothing suited him better than getting it on outside behind the bushes."

"Everybody loves that place, and it's great for spying on other people, too, if you know what I mean. Send them there, and I think they'll be fine. We can step in if things get squirrely." Grinning, he quirked an eyebrow up and down.

"Guess it couldn't hurt. Now that I think about it, I'd kind of like to see him in action with someone else."

"And Vivian can hold her own, or will by the time I'm through with her. Remember how my admit Rose handled Joe?"

Daria laughed. "An admit who practiced what she'd learned. What a scream! Yeah, I remember her taking control of him. Joe had more respect for us up here after that. Then let's plan on it. You work with Vivian some more while I'm taming Bad."

Thomas smiled and mouthed a kiss toward her. "I love it when we come up with snazzy ideas."

CHAPTER 5

Quit wagging your ass." Daria smacked Newton on one of his buttocks and turned her attention back to examining his asshole, rimming the outside and gently working in two of her fingers. He let out a groan. "I've stretched you nicely over these last few weeks, but I think you need a little more."

Newton's cuffs rattled against the iron screen, filling the tub room with harsh clanking sounds. Positioned on all fours, he shook his head and struggled to speak against the ball gag in his mouth.

"No?" She wiggled her fingers, thrilling at the sight of his twitching, upturned ass. "You're lying, dear. You've enjoyed wearing larger plugs, but you can be stretched some more. And there's one more thing I forgot to tell you." She leaned around, catching a glimpse of his face. "I know you slipped out and went to Vivian's room."

A barrage of unintelligible protests filed out of his mouth, and he shook his head with more vigor than before.

"Yes, I know you came on back and nothing happened. Still, standing there gawking through the door, hoping she'd see you still doesn't absolve you from this little transgression. You never should have done that. Didn't I tell you that seeing her without permission was a no-no?"

Newton responded with a grunt, trying to wrest his hands free.

"You're not getting out of those, so just stop it. You like challenging me just so I'll do something, is that it?"

He nodded lightly a couple of times, then shook his head while emitting garbled sounds.

Daria laughed. "Can't decide, eh? Either way, your ass gets it—along with a little present from me, but more about that later." She removed her fingers and headed toward the cabinets. If she wanted to move him onward in his treatment and time with Vivian, every experience she gave him counted, and just about every admit learned to wear plugs. He was no exception. She and Thomas had found much excitement in setting up a play activity between their admits, and couldn't wait to set a date, but the admits needed more training.

Despite his contrary nature, Newton had been mostly cooperative since their time in the garden, with occasional relapses of obstinacy. At The House, attendants became wary of admits who deliberately transgressed in hopes of receiving a certain punishment as their reward. With Newton, however, she doubted he used this technique. He simply wore his innate trademark of stubbornness with great pride.

From the drawers, she pulled out some lube, a speculum, and a larger plug than the last one he wore. Grinning at the craftiness of her plan, she selected a special device, one she'd use for relieving an aching bladder. There had been a reason for drinking an extra glass of water at lunch. Despite his unintelligible answers, he was comfortable, hands and knees resting on a sufficient padding of towels.

She'd selected the best punishment for him. Stretching his ass open, creating a gaping hole for her viewing pleasure, gave her the upper hand. Like most admits, he disliked the discipline process, but another part of him liked the physical sensations that came with paying the price for transgressions.

Supplies in hand, she made her way back to Newton and kneeled behind him, caressing his buttocks. Once the speculum had been coated with a generous amount of lube, she spread him apart.

"I need you to lift your ass higher so I can get this in."

Pausing a few seconds, he slowly bowed his head down to his hands, and thrust his buttocks upward.

"See, I knew you wanted this. You're too proud to admit it." She pressed the speculum against his anus, the coolness of it startling him.

"Easy, now. It's not all that bad." Working the end gently, she pushed the metal slowly inside him, loving every moan and growl seeping out of his mouth. "You like getting your ass filled? You don't seem to mind too much."

Daria glanced around, noting his eyes had closed. Between his legs, he bore a stiffened cock. Smiling, she grasped the speculum with both hands and opened the blades, taking her time, watching as his eyes squeezed tighter, ragged breaths tumbling from his throat. Her attendant had done this to her several times and she'd loved it, the sensation of cool metal sliding against her anal walls and the parting of flesh as he forced her open. She locked the blades open and peered inside.

"You look fresh and ready to me, Newton, with a nice hole for holding what I have planned for you." She squeezed one of his buttocks, rolling the flesh between her thumb and forefinger. He let out a small whimper. "When you first walked down the halls of The House, you mentioned seeing men humping ass. Do you remember?"

Another groan in reply.

"Do you know what the guys make those ladies do?"

He shook his head. His face had turned a light pink, and he started swaying his hips. Daria smacked his rear, a command to stay still.

"They make the ladies hold their cum in their ass. It reminds them who's boss. When I asked you to stay away from Vivian, you didn't."

Newton bellowed out a few sounds and lowered his head.

"What's that? You want to hold something in your ass?" Daria rubbed his butt cheeks with one hand while squeezing his balls with the other, grinning as he bucked a couple of times. Her bladder burned inside; it was time. She picked up the plug and the other device, a female urination cup. Positioning the cup snugly over her pussy, she angled the cup's spout so it rested close to the open metal handles.

"I don't have cum, Newton, but I have pee, and I made sure I had enough for you."

She relaxed her muscles, sending a stream pouring between the open blades. Newton let out a loud groan, pushing his hips higher in the air. Daria sighed as the burning subsided, watching her flow with enthusiasm.

Nothing more satisfying than seeing your own fluids enter a man's behind, and a few small turns allowed some spattering against his butt cheeks. Her admit definitely didn't mind, holding his ass up so he could catch every drop. Having emptied herself, she removed the speculum and quickly inserted the anal plug. He held enough of her, she knew. The speculum had been opened wide enough and deep enough to do its job.

"Now, you'll hold part of me for a while." She smacked his ass, satisfied at the sight of his thighs quivering. "I'd wipe you off, but we're not done. Not by a long shot." Daria whispered in his ear, "I'll leave you here for a little while, to think about what you've done." Ending with a quick squeeze of his balls, she quickly cleaned up around him and left the room.

He'd be safe there alone for at least thirty minutes or more. She'd check on him, and so would The House staff who kept an eye on admits when their attendants weren't around. Now she understood why guys liked the ladies holding their ejaculate. Thoughts of Newton holding her urine inside him filled her with a sense of satisfaction, a good punishment well-executed. Nothing like a little discomfort and a whole lot of humiliation to keep him in line. Other people passing by always had the opportunity to stop in and inspect the situation. How would dear Newton feel now, with others breezing by, stepping in and viewing the plug in his ass? Everyone knew if a lesson occurred in the tub room, more intense treatment had been given.

§§§

Forty-five minutes later, Daria returned, only to find Newton grunting, swaying his hips back and forth. She smiled. Her personal enema appeared to have worked its charm.

"Just in time, I see," she said, popping his rear end with her hand.

He glanced up, a pained look in his eyes. "Don't worry, you'll feel much better in just another minute." Stooping down close to his face, she grinned. "Ready to get that infernal thing out of your ass, I imagine. But I need to get something else." One of the cabinets held a supply of old-fashioned porcelain chamber pots. She availed herself of one of them, along with some damp washcloths and towels.

A triumphant smile crossed her lips as she watched him question her with his eyes. "Yes, it's exactly what you think it is. I'm sure your little mind is whirring about what I'm going to use it for, though you don't have to think too hard." She winked at him. "When I pull this plug out, you need to squat over this pot." Daria placed the pot between his legs and gently removed the plug while pressing above his pubic bone. With a light tug and twist, the plug slipped out, followed by a river of fluid and waste.

She stepped back, alternating her gaze between his rear and the expression on his face, which had flushed a bright pink. From the tightness of his jaws, she imagined his teeth clamping down on the gag. His obvious embarrassment sent a jolt of pleasure radiating to her clit. Quickly disposing of the bowl's contents, she hurried back and cleaned his skin.

"I think you're ready for the next step. I've been waiting for the right time to do this, but I think you've more than earned it. You did a good job, expelling all the bad stuff. Hopefully you won't try sneaking out again when I've told you not to." She removed the gag.

He didn't say anything, but flexed his muscles to relieve the tension. Daria returned to the cabinets and pulled out a strap-on and some lube.

"What the hell are you doing now?" Newton's voice came out in a light growl.

"Oh, my, still huffy? Don't deny you liked holding my piss in your ass. You sure hiked your bum up high enough for everyone to see. Plenty of folks watched you hump back and forth, trying to relieve yourself." She smacked him with a firm stroke, grinning as he flinched. "Or is it that you really liked being filled, and every move tickled your special place. Don't lie. I can tell." Sure enough, his cock had lengthened.

The strap-on soon found its rightful place. Daria stroked the phallus before applying a large amount of lubricant over the shaft and tip. "Since you did such a wonderful job getting rid of all the meanness inside you, I at least want to reward you for being such a good sport."

"Like everything else, I guess I'm not getting out of this. So do what you gotta do." He turned his head away, scowling.

"Glad you like learning your lessons, Newton. You'll only be a better lover because of it." She placed one of the remaining towels on the floor, motioning him to get on it. The last towel, she positioned under her knees.

Kneeling down behind him, she spread his butt cheeks apart, aimed the tip of the strap-on at his anal entrance, and gently pressed in past the resistance, sliding in easily until the phallus rested deep inside him.

"Fuck. Not bad." He let out a light whistle before sounding out a heartfelt groan.

She began moving with slow, even thrusts, ensuring he acclimated to the girth and length. The smoothness and ease of the phallus gliding back and forth encouraged more groans and a stiff cock sporting pre-cum in the slit of his tip. Should she free one of his hands and let him jerk himself off while she hammered him from behind, work him with her own hands, or would sweet internal torture be more fun? Ah, such choices one had to make when finding themselves in the lucky position of attendant!

The rhythm of her hips increased, and from the frustrated movements of his hands straining against the cuffs, he wanted to pound his dick just as much as she would have liked to do. She knew how the gliding motions from behind created a perfect buildup for setting off a strong release.

Torture him from the inside. What fun it was to fuck him up the rear and let him come without hand strokes. She enjoyed watching her admits struggle with gaining their own pleasure while she enjoyed hers with ease. The steadier her thrusts, the more Newton had settled into the feel of it. He'd stopped tugging against the cuffs, defeated. He stilled, allowing his body to absorb each pass. She paused a second to view his face.

His eyes remained closed. The skin of his cock had grown more taut and the head had the characteristic hue of one in an exquisite, engorged state. Daria, giving into temptation, reached out and pressed up and down the length of a swollen vein. He let out a passionate roar, and bucked a couple of times before settling down again. She slowed her pace, reaching around his chest to fondle his nipples, alternating between gentle caresses and earnest pinches of the nubs.

He bowed his head, taking in a deep breath and forcing it out. She upped the pace, undulating her hips. The phallus had settled nicely against her slit, and she opened her thighs just enough for the end to rub her clit with each push. If she kept this up, they just might come together. Struck with an idea, she pulled out.

"Hey, don't stop now!" He grimaced. "I was starting to enjoy myself."

"Hush up!" She smacked his thigh before unfastening the cuffs. "Roll over for me."

Newton repositioned himself on his back.

Grinning, Daria added additional lube on the phallus. "Lift your knees and spread them. Time to take it like a woman." She entered inside him and thrust her hips with a steady rhythm. His erection remained as strong as ever, and she'd become obsessed with wanting to see him come. He'd closed his eyes again, accepting her penetrations.

She stared down at him. No wonder guys loved their dicks so much. Wearing a likeness gave her power of a different kind. Fucking someone like a man was personal. It was intimate, went deep, and sent the message that you meant business in the most direct and undisputed way.

The phallus continued moving over the area near his prostate while the end of it grinding against her sent a new fullness and ache in her clit. His face contorted into one experiencing intense pleasure, and his mouth had opened ever so slightly. She slowed her pace, not wanting him over the edge just yet. Fondling her nipples, she closed her eyes. Each flick of the rings and gentle squeezes from her fingers sent a surge radiating to her pelvic region. Her speed increased little by little. Neither would last long now. With a few more thrusts and a circular motion of her hips, it happened. A rocking orgasm filled her pelvic region at the same time Newton tensed. Intense and immersed in the moment, she watched with eager eyes as his ejaculate pulsed out thick white streams onto his abdomen.

The beauty of a swollen cock heaving out its cum never ceased to fascinate her. And his cock was beautiful, measuring a little more in girth and length than average, and topped with a pert, beautifully shaped tip. Out of the corner of his eye, she caught a tiny tear trickling out. He resumed regular breathing while a new smile covered his lips.

"Damn, that was hot as hell!" Newton let out a loud whoop. "But you know what?" A sober expression replaced the smile.

"What?"

"I liked it when you but that tube in my dick." He grinned.

She raised her eyebrows. "You liked being catheterized? Most admits feel squeamish and hate the lack of control."

"It felt good going in, kind of like getting fucked in a tiny hole. I'd have never guessed it."

"Most people outside these walls don't go around sticking tubes in each other when they have sex or play around, but The House has ways to heighten pleasure. Some of our tools and supplies are ahead of their time."

"Will you put it in again? I'll do whatever you want and try to be extra good."

That look of innocence again. At times, it worked a certain magic over her.

Daria ran her fingers over his chest. "You like things inside your dick? Tell you what, if you're extra good, I'll see what else I can do. Maybe something that's similar, but different."

Newton pulled her face over his and delivered a deep kiss, teasing the inside of her mouth with his tongue. "I'll be good. I promise."

§§§

The hour was three o'clock in the afternoon. Daria lay napping soundly, giving Newton ample time to sneak away again before dinner. He'd done it several times when he could steal away while she carried out other duties or slept. His promises be damned. It's not that he didn't want to keep them; he just couldn't. His strong urges stood in the way. Quietly, he stole down the hall, looking ahead with purpose, barely nodding or acknowledging anyone who passed. If he could reach the desired room and spend only a few minutes viewing the inside undetected, he'd feel happier when he returned back to his own room, and perhaps rest a little easier.

Luckily for him, the occupants were inside. Just as he'd hoped. His heart pounded with anticipation. As Daria had mentioned on his first day at The House, anyone could peek into rooms, and most likely the ones being viewed hardly paid attention, especially if they were so engrossed with each other. True enough, Thomas and Vivian didn't see him while he stood and gazed.

How attentive and tender Thomas behaved toward Vivian, stroking her hair, smiling at her. Every look, every finger sliding over her skin, each kiss bestowed as if she were the most important person on earth. When they walked down the hall together, he held her close as if someone might snatch her away. When he'd seen them in the tub rooms, she lay back in his arms while he fingered her clit. He'd often spied her sucking Thomas's cock and squeezing his balls, returning the attention he'd given her. If Thomas treated each of his admits this way, he undoubtedly convinced them, for the moment, that only they occupied his world and his mind.

Could he, Newton Grenfield, pull that charm off with dozens of other women? His father managed, Thomas managed, and all the male attendants who worked here. Their motors ran hot, cocks stiff and charged, ready for the next round of fucking. But unlike them, he felt out of control, and no matter what Daria did, he wanted more. He wanted it bad, hard, soft, good. When she'd dished it all out, he wanted more, all over again. For once he'd like to feel relief, true relief where he could rest a while, knowing pleasure could be obtained at any time with a willing person. Better yet, that he didn't necessarily require pleasure for the moment or several moments or hours, maybe a day or two, maybe longer.

He closed his eyes and opened them, refocusing on the couple in the room. His cock stiffened and he sensed the heat flair in his face. Vivian had spread her thighs, reveling in Thomas's attention to her pussy. When his tongue flicked at her clit, Newton saw her breath hitch and her face draw up in pleasure. Thomas inserted a couple of fingers inside her center, and Vivian arched her back and lifted her hips.

For a moment, Newton imagined himself in Thomas's place, going through the exact same motions, lavishing the exact same attention. He thought back to the time he'd seen his father. Like Thomas, his father always seemed to be the one in charge, the one who led the way. As he'd spent time with Daria, she led the way, with him following suit. Her attempts to appease him and provide him frequent relief garnered his appreciation. Like Thomas, she cared for him, tended to him, protected him, though he knew he could crush her in an instant. Did he ever take pride in seeing Daria's face draw up in pleasure, marvel at making her buck like an untamed bronco?

Of course he wanted her happy with him, happy with the way his body filled hers, happy with the way his lips and fingers touched her. Her opening up to him on the first night had scared him as much as it had touched him. For a moment, he likened himself to a prisoner set free on the first day of release. Too many choices. The only time he had taken initiative since then was in the wee hours of the night, the ultimate time for submission, when she lay sleeping next to him, trusting, unguarded.

He liked those moments of making the move, like he always tried to do before he came to The House, like the old nighttime fantasies he had of slipping his fingers deep inside the lady next to him while she spread her legs for him, eager and willing. That's what Daria did.

During the day, she took charge. No matter how much she asked about his feelings, he had a hard time admitting them. He still held fear and unrequited urgency close to him, and doubted any amount of talking would fix it. At the same time, some of her punishments were wearing him down by slow degrees, but still not achieving that peace he wanted and so desperately needed. His body had controlled him in a tight grip since his teenage years, never loosening its hateful fingers. Now he wanted control. Total control.

Watching Thomas sliding in and out of Vivian's slit had resulted in a cock needing relief. He took several deep breaths, trying to calm himself, and he knew the quicker he got back to his own room the better. From this moment forward, he'd do things differently while he still had time here in this odd, wonderful place, The House. He'd try taking charge, use the skills taught by Daria. Most of all, he'd try not to cross her anymore. She didn't deserve a hard time. Without her, he'd be the hungry beast, never finding enough food. Without her, he'd be a wild man in the elusive search for a lover.

Newton reached his room and slipped quietly into bed, glancing over at Daria, who slumbered beside him, oblivious to anything around her. The hallways had quieted down. Dinnertime was still an hour and a half away, and he looked forward to another good meal and all the debauchery surrounding it. Daria took in a deep breath and let it out. Newton watched her chest rise and fall. She'd removed her dress.

The golden nipple rings flashed in the evening sunlight streaming through the window, and her out-turned knees had opened her slit. He sat up and gazed at the moisture pooling between her nether lips. Even in sleep she was wet. He'd start his plan now. Nothing better than a little play before dinner. He slid into a comfortable position. Grasping each side of her pussy, he spread her apart and darted his tongue around her folds, he tasted her, warm, slick, musty.

She stirred. He found the entrance to her core with the tip of his tongue and pushed, pressing in as deep as her body allowed. When he lapped at her clit, she let out a whimper, her thighs quivering. His own cock felt ready to burst. He spent the next few minutes tormenting the space inside her cleft, licking and sucking her clit until her hips jerked. A pool of pre-cum had pooled in his slit. Closing his eyes, hot and ready, he paused and took a quick breath.

CHAPTER 6

The forest spread far and wide. Trees with their massive branches and thick green leaves stretched toward the sky, inviting the sun's grace of warmth and light. Pines exuded a rich perfume as their resinous essence filled the air. A gentle breeze swirled all around, and in the distance, various birds called out to one another. Several yards away, a stream gurgled, leading onward deeper through the trees. Not far from this stream, Newton had led Daria to a section of the forest where beds of moss covered the ground, carpeting the woodsy floor in rich green.

This trust walk had been his idea, and he'd done a wonderful job, guiding her, telling her where to step up, where to watch when the ground changed, and she heard him kick away larger rocks so she wouldn't stumble. Too bad the blindfold kept the vision a secret, but she'd know where she was soon enough.

Thomas had taken her on several nature romps, showing her the layout of the land while performing a number or two on her body where it counted most once they'd found a resting spot. Newton had surprised her that morning, taking the liberty of cuffing her wrists to the bed while she slept. He'd coaxed her to waking, using his tongue and fingers to tantalize her to the point of orgasm. Just as he'd brought her to the brink, he'd stopped, leaving her with an aching pussy. When breakfast arrived, he'd fed her every bite. The attention left her intrigued and horny. She played along the whole time, not knowing what to expect. He'd filled a leather bag with some toys, leaving him armed and ready for a pleasure-filled day.

"Sit down here." Newton helped her to a sitting position. "And now for these." To her surprise and joy, he guided her to a supine position on a large, mossy bed and cuffed her wrists together. He tweaked one of her nipples, nearly taking her breath away. Yes, he'd come up with the dandy idea of stripping off her dress once they reached the forest line several yards away from The House. With the breeze caressing her naked flesh and the stroke of his fingers, she barely kept herself in check, preferring more than anything to lift up her hips and let him fuck her good and hard right then and there.

"If you were mine, I'd have you naked all the time." His rich voice settled into her ears, soothing and sexy at the same time. He delivered a kiss on her lips, sinking in his tongue and roving over the roof of her mouth. The work of his fingers over her flesh sent a surge of pleasure straight down between her legs. Before she realized it, she'd spread her thighs wide, hoping he'd sink himself deep inside her.

"You can just close those for now." He pushed her thighs together. "And I see those pretty lips of yours pouting."

"Aren't you going to take this blindfold off so I can see you?"

"Nope. I'll take it off when I'm ready."

Just as she let out a huff in protest, she startled at the sensation of his mouth suckling her nipple, gently flicking the ring at intervals. His fingers strayed over the inner side of her thighs, and just when she thought he might at least plunge a couple of fingers inside her wet slit, he stopped. She frowned.

Newton ran a finger over her cheeks and through her hair. "You've never really told me much about yourself. I thought maybe on such a pretty day like today, you could do it."

"Now? I'm not that interesting. Telling me what you're up to today would be more fascinating."

He kissed her forehead. "I don't think so."

"You've been acting strange the last few days."

"Strange? How's that?"

"All lovey-dovey. You've never done this before. What's gotten into you?" She smiled in spite of herself.

"You've been awfully good at trying to keep me in line. I just want to show how much I appreciate you." He kissed her lips. "Tell me, what made you decide to get a job here at The House? Why didn't you become a teacher or nurse?"

She turned her face toward his voice. "I feel like I do enough teaching, showing people how to enjoy their natural urges. Whether or not you'll ever believe me, I heal people in my own way. Rather, all the staff here heal. So there you have it, two occupations covered."

"But what led you here?"

She gritted her teeth. His fingers roving over the lower part of her abdomen created a huge distraction. "I was a pretty precocious child, understood grown-up things probably much earlier than most girls my age. During my teenage years, I found myself looking for opportunities to be alone with guys. When those moments occurred, I took full advantage of them." Her stomach clenched. Newton had slid a long, thick finger inside her cleft, intent on lodging it deep into her center. With a light exhale, she continued. "Soon, I didn't have to go looking anymore; the guys found me. Fondling a stiff cock with my lips and fingers or holding one inside me became an obsession. When I found a job that fed my body and soul, I simply couldn't pass it up. Not sure when I'll leave here."

"You and that Thomas guy seem sweet on each other. Don't think I haven't noticed the looks between you two, and I know you slip down to see him sometimes."

"You're a sneak, you know that?" She grinned.

"See, I bet if I took that blindfold off, your eyes would be shining like a million stars. I'll say this, unless you've been pissed at me, I've never seen your cheeks this pink. Do you ever see a future with him like I do with …"

"With who?" Daria moved her hands as if trying to take off the blindfold, but the cuffs hindered her.

"Never mind about me. We're talking about you and Thomas."

The last thing Daria wanted to discuss was her relationship, professional or otherwise, with another attendant. She shook her head. "I don't think there's really much to say about him and me. We work together."

"Say what you want, but I disagree."

Her pulse sped up on hearing him open the leather bag. Finally, enough chitchat and down to business. Her clit had ached since he'd brought her here to this spot, wherever they were.

"Newton?" He'd grown quiet, and the rustling in the bag had stopped. When the shock of freezing cold touched one of her nipples, she let out a shriek.

"Like that? That's for clamming up about yourself. You don't come off information easily, do you?"

"Oh, my god!" Daria flinched. Newton ran what felt like a piece of ice over the other nipple, droplets of water trickling down the sides of her breast as her skin warmed the frozen liquid. "Damn, that's cold." She let out a loud laugh.

"You think it's cold there?" His voice teased her.

Daria sucked in her breath and spread her legs. He'd slipped the ice inside her cleft, wedging it inside her passage. She strained, sending the piece sliding out, wriggling as water ran down her anus.

"Since you don't like to talk, I have to find some other way to entertain myself." More rustling sounds through the bag. By this time, her curiosity had kicked in. "One last chance. Tell me something about you and Thomas or about a wild time with a guy, or I use this on you."

"What's this?" Daria kept her thighs spread apart. No need giving up yet. If she knew him, he couldn't outlast her.

"I'm not about to tell you that. You're sneaky, aren't you?" He tapped an unknown object against his palm, sending out a faint rattle.

Try as she might, Daria couldn't discern what mystery item he held in his hand. Keep quiet she would. A few seconds of silence passed, with nothing but the breeze and the stream filling her ears. She gasped. Over her nipple he ran a series of sharp pricks, which trailed over her side and cut over her pubic bone, stopping at the edge of her slit. He'd selected the wheel of spikes, a circle of tiny pics with ends sharp enough to tease someone, but not sharp enough to break the skin. When he tipped a spike gently against her clit, she let out another cry.

"Don't hurt me, Newton. Those things are sharp." She caught her breath and tried to calm her voice. He hadn't come near hurting her, but the quick pricking sensation did nothing but flare up her lust to unbearable heights.

"Tell me just one little thing, just one." He ran the wheel over the inside of her thigh. She undulated her hips.

Damn! Would he ever remove this blindfold? And was he playing with himself while tormenting her? His breathing seemed heavier at times, and somehow she swore he was moving his hand against his own flesh. "If you slip inside me real qui-i-i-ick, I'll tell you something when you're fi-i-i-inished." She smiled.

"Nah, not doing that. Do we have a deal, or do I pull something else out of this bag?" She clenched her teeth at the movement of his wet tongue wiping over her nether lips.

"I have to ask, Newton. Are you jacking off?" He stopped just as the tip of his tongue wiggled inside her slit, dangerously near the pulsing bundle of nerves resting at the top. She caught her breath. "Damn you," she whispered.

He remained silent, but delivered a sharp tweak to one of her nipples. She whimpered. "I learned from the best," he said, brushing his lips against her ear. "Tell you what, do what I asked you, and I'll reward you."

She licked her lips. "Can you take off this blindfold? I'd like to enjoy the afternoon just like you."

"No, don't think so." Another sound of him moving through the bag.

"Oh, god!" Her pulse quickened at the shock. He'd placed a clit clamp on her, the gentle squeeze setting off a pang of lust throbbing between her legs.

"Just one little tale. That's all I'm asking, really." He took her earlobe in his mouth and sucked and licked the flesh, sometimes dipping his tongue in her ear. "You want your pussy fucked?"

Daria nodded.

"What did you say?" He ran his finger over her lips.

"I said yes." Her words came out a little cross.

"No you didn't, and you seemed a bit snippy too." His finger dipped inside her navel, the circular motions and manipulations there driving her nearly insane. "For a gal who wants a cock in her pussy, you're mighty stubborn. So tell me you want your pussy fucked, and then I want a quick story."

A flash of irritation shot through her, but she caught herself before she barraged him with some choice words. Today he'd put himself in charge, and taken his sweet time, the exact thing she'd been wanting him to do. Clenching her fists, she took a deep breath.

"I want my pussy fucked. One time when Joe and I spent time together, he fucked me with one of his pet snakes. And I liked it, the way the tail filled me up like a man's dick. I liked the feeling of it slithering out of me."

In seconds she found herself staring up into Newton's face, his lips turned up into a triumphant grin, his eyes shining. "That's a pretty wild story. Did that really happen, or are you just putting me on?"

"I swear it's the truth. Joe, one of our attendants here at The House, is pretty hard-core."

Newton edged her thighs apart with his knees. "Get ready for me to fill you up. And just for the record, no I wasn't jacking myself off." He grinned, and removed the clit clamp. She bucked a little as the blood rushed to the bundle of nerves, creating a pleasant throb. His stiff cock bobbed against her, and the anticipation of him impaling her overrode everything else. Her legs opened and he slid in, nice and smooth.

Each thrust of his hips sent her body humming, a smooth and frenzied vibration building her up for a hard release. The ache swelled inside her pelvic region, and every muscle tingled. She tightened down on him, working her muscles until she caught the sight of a faint grin across his lips. She watched the way his face contorted with pleasure, the way his eyes closed, the way his breath hitched in his throat. He stiffened, his jaw tightened, and his eyes flew open for a brief moment. Inside her darkest regions, she felt him pulse out his lust.

"Don't move." He gazed down at her and smiled. Slowly he pulled out, reached for the bag, and brought out a smooth egg-shaped glass phallus. "Open up for me." She did as he instructed, luxuriating in the touch of the glass against her walls as he slid it deep inside her. "There, now. You can just hold that inside until we get back to The House." He rubbed her abdomen. "Think you can do it? It's awfully smooth. It slips out, and your pussy goes without anything until this time tomorrow. As for me, I'll get myself off one way or another—and you can just watch."

She grinned. "You're on. And what if I make it without a hitch?"

"Your pussy get's another round of fucking. Now open your mouth." Newton reached into the bag, pulled out a bowl, and removed a strawberry. Daria licked at his fingers, sucking them as he pulled them from her mouth. At last he unsnapped the cuffs, massaging her arms, wrists, and fingers. He slipped a piece of melon between her lips, teasing by pulling away the fruit each time she moved to take the whole piece in her mouth. She lapped shamelessly at the juice, and when she'd licked to his satisfaction, he pushed it in her mouth.

They spent the remainder of the day roaming through the woods, with Daria pointing out the places where she and Thomas had made love. Newton had shed his trousers and joined Daria in the spirit of total nakedness, letting the breeze kiss every inch of his skin. Sometimes they stopped and pleasured each other, Daria sucking him off while he tormented her clit with his tongue.

They even watched each other release their bladders, each one taking a willing turn. Newton squeezed his balls and tweaked his own nipples as he shot out his stream. He made Daria stand and spread her labia apart, grinning with eager interest as he held the glass egg in place himself when she released a steady flow.

"I'd still rather see you pee. I'll give you a pass on holding this thing in until you're done."

Each washed off in a nearby brook. As a reward for his change in behavior and generosity, she rummaged through the bag and pulled out a prized tool, one she'd never expected. A beautiful rosebud sound, a bulbed-shaped drop, polished to perfection, resting solidly on the end of a steel rod.

Daria's pulse sped up. She adored sounding men, the simple act of sliding a special metal rod inside their holes. The sensation was like no other, and while standard rods filled them up, the rosebud opened them slowly, pinpointing the sensation as it traveled down the urethra. She knew, because her attendant had sounded her.

"I've seen the ladies use these on several fellows. I'd hoped you'd try it on me." He'd smiled an almost-shy smile, one tinted with humility.

"I'd love to, Newton. How about we settle down here by the stream, and I'll get everything ready. You even remembered to bring gloves and some cleanser. Smart move."

"Thomas let Vivian do him. I saw everything from start to finish." Blushing, he averted his eyes. "I promise I'll try not to go back there, and I've been really good, too. Haven't been back in the past three days or so."

Daria started to answer, but thought the better of it. No point in spoiling a surprise or giving him a reason for any kind of relapse into defiance. Newton reclined back on the grass, cradled his head in his hands, and let her work her magic with the sound. She glanced at the expression of pleasure on his face, the way his lips curled up into a light grin when she snapped on the gloves and cleansed his tip. When she removed the device from its packet and inserted it inside his shaft, he let out a loud groan as the rod sank deeper inside with a few manipulations of his shaft. With each progression of the metal bulb, he opened himself to the sensations, spreading his legs and squeezing his own nipple.

"No wonder the guys like this. It's the best cure for horniness." He drew out a loud sigh as she moved the rod in and out, taking care to lift and let the weight of it fall in place. Newton clenched his fists, closed his eyes, and took several deep breaths. Daria moved the rod over the area near his prostate with slow, calculated strokes, enhancing his sensations. She smiled, paused, teased a little longer. No sooner than she removed the rod had he spilled his cum onto his abdomen.

Daria had known the sensations all too well, remembering when this form of pleasure had been introduced to her. She'd marveled at the way the steel rod kissed the walls of her most sensitive and private part, and she loved reciprocating, watching the way her attendant's eyes glazed over with pure bliss as she invaded him. If Newton kept up his good behavior, his true reward lay ready and waiting down the hall from their room.

With all used toys placed in a special bag denoted for cleansing, Newton wiped himself clean and tossed the leather bag over his shoulder. Hand in hand, he and Daria headed back to The House. When they reached the edge of the lawn, they quickly slipped on their clothing.

She grinned at him. "I've held this egg, without dropping it. Do you still aim to pay up?"

"Wouldn't have it any other way. Like you, I keep my promises." He took her hand, leading her to the front entrance of The House and up to their floor. Daria caught sight of Thomas and Vivian walking down the hall, and, out of the corner of her eye, she noticed the quicker pace Newton had picked up. He and Vivian exchanged wide smiles, with Vivian offering him a light wave.

"Well, well, looks like you two have enjoyed yourselves for the afternoon." Thomas stopped, nodding toward the bag around Newton's shoulder. "Are you keeping her in line now?"

"Yes sir, she's taught me all about keeping things in line. And I'm rewarding her for good behavior." Newton bounced his gaze from the attendants to Vivian.

Thomas and Daria exchanged knowing glances. "Fantastic. My dear girl here needs a good reminder every now and then." He grinned and patted Daria's shoulder. "Come see me," he mouthed, and kept walking, pulling Vivian away with him.

CHAPTER 7

aria seated herself in a comfortable spot behind the thick green box hedge separating her from the adjoining section. She'd discovered a convenient opening among the branches giving her a brilliant view straight ahead, a line of sight falling on the couple situated only a few feet away. Luck worked in her favor by sailing all dialogue between the two right into her listening ears. Beside her sat Thomas, who'd already found another opening.

Everything had progressed so far according to plan. Their charges had settled into an amiable conversation. With any luck, Newton would spend a little time getting to know Vivian, easing into any action before jumping in without a care. Would he take charge, or would she? Would they do nothing else but talk? In this case, it didn't matter, only that Newton conduct himself amiably and act interested in anything Vivian said or wanted.

Thomas and Daria had left their admits together, pretending to go away and leave them alone. After five minutes, they'd returned. No admit spent time without an attendant in charge or other staff member minding their care. Just because she and Thomas agreed on this meeting between Newton and Vivian didn't mean exemption from the rules. Thomas glanced over at Daria, gesturing with a proud thumbs-up. Turning their attention back to the couple, they watched with heightened eagerness.

§§§

Newton stretched himself out on his side, a wide grin on his face. Vivian spent a few seconds fluffing out her hair. He watched with fascination. She could have been in pictures, with her cherubic face and kissable lips. If he had his way, he'd kiss those sweet red lips right then and there. To hell with decorum and civil talk. Taking a few breaths, he calmed himself. He'd made a promise since his last trek to Vivian's room, seeing her and Thomas engaged in lusty play. He'd try and use some manners, feel her out, see what she was really like.

"Are you happy they let us get together like this?" He plucked at a piece of grass.

"I'm more than glad. Thomas is a sweetie, but I know I've bugged him to death mentioning you all the time." She smiled at him, snuggling closer.

"It's hard to believe that just seeing you one time would be such a big deal. I've thought about you constantly since then." He ran a few fingers through her hair.

"Me too. I'm surprised they let us do this. I don't think that's the norm."

"I'm not sure what's normal around here, are you?" He shifted a little, fidgeting, trying to get comfortable. This idle chitchat did a number on his dick, which had stiffened inside his trousers. Surely she saw it.

"So why are you here, Vivian? Such a sweet, pretty thing like you, I wouldn't have guessed it in a million years." Newton leaned over and buried his nose in her hair, leaving a light kiss. He knew everything wasn't under total control. Had he been on a date outside The House, touching the woman would have been a no-no until many dates had passed. Thank heavens he could fudge much easier here.

Vivian cuddled up next to him, hesitating before quickly running her fingertip over his chest. "I'm not so sweet, if you want to know the truth."

"Tell me the truth, then. I'm all ears." Newton moved his arm around her, pulling her closer.

"I don't know about you, but I like sex. Can't explain it. But even as a very young girl I played with myself, touching, feeling everything.

When I discovered my clit and how that set off a whole slew of sensations, I didn't stop. As I got older I couldn't resist inserting things inside myself, handles of hairbrushes or mirrors. One time a male friend and I got together. He was just as curious as I was. He told me about having some wet dreams and how he spent nights fondling himself. I'd never seen a guy naked before, so when he suggested getting together to see what it was all about, I jumped at the chance.

"We slipped off one afternoon and ended up in a graveyard, of all places. And it didn't take him but a few seconds to drop his trousers, with me slipping down my panties just as fast. I don't know how long we spent fooling around with each other, but I knew I liked his fingers inside me while I stretched and rubbed on his dick. Fingering his head turned me on as much as it did him." She glanced up at Newton. "Are you okay with me rambling on? You look really flushed all of a sudden."

"No, I'm fine. Interesting story. What happened next?" Newton stretched his neck from side to side, glancing up at the sky and back down to Vivian.

"Well, I squeezed his balls, rubbed on him some more, and got him real hard, at which point he wanted to go all the way. So we did. Heck, why not? I just spread my legs wide open, and he went for it. It wasn't much fun the first time, but we made a pact to go back to the graveyard and practice some more. We were young teens then. As I got older, it just got worse. My parents got tired of me coming home late at night when I went out. So, long story short, I ended up here. This day and age, it doesn't take much to get thrown into a place like this."

"It's hard, isn't it, having to watch everything you do and say? But we're lucky we ended up on a side no one knows about." Newton kissed the tip of her nose. She nodded.

"What about you, Newton? Are you one of those bad boys?" Her lips curled up in a mischievous smile.

"Um, I could be. Some think I am." He chuckled. "I could have easily been your friend or one of those men you went out with at nights.

It's actually a shame we didn't live in the same town. I think we would have hit it off really well, don't you think?"

"I think we've hit it off fine right now. I've always been one to take advantage of a moment, never hold back." Her hand had found its way to his hip and over his ass.

"And unfortunately, I'll confess that I tend not to hold back, either. As a woman, you have it lucky. It usually costs me." He gave her an intent stare. She gazed back at him in silence.

"How did you end up here, Newton? It's your turn." Her hand moved over his thigh, inching over until her fingers brushed over his crotch, tracing the outline of his cockhead. His face turned scarlet, jaw clenching as he struggled for composure.

Swallowing hard, he croaked out his words. Instead of pulling away, Newton bent one leg up, leaving the other stretched out. "There's not a whole lot to say," he said, giving her a wan smile. "I guess my old man didn't like me being a chip off the old block, thought I had a problem." Newton chuckled. Vivian continued gazing at him, serious, wide-eyed. He licked his lips, thinking of what to say next. "Let's just say I had certain women who were nice, but simply not my type, not someone I could see myself settling down with."

"Uh-huh." Vivian nodded, encouraging him to go on. Her fingers traced the length of his cock as he narrated his story. Up and down she worked, circling his cockhead with her forefinger.

"Anyway, I think I basically moved too fast, thinking that once they started paying attention to me, they wanted one thing. As a result, I spent a lot of time alone, being my own best friend." He grinned at her.

Vivian stared off into the distance before turning her focus back on him. "So what do you plan on doing when you leave here?"

"I'll head on back to work, maybe start looking for a house of my own. I think it'll be time to do that. A grown man needs a place to call his own, don't you think?"

"True. I'll most likely try to find a job in a dress store. I like fashion, jewelry, all the pretty things." She grinned up at him.

Newton blinked several times, rubbing his finger through the grass faster, more urgent, pulling out blades of green every now and then.

She leaned her head sideways, eyeing him carefully. "Is this something you want to talk about right now, or we could talk later? You look distracted."

"To tell you the truth, this is my problem. I tend to ditch the talking and get down to business, or try to. Like I mentioned earlier, most girls don't like it, and simply ditch me. My old man got tired of hearing complaints later and watching me fall flat on my face. So he thought sending me here would fix everything." He sat up. "Here's the thing. I don't know about you, but I'm always in the mind to do what you and your friend did in the graveyard." He gave her quick wink.

"I won't think any less of you if you get right down to business." Vivian reached up for the straps of her dress. "I'm all yours."

"You sure?" Newton raised an eyebrow.

"Of course. Right now I want it as much as you do.

"I'm on it, then." He chuckled, grabbing her hands and rolling her over on the grass. "You just keep those hands above your head and don't move. Lie back and lift those pretty hips. I'll take care of business." He repositioned himself on his knees, eyes taking in a quick view of her feminine bits. With deft hands, he pushed up the dress, exposing her in the afternoon sun. His face held the expression of one eyeing a feast after days of starvation. The gleam in his eyes burned with a strong inner fire as he glossed his tongue over his lower lip. At last she was his, the moment he'd always wanted.

Vivian offered herself, ready for him as his fingers spread her apart. His tongue darted out, a hot wet tip prodding at her clit. Quickly he moved, flicking, teasing, fastening his mouth on her flesh and sucking firmly. He repeated the series of moves several times, each round faster than the first. Groaning, she clenched her fists, pumped her hips a little, and spread herself wider. He worked the tip of his tongue inside her entrance, pushing firmly, sliding in as far as he could, wiggling the tip over her walls, lapping at her fluids. When he gently grazed her clit between his teeth, she let out a cry. He lifted his face, watching the undulations of her hips as pleasure racked her body. On her lips, she wore the smile of one suspended in pure ecstasy.

He leered down at her. "You like me tonguing your pussy?"

"Put it in … something … your finger … cock." Vivian gasped for breath. "Oh, god, it hurts, but it feels so …" She winced. Newton obliged, slipping in two thick fingers and spreading them.

"You're so wet. Juicy and sweet." He leaned over her face. "Yours is the best pussy I've ever tasted." Without another word, he dropped a kiss on her lips. Just as her hands moved in the direction of his trousers, he backed away, slipping his fingers from the inside of her nether regions.

"Oh, no you don't." With a laugh, he sat on his haunches. "You don't get a shot at this baby until I say so." Her eyes widened. Newton reached down, placing a hand over the outline of his cock, thickened to full length and girth. He grasped himself through his clothing and gave a firm squeeze. Laughing he continued rubbing himself, squeezing at his cockhead. "I'm a lot to hold Viv, but I think you can do it. Do *you* think you can?"

She nodded, reaching out for him.

Newton leaned over her, flicking his tongue over her earlobe, nibbling the flesh before kissing her neck. His fingers moved over her nipples, teasing the nubs beneath the dress. Vivian moaned and arched her back.

"You ready for all of me? I'm a big man, Viv. I need to make sure you can hold a nice fat one. I need to hear you say that holding a big one like me is no problem." He placed a quick kiss on her lips. "Say it, Viv. I'm dying here."

Vivian flashed him a wide smile. "I can hold a big man like you inside me. I'm not scared of you." She bent her knees up and spread her legs.

Newton unsnapped his trousers, releasing his engorged flesh, holding it down a bit so that it bobbed back and forth, teasing her.

He landed his hands on either side of her shoulders, settling easily between her thighs. With a smooth push, he impaled her, moving his hips in small circles followed by short, powerful thrusts. "You feel good, all hot and wet." His cock slid in and out of her with ease.

Vivian reached up, working the nubs of his nipples. He paused, reveling in the sensations.

"Push the top of your dress down. Show me those tits."

She needed no further encouragement. Her fingers tugged apart the straps, and down came the top of the dress. Newton dipped his head, catching a plump nipple in his mouth. He drew out another series of cries, feasting on both her breasts, licking, biting, and sucking. At one point, he stopped, closing his eyes and catching his breath.

"You like fingering my ass hole?"

The only answer Vivian gave was the movement of her fingers wedged between his buttocks. She'd managed to work the front panel of his trousers all the way back, taking full advantage of tantalizing his ass with skilled fingers.

He grunted and bucked his hips. "Yeah, nothing like being finger-fucked in the ass, especially if it's you." Newton began thrusting, starting slow and building up into the final crescendo when he let out a cry as he pressed hard against her, shuddering while his cock landed a thick load deep inside her core. Vivian closed her eyes and nodded.

"Come on, give it all you got." She chuckled, and gave his firm buttocks a good squeeze as he pushed out the last drops of cum.

$$§§§$$

From behind the hedge, Daria held her breath, eyes fixed on the two admits as they descended into the afterglow of passion, holding each other like one or the other might disappear. She sat back in amazement. This wasn't the same man she'd first met. Had all her teaching finally reached him? Hearing Vivian's story had set him off, she knew. She'd watched him struggle with listening, but he'd held back beautifully, asking her questions, appearing interested in her. The sight of Newton working Vivian had sent her own crotch into a maddening ache. She glanced at Thomas, who'd inched his way over to her. He flashed Daria the thumbs-up signal. From the view of his face, tight-lipped and glinting eyes, she knew he wanted to unload a full cock. Watching Newton go at it with his admit had sent his testicles in overdrive.

"It's our turn. We're allowed, you know." He wrapped his arms around Daria, kissing her lips.

As he unsnapped his trousers, she lay back, shifted up her dress and spread her legs. Her gut clenched at the sight of a thick dick that rivaled Newton's, including the sizable cockhead that sent her fluids pooling inside her slit.

Daria always looked forward to these moments when she could hold Thomas in her arms, and his luscious dick inside her. She like him gliding in and out, coating her hidden walls with his cum. When it came to Newton's fancy tongue work inside Vivian, she knew where her admit had seen those moves. Nobody's tongue flicked and bumped like Thomas's, the master clit teaser of them all.

She closed her eyes and waited with sweet anticipation for the moment he would make a nosedive for her clit. Daria clenched her jaw to keep quiet. No need to make Newton and his newfound love suspect they were being watched by their own attendants. The sweet pain swelled in her pussy as Thomas coaxed her clit from its hood, stabbing at her hot button before flicking and sucking, washing over it until she succumbed to the hardest spasms she'd ever experienced. Even the muscles in her backside clamped down.

With his cock near the bursting point, Thomas settled between her legs, burying himself to the hilt. He sucked in his breath and moved with beautiful precision, a deliberate rhythm of slow advances, quick circular twists of the hip, and a burst of speedy thrusts. In return, her internal muscles grasped his shaft until he pulled out a limp piece of flesh, happily spent.

Inside her hidden depths, she held his lust. Resting, she savored the moment, marked, used for his pleasure and hers. Thomas held her close, his hand wedging its way inside the top of her dress. For the moment, he entertained himself some more, squeezing her nipples, nudging the rings piercing her skin.

"I think our experiment succeeded, sweetheart," Thomas whispered.

Daria's eyes shined as she viewed him. "Do you think we could let those two spend more time together, do some different things? I really think Newton needs this. He needs someone he can really call his own."

Thomas smiled at her. "I don't see why not."

"I've told you all about Newton and what's in store. I think having a special someone who understands is more important than ever." Her finger grazed his cheek.

"I couldn't agree more. He'll have a hard enough time dealing with a bad hand that's been dealt. We can only hope she'll be understanding when she finds out." Thomas gave Daria a sober look before peeking through the hedges again. "Would you believe it. They're at it again."

"Come on, sweetheart." Thomas grinned, tapping her on the shoulder. "Let's let those two get off one more time before we drag them back to The House. I think they'll miss each other."

"Maybe we can come up with a way to pacify them a little longer once we get back. And when we do, maybe we can …" She ran her finger over his sac, giving him a gentle squeeze.

"*Operation Matchmaker*, part two. Couldn't agree more." He snapped up his trousers and peeked through the hedges one last time.

CHAPTER 8

I never imagined eating food could get so creative." Newton sat in the corner of the dining room with Vivian curled up next to him, playing "Eeny, meeny, miny, moe" with the selection of food spread out before them.

"It's kind of fun, don't you think?" She grinned, dipping her dainty finger in a bright red sauce.

His eyes narrowed. Admits and attendants dined off of each other, licking nipples and cocks. Men inserted tasty bites of fruit into their lady's hidden bits, feasting with gusto as their dining partners spread themselves wide for eager lips and hot, swirling tongues. If he'd joined this carnal scene the first night, he would have devoured Daria in bed, and spent the rest of the night masturbating until he ran dry.

"Here, taste this." Vivian held out her finger.

Newton licked it, swirling his tongue while she laughed at the sensation. He sat back, surveying everyone around him. As Daria had mentioned on his arrival, The House dining room was the one place where everyone congregated at mealtimes, nude, bringing on their enthusiasm for debauchery. No wonder she'd made him wait a few days. The sight before him would have been sensory overload. Even now, his balls throbbed. He held back, the need for attempts at self-control conflicting with the urge to make a dive for Vivian's pussy with every ounce of energy boiling inside.

She would never mind him sucking and licking her feminine parts, invading her with the hard, eager tool between his thighs. Why so cautious now? True to his promise, he'd used Thomas's example and Daria's teachings, curbed the lust, and courted his lover. Did this step make a difference in winning her over? Or had this whole ordeal been a waste of time, with her not caring how fast he'd moved? And what made her different from willing girls in the past? He wrinkled his brow, deep in thought. Regardless of the past, The House had changed both of them forever, giving them and others who left this place special knowledge that would leave the prudish majority cringing. He and Vivian didn't cringe, but gripped sexual pleasure by the proverbial horns and embraced it, loved it, would wither away and die without it.

"What's wrong, Newton? You don't look content right now. Would you rather be with someone else?" Vivian stroked a few locks of his hair, the smile fading from her face.

He shook his head. "I'd rather be with you than anyone else."

"Then what are you thinking about? I sometimes get a funny feeling something's bothering you."

"Viv, do you ever get tired of seeing all this carrying on, or have moments when sex doesn't even cross your mind?"

"That's an odd question. Of course I have times when I'm not thinking about it." She thought a minute. "Why? Don't you?"

"Maybe when I'm asleep." He frowned, casting his gaze over the dining room. "I sometimes wonder what these people are really like, what they'll be like when they leave here. Will they have a normal life where work, family, and sex blend in a nice, easy mix? Control that drive, curb that urge to fuck until it hurts, until you don't want another thing in you, or you think you you'll never shoot out drop of spunk again because you're all dried up?"

"I'm sure they will. It's nothing but a balancing act, feeling comfortable with yourself and the one you're with, going on and living life." Vivian leaned in close to his ear. "Do you feel comfortable with me?"

"I'm my best with you. I stop and think. I care. But I think it's because I've learned how to do all that here. I never did it before. I couldn't. I still …" He curled his fingers, jaws clenched.

"You still what, Newton?"

His eyes roamed the floor, fingers fidgeting. "Nothing … I lost my train of thought."

"I don't think it'll be quite this intense when we leave. There's a lot of distraction here."

"Yep, you got that right." He chuckled, fingering the fruit inside a small bowl. "Hey, why don't we try our hand at what some of these folks are doing?" Newton leaned his head toward a gentleman and his lady playing with chocolate and strawberries.

"I'm game." Vivian stretched out on the floor, opening her thighs. "Go ahead."

For the next few minutes, Newton concentrated on inserting an assortment of berries deep inside her core until she couldn't hold any more. He dripped the luscious juice over her breasts, sucking hard at her nipples and licking over her skin to make sure he got every drop. For a final topping, he spread her nether lips apart, pouring a little honey over her while she flinched and giggled at the tickling sensation.

When he fixed his lips between her thighs, she became still, clenching her jaws as he moved inside her, tongue flicking as he ate each piece of fruit she offered. Newton cast his self-questioning aside, reveling in feeding off Vivian, swirling his tongue in the sweetness of woman and fruit. He liked running his tongue over wet, smooth flesh as he moved in and out of each hidden spot inside her.

Knowing she genuinely wanted him made the best difference of all. From the sparkle in her eyes the moment they met, he knew she wanted him—really wanted him. With this woman, there never would have been an issue of coming on too strong, losing her because of an overeager urge to consume her.

He'd learned one thing. Taking time and slowing himself down enhanced the outcome, whether or not he wanted to admit it. The slow ride and teasing touch made the buildup and subsequent climax worth the wait. He understood now the beauty of courting, holding back, but with an end purpose in mind, one mutually desired. In the wait was rich reward, soft and sweet on lips and tongue. He closed his eyes, paying special attention to the hot button that set her body rocking with spasms of sheer bliss.

§§§

From across the room, Daria and Thomas supervised, observing their admits in between kisses and fondling each others' nipples and sensitive parts below the belt line.

"I think they're really getting into each other." Daria looked out at the two, absorbing the view of Newton bearing down on Vivian.

"I'm getting into you sucking me off. Please, don't stop." Thomas undulated his hips, groaning when Daria gave his sac a firm squeeze. "Gotta hand it to you, your tongue knows no bounds." He lay back, eyes closed, while she tongued his cockhead.

She didn't say anything, but kept tormenting him, licking and swallowing his cock until he shuddered, feeding her every drop of cum. "You're tasty all by yourself."

Thomas sat up, cradling her in his arms. He placed small pieces of food in her mouth, offering her a sip of drink from an elegant cut-glass goblet. Daria relished the way he cared for her, his tenderness a stark contrast to the dominant side of his nature, which he displayed with ease and finesse when he wanted to. She hadn't forgotten what it had been like as an admit under his watchful eye. No wonder Vivian could handle Newton after Thomas's training. Newton and Vivian held promise.

"Does Newton have any idea what's in store for him?" Thomas sipped from his own goblet as Daria answered.

"I haven't said anything to him yet, but I'm wondering if I can't get him to see the benefit since he's admitted his lack of control." She gave Thomas a wry smile. "I'll use any argument to my advantage. How do you tell a guy that he's about to change permanently, and there's nothing he can do to stop it?"

Thomas studied her, thoughtful, nodding as he considered Daria's task. "Definitely turn it into a positive if you can. Try to help him buy into the procedure as a way to solve a lot of his problems."

"I just wish his treatment here didn't involve something so drastic, that's all."

"You never know, sweetheart. Sometimes everything works out for the better, even a situation as dire as this one."

"I wonder what he'll be like when he leaves here, whether or not she'll still care for him after she finds out."

"Don't know." Thomas popped a strawberry in his mouth and ate it. "I think he'll get past the experience of The House, blending what he's learned here into a new life once he's home. This place is only a chapter in his life. The ending is yet to be determined."

"You think that's the whole point of The House, discovery, immersion, integration?" She squeezed her eyes shut, laughing at her philosophical self. Thomas's serious expression restored her sober side.

"Couldn't have summed it up better myself. That's exactly what it is. When it's time for integration, it's time to leave The House."

Daria nodded, turning her face toward Newton. Vivian had taken her place between his thighs, her mouth encasing his cock while he lay back, eyes closed, a satisfied grin sprawling over his face. She watched longer, taking in the sight of his muscles contorting as Vivian imbibed a healthy dose of lust. Like Thomas, Newton enjoyed nothing better than surrendering to earnest tugs and teasing licks of a tongue.

Her breath hitched. The suckling sensations from Thomas as he encased her nipple in his mouth encouraged the flow of juices inside her. In her pelvic area, a dull, pleasant ache filled her with anticipation for the moment his tongue would trip and dance over an urgent clit, casting her helplessly into the abyss of a heady climax.

§§§

"There you are. I've been looking all over for you." Daria slipped up behind Newton, touching him on the back of the shoulder.

He jerked his head up, frowning at the intrusion. In silence he turned away, staring at the pond.

"What? Fish aren't biting today?" She grinned and sat down beside him.

He didn't answer, but stared into the water, eyes smoldering. For such a glorious, sunny day, his face reflected an internal storm.

"What's wrong, Newton?"

"Do I get to write some more about why I shouldn't sneak out, or something like that?"

"No. Only because you've been acting odd lately, and I know something's eating away at you. You need to talk to me."

Newton turned his eyes upward a second before staring off across the water. "I don't know what to say. Not even sure I really feel like getting into it. It's too much."

"What's too much?" Daria placed a hand on his back, rubbing up and down with small strokes.

Silence.

"I'll tell you what I think's the matter. It may be nothing but my own crackpot theory, but I need you to tell me if I'm right or not. Your engine's running full speed, and you're powerless to stop it. Your key's locked in the car, and not a soul in sight who can help." She turned his face so they stared each other in the eye.

"Don't know how much I can take. You'd think being here, seeing all the craziness, getting a chance to go at it whenever I want … having a woman I adore who wants it as much as I do …"

"But that's not the real issue, is it?" She took his hand in hers.

Newton shook his head, licking his lower lip. "Nah, it's not the real problem, getting some whenever I want. I used to think it was, but it goes deeper than getting your balls pumped by some pretty lady sucking cock."

"What do you think the real problem is?"

"There's something driving me, something on the inside, an urge that never stops. No matter how much I try to satisfy the drive, it only comes back in a matter of hours. To try and go days or weeks without any satisfaction is useless. All I end up doing is finding a place where I can jerk off without anybody suspecting what I'm up to." The corner of his lips turned down in dismay. "A person can claim they need to pee only so much before they start looking like a weirdo."

"How much do you pleasure yourself in a day?" Daria rested her head on his shoulder.

"I can go five times in a day, so much my balls ache like a son-of-a-bitch when I'm done. I almost swear they'll shrivel up if I squeeze out one more drop. Even here at The House, we don't go that much. Restraint and control sets the limits. But for me, there's no fun in waiting for it. It kills me. I'd give anything to tame that fire inside to a dull roar, where it's the submissive, and I'm dominant—over me."

For the first time she took in the defeated look on his face, the anguish. She'd hoped the trysts with Vivian had solved the problem, but the fact that it hadn't didn't totally surprise her, either. Dr. James had given her the warning on the first day Newton stepped foot inside The House. The alteration. The transformation.

"Newton, I think there is a way we can fix this problem."

CHAPTER 9

The air in the room filled her body with a creeping, relentless chill, wrapping icy fingers around her heart. Any minute those ghostly fingers threatened to pull the beating core of life right out of her. White cheery streaks of light from the afternoon sun mocked the future as time ticked onward for a troubled man who would be forever changed. Bound naked to a cold steel table, the point of no return, fear infiltrated the man's eyes, despite his fortunate agreement to the scene where he found himself now.

Fortunate because neither Dr. James nor Daria had been forced to deal with a potential crying and gnashing of teeth that would have occurred had the admit outright refused the grim hand dealt to him. Newton didn't need to know his father's specific orders: "do something or else." His own desperation to try anything had lessened the blow. Dr. James's assurance that sex would be totally under his control from this moment forward gave Newton some encouragement, and freed the doctor from further straining the relationship between this admit and his father.

"Look at yourself like the famous Italian opera singers of the past who had this done on purpose," the doctor had suggested. "They had more women than they could handle, lives filled with clandestine trysts in the bedroom, and women fighting to be with them. These men still functioned. You'll drive the sex instead of it driving you."

With this strong reassurance from the good doctor, Newton made his choice. Daria closed her eyes, silently constructing a prayer as her admit's trembling radiated through her hand on his chest. Newton had asked her to be with him for moral support. During this important time in his life, she had no intention of leaving him alone. Between his thighs a flaccid shaft perched on a set of plump balls. A white towel underneath added to the horrific clinical ordeal waiting to happen. Newton's eyes cast a cold, almost lifeless stare on the plastered ceiling. Daria knew the finality of it all still riddled him with fright. If it weren't for the occasional twitch of nervousness, she'd swear a corpse rested in front of her. Overcome with an urge to try and make it all better, she leaned over and placed her lips squarely on his, slipping in her tongue for a quick caress over the inside of his mouth. He didn't move.

She whispered in his ear, "A kiss for you, Newton, with all my heartfelt wish that you'll be able to find some peace, and that love truly is in your grasp. You deserve it, after all." A few tears pooled in his eyes, and he swallowed hard in a feeble attempt to keep his emotions in check.

"Can you please pass me that small bottle and the syringe?" Dr. James leaned his head toward the items situated within her reach. Daria nodded, handing the items to him one by one. She watched as his gloved fingers inserted the needle into the bottle, drawing up some of the liquid.

Her voice came out in a small squeak. "Dr. James, are you sure there isn't another way?"

"My dear, I don't believe there is, and it looks like our admit has reached the end of his rope." He caught Newton's gaze. "Mr. Grenfield, doing this at your age is a saving grace, because you can still function sexually. Might take a little extra effort, but with all you've learned at The House from Daria and others, you should still have a better-than-average intimate life. Don't you think, Mr. Grenfield?"

"Hope so, Doc." Newton's voice trailed out faint, raspy, his face pale with fear.

"Okay, Newton, this is it." The doctor turned his eyes toward Newton's face.

Newton winced. His thighs tensed, and he let out small grunts as the needle pierced his flesh in different locations, including the soft flesh between his thighs.

"There, we'll just give this some time to numb things up before we begin."

At the sight of Dr. James reaching for a scalpel, scissors, and the metal basin, Daria wanted to run far away, into Thomas's arms. Would this change things between Newton and Vivian? Had he gained a true shot at something special, only to have it snatched away at the last minute? She gulped, forcing the tears back.

After several minutes, Dr. James tugged, rolled and squeezed the spongy orbs between his fingers. "Newton, do you feel any of that?"

Newton shook his head.

"We're ready." The doctor poised his scalpel in preparation for the extraction of a man's most precious treasures. He began the incision, cutting sure-handedly through the flesh. His eyes, intent on their target, didn't blink; a hint of sadness covered his face. A firm mass of tissue slid through the opening as the doctor gently squeezed it out. He quickly tied off a longer stretch of cord-like matter. 'The spermatic cord,' he'd said. Daria swallowed hard, averting her eyes. She studied Newton's face, how the muscles had relaxed, his jaw slack. The sounds of blades coming together sent a wave of nausea shooting through her stomach; her blood ran cold. A sudden onslaught of dizziness overtook her, and her knees weakened.

"Daria, can you hold steady, or do you need to leave? Our young man and I will be fine on our own." She closed her eyes. "I'm ... fine." She placed her hand in Newton's. He gave her a forced light smile. "It's just that I'm not used to ..." Her teeth clamped shut on hearing the blades come together a second time, meaning the other testicle had been removed.

"Just try and remember the good we're doing here. All's not lost, and Mr. Grenfield, we'll make sure you know that, too. You won't leave The House, shall we say, empty-handed."

The clanking of the scissors and scalpel in the metal basin signaled the end of the horrid procedure.

Avoiding a view of the basin, she let out a sigh of relief. "Are we done, Dr. James?"

"Yes, we're done. Just a few stitches and this gentleman can rest back in his room. I'll check on him later. Newton, you'll need about three weeks to heal, so no funny stuff. After that time, you can start trying things out a bit."

§§§

Newton glanced at Vivian, who maintained a thoughtful gaze as she stared back at him. Telling her why he'd made such a drastic decision had been difficult. Explaining his feelings to Daria in the beginning had helped somewhat, but pouring out your heart to someone who could easily walk away from you had created a greater struggle. If she'd walked away from him, this abandonment would have wreaked havoc on his psyche, creating an internal darkness he may never have fully resolved.

"How do you feel about me now that all this has happened? Is this a turnoff for you?"

She rubbed his arm, staring off in thought. "I'm shocked. I won't lie. Part of me will always wonder if you had to go this far. But the real question should be, how do *you* feel?"

He lay back, running his hand over his cock, fingering the head as he thought. "I don't know. Feels kind of strange not having balls to squeeze anymore. I miss them, but then again I don't think I do, either. It's hard to explain. I feel calmer, more in control, more like I can take life easy and not get so riled up. Dr. James told me it would be like this."

Vivian snuggled closer beside him. "It's a drastic step, but if you thought doing this solved a problem, then you made a right choice. You seemed so unhappy at times."

"This is why I've kept a low profile lately. It's another reason why I haven't felt like going into the dining room. Didn't want all those studs in there laughing at me."

"I doubt they'd ever laugh. These people here aren't silly school kids. They're serious about what they do. Thomas said he's seen people in your situation before, and is seeing it more as time goes on." She leaned close to his ear. "You know we can keep up with what we've learned here, don't you? I mean …" Her face flushed.

Newton beamed. "Of course we'll do that. It's three weeks since the operation. I'm ready now. Do you want to try? I'm willing if you are."

"Of course. Daria and Thomas both agreed we'd be spending several nights together, and I'm happy about this. No matter what, I care about you, Newton."

He stroked her cheek. "The same here, Viv. While we're here, I want to see what I'll be able to do. Getting through this ordeal with you beside me is what I need." He kissed her, squeezing her nipple gently between his fingers. Vivian let out a moan and fell back on the bed. Newton pushed her thighs open before slipping a couple of fingers deep inside her. Her breath hitched in her throat.

"I haven't forgotten how to please a woman. But I'll let you in on a secret. For the past few days, I've been able to get it up a couple of times. Have to work at it more, but I can still do it. Besides, squeezing a good set of tits and playing in a hot wet pussy is still fun, no matter what, especially if it brings a smile to a woman's face. Daria has been a big help, letting me fool around with her most every night, just to keep my head in the game. She's a good teacher, and that's what she's supposed to do, help people like me. Honestly, though, my mind kept going back to you."

"Keep going, then. Your fingers drive me mad." Vivian smiled.

Newton swirled around her fluids, noting the swishing sounds when a woman is wet and ready. Somewhere in his depths, he felt the old urge again, the rush of blood filling his cock. It came slowly, receded, came again. He took some breaths and focused on how it used to feel, how squeezing a pair of plump nipples and sliding over an eager swollen clit filled him with a sense of urgency.

The smell of a woman alone used to excite him. That uncontrollable urge didn't come anymore, but a reassuring sense of pleasure and control did. The scent of Vivian would always instill some form of excitement for him. He could do this if he put his mind to it, if he concentrated hard enough. Most important of all, he could do this if he had Vivian rooting for him, loving him without judgment.

Spreading her nether lips apart, he landed his tongue on her clit, flicking the nub of flesh with determination. When he sucked her, she cried out. He kept at her, fingering inside her hot core, flicking and sucking until she came, lifting her hips with each spasm.

"Looks like you're ready." Vivian had caught her breath and reached out, running her fingers over a hard cock, squeezing the cockhead in all the right places.

He closed his eyes, taking in the touch of her fingers over his flesh. To his relief, the absence of balls didn't seem to matter to her. She kept right on strumming over him, still wanting him. His heart raced, and his cock held a light throb, not the uncontrollable fiery one that never knew full satisfaction. Desire came when he wanted it, not in spite of him. This ability brought him satisfaction each day he realized the truth.

His hard cock was the result of loving Vivian, wanting to satisfy her as much as anything. And that's what Daria had been teaching him all along, to enjoy and please your partner.

Newton lifted himself up and settled in between her thighs, aiming his tip at her entrance. With a quick move, he slid inside her, the cry from her lips filling his ears like sweet music. With slow undulations, he glided in and out, enjoying the sensation of her hugging his cock. He wasn't in any hurry, but measured each thrust of his hips, speeding up at times, slowing down nice and easy at others. He paused to suckle her breasts, taking his time in biting, sucking, and flicking his tongue over her nipples.

When he was ready, he gave himself over to the release, one that filled him with a bliss he'd never known, a slow heat radiating throughout his body, leaving him refreshed and definitely satisfied. Instead of pulling out, he remained connected, smothering her lips with kisses. He'd done it at last in his new state, with Vivian, giving her what she wanted, and taking what he wanted—her happiness, his control.

Settling beside her, he cradled her in his arms. "I've been thinking a lot, lately. We won't be here forever. When we leave, would you be interested in …?" He stared off across the room.

"In what, Newton?" She rested her head in the nape of his neck. "What do you want?"

Licking his lips, he drummed up every ounce of will to speak his mind. "I'd like to have a life with you, that's what. I want to wake up every morning and know you're with me. I want to fall asleep every night with you."

Her eyes lit up, along with the smile stretching across her face. "Would you, really?"

"Vivian, I fell in love with you the moment I met you. Of course this … thing … has happened, and I'm hoping like hell it won't bring us down. I'm hoping with patience, time, and work, we can still keep things nice and hot, like before."

She ran her fingers through his hair, taking in each word. "There's more to life than doing it all the time. At least we know how to get creative, and we'll come up with ways to make things work. I know we will."

"We won't be able to have our own children. I know most women want them." He stared at the bed covers, dreading she might have second thoughts.

"I'm not most women, and there's always nieces and nephews. I have brothers and sisters." Vivian landed a light kiss on his lips. "You never know what life has in store for you, and I'll keep busy doing other things. It's all okay."

"I love you, Viv." Newton took a deep breath, holding her close.

§§§

Daria lay next to Thomas, this time finding little comfort in his finger lodged deep inside her as they relaxed on the floor of his room. She'd wanted more than anything to find a way to spy on Vivian and Newton—just a quick peek. How were they doing? How would Vivian handle his new state? She adored sex. Would a castrated male send her into the arms of someone else?

"You've got to stop worrying about those two." Thomas chided her again, like he'd been doing since they hooked up after sending Vivian to Newton. "They're adults. They'll find their own way and work it out. If it doesn't work, it doesn't work."

"I just want it to work." Daria shot him a frustrated look.

"Me, too, sweetheart." Thomas grinned as his strokes over her clit brought out a momentary flicker of lust. "Newton wasn't getting out of his situation no matter what, with or without Vivian. Having her hang in there with him will take the bitterness down to a more tolerable level. I agree that much."

"What do you think they're talking about down there? Do you think he'll be able to satisfy her? Satisfy himself?"

Thomas shrugged. "Don't know. They say the Castrati had healthy sex lives, and they got cut way younger than our friend Newton. So he has a good shot at keeping things going. Vivian has been a wonderful admit, and a quick study. She'll keep the embers burning in their love life."

"You think so?" She smiled at Thomas. He always said the right thing, making her feel better.

"I know so. But for now, let's just concentrate on having a good time, like we used to do when we found free moments."

"We managed to find them, didn't we?" Daria laughed. "I enjoyed my attendant, but I wanted …"

His eyes bore into her, as if staring into her soul. "Same here." His fingers moved faster, sliding deeper into her center.

Shifting her position, she lost herself in the sensation of his movements, deliberate, urgent, gentle.

He stopped, took her in his arms, smothering her with a deep kiss. A rigid cock nudged her flesh. For a moment, Daria forgot about the two admits down the hall.

CHAPTER 10

Newton stood outside the entrance of The House, suitcase in hand. After a few months, he'd received the call that his father was on his way to pick him up. Vivian had already left The House a week earlier, nearly sending him into a fit of depression. He'd remembered the tears in her eyes, soothing them away with promises he'd come for her once he got out. He intended to keep that promise. With a heavy heart he'd watched out a window as she walked with her family, head bowed, down the steps and into the car. When she turned around one last time, offering him a last wave good-bye, his own tears came hard and fast.

One call from the steward, and his father had put up no argument once he'd been informed of his son's successful treatment. The fact Vivian was waiting for him sweetened the bargain even more.

His old man may have thought himself quite worthy in the love department, but even in his tamed state, Newton knew his skills would put most men to shame. He'd given Vivian one last hurrah, sending her gasping and bucking before he'd totally finished. Now his thoughts turned toward the future, his own home, and her.

Inside his suitcase, he'd stowed away some precious toys. She'd had her own toys given to her when she'd left. That's what the staff at The House did, provided their admits with a special take-home package when they left, tokens reminding you of where you'd been, what you'd learned. He and Vivian would indulge together.

But most of all, he'd see her shining eyes every day, hear her sweet voice. Together, they'd get through anything. He was sure of it. He turned around and scanned The House one last time before the sight of a car coming up the drive stole his attention.

Mr. Grenfield pulled the car to a stop in front of the steps and got out. He surveyed his son up and down. "You're looking mighty fine, son. Did you get on all right here?" He turned his face up, eyes roaming over the facade looming in front of him. "Sure is a big place. Did they treat you okay?"

"Like you give a damn." Newton gave him a sour look as he headed to the trunk.

"I see they didn't do much for your mouth."

Newton stood face-to-face with his father. "I want to know something once and for all, old man. Why did you send me here?"

His father's face reddened. "You had a … problem, that's all." He glanced around, eyes darting over the lawn and back to Newton. "Look, I just wanted you to be better, not so …" Running his fingers through his hair, the older man stared back at his son. "Listen, they took care of you, didn't they? I couldn't get them to tell me much."

His eyes remained fixed on the man in front of him, mentally cursing and thanking him. Whether or not Newton wanted to admit it, The House had been his salvation, but he'd never say it out loud. "Let's just say, 'problem solved,' and leave it at that."

Without a word, Newton tossed his suitcase in the trunk and made his way to the passenger's side. Mr. Grenfield started the engine, and the two men rode down the drive, leaving The House nothing more than just a memory.

"Any thoughts about the rest of your life now that you're out?" Newton's father kept his gaze focused on the road while they drove.

"As a matter of fact, I do."

"Like what?" His father cast Newton a quick glance.

"Like getting on with things, taking care of myself, making a living. Much of the same things I did before you dumped me off."

"Oh, come on, boy. Like I've told you before, it was for your own good. Are you going to hold a grudge against me forever?"

Newton cast him a smug smile. "I'll say this, I'm better than ever."

His father shot him a quick, wary glance and turned his attention back to the road.

All in good time. His father would learn about Vivian soon enough. No need to fire up his old man with talk of settling down with a good woman. At least not right now. His father most likely would have plenty to say once he learned Newton still aimed to have a woman in his life. Maybe running away and eloping with Vivian would solve the whole dilemma.

He smiled as he gazed out the window. Why not? Something deep inside suggested he needed a fresh start, to leave the past behind with all its frustrations and heartache. If he planned it right, he and Vivian could sneak away together and never look back. The thought of it thrilled him, sent his pulse racing. Sometimes a man needed to run away, far from family where he could be a man, work like a man, and make love like a man unencumbered. His time at The House had given him that strength, the confidence he needed to make life worth living, more exciting. The afternoon sun blazed through the window. Out on the open road, headed toward home, the future held the promise of new beginnings, days filled with heartbreaks and joys life threw at a person. No matter what happened, he'd handle everything with a clearer head and an eager heart.

ABOUT THE AUTHOR

Scarlet Darkwood wields a mighty pen, or at the very least, delivers mighty punches to the computer keys when she's typing furiously on a story. She likes dark and twisted, and the weirder, the better.

Always preferring avant garde themes, her stories take the reader on unusual adventures, exploring the darker parts of the human psyche as she whips out cunning prose wrapped in provocative themes. Sometimes she veers from her beaten path and takes a happy-go-lucky romp in the brighter sides of life, kicking up her style into sharp, snappy dialogue and clever descriptions.

Writing in several genres unleashes her imagination so she never grows bored. From a young age, she's enjoyed writing and keeping diaries, but didn't start creating novels until 2012. She's a Southern girl who lives in Tennessee and enjoys the beauty of the mountains. She lives in Nashville with her spouse and two rambunctious kitties.

For more information about the latest concerning Scarlet and her work, sign up for her newsletter: http://eepurl.com/Rt5HP

Visit her Blog: scarletdarkwood.com
Follow her on Google+: google.com/+ScarletDarkwood
Follow her on Twitter: twitter.com/ScarletDarkwood
Follow her on Facebook: facebook.com/scarletdarkwoodauthor

MORE FROM SCARLET DARKWOOD

Erotica:
Pleasure House
Dance Of Desire
Supernatural Romance:
Words We Never Speak
Erotic Romance:
Master Of The House
Mistress Of The House

Erotic Shorts:
Hard Way In
Fun with Dick and Peter
Naughty And Nice

If you have any questions, comments or suggestions,
you can reach the author at sdarkwood@gmail.com